PRAISE FOR *LOVE'S A WITCH*

'Heartwarming, delightful and enchanting – *Love's a Witch* is everything you want from a witchy romance and more! Full of family, small-town Scottish charm and an absolutely wonderful cheese-loving familiar, you'll want to sink into this book and never leave!'

Sarah Beth Durst, *New York Times* bestselling author of *The Spellshop*

'*Love's a Witch* is a hilarious cosy romantasy brimming with small-town charm, witty banter and a quirky cast of characters I fell in love with from the very first page. Tricia O'Malley seamlessly weaves a magical world of witches, romance and sisterhood in this enemies-to-lovers romance'

Helena Hunting, *New York Times* bestselling author of *Pucked Up*

'Steamy men in kilts, lightning-quick banter and ancient curses – this is pure dopamine!'

Elizabeth Hunter, *USA Today* bestselling author of *A Hidden Fire*

'A cosy, witchy romcom overflowing with quirky witches, hilarious mishaps and the powerful alchemy of friendship. This spellbinding tale that will delight enemies-to-lovers fans is pure enchantment from start to finish'

Linsey Hall, author of *The Modern Girl's Guide to Magic*

TRICIA O'MALLEY

THE SCOTTISH CHARMS SERIES – BOOK 1

LOVE'S A Witch

SIMON & SCHUSTER

London · New York · Amsterdam/Antwerp · Sydney/Melbourne · Toronto · New Delhi

First published in the United States by Gallery Books, an imprint of
Simon & Schuster, LLC, 2025
First published in Great Britain by Simon & Schuster UK Ltd, 2025

Copyright © Lovewrite Publishing LLC, 2025

The right of Tricia O'Malley to be identified as author of this work has been asserted in accordance with the Copyright, Designs and Patents Act, 1988.

1 3 5 7 9 10 8 6 4 2

Simon & Schuster UK Ltd, 1st Floor
222 Gray's Inn Road, London WC1X 8HB

For more than 100 years, Simon & Schuster has championed authors and the stories they create. By respecting the copyright of an author's intellectual property, you enable Simon & Schuster and the author to continue publishing exceptional books for years to come. We thank you for supporting the author's copyright by purchasing an authorised edition of this book.

No amount of this book may be reproduced or stored in any format, nor may it be uploaded to any website, database, language-learning model, or other repository, retrieval, or artificial intelligence system without express permission. All rights reserved. Enquiries may be directed to Simon & Schuster, 222 Gray's Inn Road, London WC1X 8HB or RightsMailbox@simonandschuster.co.uk

Simon & Schuster Australia, Sydney
Simon & Schuster India, New Delhi

www.simonandschuster.co.uk
www.simonandschuster.com.au
www.simonandschuster.co.in

The authorised representative in the EEA is Simon & Schuster Netherlands BV, Herculesplein 96, 3584 AA Utrecht, Netherlands. info@simonandschuster.nl

Simon & Schuster strongly believes in freedom of expression and stands against censorship in all its forms. For more information, visit BooksBelong.com

A CIP catalogue record for this book is available from the British Library

Paperback ISBN: 978-1-3985-4952-4
eBook ISBN: 978-1-3985-4953-1
Audio ISBN: 978-1-3985-4954-8

This book is a work of fiction. Names, characters, places and incidents are either a product of the author's imagination or are used fictitiously. Any resemblance to actual people living or dead, events or locales is entirely coincidental.

Typeset in Warnock Pro by M Rules
Printed and Bound in the UK using 100% Renewable Electricity
at CPI Group (UK) Ltd

TO MY *ANAM CARA*, BLUE.
SLÁN ABHAILE.

*The heart aye's the part aye,
That makes us right or wrang.*

—**ROBERT BURNS**

PROLOGUE

Bonelle MacGregor

A day for celebration should never end with a curse, but one cannot always see the future.

No matter how much magick they have.

Mabon heralded the arrival of autumn, honoring the balance of light and dark, and for one magickal town nestled in the hills of Scotland, the long-awaited return of their prince. Briarhaven, a home to witches, fae, and humans alike, bustled with excitement over the arrival of their dearly beloved—and notably *single*—prince.

It was said this year he would choose a wife.

More than one woman had awoken with a smile on her lips and hope in her heart. Maybe, just maybe, this day would end with a crown upon their head.

There was one budding witch, however, for whom the prince's return was of little interest.

At the age of four and twenty, Bonelle MacGregor cared little for the whims of love or arranging for a husband. Instead, she eagerly awaited the bloom of her magick in the coming year. She could already feel the first tendrils unfurling in her, hinting at what was to come. Bonelle welcomed, no, *ached*, for its arrival, as she had written books upon books of spells she was dying to try. She sensed she could do great good for her people, once her magick flowered.

Unlike her best friend, Vaila, who cared little for using her magick to help others when there was a prince to be wed. Vaila was so focused on the prince's return that she'd cried twice that morning about which dress to wear for the bonfire dance. After the third time switching the ribbons in Vaila's hair, Bonelle had begged off so she could go investigate a rumor she'd heard.

A mysterious traveler had arrived.

Hopeful for new books, particularly if they carried exotic spells from faraway lands, Bonelle slipped away from where fading wildflowers festooned a field outside the village, the beat of the drums matching the thumping of her heart. A wagon was tucked in a shadowy grove of trees, a man, broad-shouldered and lean from travel, arranging his goods.

"Good day, sir." She bobbed her head lightly. The wagon, though appearing to be of humble nature from afar, glittered and glimmered once close.

"Good day, miss. May I interest you in my wares?" The man was dirty in the way of men who have been on the road for ages, his face covered in dust, his nails caked with mud. Yet she couldn't look away from his enchanting azure eyes. A thousand truths swirled there, magick and mystery and might, and her words were lost to the ether.

"Perhaps a shiny bauble for a bonnie lass?" The man shifted, lifting a swath of velvet fabric to reveal a tray of gold jewelry. At that, she wrinkled her nose, her captivation broken.

"I've not one for baubles, no." Bonelle pursed her lips, deliberately trying to avoid looking at him lest she did something stupid like ask him for the secrets of the universe. "But I do love books. Do you have stories from strange lands, sir? I'd love to expand my library. Books hold infinite worlds and many new companions."

"I feel much the same, witchling." The soft burr of his voice rippled across her skin, awareness tugging her closer. "You may enjoy these."

The traveler handed her three books, bound in leather, dyed in the same beautiful blue as his wagon.

"I certainly can't afford these," Bonelle said, surprised at the quality of the bindings.

"A gift."

"Ah, I'm not so green to the ways of the world as to accept a gift from a strange traveler." She laughed up at him. He must be fae, always up to tricks. "I do have coin."

Digging in her pocket, she laid three silver coins in his hand, and jolted when a spark of energy shot up her arm.

"If you insist." The man closed his hand over the coins, and when he opened it again, they had disappeared.

Before she could ask him about his travels in strange lands, voices of approaching customers sounded at her back, and Bonelle turned blindly, running home to store the books in a safe spot in her cottage. Though she ached to dive into every story found in those delicate pages, she reluctantly tucked them away and returned to the festivities, having promised Vaila she would dance around the bonfire with her.

"There you are." Vaila grabbed her arm, hurrying her toward where dancers circled a merrily crackling bonfire. "Don't look, but the prince is here! I'm told he's going to invite one of us maidens to sit by his side at the head table tonight."

"And that's a good thing?" Bonelle asked, in all seriousness, but Vaila just rolled her eyes and dragged Bonelle forward.

The drums struck up, the piper stepping close, and Bonelle lifted her head as an icy breeze danced across her cheeks, the promise of winter swirling in its depths. Gilded leaves fluttered in the wind, and the dancers fell into motion. Awareness prickled, needling her in the shoulders, and she slanted a glance over her shoulder to see the traveler standing, arms crossed, his head bent in conversation with another man.

The prince.

He wore a simple gold circlet in his hair and a rich red tunic, honey-blond tresses rippling in the breeze. His icy-blue eyes stayed on the dancers, even though he bent his ear to the traveler.

Before she could ponder more deeply how the traveler knew the prince, the dance came to an end when the prince stepped forward, clapping his hands. Bonelle fell silent, the fire crackling and spitting at her back.

"This is it," Vaila hissed at her ear.

"Why did he stop the dance before we were finished?" She glared, annoyed. This was a time-honored tradition.

"Because he was so taken with my beauty that he's going to choose me as his maiden for dinner tonight—maybe even his *wife*." Vaila's nails dug into Bonelle's arm, and she winced and forced herself to paste a polite smile on her face.

"My lovely gentlewomen . . ." The prince swooped his hands out in front of him, a smile on his lips. "I must apologize for interrupting your beautiful dance, but I was so overcome with admiration for one of you fair ladies that I quite simply had to claim her as my companion for the evening."

Bonelle's shoulders tightened at his words. Her magick rippled, the high levels of emotion threading the air bringing it to the surface.

The prince strode forward until he stood in front of them, and Vaila gasped, tossing her head back, chin held high.

"My enchanting mistress, will you join me this evening?" The prince's hand reached forward.

"Why, of course—"

Vaila's words dropped away as the prince's hand stopped just below Bonelle's breastbone, waiting for her to take it. Bonelle stared down at the hand, where a thick gold ring with an intricate insignia was nestled at the base of his index finger. She struggled for a breath as Vaila gasped beside her.

"No." It was soft, a simple word ripped away on the wind, but she caught it, her heart twisting at Vaila's distress. Once more, her magick heated beneath her skin, as though imploring to be released, yet it was bound by the rules. Unlike Vaila, who'd stepped into her magick a year prior, Bonelle was forbidden to free her magick until the age of five and twenty.

Time slowed.

Lifting her head, Bonelle ignored royal protocol and turned toward her best friend. Already, the words were at Vaila's lips, her face twisted in rage, dark magick seeping from her skin.

"By thorn and thistle, by curse and bane,
Your magick's strength shall wax and wane,
Misfortune shall haunt each town you claim,
Bringing ruin, grief, and endless blame."

The curse fell upon Bonelle, as though she'd walked into a sticky cobweb, and she floundered backward, her hands raised as though she could stop the blood magick that poured from Vaila's broken heart.

Shadows fell, the murky clouds having turned murderous, and a shriek split the sky.

Bonelle's blood ran cold.

Her foot caught on a root as she turned to run. She stumbled, but an arm looped through hers and dragged her into the shadow of the trees, where she was unceremoniously dumped on the ground. She went to her knees, her fingers clutching the damp moss that coated the forest floor. Tears welled, and she blinked them back, her thoughts whirling as she gasped for air.

"The emberwolves approach. You must go."

At that, Bonelle sprang to her feet, fear rippling through her.

"She called an emberwolf?" Bonelle gasped. Her heart skipped a beat when her eyes finally landed on the man who'd dragged her to the forest. Not just a guard, *oh no*, but the traveler himself.

"Her curse did. Harm will befall any town in which you stay."

Bonelle gaped up at him before turning to look out at the festival grounds, where the people had scattered, fallen leaves strewn across the grass in their wake. The shadow of an emberwolf drifted across the field, and her stomach twisted.

"Who are you?" It was an inane question at an impossible time, but still Bonelle had to know the name of the man who was banning her to exile.

"Eoin Douglas. First Knight of the Iron Thistle Order, protector of Briarhaven."

"Protect *me*. Please," Bonelle begged.

He stilled, his eyes darting between Bonelle and the field, but when another shriek rattled the branches canopying above them, he decided.

Bonelle knew before he spoke.

"Run, MacGregor. Take your curse with you and run."

PRESENT DAY

CHAPTER ONE
Sloane MacGregor

"Welcome to Briarhaven, Scotland's most magickal town."

I glanced at the video playing on my sister Lyra's phone to see a woman in a blush-pink pantsuit and perfectly coiffed blond tresses beam into the camera. Her smile fought the tight skin of her face, and her widened eyes held a slight maniacal glow.

"She seems a bit tense," I said, returning my gaze to the road that curved through a canopy of trees with twisted branches arching overhead.

"She looks like a fembot." Nova, the youngest of us three, leaned forward from the back seat.

"Be sure to book your tickets in advance for the VIP Briarhaven experience. If you're lucky, you might even get upgraded to our full moon package!" Pink Pantsuit's voice sounded as plastic as she looked.

"She's like the people who harass you to buy time-shares anytime you book at an all-inclusive hotel," I said.

"And remember . . . in Briarhaven, we believe in three things: magick, mirth, and mystery! Charm on, witches!"

"'Charm on, witches,'" Nova mimicked, easing back. I snorted.

"Mirth?" Lyra turned the word over on her tongue. "When was the last time you heard someone say 'mirth'?"

"Mirth happens," Nova said, winking at me in the rearview mirror.

"For what it's mirth, I think it's an underused word." I slowed the car as we approached a tight turn in the hills.

"Mirth you." Lyra glowered, letting out a little huff as she settled back against the seat.

I grinned at my impossibly beautiful sister.

Lyra had the kind of looks that made men and women alike stop in their tracks, police officers fumble their words and never issue tickets, and grown men send extravagant gifts. The most extravagant gift *I'd* ever received from a boyfriend was a coupon for a buy-one-get-one-free ice cream at Dairy Queen.

As if on cue, we rounded a corner to see a rustic wooden sign, covered in vines and thorns, tucked next to the road beneath the shaded bower of trees that had grown tighter and darker upon our approach.

"Briarhaven. Population 3,333."

"Repeating threes, how original." I could all but hear Nova rolling her eyes in the back seat.

Nova had an edgy beauty that reminded me of thorns tucked among rose petals. A budding tattoo artist who was developing a rabid following online, she'd come out of the womb far cooler than I could ever aspire to be.

"Okay, but, wait a minute . . . would you just *look* at this? Bloody hell, I think they've given the town an actual makeover." Lyra leaned forward as we left the tunnel of trees and Briarhaven spread before us. Tucked at the base of sharply edged mountains, the village was colorful and charming, like someone had flicked a paintbrush full of color against a rich green canvas. Golden trees with leaves just on the cusp of turning amber blanketed the hills, and a stunning loch shimmered in the distance. Since we'd last been here, it seemed the town had quite literally been made over into a theme park–like tourist attraction.

Shocked at the transformation, we could only gape as I drove slowly past the main square, gilded sunlight spearing through puffy white clouds, sidewalks busy with tourists, some dressed in cosplay with witch hats or fake fae ears. A breeze blew a scattering of amber leaves down the street, and a stall selling freshly picked apples was set up near the sidewalk. A poster for an upcoming Halloween costume contest was taped to a black light pole with an old-timey lantern at the top, and I shook my head. *How would tourists ever compete with magickals when it came time to dress up?*

"It's incredible what they've achieved in the last eight years. I mean, I can hardly recognize the place," Nova said. I nodded, my nerves kicking up as I turned down our childhood street—memory lane, so to speak. We all went silent as I pulled to a stop in front of a run-down cottage tucked in a row of detached houses that had also experienced the same glow-up as the rest of the town. Ours stood out like a sore thumb.

"Well, this is a hot mess."

"It's not a hot mess, it's just . . ." I trailed off as we looked out the car window at our childhood home. A two-story cottage, overgrown ivy obscuring the gray stone exterior, with one shutter slung askew, barely hanging on. *Same, shutter. Same.*

"A dumpster fire?" Lyra suggested. Nova nodded her agreement, and I sighed.

"A project." Unbuckling my seat belt, I cracked the car door open, stood, and stretched. A crisp autumn breeze teased my hair, and burnt-umber leaves fluttered to my feet. Nature's glitter, throwing a goodbye party before the plants slept for the winter.

If I looked closely enough, I could see the threads of memories wrapped around the house—snatches of arguments, broken magick misfiring, rare moments of laughter. It was home because it was the longest the MacGregor clan had managed to stay in one spot, together, before the curse that plagued our bloodline—like a mosquito buzzing when you're desperate for sleep—forced us to move on.

It had been years since we'd been back to Briarhaven, and I never would have returned if not for one very specific reason. The one woman I couldn't refuse had called me home to break our family curse.

The same woman who now stood in the open doorway to our dilapidated home, her walker wrapped in silk ribbons, both her housedress and eyeglasses dripping with sparkles. A sleek gray bob of hair framed a happy face just giving over to age, and a falcon preened its feathers at her shoulder. Broca MacGregor, ladies and gentlemen. The legend herself.

"You look like you're waiting on news of the mysterious passing of your rich husband," I called.

"Husband?" Broca said in the same tone as if I'd just pointed out a cockroach. "Why marry them when they're so much more fun when they're courting you?"

"Says the woman with five ex-husbands." I rounded the car and popped the trunk for our luggage while Lyra and Nova bounded out of the car to go embrace our grandmother, who had arrived to town earlier that day. Likely being carried on a throne by several strapping males. As matriarchal witches, Broca was plagued by the same curse as us. She'd spent the last eight years methodically working her way through the men of Europe, each suitor more extravagant than the last.

"Which is how I know men are easily digestible as lovers, but barely tolerable as husbands."

"Must we discuss your lovers already?" We'd only just arrived, having traveled all night, and I'd need a glass of wine before I could handle such a conversation. Reaching in the trunk, I pulled out a suitcase and put it on the ground.

A flurry of snowflakes landed beside it.

Shite.

Groaning, I straightened to see all three women glaring at the sky. Broca's falcon—her familiar, named Iris—cried out in protest and took to the air, disappearing toward the hills.

One very brokenhearted witch, centuries ago, had cursed our ancestor with a highly inventive, if not deeply annoying spell. The result of which had forced every MacGregor since to never be able to fully settle in one spot for very long, as natural disasters and oddball curses would descend upon any town we were in. Even better? When we did step into our magick at the age of twenty-five, we'd often have to deal with it being unpredictable.

"Does it have to be snow?" Lyra asked, stomping the heel of her Christian Louboutin stiletto into the ground.

"It's better than the caterpillar infestation." Nova zipped her leather coat, squinting at the dark clouds that now clustered over us.

"Ew." Lyra rounded on her. "I thought we'd agreed never to bring that one up again. I couldn't sleep for months after."

"Likely due to the caterpillars that had nested in your hair. Maybe they burrowed into your brain."

Lyra gasped and patted her luxurious tresses. It had taken a three-day weekend at a high-end spa to ensure not a trace of caterpillar slime could be found on Lyra before she was able to move on from *that* particular iteration of our curse.

"Caterpillars don't burrow. They go into their closet and come out looking fabulous."

"It's a chrysalis, not a closet, Lyra."

"To-may-to, to-mah-toe." Lyra shivered as a blast of wind tossed snow at their feet.

Grinning, their bickering an odd source of comfort for me, I reached the front door. "Broca, let's get you inside and get the heat on."

The house itself was a simple rectangle, with four bedrooms and two bathrooms upstairs and an open living room, kitchen, and dining room on the first. Though the house had been built in a time of small rooms and closed doors, likely to keep heat in, somewhere along the line walls had been removed to create one big living space, and two brick pillars acted as the main foundational supports in the room. I used to run circles around those pillars as a kid, my father chasing me—on a good day, that is—while my mother drank coffee in her chair by the window where sunlight spilled inside for a good portion of the morning.

Leaving the suitcase at the door, I walked slowly next to Broca as she navigated toward that same chair and helped her sit. Lyra crossed to the kitchen to dig in the cabinets, likely looking for tea, while Nova checked if the water was running. Looking around, I sighed. Dusty sheets covered the rest of the furniture, cobwebs clustered in corners of the windows, and more than one light bulb had long ago burned itself out.

A knock sounded at the door, and we all turned. Before I could cross to answer it, let alone fully take stock of the condition of the room, the door swung open.

"Who just opens someone else's door?" I asked, already crossing the room, ready to do battle.

My mouth dropped open.

The sexiest man I'd ever seen in real life filled the door.

A face made for fairy tales, with muscular arms shown in their best light under a T-shirt, never mind the snow swirling outside, had me frozen to the spot.

I gaped at the gorgeous man that hulked in the doorway. Unruly dark hair, those soul-searching blue eyes, and a sharp jawline marked with dark stubble made me want to look twice. And a third time, for good measure. The man was made for fantasies, not real life.

"Oh my," Lyra breathed from across the room, and I silently nodded in agreement.

"Ladies." This man's voice, like whisky-soaked sugar, made heat bloom in my chest. My magick unfurled inside me, as though stretching after a long rest, ready to greet the world. It may be ready, but *I* was not. And the last thing I needed was for it to make its first appearance ten seconds into my unwanted return to Briarhaven. Though my twenty-fifth birthday was still two days away, the knowledge that I was about to step into my power had been humming through me for years now. For most witches, it was meant to be a celebratory day. For me? It was like waiting for a gavel to slam down as a judge declared my sentence.

"Unfortunately, I'm going to have to ask you to leave."

With that, the man bent and picked up my suitcase, trudged out into the snow, and deposited my luggage back in the trunk of my car.

Never had my opinion of someone changed so fast. Turning, I glared at the others.

"See? I knew coming back was a mistake."

With that, I stormed outside.

CHAPTER TWO
Sloane

"You can't stay here."

His rumbly voice sent shivers across my skin as I skidded to a stop at the side of our hastily purchased car that had seen better days. I looked up, up, up, until frowning arctic-blue eyes speared mine.

Of course, he was also unbearably tall. It was unfair, really, how some people, like Lyra, hit the genetic jackpot. Granted, beauty was subjective and all, but I suspected I would be hard-pressed to find someone who didn't find this man attractive.

"Excuse me? I can do whatever I want, thank you very much." I blinked up at him, snatching my suitcase from the trunk, and forced myself to break the hypnosis thing that beautiful people unintentionally seemed to do to others. They couldn't help it, which was something that I'd learned with having Lyra as a sister. But if you wanted to get through a meaningful conversation, it was best not to look directly at them. Like the sun.

"But you see, you really can't. You have to get out of Briarhaven." *Prince Charming himself here.* I gaped as he tugged the suitcase from my hand and once again lifted it back into the car.

Here's the thing about having a curse that plagues your bloodline and forces you to move frequently—I'd learned that I didn't tolerate bad behavior from people well. I didn't *have* to tolerate it. In small towns, people needed to, for the most part, make nice with their neighbors even if they held differing viewpoints or were unlikable. But *I* didn't have to do the same. We never lived somewhere long enough to have to work things out with a neighbor or rely on them during a town catastrophe or whatever, so when people were being assholes, well, I could just call them out on it with little thought to what damage that might do to my reputation.

Just like I did now with my new least favorite person in the world.

"Perhaps you didn't hear me the first time? I can do whatever I like. Touch grass, Charming." I yanked my suitcase from the car and barreled up toward the house.

"You think I'm charming?" I turned to see a corner of his mouth quirked in a sexy half smile, freezing me in place as I tried to ignore the tug of lust.

I squeaked as he brushed in front of me, stopping me steps from the door, and grabbed the handle of my bag. Jerking it from my grip, he proceeded back toward the car, waving me away like I was a gnat. Fury filled me. I lunged and took hold of the other side of the bag, forcing him to slow his forward momentum. A look of confusion crossed his face.

"Just what the hell do you think you're doing?" I asked, tugging harder.

Charming pulled the luggage forward, as though it was a foregone conclusion that he would get his way, and I slipped in the snow that was already accumulating at our feet.

"Watch it, buddy. I'm going to—"

My feet went out from under me and air whooshed from my body as I flung my arms out, trying to catch myself before I landed in the snow.

Unfortunately, or fortunately, depending how one looked at it, the thing I happened to catch hold of was none other than Charming's crown jewels. He gasped in surprise, somehow managing to still catch me with one arm before I hit the pavement, while also reaching for his goods with the other.

And let me tell you, from a completely objective standpoint, *they were good*.

No man should be blessed with this many positive physical attributes.

Which meant there must be serious issues in other areas. Likely his personality. Or his apparent expectation that everyone should follow his orders. Focusing on the negative so I could ignore the desire that fluttered in my chest like a butterfly trying to escape, I glared up at his perfect face. His arm was still wrapped around my waist, and I couldn't help but notice he was basically made of muscle.

Because *of course* he was.

Charming subtly adjusted himself, wincing lightly, and I steeled my gaze.

"I'm not going to apologize for that. You brought this upon yourself."

"Noted." A faint wisp of the Highlands hovered in his voice, and my insides curled at the soft burr.

The man had the gall to turn and move toward my suitcase again, and I almost drop-kicked him off the pavement. Almost, because, well, I'd likely break my foot against all that muscle. Nevertheless, maybe I could sneak a karate chop into his collarbone to deter him. Sighing, I placed myself between him and the bag and waved my hand in front of his face.

"Hello? *Sir?* Is there anyone in there?"

He raised an eyebrow at me but said nothing.

"No? Nothing? You're just the strong and silent type, eh? I'm sure that works for you on most of the women around here, but that shite doesn't fly with us. Whatever this is you're doing, just stop. This is our grandmother's house, and we have every right to visit her."

"I know exactly who you are, Sloane."

Why, *why*, did my name sound so good on this man's lips? I wanted to arch my back like a cat and nuzzle in for a cuddle. This was ridiculous.

"Then you have me at a disadvantage. And you are?" A shiver ran across my skin as the wind gusted, snow melting against my cheeks.

"Knox Douglas."

"Knox?" My mouth fell open. The last time I'd seen Knox Douglas, he'd been a scrawny private school boy, but even then, all the girls in town had crushed hard on him. It was unfair, really, the glow-up this man had enjoyed since I'd last seen him. The only thing about me that glowed was the sweat on my face after Lyra dragged me to the seventh circle of hell—her Pilates class—and I came out gasping for air and promising my firstborn if I never had to attend another session.

Before I could do much more than blink, he'd grabbed hold of the luggage once more. Blocking him, I rammed a hand into his stomach, pushing him back from the luggage.

"You're one of those people nobody says no to, aren't you?" I asked.

A bewildered look crossed Knox's face as though he'd never really considered the option of someone refusing to do what he wanted before.

"Och, lass. I reckon not. I am the provost, after all."

"Run unopposed, have you?" I gave him a sarcastic smile as I heaved the luggage from his hands and dragged it inside, where everyone hovered a few feet back and away from the snow that gusted through the open door.

"Aye, largely." Knox filled our doorway.

"Shocking." Men like him annoyed women like me. They didn't annoy Lyra, as those two spoke the same language where doors opened unaided, presents showed up on doorsteps, and dinner bills were always miraculously paid. But for me? Life didn't run so seamlessly.

"Well, if it isn't wee Knox Douglas, all grown-up. It's been ages since I've seen you." Broca came as close to a sashay as she could with a walker, and Knox grinned at her.

It was the grin that did me in.

Coherent thoughts scattered from my brain.

"If it isn't the notorious MacGregor witches back in Briarhaven. It's good to see you, Broca, even if you've taken a bit of a tumble, it seems."

"Och, it's just a wee bruise. Nothing much to fuss over." Broca flirted up at Knox, and I raised an eyebrow. A hip replacement was certainly *not* a wee bruise.

"If it's good to see her, why are you trying to kick us out, then?"

Knox turned back to me, the smile sliding neatly off his face, and I silently applauded my ability to annoy even the most handsome of men.

"It's good to see you all are doing well," Knox amended. "But, since you *aren't* good for Briarhaven, I really must insist that you go."

"Who says we're not good for Briarhaven?" This from Nova, who, with her sullen glare and tattooed arms, looked every inch the badass she was. She could have followed it up with *You want a piece of me?* and actually pulled it off.

I would have looked like a cranky librarian scolding someone for returning a book late.

"Yeah, what she said." *Yup, didn't quite land that.*

Knox's gaze drifted back to me, my breath caught, and I found myself leaning, honestly leaning, forward, as though his very nearness somehow was pulling me into his gravitational force. Was this some kind of magickal charm he was using on me to sway me in his favor? If so, I was even more deeply annoyed because I didn't take well to people using magick, or coercion of any sort, on me.

Knox turned and pointed out the front door, where snow swirled wildly behind him.

"Exhibit A."

"Hardly unusual for Scotland," Nova scoffed, crossing her arms over her chest. "Or is a little snow enough to send you scurrying back to your drafty castle?"

"I don't scurry, and my castle is cozy as can be on a snowy winter's night."

I'd forgotten he lived in the castle. Now I was even more annoyed.

"Ladies, while I can appreciate you want to be home to help Broca, having you here is bad for tourism. It's been a while since the MacGregors have lived in town, and things have changed since your family left. We've worked tirelessly to build up our reputation, to design a careful, thoughtful, and well-planned town with a theme that allows people like us to live here safely as well as to entice humans to spend tourist money. It's a win-win for everyone that has been hard fought for. The last thing I need, or want, is a trio of messy witches screwing things up for us."

"Messy?" I arched a brow at him, pushing Lyra out of the way and getting in his face. Vaguely recalling something from childhood, I poked Knox in the chest. "You're no longer welcome in this home."

To my absolute delight, the magick in the old house held strong. Knox was sucked backward onto the front porch, and the door slammed resoundingly in his face.

"Well, now, that's a neat little party trick," Nova decided.

"Is he a vampire? Doesn't that only work on vampires?" Lyra turned to me, shock on her pretty face.

"It's a protection spell," Broca said, waddling forward. "I recharged the wards when I returned, and I have to admit I'm quite chuffed with myself. That worked nicely. Well done, Sloane."

A knock sounded at the door.

"Go away!" we all shouted at once.

"Ladies, we have to talk about this. Your curse is going to destroy this town. I can't allow that to happen. How much will it cost?"

At that we looked at each other.

"He's trying to buy us off?" I gasped.

"I wonder how much. I did have my eye on a new stand mixer." Lyra tapped a manicured nail against her lips. A natural-born influencer, her talents lay in the kitchen, and she ran a successful cooking YouTube channel that could more than pay for as many stand mixers as she'd like.

"Enough to open a tattoo shop?" Nova considered.

"We don't need his money," Broca reminded them. Being a witch had its benefits, and one was that our family had been incredibly good with timing particular investments through the years. I wouldn't say they dealt in insider trading *specifically*. But I also wouldn't say their investments didn't have an added boost of a magickal inclination here and there.

The knocking continued.

"I'm not leaving."

I pictured him, sitting on our porch and getting covered in snow, and my heart thawed slightly. Sighing, I cracked the door open and looked out. The snowfall continued, fat fluffy flakes dancing in the light from the streetlamp, dusting across Knox's perfect jawline.

"One would surmise that it would be stupid of you to sit on a porch and freeze to death in a snowstorm, so I would like to think that you have enough self-preservation to see yourself home."

"I'll leave once you leave." Knox lifted his chin, a stubborn look in his eyes.

"What are you, twelve? *I'll go if you go*?" I threw up my hands. "It's true, isn't it? People never tell you no, do they?"

Knox blinked at me as frustration flashed in his eyes.

"As I believe I mentioned, it is not a common practice around here."

"Consider this a lesson in growth, then." I had the gall to reach through the door and pat Knox's cheek in the most condescending manner I could. Frustration shifted to annoyance on his handsome face, and I couldn't have been more pleased with myself. "For your information, we're here to break the curse. We'll get it sorted soon enough, and your precious town will be none the worse. In the meantime, might I suggest you pull out your ice skates and enjoy an early winter?"

His eyes narrowed. "Cute." The word dripped with sarcasm. "Though I much prefer the easier solution—you leaving."

"We can't always get what we want, can we?"

"Again, not a problem I usually have."

"Arrogant, aren't you?" Was he seriously not going to leave us alone? This was moving past annoying to infuriating.

"No, I don't think so." Knox crossed his arms, considering my words. Like, *actually* considering them, not just pretending to in order to blow me off. "Things just usually go my way."

I didn't doubt it, what with his charm and good looks.

"I totally get that," Lyra agreed from behind me.

"Listen, Knox. We've been in Briarhaven for about three seconds. In that time frame, I've barely been able to hug my grandmother, let alone figure out how or when to break the curse. So, may I kindly suggest you back the hell off and give us a moment to breathe? Legally, you have no right to evict us, and if you're going to insist on being a nuisance, I'll call the police."

At that, Knox grinned, a dimple forming on one side, and I sighed, banging my head lightly against the doorframe.

"Please don't tell me you are also the police?"

"There's not much call for a police force here, Sloane."

Ugh, there it was again: my name on his lips. Why did it just sound so good?

"Please, just leave. I'm begging you. We've been traveling for ages. I'll update you on the curse-breaking as soon as possible. But you know what won't help break the curse?"

"What's that?" Knox crossed his arms over his chest.

"You. Being here. Interrupting us." With that, I closed the door, and when silence followed, I let out a shaky breath. A dull ache pounded at my forehead, and I realized I wanted nothing more than to go face-first into a pillow for ten straight hours.

"I'm going up to bed. I'd politely request everyone leave me the hell alone."

I stomped up the stairs, automatically following the way to my childhood bedroom, Nova's voice trailing after me.

"Don't mind Sloane, Broca. She's in one of her moods. And, in fairness, she has been driving for hours. She'll be better after a good sleep."

"I suspect that's not what has her in a mood."

CHAPTER THREE
Sloane

I woke up fast, moving quickly from sleep to alert, as was my habit after years on the road. I blinked at the plastic glow-in-the-dark stars stuck to the ceiling over my head and took a moment to recalibrate and figure out my surroundings.

Briarhaven.

And in my childhood bed, which was surprisingly comfortable given how long it had been since I'd slept here. Breakfast smells teased my nose, the chatter of voices reaching through my bedroom door, which was slightly ajar, and for a moment I let my mind drift to memories of childhood mornings.

On the good mornings, disco music would be playing, and Broca would be singing, and likely dancing along with the radio, shimmying her hips in whatever colorful or sparkly outfit she wore. She was a horrific cook, but a delightful grandmother, and my love of music and unrefined cuisine came directly from her. When most people thought of their favorite childhood breakfast meal it was likely something like pancakes or waffles. Mine was cheese in a tube—Primula was the best, naturally—on top of Ritz crackers with one tiny piece of bacon on top. Paired with a steaming cup of tea, that was my breakfast sorted.

Broca wasn't one for paying attention to details like recipes and basic housework. Why would she be when there were more fun things to do like dance and teach magick?

On the bad mornings, my mother would be shouting at my father, or vice versa, and at least one dish would always break. My mother did have a flair for the dramatic, and sometimes I wondered if she enjoyed having a fight just for the sole reason to smash a dish. Her magick cleaned it up, so there wasn't really any repercussion to her shattering plates other than a seriously mismatched dinner set. That and scaring her daughters, but some people broke things just to watch them shatter.

Spotting my bag at the foot of the bed, I sighed in relief. Nova, likely, had braved the snow and lugged my bag up the stairs. Stretching, I took the blanket with me as I went to stand by the window and looked out at Briarhaven in the daylight. Snow drifted down, lighter than the night before, and an old man shoveling his front walk saw me in the window. Straightening, he held two fingers up—not the peace sign, mind you—and glared from beneath bushy brows.

I smiled brightly, waving enthusiastically at him, deliberately misinterpreting his rude gesture.

The snow had easily accumulated to at least a few inches, deeper in some places, where the wind had pushed it into drifts, and the gritters were out tossing salt on the streets. Sir Plows a Lot drove by, and I huffed out a laugh, remembering Scotland's penchant for naming their gritters fun names. A particular favorite of mine was Blizzard of Oz, though Lyra preferred Gritney Spears. Nova favored Melter Skelter and Spready Mercury, and I couldn't blame her. Both of those names were strong contenders for top gritter names. Salt spread across the freshly cleared street, and the snow intensified, as though annoyed that anyone had tried to clear a path.

I sighed. Living with a cursed bloodline was something I'd grown used to, but that didn't mean I particularly cared for it. I couldn't blame Broca for ordering us home to try to break the damn thing and live a life free of rules placed on us by one very angry and heartbroken witch centuries ago. Moving frequently was getting old, and that was only one part of the curse that shrouded our family name.

Pretty cool, right? Not.

I tightened the blanket around me, apprehension kicking low in my core, as I thought about the next part of the curse, which, from all accounts, was going to land at my feet in a day.

My twenty-fifth birthday. When all witches came into their power.

From my vantage point, Briarhaven spread out in a twisty-turny way, with winding streets creating a maze of sorts beneath the castle that jutted from the hill overshadowing the town. In the daylight, with snow-covered roofs, smoke piping from chimneys, and sun peeking through heavy clouds, the town looked quaint and cozy. A sanctuary for magickals—witches, fae, pixies, and more—with humans none the wiser, and the only place the MacGregors had ever managed to live for longer than a year. Now, a part of me itched to settle in, as much as depressing childhood memories made me want to leave, largely because I was just so tired of hitting the road all the time.

Maybe Broca was right. Perhaps her vision about the three sisters breaking the curse was meant to come to fruition. It wouldn't be the first thing she was right about, though I tried my hardest to never let her know that. A bit of a diva, she was.

My eyes strayed to the castle. Was Knox standing in his window? Looking out over his domain and silently hating us from afar? I'd dreamt of him. Much to my irritation.

He pinned me against the car, icy snow melting against heated skin, his mouth a sin against my throat.

"Sloane? You up?" Nova's voice trailed up the staircase.

"Yup, coming down." Best to cut that train of thought off immediately, because clearly, I was just in the dry spell of all dry spells. Throwing on a tattered hoodie I'd left behind in my room, with Keep

Calm and Carry a Wand scrolled across the front in sequins—a gift from Broca—I tugged on leggings and thick wool socks before padding downstairs and into chaos.

Broca sat in the armchair, legs propped up, wearing a screaming-pink dressing gown with feathers at the cuffs and dripping in diamonds. She could have as easily been lounging on the deck of a yacht somewhere as she was on the faded armchair tucked under the front windows in the living room. Disco music jammed in the background, and Broca held a hand in the air, lightly maneuvering dishes with her magick, while Lyra and Nova dove out of the way in the kitchen.

"This is not helping," Lyra barked, annoyed.

Everything clattered to the counter as a knock sounded at the door.

"Why? *Why* are there people knocking at this door? It isn't even eight in the morning. Don't people have to work?" I mimicked a throat punch as I envisioned Knox at our door once more. I stomped across the room and swung the door open, prepared to give him a piece of my mind, only to find a woman in a pale pink pantsuit, with perfectly coiffed blond hair, a plastic smile on her face. Behind her, two women clustered, one smiling and one giving annoyed looks to the snow.

"Welcome to Briarhaven!"

"Holy hell, it's the fembot," Nova hissed, gripping my arm from where she'd followed me.

"We're just so delighted that the MacGregor witches have finally returned, particularly because we've taken up your slack in the Charms. I'm sure you're tired from your travels and based on the condition of this house"—the woman looked past us at the dusty sheets covering much of the furniture in the front room, open disapproval radiating from her face—"I figured you wouldn't want to cook. Here's a casserole to sort you out for today."

"The Charms?" Nova whispered to me. I just shrugged, uncertain of making any sudden movements around the fembot. I eased back as all three women stepped inside.

My eyebrows rose as the woman reached inside her tiny pocketbook and pulled out a steaming casserole dish easily triple the size of her purse.

"Well, that's a fancy trick," Lyra said.

"I'm Mandy Meadows, head of the Charms, and your official welcome wagon!" Mandy exclaimed in an upbeat robotic voice. "While your grandmother has managed to keep your legacy seats open by attending our coven meetings by Zoom, it's so much better now that you're here."

I tuned back in to what Mandy was chattering on about, zeroing in on her tight smile and wide blue eyes.

"Wait. What? Legacy seats?" I swiveled to look at Broca. "What is she talking about?"

"Och, darlings, it's your coven, of course."

"Our coven?" Lyra sucked in a breath of excitement. She'd always been more into the witchy stories our mother had told us than either Nova or I had been. It had suited me to ignore our bloodline, seeing as the only thing that had come from it so far had been misery and disrupted routines. The appearance of one Mandy Meadows, looking like a country club woman hopped up on speed, had slammed our heritage back to reality for us.

"Your mother didn't tell you about your coven?" Broca's face fell.

"No." The word almost came out on a growl.

"That's right." Mandy beamed and nodded, a touch too effusively for my taste, like one of those bobblehead figures you picked up at a petrol station and attached to the dashboard. "You have legacy seats in the most elite coven in Briarhaven—the Charms."

Right, time to nip this in the bud.

"I have no idea what you're saying to me." I stepped forward, gripping Mandy's arm lightly, and propelled her toward the door. "But I'm sure we can find another time to talk about this. We've had a long few days of travel and haven't seen our grandmother in years." Mum had done her best to cut us off from Broca, dragging us around the States, and by the time I'd been old enough to take charge of my sisters, we'd just been trying find our feet on our own. And frankly, none of us had been quite ready to come back to Scotland. Now, seeing Broca again in person, I realized just how much we'd missed her.

"I know a great house cleaner." This from a woman who looked eager to please, in a neon-pink jumpsuit, chaotic hair, and huge tote bag at her shoulder that looked like it could carry enough weapons to take down a small army. "I'm Felicity Sheridan, vice president of the Charms. Never harm, always charm!" I swear she almost saluted.

I glanced over my shoulder at Nova, who mouthed to me, *Never harm, always charm*. I bared my teeth at her like a cat hissing, and turned back to the third woman, who gave me a knowing look.

"Tam Sullivan. Treasurer and all-around badass, if I do say so myself." Tam pumped my hand so vigorously my bones rattled. A woman in her early fifties, she wore an Adidas tracksuit and had close-cropped hair and lively, intelligent eyes. "Don't let these two indoctrinate you."

"Oh, for goddess's sake, Tam. You've just met them," Mandy hissed, turning to glare at Tam.

"Someone's got to dull the brunt of you two."

"Really? Are we that difficult? I like to think we're everyone's favorite witches. Like fairy floss and lollipops." Felicity put her hands on her hips, looking like an enraged gnome, with her messy bun of hair wobbling on top of her head.

"Who says fairy floss is everyone's favorite?" Tam tucked her hands in her pockets.

Felicity gasped like Tam had just told her she drowned kittens before breakfast every morning.

"Is fairy floss . . ." Lyra began. There hadn't been any happy family trips to the circus when we were children. Something I'd remedied once we were in the States, and I was the one in charge.

"Cotton candy," I supplied, not turning from the spectacle of these three women.

"Yuck," Nova said.

"I thought you liked cotton candy?" Lyra asked.

"I mean it's fine. It's not in my top five fair treats. Or maybe even ten. It's just sticky and annoying, really."

"I think it's fun," Lyra said, and Felicity zeroed in on her.

"Yes, see? It is fun. And that's what the Charms are. Fun! Speaking of, I'm so excited because we're here to—"

"Maybe they could invite us to stay for a cup of coffee?" Mandy's unwavering grin was beginning to remind me of a flight attendant asking an unruly passenger to pull themselves together before she got out the restraints.

"Is it mandatory?" I asked, leveling a look at Mandy. I wasn't my best before coffee, even less so when I felt like I wasn't in charge in my own space.

"Sloane. That's not the kind of hospitality we raised you with." Broca arched an eyebrow at me and waved the women toward the dining room, crystal bracelets clinking at her wrist. "How do you feel about cheese and Ritz for breakfast?"

Mandy gave us a look like we'd just offered her cocaine, while Felicity looked positively cheered at the possibility of cheese. Tam shook her head and made a small tsking noise with her lips.

"Och, ladies. Best to start your day with a healthy breakfast and a good workout. Get the blood flowing."

Nova nodded in agreement. She was one of those people who woke up refreshed and went for a morning run before her coffee. It was my least favorite thing about her.

"I keep telling them that." Nova and Tam beamed at each other, kindred souls apparently, while Lyra gave a delicate shudder.

"They never let me prepare a proper breakfast for them." Lyra pulled mugs from the cupboard, rinsing the dust, and shortly, the women all had cups of coffee and were settled at the table. My brain had finally decided to wake up a bit and check into the conversation, which was currently, from my estimation, about the price of a pack of biscuits.

"Such a shame." Felicity shook her head, pressing her lips together, a pinched look coming over her face. "The kids are desperate for more, but I'm not made of money, am I?"

"Too much sugar in biscuits," Tam declared, sipping her black coffee. "Hidden sugars in everything these days."

We sat around the dining table tucked in an alcove off the main room of the house, while Broca reclined on the armchair nearby. In the morning light, I could easily see the dust that had accumulated, and I couldn't fully blame Mandy for her disapproving looks. As it was, she barely relaxed into her chair, sitting on the edge like it was going to explode at any moment, never resting her arms on the dusty table. Instead, she clutched her coffee in front of her, her fixed smile beginning to make me wonder if this was her resting Barbie face, likely contemplating how her life choices had landed her here, in this dirty house.

"Was there something you needed to talk about?" I asked, forcing my thoughts away from all the things I needed to do to make this space homey again, starting first with a good solid clean, and realized that I'd, once again, shoved my foot in it. The conversation halted, and everyone gave me those pained looks that people get when you don't follow the correct social niceties. Fine by me. Niceties came in the afternoon, when it was a proper time to visit, not at first blush of morning.

"Yes, of course there is." Mandy gave me a disapproving look and clutched her coffee cup hard. I began to worry it would shatter and stain her pink pantsuit. Did she sleep in that outfit? I pictured her stepping into a closet and hanging herself up by the loop in the back of her suitcoat, powering down for the night. I chuckled. The other women looked at me with concern. At least I found myself humorous. "Now that you're all here, we'll have our first Charms meeting next week once you've settled, but in the meantime, we have a more pressing issue to address."

"Mm-hmm, we do." Felicity nodded. "We really do."

"And that is?" Just what I needed, more people complaining about the snow.

"Your magick, of course." Mandy's hands were growing white where they gripped the cup. "Your birthday is tomorrow, and we'll need to discuss how we deal with it."

"Och, that's a grand way to put it, isn't it? If she wasn't already nervous, you're certainly going to make her so." Tam rolled her eyes, slouching backward in her chair, fingers tapping on her leg.

"Why would I be nervous?" I mean, of course I'd given thought to my twenty-fifth birthday and the potential magick I'd receive. Every witch did. Had I made spreadsheets and run probability tests? Maybe. But that was neither here nor there. As Broca gleefully reminded me, the magick I ended up with was one thing that I could not manifest myself.

Much to my deep annoyance.

Maybe I needed to change my middle name to Sloane Annoyance MacGregor, because as of late, I'd been leaning far more into the tetchy side of my personality than ever before. I hated not being in control. And the more I tried not to focus on my looming birthday, the bigger the expectations grew in my head.

"As we all know," Mandy began, placing her coffee cup on the table—thank goddess—before she actually broke it, "the MacGregor bloodline carries a very unfortunate curse. One that has ramifications for all involved, including those who could be exposed to collateral damage."

"Collateral damage," Felicity repeated, nodding vigorously, eyes widened.

"It's imperative we handle this situation before it gets out of hand," Mandy continued, tension beginning to band my jaw as I grit my teeth. She gave me a tight smile. "Of course, we wish you the happiest of birthdays and all that, but we'll need to keep you closely monitored at all times tomorrow."

"Oh, you're getting a babysitter," Nova singsonged, flicking the back of my hand with her finger.

"I most certainly am not," I said, glaring at her.

"More like a security detail," Lyra said, grinning at me. "How very chic."

"More like assets," Mandy interjected. The smile stayed cemented in place, but I was beginning to suspect it was taking magick of major proportions to do so. "Having a coven to assist you during your change is a huge asset to any burgeoning witch. That way we can quickly disperse any . . . abnormalities."

"Yes, abnormalities. Wouldn't want that." Felicity shook her head, hair spilling from her messy bun, and she shoved it back into its scrunchie in a practiced move.

My eyes rounded, horror filling me.

"Bloody hell, Mandy. Have some tact." Tam leaned forward, snapping her fingers to bring my attention to her. "What Madame President is trying to say is that because we don't know how your magick is going to manifest, the very least we can do is be here to help—just in case things go a little haywire—and we can corral any . . . issues . . . that may arise."

"And we're throwing you a cèilidh!" Felicity bounced in her seat, clapping her hands.

"Wait . . . what?" I gasped. I hated parties where I was the center of attention, let alone parties that required dancing and paying attention to instructions.

"We've invited the whole town. The Charms are all very excited," Felicity continued. "I'll make banoffee pudding, as it's the kids' favorite."

"Wouldn't you make Sloane's favorite? It's her birthday." Tam raised an eyebrow, and Felicity's face fell.

"Oh, sure. Right. Well, Sloane? What's your favorite birthday treat, then?"

I just gaped at the women, my brain bouncing between potential magickal abnormalities and types of birthday cake.

"How can the whole town be invited to something when you didn't even know we'd be arriving?" I asked, my mouth finally spitting out a thought.

"It's not a large town," Tam said as she finished her coffee. "You'll learn quickly that people will know when you run out of toilet paper."

"*Delightful* imagery, as always, Tam," Mandy said, annoyed.

"I'm not wrong—"

"Nevertheless, we can move on. Sloane, please. There's a small matter of the MacGregor curse. The truth is that your magick will likely misfire when it manifests tomorrow. This shouldn't come as a surprise to you, and the Charms are here to assist you during this difficult transition."

"Are you changing into a werewolf or something?" Nova slanted a look at me, barely constrained glee behind her eyes. "Transitioning and all that."

"I do love dogs," I admitted, and she snorted.

"Old Mr. Sturrock accidentally did. Remember that one Samhain?" Felicity shivered, crossing her arms over the large tote she still held in her lap. Maybe it was her emotional support tote, as I'd yet to see her stop hugging it.

"Ladies, if I may?" Broca interjected from the armchair, though it wasn't really a question. Conversation ceased, and we all turned to look at Broca, who was calmly filing a painted green nail into a point just short of a talon. "Sloane will be delighted to have your assistance tomorrow as she celebrates stepping into her magick. The cèilidh sounds like great fun. It will be the perfect way for the girls to meet everyone in town while also reassuring people that there is nothing to worry about now that we are home."

"But—"

"And she just loves banoffee pudding, don't you, Sloane?" Broca gave me such a sharp look that I shrank back into my seat.

Mandy nodded curtly.

"It's settled, then. We'll see you tomorrow, ladies, and remember—"

"Never harm, always charm," Nova sang too sweetly, and Felicity clapped, jumping out of her seat in excitement.

"Oh, goodie, I can't wait. The kids are going to be so excited. Charm on, witches!" Felicity fluttered her fingers at us, and I internally groaned.

Tam patted my shoulder as she passed, before lecturing Felicity about the sugar levels in the pudding. At the door, Mandy stopped and turned back to us.

"Well, now we have that sorted, I'm sure tomorrow will go swimmingly." Glaring at the snow that swirled through the front door, Mandy left. I noticed not a single flake dared to land on her pantsuit, and I had to hand it to her—the witch had power. Even if it came in the form of magickal Scotchgard.

"Well, if you weren't nervous before . . ." Lyra grimaced in my direction.

"Now I'm terrified." And I was at that. And nowhere in my calculations had I even considered the potential of me turning into a werewolf, and while, logically, I understood that wasn't the way our witchy magick worked, it now felt like anything was possible.

"Is that a hair on your chin?" Nova leaned forward and squinted at my face, and I gasped, jumping up from the chair.

"I hate you." Stomping across the room, I made for the bathroom.

"Girls, leave her be. It's tough not knowing what your magick will be." Broca's voice floated after me as I climbed the stairs.

I hated uncertainty—hated not knowing. It unsettled me in a way that excited other people. But, maybe, just maybe, the ability to see the future would be my magick. I held on to that hope as I slammed the bathroom door and turned on the shower.

Surely it wouldn't be all that bad, right?

CHAPTER FOUR
Sloane

"That poor tree," Nova said, nodding to the massive yew tree in the center of the town square, its leaves now leaden with snow.

After breakfast, Broca had promptly ordered us into town for supplies, claiming she needed a nap to have the energy to deal with all of us. I suspected it was more to ease the pain from her recent hip surgery but agreed to get out of her hair for a while. Largely because I knew she was going to hate me later when I started her on the daily walks detailed in the physical therapist's instructions Broca must have hidden in a kitchen drawer. I was glad to do it, too, because never once had Broca asked for help. She'd been a constant in our lives, even when our mother had dragged us away, and we'd always stayed in consistent communication.

Cobblestone streets, black Victorian-style streetlamps, and strands of string lights surrounded the interior of the square that showcased the ancient yew tree. It felt like stepping back in time, which I supposed helped with the magickal vibe the tourism board was going for, and haunting music drifted in the air.

"I can't believe it. Did they pipe spooky music in?" Lyra pointed to small speakers built into the base of the light pole. "The streetlights have speakers attached."

"Setting the mood. Okay, okay, I dig it. They're committed," Nova said.

Snow swirled under the streetlamps, a frolicky little dance of flakes, and a woman glared out from a shop window.

"'The Dragon's Hoard.'" I read the black sign over the window, the letters etched in gold with tiny flame scrolls. The window showcased all things shiny and sparkly, a gift shop catering to what I assumed most dragons would love—all that glitters—and I smiled at a black crystal dragon figurine with glittering ruby eyes. "I'm not going to lie, I'd buy that dragon in a heartbeat."

"Do you want it for your birthday?" Lyra bounced on her feet. I rarely let them buy me anything, largely because we had to pack up and move so often. What was the point of acquiring trinkets if I had no place to put said trinkets?

"Mmm." I wavered. The dragon was pretty cool.

"You know she'll say no. She always does." Nova tucked her scarf into her leather jacket.

I wasn't that boring and predictable, was I? The dragon gleamed in the light, and I sighed, coveting it. If it weren't as large as it was, I probably would have let them buy it for me immediately.

"How about this? If we break this curse, that dragon will be my reward. You can gift it to me then."

"That's fair. I'll allow it." Nova patted my back like an approving schoolteacher, and I shrugged off her touch, moving to the next store.

"'The Veilcrest School of Spells.' Huh. Imagine that. A spell-casting school, of all things. Sloane, you can enroll once you get your magick," Nova said, her tone gleeful.

"'The science of spell-making. Harvesting ingredients. Full moon rituals,'" Lyra read from a sign on the window. "This sounds really interesting."

"I'm not going back to school." I'd hated school, hated being on someone else's schedule, hated learning about subjects that didn't interest me. But if I loved something, like literature, then I leaned all in. My biggest regret about moving was that I couldn't take my books with me.

"Look, an enchanted bakery. 'Mystic Munchies.'" Lyra snickered. "'Charming cakes and bewitching biscuits.'"

"This is nothing like I remember it. Briarhaven really has turned itself into a theme park, hasn't it? But, like, kind of classy? It's not like Disney." Nova said as we all tilted our heads to watch a chocolate fountain situated in the front window of the bakery. The chocolate poured from the mouth of a croissant dragon and coated tiny bubbles that floated up from what had to be a cauldron of dry ice perched beneath it.

Except I was fairly certain dry ice didn't send bubbles into the air. Let alone bubbles strong enough to be coated in liquid chocolate.

"They're using magick out in the open," Lyra breathed, fixated on the window. "How are they getting away with this?"

"Sometimes, hiding in plain sight is the easiest way to go unnoticed," I murmured, transfixed on the chocolate-covered bubbles.

I wanted to reach in and pop one.

"This is really working for the town." Nova looked up as a trio of tourists, speaking Spanish, pushed past us, their arms laden with shopping bags despite the snow.

"It really is a safe spot for magickals to live," I said. "Broca told me they dreamt it up after Airbnb became so popular, particularly with people wanting holidays based on unique experiences. It was a way to bring tourism money to the town, while also allowing those with magick to live openly."

"Bloody brilliant, really," Lyra mused, still transfixed on the bakery window. I was certain her head was already running with about a million ideas for new recipes.

Continuing on, we stopped across the street from a pub called the Rune & Rose. A handsome man, a winter hat pulled low over his brow, shoveled the walkway in front of the pub. He glanced up and then gave us a narrow-eyed look. Our reputation had preceded us, I saw.

"Friendly neighbors, as I recall." Nova waved at the man shoveling, who turned his back and stomped inside. "Or not."

"Can you blame him? We'd just gone into a bonnie autumn, and now endless winter is upon us. I'd be pretty annoyed too." A blast of icy wind splattered snow across my face. "Scratch that. I *am* annoyed."

"It's hardly our fault that our bloodline carries a curse. And a stupid one at that. We're bad-luck charms for every town we live in, and we get crappy magick. It's not fair," Lyra complained.

The three of us were each born eleven months apart. And as the oldest, I had more misgivings about returning to Briarhaven than my sisters, mainly because I recalled my childhood having been deeply chaotic until my mother had kicked our father to the curb and dragged us to the States, swearing to never step foot here again. She'd held true to her word, stopping short of making us promise not to return, but those early days of misfiring magick and high tension had instilled in me a deep need for routine and calm in my life.

Which makes moving every year or so one of my biggest frustrations in life.

And I also couldn't really blame Briarhaven for not rolling out the welcome mat upon our return. Our family had been notoriously difficult, largely due to my parents and their deeply toxic relationship. How we'd managed to stay in one spot as long as we had without blowing the entire place up was still a mystery to me.

"And I don't see what the big deal is, anyway." Lyra went on, squinting into an engraved gold makeup mirror—given to her by a besotted boyfriend—and swiping on a plum-colored lip tint despite the snow. "There's always been magick in Briarhaven."

"Yeah, but everyone had to hide it. Guess they got tired of living a lie," Nova said.

"It wasn't a lie. It's just that historically the real world hasn't taken too kindly to witches."

"And werewolves. Your new brethren." Lyra leaned closer and squinted her eyes at my chin. "Are you certain those aren't whiskers I see sprouting?"

"I swear to the goddess I will break that fancy mirror of yours." I dove for the mirror, and Lyra squealed, dropping it into her purse.

"Lorenzo would just replace it if you did."

"Of course he would." I couldn't help myself and ran a hand over my chin. No hairs to be found. "Let's just get this list done and get back home. I'm feeling . . . weird."

"Weird how?" Instantly, both my sisters leaned forward, taking me seriously. I wasn't one for dramatics, so if I mentioned something felt off, they usually listened.

I rolled my shoulders.

"I don't know. Ever since we've been back in Scotland, it's like . . . like I have an itch between my shoulder blades I can't scratch. I feel on edge." I twisted my purse strap in my hand. "I'm so used to being untethered, yet we have roots here. I don't know how to match up what was with what is, if that makes any sense?"

"It's like trying to attach a fallen branch back to a tree." Nova nodded and patted my shoulder.

"Yeah, kind of like that, I guess. I don't know."

"Like it or not, your magick is about to appear. And we all know just how much you like being in charge."

"Here's your informational packet on our new town, ladies." Nova's voice took on a lecturing tone, mimicking me. "Color-coded with safety warnings, cultural nuances, and a few key phrases in the local language."

"Remember never to shop too much, as we'll have to pack up and leave," Lyra chimed in.

"And above all else, tell your sisters where you're going," Lyra and Nova said together, and I rolled my eyes.

"You make me sound like an overbearing mother."

"Not overbearing, no." Lyra reached over and squeezed my arm. "It's nice to have someone who cares. But, you know, it wouldn't hurt to have you loosen up a little bit."

"I just don't want to see anything bad happen to you both."

"You can't protect us from everything. Hell, it's not like Mum ever bothered to." Nova's voice held a cool indifference that I knew well enough hid the hurts she harbored.

That we all harbored.

"Did you tell her we were coming back here?" Lyra asked, and I closed my eyes, replaying the conversation in my head.

"Small towns breed small-minded people. If you go back there, don't bother contacting me again."

I disagreed with my mother. Small-minded people could be found anywhere. But, somewhere along the line, Briarhaven, or our father, had hurt our mother so deeply that she was taking our return as a personal betrayal.

"Yup. It went as well as could be expected." I shrugged, hiding the brunt of what Mum had said from my sisters, as I always did. I'm not sure why I still shielded them from her, as they were grown adults. Yet there was something about a mother putting herself first, over and over again, that reopened those childhood wounds that we had all done our best to heal from. "Shall we crack on? Divide and conquer?" I held up the list, signaling the discussion about our mother was done.

What was there to discuss, anyway? Mum wasn't speaking to us, and Dad had disappeared without a trace years ago. We could go in circles about it or get on with living our lives. But as the snow piled up around us, I knew I'd rather move forward and get us back to cozying up before the fire while we shined up our childhood home.

"I'll hit the Silver Quill for books," Nova said, studying my list.

"I'll go to Cauldron's Cupboard for groceries." Lyra rubbed her hands together in anticipation. "And a quick stop at Mystic Munchies, of course."

"Right, then I'll take the Pixie Dust Apothecary for medicine." Despite myself, my lips quirked. "I do like the names."

"Me too. I mean, if you're going to be a theme park, might as well lean into it, right?" Nova agreed, waving to the man who now looked at us from the front window of the pub.

"Meet back here in an hour." My sisters scattered, likely ready to be out of the snow, but I lingered a moment, studying the pub across the street. Last I could remember, it had been a community center of sorts. I supposed it still was, just now with food and beverage.

The Rune & Rose.

A pretty name for a pretty pub. Two arched windows, with paned glass, shone warm light against the snow that swirled outside. The pub was cream brick, with a bright red door, and the black-and-red sign had gold painting on the letters. A rose twisted around a dagger, with runes down the blade, and a shiver of knowing filled me. Celtic music lilted, muffled from inside, and a few people sat before a thick stone fireplace. Homey, warm, and welcoming.

Yearning filled me. It was true, what I'd said about being used to being untethered. That didn't mean I had to like it. I'd long ago accepted that we needed to keep moving, that ours was the life of a nomad, yet that didn't necessarily have to sit well with me. A part of me craved the predictability of being rooted in one spot, the sameness of small-town life, the ability to build a community of sorts.

"Never harm, always charm!"

I snorted as Mandy's voice rang in my head. Okay, maybe not *that* community. I could never imagine myself being friends with the fembot of a coven leader, as she and I were worlds apart.

Turning, I wandered down the sidewalk toward the apothecary, breathing a sigh of relief when the snow lessened and a few shafts of sunlight split the blanket of moody clouds above. Crouching at a trio of pumpkins displayed by a front door, I brushed snow from the grinning jack-o'-lantern faces. I hoped the snow wouldn't impact the Halloween festivities too much. It wouldn't be entirely unusual, as I recalled a time or two when we went guising as children when we'd had to bundle up with warm jumpers under our costumes.

A memory of Broca, dressed entirely in sequins as Glinda the good witch, accompanying us as we went guising from house to house, brought a flicker of warmth to me. It hadn't been all bad,

I reminded myself, and pushed through the front door of a brilliant pink building with a turquoise door and mustard-yellow trim. Pixie Dust Apothecary was everything it promised to be, with mirrored glass shelves holding hundreds of bottles and vials of all shapes and sizes, and long wooden tables clustered with charming boxes of herbs and teas. Soft harp music played in the background, and a stunning woman wearing a shimmering velvet green dress slinked forward. Her blond hair tumbled past her shoulders, a tiara of rose quartz crystals pulling it back from her face, and diamonds winked at her ears.

"Raven O'Ryan!" I exclaimed.

"Sloane MacGregor. I knew you bitches had to be back in town when the weather turned." Raven threw her arms around me and gave me a hug, rocking back and forth three times as I inhaled the scent of lavender. Pulling back, she held me at arm's length and studied me.

"Bloody hell, Raven. You're gorgeous." I blinked at her. Raven had been an awkward child with buck teeth, messy hair, and a propensity for wearing the baggiest clothes she could find.

"Yes, much like Briarhaven, I've had a bit of a glow-up." Raven twirled, her arms outstretched. "You like?"

"Knocked it out of the park," I said. "This is *your* shop? I'm impressed. It's so pretty, Raven."

"It is, it is. When the Douglases came up with the plan to revamp Briarhaven, I jumped at the chance to get my own shop. They held it for me until I was old enough to sign a lease, and I've been here ever since."

"Is that right? That's unusually nice of them."

"They wanted the locals to invest in the town. And since they knew that all I did was study spells and medicine, well, it was a natural fit." Raven came from a long line of healers, so much of her education wouldn't have been found in books either. It was a smart move on the Douglases' part, keeping her and her family tethered here, as the NHS was so backed up lately when it came to medical appointments. "It's good to see you, Sloane."

"Is it?" I nodded toward the snow that fell in fat flakes outside the window.

"Och, it's nothing we haven't dealt with before." Raven waved away the snow like it was not an issue at all. "We'll get it sorted, much like we do everything else that comes our way."

"That's a relief to hear, as not everyone has taken so kindly to our arrival."

"Screw 'em," Raven said, and I burst out laughing.

"I've missed you," I blurted.

Raven looked up from where she'd begun to unbox sachets of lavender.

"I haven't gone anywhere, have I, then?"

"No, that's on me," I admitted, moving farther into the shop, the coziness easing some of the tension at my shoulders. "I was so busy taking care of Lyra and Nova that I was horrible at keeping up with everyone. It felt like one too many things to handle, you know?"

"I don't, at that. But I also don't have an impossible mother and a disappearing father. So for that, I'll be giving you a wee pass. *This time.*" Raven gave me a stern look. "But next time you just up and disappear on me, don't expect me to be so welcoming."

Tears threatened, surprising me, and I turned away so she wouldn't see them. Forgiveness, coming so easily, touched my heart.

"Understood."

"The Charms could use you, as well."

I whirled, surprised. "You're a part of the Charms?"

Raven put both of her hands beneath her chin and fluttered her eyelashes. "Never harm, always charm!"

I snorted. "How did they rope you into that?"

"All the women in my family have been in it. Kind of a legacy seat situation, like yours. It's not so bad if you can get past Mandy's head cheerleader mentality."

"She's terrifying. Her smile never breaks."

"It's a real feat." Raven chuckled. "Not to mention her strict adherence to the rules. We bring *this* casserole for Mabon and *this* casserole for moon baths. She's wound so tightly I'm surprised she doesn't explode into a ball of pink glitter."

"I really don't think I want to be a part of a coven, Raven. It just doesn't sound like something that's for me." Joining, well, anything, really, was far outside my comfort zone. I'd made the mistake of joining a netball team once in high school, only to have to miss several practices due to my unreliable parents. And by the time I'd finally gotten them to pay enough attention to what I needed, Mum had uprooted us from town. After that, I'd found it had just become easier to abstain from group activities than to become a part of a community.

Raven gave me a knowing look. "I hope you'll change your mind. It would be nice to have you at the meetings."

I shrugged, noncommittal, picked up a green vial, and held it to the light. "Broca's had hip replacement surgery and doesn't much want to take any pain meds for it."

"Sure, and she has the right of it. The pain lets us know when we're doing too much. Nevertheless, I have some things to aid the healing process, which will in turn ease her pain." Raven strode to her shelves and began to gather a few jars and bottles. "This one, the arnica cream? Great for aches and pains. I've added a dose of thistle, harvested under a full moon, to aid its power."

I leaned against a wall as Raven went to work, picking up a strand of amethyst stones and running them through my fingers like worry beads.

"How's it been here?"

"Since you've left?" Raven glanced over her shoulder. "Same. And not the same at all, I guess. Obviously, Briarhaven basically shut down for a year as we completely rehauled the downtown and turned it into what you see today. That was kind of a wild time, everyone picking colors for their buildings, voting on shop names, that kind of thing. It was fun, in its own way, even though it took ages to make decisions. I swear, everyone has an opinion on something. Och, it went well enough, though, I suppose, considering how quickly it moved. Knox did a good job with it."

"Did he?" I twisted the strand around my finger. "He's young to be provost, isn't he?"

"Is he?" Sloane shrugged as she brought jars over to the counter. "I guess, not too much older than us. He does a good job, and people really love him."

"I don't." I closed my hands tightly around the stones.

Raven glanced up at me, a considering look in her eyes.

"I didn't say you did."

Caught, I looked up at her and then gently unwound the strand of beads I was mangling between my hands and put it on the counter. "He tried to kick us out yesterday."

"Ah." Raven's lips quirked and I stepped forward.

"What's that look for?"

"Nothing . . . och, it's just . . ." Raven waved a hand in the air with a laugh. "Didn't you fancy the lad a bit back in the day?"

I drew myself up. "I most certainly did not."

"I mean, we all did, right? He was kind of the golden boy of sorts. Still is, I guess. Hell, I'd make a play for him if I didn't have my sights set on another."

"Who do you like?" I asked, desperate for a change in conversation.

"That, my friend, takes more than breezing back into my shop after years of silence." Raven nodded to the front door, where bells jingled and new customers arrived. "I'll tell you over a pint sometime. Call me. We have a lot to catch up on."

Raven packaged everything neatly in an eggplant-purple bag, with a pretty sparkling black bow attached to it. She tucked her card inside, along with her number, and gave me a quick hug before attending to her new customers. Bundling the bag under my coat, since it was too pretty to get wet with snow, I beelined for the car, my mind whirling.

Had I fancied Knox? More so than anyone else?

It was weird how my mind had blocked out many memories from that time in my life. It had been so chaotic, my parents constantly fighting, and I'd tried to spend as much time away from home as I could. Then, when Mum had taken us abroad, well, we'd flitted from town to town so fast that everything had blurred together. Call it trauma or call it a blessing, but either way, the memories lay hidden behind the veil of time. Including any supposed crush I might have had on Knox. That certainly won't be rekindled, that's for sure.

Picking up my pace against the icy wind that shoved me back, I pushed toward the parking lot. I blew into the car, slamming the door behind me, a flurry of snow and packages, to find my sisters already there.

"Sorry about that. Were you waiting long?" I gasped, my cheeks stinging from the snow.

"Not too long at all. But it's cold." Lyra rubbed her hands together and blew on them, nodding toward the ignition. "Can you start the car?"

"Aye, nae bother." Already my Scots was coming back to me. I'd largely been Americanized since I'd left, finding it easier to blend in at schools when I'd let my accent drop, but it was slowly coming back now that I was here.

Home.

Turning the key, I blinked at the clicking noise that emanated from the steering column. Lights flashed on the dashboard, but the car didn't start.

"Damn it," I breathed, slamming my fist on the steering column. "Battery's dead."

"Noooo," Nova wailed.

"I didn't pack for this weather."

"How can we have a dead—"

Something pounded my window, and we all screamed.

CHAPTER FIVE
Knox Douglas

I wasn't sure what the MacGregor sisters were doing huddled in their car, which looked to have its bumper being held together by duct tape, but I could surmise pretty easily that there was a problem when it didn't immediately start and leave the car park. Slanting a glance up at the murky gray clouds and sleeting snow, I sighed and pulled my waxed canvas jacket on.

I'd taken a seat at the Rune & Rose, needing a moment to decompress with my mate Liam, who owned the place. He was as tall as I was, with lighter hair than me, and bright blue eyes that had melted more than one woman's heart.

"How you getting on, then?" Liam nodded out the window toward the snow.

We'd known each other since after high school, and nothing had made me happier than when he'd decided to stay here and open his own pub. His witchy-themed cocktails were infamous, and a huge draw for his clientele. Even now, as he poured dry ice into a glass of gin, and the drink bubbled and steamed, his customers laughed and filmed the display for their social media. His drinks were innovative, each one being named after a different type of magickal potion or a famous witch, like Isobel Gowdie, condemned to death in Scotland's history.

"Och, it's a bit brisk, isn't it?" I said, downplaying the calamity of winter weather wreaking havoc on our town. Ever since Sloane had slammed the door in my face the night before, I'd been dealing with one issue after another, as the snow caused chaos through the town. A hot coffee and a cuppa soup was what I needed.

Not more problems with Sloane.

A memory surfaced. Sloane, sullen and angry, kicking a football down an alley behind her house, shouts sounding from the open window.

A plate had smashed, the noise echoing across the cobblestones, and Sloane had whirled, wiping a tear from her cheek.

I'd stopped, unable to resist offering help to someone, particularly *this* someone.

Sloane MacGregor. I'd seen her at my football practice one day, walking past the pitch, and I'd quickly grown fascinated. We didn't go to the same school, and were a few years apart, so I'd started detouring on my walk home to go past the street I'd learned she lived on.

Hoping for a glimpse. A chance run-in.

But I'd never hoped for it to be like this.

I had paused, uncertain what to do, and Sloane had kicked the ball forcefully against the wall. The ball had bounced, ricocheting wildly, and landed at my feet.

Picking it up, I'd waited as she'd stomped toward me, all teenage angst and stubborn beauty.

"You all right?" I'd asked, worried for her.

"Aye." She'd grabbed the ball, and I held it a moment longer than necessary, wanting her to meet my eyes. When she'd finally looked up, I'd glimpsed worlds of pain in her depths, and I wanted to reach out, to hug her, to offer her some sort of solace. Yet I'd been just an awkward teenager, unversed in the ways of navigating troubled families.

"If you need . . ." I trailed off as she yanked the ball from my hands and stomped away.

I'd been privy to a private moment. It wasn't my burden to share.

Frankly, all of the MacGregor sisters were beautiful, but it had always been Sloane that had caught my eye. Moody greenish eyes, lilting toward gray, a stubborn chin, and a mouth made for kissing.

Not that I'd ever tried. Our paths had only crossed a few times in childhood, but the girl she had been paled in comparison to the woman she'd bloomed into. I'd been stunned yesterday, having difficulty finding my words as she'd angrily waved her hands in front of my face.

Sloane MacGregor. My secret teenage crush had blossomed into one hell of a woman.

Not that it much mattered what I thought one way or the other. She needed to leave. Along with her family.

"Put it on my tab, mate." I nodded out the window to the car that was currently being covered with snow.

"Och, it's a dreich day, lad. I heard it's the MacGregors we have to thank for this lovely weather," Liam said, clearing my soup bowl.

"It's not their fault." I surprised myself by defending them. I needed them to go, didn't I? It would be easier if the town was on my side. I'd worked too hard to bring Briarhaven back from the brink of desolation to have the sisters and their blood curse mess things up.

"Aye, it's a right shite curse, isn't it, then?" Liam mopped the bar with a towel, squinting out the window.

Shrugging, I left the pub, nodding at a few people on the way out. Tugging my wool cap from my pocket, I pulled it over my hair and zipped my coat against the wind, stomping through the snow that had accumulated on the path to the car park.

I could hear the starter clicking, indicating a dead battery, from across the lot. Sighing, I stopped outside the car and knocked on the window.

Screams rose from inside.

Despite myself, I laughed, and brushed the snow away from the window until Sloane's glaring face appeared.

My heart tripped as I took in her scowl, the pretty curve of her lips. The door cracked open, and Sloane leaned her head out.

"Car troubles, lass?" I asked, fully knowing there was, indeed, a problem.

"Nope." Sloane sniffed and moved to close the door. I caught the frame with my hand and held it open, easily enough, and Sloane glared up at my hand.

"I could break your fingers if I slammed them in the door."

"I would advise against doing so," I suggested, leaning closer.

"Then take your hand off my door."

"It's clear you need help. Your battery is dead."

"Yesterday you wanted to kick us out and today you want to help us?" Sloane arched a brow at me.

"Can't leave town with a dead battery, can you now, lass? Go on, then, lift the bonnet for me."

"Just let him do it, Sloane. It's freezing," Nova hissed from the back seat, and I leaned in farther to see Lyra and Nova, matching scowls on their faces.

"I should be able to get you sorted shortly, ladies."

"Thank you. Our hero." Lyra fluttered her eyelashes at me, the warmest one of the bunch, and I grinned at her. Sloane rolled her eyes.

"A little warmth goes a long way," I said, helpless not to poke at her.

"And was that a warm welcome you were giving us last night, then?" Sloane asked, her eyes widening as she crossed her arms over her chest.

"Touché."

The bonnet popped open, and I moved around the front of the car, angling my face away from the arctic wind. While it would be easy enough to go get my car, jump the battery, and get the women on their way, it would take a lot more time than what I wanted. Glancing over my shoulder to make sure there were no wayward tourists wandering about, I held my hands over the battery.

A current of magick rolled through me, and the battery briefly illuminated before returning to normal.

My magick had always worked that way. It hummed inside me, like being plugged into an electrical socket, and the first year after I'd turned twenty-five had been wild as I'd learned how to harness it. I was best with elemental energy, invoking electrical currents, lighting flames, redirecting water—that kind of thing. But I'd also learned that I had strengths in many areas. Turned out, as I was a protector of Briarhaven, my magick had arrived as a jack-of-all-trades. It was useful, in many situations such as this one, and I'd been grateful for my gift many times since.

Slamming the bonnet, I rounded the car as the door cracked open again.

"Go on, then, give it a go."

Sloane bit her lip, annoyed with me but clearly wanting her car to work. She turned the key, and the engine caught easily, much to the joy of her sisters.

"Thanks, I guess." Sloane slanted me a look.

"I meant what I said, Sloane. I need you all to leave before this gets much worse."

"That sounds like a *you* problem, not an *us* problem," Sloane said, and yanked the door shut. I pulled my fingers away just in time and stepped back as she reversed from the car park.

Her snotty attitude should make me dislike her more, and yet for some reason, it made me want to break through her walls and peel back her layers. Which, frankly, was infuriating. The Douglas family had prided itself on keeping peace here for centuries now, our duties taken seriously, and I wasn't going to be the one that would allow our perfect record to be broken.

Or so I'd been not-so-gently reminded by my overbearing parents last night.

They'd phoned me from their riverboat cruise in Vienna, noting a disturbance in the force, and I'd had to listen to them rant about the

MacGregors and how they should have exiled the whole family from town years ago. By the time they'd clicked off, my mother on her third martini, I hadn't spoken in almost forty minutes. It had always been that way—my parents ordering us about—while we'd all had to fall in line. And the message had been clear. Sloane was the enemy, at least according to them. Who was I to even consider standing up to centuries of Douglas family tradition? What was good for Briarhaven always came first.

No matter what.

Duty weighed heavily on my shoulders. As firstborn, the responsibility had fallen to me to take up the helm when my parents had decided they wanted to see more of the world than tiny Briarhaven. They hadn't even asked. As soon as I'd finished uni, I'd been brought back to Briarhaven and installed as provost, and they'd left. My two brothers, on the other hand, got to backpack through Europe and find themselves. Whatever that meant.

Instead, I'd put my business degree to use. If I was going to be stuck in Briarhaven, I could, at the very least, solve some issues that the town struggled with. A glaring oversight on my parents' part. Not that I'd ever bring it up to them. Their wrath wasn't worth pointing out that I thought they'd rested on their laurels, allowing the town to descend into an almost state of disrepair, as a tough economy had made everyone tighten their belts. Coupled with a reputation that Briarhaven was boring and decrepit, and the village had started to become a "must-miss" on a tourist's itinerary.

Instead of railing against the reputation, I'd decided to lean into it. One night, after a few too many whiskies, I'd been moaning to Liam about the town's woes when we'd stumbled upon the idea of making it a theme park of sorts—more attraction than theme park, really, as we didn't have rides. A tourist destination for those who love all things magickal. I'd spent weeks drawing up the presentation and the zoning plans, and had even offered small business loans at zero percent interest for the townsfolk who were ready to invest.

To my surprise, my parents had given me the go-ahead, and mostly everyone had embraced the new vision for Briarhaven. Not only has it been a roaring success, but it has also provided a much-needed refuge for the magickals in our world.

Gone were the days where we could live freely.

Briarhaven had been the home to a variety of magickal families for centuries. Witches, fae, broonies, and elves . . . all sorts of creatures with power resided here. As the years crept by and the human population grew, magickals—some feared, most untrusted—were forced to live in hiding lest their kind be hunted. The people of Briarhaven had long ago assimilated to the human world, but there was only so much we could do to hide the wisp of "otherness" that clung to our town. By turning Briarhaven into a destination, I'd been able to explain away many of the unexplainable happenings in our town. It was a point of pride for me, because I did feel that everyone should be allowed to live in peace, without persecution for what they were.

Briarhaven was happy, healthy, and thriving.

The return of the MacGregors didn't bode well for this prosperous town. As for the pretty Sloane MacGregor, no matter how very much I wanted to trail my lips over that stubborn point of her chin and sink my teeth into that full bottom lip, I needed to stay focused on the one thing that mattered the most. Protecting Briarhaven at all costs.

CHAPTER SIX
Sloane

"I think Grumpy McProvost has the hots for you," Lyra said as I drove us carefully home through snow-slicked streets.

"Totally does," Nova agreed from the back seat, where she'd opened a package of blueberries and was popping them in her mouth one by one.

Heat rushed through me, the mere thought of Knox's hands on my body doing strange things to my insides, and I shook my head.

"You're too used to seeing love everywhere. You can't help it."

"I'm used to seeing people fall for *me*," Lyra clarified, not being remotely arrogant. She was just stating the facts. How she remained down-to-earth, I did not know, but somehow my stunning sister was just as sweet as she looked. "His eyes weren't on me, Sloane. They were on you."

"That's because I'm in the driver's seat."

"Hardly. It's because he wants to play spin the bottle with you." Nova made kissy-faced sucking noises.

"What are you . . . a child?" I flicked a glance at the rearview mirror to see Nova enthusiastically kissing her hand. "Who even plays spin the bottle anymore?"

"I don't know. I figured it was something you ancient folks played at parties in high school."

"Ancient? Kindly go screw yourself, Nova. You're barely two years younger than me."

"Aww, did I strike a nerve, darling?" Nova beamed, happy with herself. "I'm told werewolves are quite bitchy around that time of the month."

"I'm not going to be a werewolf!" I slammed the brakes a touch harder than necessary in front of our house and slid the front of the car neatly into a snowbank. "Lovely, just lovely."

"I know a hot . . . muscular . . . dreamy"—Lyra panted the words, putting on a sex-bomb act, trailing a finger down her chest—"grumpy provost who will help you out of a jam."

"I should have left you two at home," I grumbled, getting out of the car and walking to the snowbank to assess the damage. The front of the car was tucked into the pile of snow, but not far enough that it would be an issue. At least I hoped not. Considering myself parked, I opened the back door to a grinning Nova and snagged some of the market bags.

"You love me," Nova insisted.

"Nope. Not even sure you're my sister."

"We're definitely sisters. Who else would put up with your attitude?"

"*My* attitude? You make me look like sunshine and lollipops, dear."

"Yes, that's you. Just an explosion of sparkles everywhere you go."

"Maybe not sparkles, but at least I don't make people reach for their weapons."

"Aww, thank you." Nova paused at the front door, holding a hand filled with shopping bags to her heart. "That might be the nicest thing you've ever said to me."

Rolling my eyes, I pushed the door open, looking back at Nova as I stepped inside.

"Being intimidating is not a positive personality trait."

"Maybe in your world it's not." Nova preened. Sighing, I turned and skidded to a stop, Nova slamming into me from behind.

"Surprise!" Broca sang.

The entire first floor had been transformed. Gone were the moldy sheets covering the furniture and the thick layer of dust on the baseboards. Streamers crisscrossed the ceiling, twinkle lights fell in curtains along the walls, and a pile of presents awaited opening on the living room table in front of the couch.

"Happy birthday, babes." Nova smacked a kiss on my cheek and ducked away before I could swat at her with my grocery bags.

"Broca! You were supposed to be resting up. Not doing all this." I hurried over to where Broca stood with her walker, in navy-blue high-waisted trousers and a sequined jumper.

"Pssht, it was hardly a bother now, was it? Just a smidge of magick and everything was put to sorts. Go on, go on, sit." Broca waved me toward the couch.

"My birthday is tomorrow," I pointed out, dropping the shopping bags on the kitchen counter and taking off my coat. After hanging it up, I moved to the couch and plopped down, staring at the pile of gifts. Anxiety kicked up. Gesturing at the pile, I opened my mouth—

"Yes, we know we have to move all the time, and we shouldn't have bought you so much stuff and where will you put it and there's no space and all that . . ." Nova waved away what she knew I was about to say.

"But don't worry, we thought ahead," Lyra promised, closing the front door behind her and dropping the rest of the bags in the kitchen. "This is an extra-special gift for our favorite witch."

"Sixty percent of the time." Nova slanted me a look, and I gave her the finger.

"We wanted to do something today, because we know the Charms will show up tomorrow to see what your magick is, and it's just a nice moment with us girls, isn't it? Family." Broca eased herself into the armchair, waving away my offer of help. Once settled, she slapped her hands on her thighs. "Now, shall we have ourselves a wee party?"

"Let me just put this stuff away. I was thinking maybe soup and a nice salad, some picky things, for lunch." Lyra loved putting together charcuterie boards, and she hummed as she quickly put the groceries away, leaving the ingredients out she'd need for later. Once finished, she brought a tray with orange juice, a bucket of champagne, and glasses over to the table.

"Should I drink?" I glanced at Broca, not knowing if alcohol would affect the manifestation of my magick later on.

"Don't worry, I thought of that." Lyra beamed at me. "Nonalcoholic."

"Oh, good." Was it? I had no idea. A glass of champagne might soothe the nerves currently playing the drums in my stomach. All day I'd been trying to ignore this Big Thing that was hanging over my head, the unknown of what magick—my magick—would be. As the hours crept by, the drums intensified, and I worried I'd have to make a run for the bathroom soon.

An odd snuffling sound came from the back room.

"What was that?" I made to get up, but Nova hopped up and pointed at me.

"Sit."

"But—"

"It's fine, Sloane. Nova, go see." Broca waved at Nova. I suppose since she insisted on being the intimidating one, she could be nominated to investigate the weird noise for all I cared. "Now, Sloane. Don't be nervous. This is such an exciting time for a witch. I promise you, whatever your magick is, you'll learn to love it."

"I'm sure, once I know how to work with it, everything will be just fine." At least that's what I kept telling myself.

Nova came in from the back room, cradling something under a blanket in her arms. My shoulders stiffened.

"Nova, I swear to the goddess, if you throw a rat on me or something—"

"Chill." Nova grinned at me. "It's your gift." Bending over, she deposited a warm bundle in my arms and my mouth dropped open.

I blinked down at a gray-and-white dog—just like a Boston terrier, except for one huge difference. As he stood on his wee paws in my lap, he shook his body out and the blanket fell off to reveal his wings.

Beautiful, milky gray, pearlescent wings in soft shimmery scales.

"An emberwolf," I breathed.

Emberwolves, a cross between wolves and dragons, had once been fierce predators and even fiercer protectors in Scotland. Domesticated through the ages, it was now rare to find them in the wild, many preferring the comfort and luxuries of living in houses. Still, they were an unusual and highly exotic pet, and I'd never seen one of this variation—with a soft coat, big loving eyes, and a mile-wide smile that made him look just a bit like the Joker from Batman but in a nonpsychotic way. Leaning up, he swiped his rough tongue across my cheek, and a laugh escaped me.

"He likes you!" Lyra exclaimed.

"But how? Where? Can I even have one?" I looked to Broca, my hands automatically reaching up to stroke his soft coat.

"A friend owed me a favor." Broca leaned forward to look at the emberwolf. "He was orphaned, but from what we can tell, he comes from a long line of working emberwolves, bred for their companionship. Can you believe these lads used to be as big as this room?"

"Then they learned we had couches." Nova snorted.

I couldn't take my eyes off him. He was just about the cutest animal I'd ever seen.

"And yes, you can have one."

"What about when we go?" I reached up to scratch an ear, and he leaned into my palm, letting out a soft snort of contentment. His wings stretched, fluttering out, and I waited to see if he would try to fly. Instead, he settled contentedly onto my lap, tucking his wings back at his sides, his eyes drooping closed.

"That's the whole point of you being here, Sloane." Broca's tone took on a serious note, and I finally raised my eyes from the emberwolf to her. "To finally sort out this curse nonsense. So you don't have to leave. At least, if you don't want to." Stay here, instead of leaving? Instead of packing everything into a car, saying farewell to yet another house, another set of friends, another semi-settled existence. It had been so long since we'd simply . . . stopped. Made a home become a home.

I turned to look at my sisters, who had varying degrees of emotions flitting across their faces. Our childhood home hadn't been a happy one, and staying in one place wasn't something we were used to. What if we didn't want to stay? Reading us like a book, Broca sighed.

"At least try to break the curse before you make any decisions about staying in Briarhaven. I know that I'd like to stay. I'm tired of moving, girls. I love Briarhaven, and I loved our time here, even though I know how much your mother struggled."

"You know, growing up . . . How come we could stay here so long?" Lyra asked, easing carefully onto the cushion next to me and reaching out to stroke a finger over the emberwolf's back.

"Copious amounts of magick," Broca admitted. Her eyes took on a faraway look as she steepled her fingers, flipping through the pages of the past in her mind. "The Charms. Every time a new curse emerged, we worked to distill it. We never managed to completely erase it, but we managed it, for a while at least. Until your mother got too tired of trying."

"Standard operating procedure there." Nova sniffed, coming to sit on the other side of me. Together, all three of us lightly stroked the emberwolf, none of us ever having been able to have a pet before.

"Yes, I know." Broca shook her head. She never made excuses for our mother, something I deeply appreciated, instead just accepting the facts of what was. "But now I've had my vision, and I really think you'll be able to break this curse and settle here. If you'd like."

I highly doubted I'd stay in Briarhaven, even if we did break the curse, but that was a discussion for another time.

"Tell us more about your vision," Nova said, pulling out her sketchbook to start drawing an outline of the emberwolf.

"I'd been in Portugal, actually. Delightful lovers there, you know."

"Broca! No, ew!" Nova hissed, and Broca laughed.

"How have you all turned out to be such prudes?" She marveled.

"I think it's fabulous," Lyra said, tossing her hair over her shoulder.

"Can we focus?" I asked, shaking my head, amused.

"Naturally, my love. So it was after a particularly vigorous session with—"

"Noooo," Nova whined.

"My masseuse," Broca finished with a wink. "And I was feeling loose and relaxed, and then it just came over me. It was a vision of you three, in Briarhaven, finally breaking the curse. *'Three sisters to right a wrong, a heart shattered, once again strong.'*"

"What does that even mean?" Lyra wondered.

"I have no idea, and I have tried, many a time, to get more information. But the scrying ball does not let me see." Broca held her hands in the air. Her scrying ball was a simple crystal ball, or sometimes she used a mirror, and when particularly invested, Broca could determine deep insights into the future.

"Do we have to be a part of the coven in order to break this curse?" I asked. I really wasn't keen on joining the Charms. The emberwolf shifted, letting out a snuffle, and then he rolled so his stomach was available for scratchies. We all cooed in delight.

"You are a part of the coven." I met Broca's steady gaze. "You all have legacy seats. The MacGregors have been a part of the Charms for a very long time."

"But . . ." Nova poked out a lower lip in a pout. "Never harm, always charm?"

"It's trite, but effective. As good slogans often are."

"I think it could be fun," Lyra said, twirling a lock of hair around her finger.

"I think I don't like other people telling us what to do," I said.

"Ah yes, always in charge." Broca made a tsking noise with her lips. "I don't know if that is a firstborn trait or because of your mother, but you can let others help, you ken?"

The emberwolf snorted again, a puff of smoke coming through his nose, and my sisters and I gasped, the Charms forgotten.

"Will he shoot fire?"

Broca looked at me like I wasn't the sharpest knife in the drawer. "He's an emberwolf."

"Oh my goddess, we're going to have to fireproof the place." I looked around, imagining all the streamers going up in flames.

"It'll be fine, Sloane. You worry too much. Just look at the sweet darling. He'll be just fine, won't he, then?" Broca cooed over him from her spot on the chair.

"What's his name?" Lyra looked up at me.

"Blue," I said, without hesitation. "His name's Blue."

At that, Blue let out a little rumble of satisfaction, rolled to his feet, and took off on an easy glide around the room. We all gasped, and I clapped my hands together, my heart dancing inside my chest. When he landed on the kitchen counter and promptly buried his nose in a plate of cheese Lyra had left out, I jumped up.

"Blue," I said, testing his name.

Blue looked up at me, a cheeky grin on his face, full well knowing what he was doing.

"Och, you're just the bestest boy, aren't you? Can you fly to me?" I asked, holding out my arms. Blue launched himself into the air and flew to me, slamming into my chest with all the aplomb of a sodden paper towel, and I gasped out a laugh as I caught him.

"Right, graceful you are not. But you don't need to be, do you, sweet thing?" I beamed down at where he leaned back in my arms, his tongue lolling out of his mouth, my heart full.

"Welcome home, Blue. I think we're going to be best friends."

CHAPTER SEVEN
Sloane

We only had two fire accidents with Blue, which were quickly snuffed out, and he received loads of reassurance that he was still the best emberwolf in all the land. Somehow, I had not managed to stay awake until midnight and had dragged myself upstairs, Blue flying in front of me like a fat bumblebee drunk on nectar, before collapsing in bed. You would have thought after years of wondering what my magick was going to be, I'd be bouncing out of my skin to wait for the clock to chime midnight, yet the long days of travel to get here in time for my birthday had caught up with me, and I'd crashed.

Or maybe I was just avoiding reality.

For one night longer, at least.

The smell of smoke teased my nose, and an alarm bell rang in my head. My eyes shot open to see Blue, his wings tucked around him, slumbering blissfully between my feet. His little paws moved, scrambling at the blanket, chasing something in his dream. He grunted, a small stream of fire erupting from his nostrils, and singed the fabric of the blanket.

"Oops," I said, reaching over to tamp out the burning edges of the fabric.

I could see how this might become a touch problematic. Did they make fireproof sleep blankets? He looked so cute, snoring away. When he let out a wee roar, fire once more pluming from his nostrils, my eyes widened.

The last thing I needed was to burn the house down on my birthday.

"Blue," I hissed, nudging him as I beat out the flames on the blanket. "Wake up, buddy."

Blue grunted, coming awake mid-snore, and blinked sleepy eyes up at me.

"Hey, bud. It's time for breakfast. Are you hungry? Do you want some cheese?" We'd learned last night that cheese was his favorite food, and none of us could fault him for his taste.

At that word, he shot off the bed, caught himself mid-leap, his wings springing open and keeping him from hitting the floor. From there, he did a lazy lap of the room, his wings sparkling in the sunlight streaming through the window.

Wait, sunlight. Did that mean the snow was gone?

Bounding over to the window, I peered out, only to see the neighbor from yesterday clearing his sidewalk. When he saw me at the window, he repeated the same two-fingered salute from yesterday. I waved cheerfully, *again*. This was our thing now.

The formerly rolling green hills were still completely covered with a soft blanket of pristine white snow, a few streams of smoke twirling from the turrets of the castle and into the sky, and fat cotton-puff clouds hung above us all. And the sun shone, reflecting icy diamonds across the snowcapped roofs. Knowing the respite was brief, because irrespective of our curse or not, this was still Scotland, I threw on my Keep Calm and Carry a Wand jumper over my pajamas and tore downstairs. Blue zoomed ahead of me, his tongue flailing behind him as he flew, his mouth open in a smile.

I could just picture him saying, *Wheeeeeeeee.*

It was like he was new to flying and having just as much fun with it as we were watching him fly. Broca had informed me that he was around two years old, so well past his baby years, but still quite young for his kind. A sweet old witch had taken him in and trained him before Broca had brought him home to us.

"Happy birthday!"

I skidded to a stop at the bottom of the stairs, a room full of people staring back at me, and Blue swerved in midair, caught unawares by the crowd. His wings flapped against my face as he tried to land on my shoulder, but he was too big and too clumsy to maneuver that, and we ended up tangled together in a heap on the floor. I cradled Blue to me while he nervously licked my face, shooting looks over his shoulder at the group staring in shock at us.

"Um, happy birthday?" Nova asked.

"Oof," I said, shifting Blue in my arms, scrambling for purchase as I tried to stand. Why were there so many people in our house? I glanced down at my faded pajama pants and sighed. So much for any sort of dignity this morning. Finally, standing, I nodded to the room.

"Hello, um, everyone. Quite a gathering we have here at"—I slid a glance to the clock on the wall in the kitchen—"seven thirty in the morning."

"Yes, well, no time to waste. Have you figured out your magick yet?" Mandy Meadows—for some reason I could only think of her by her first and last name—stood and crossed to me. She'd changed her pantsuit. Today's was a rose-petal-pink tweed with black and white stripes, and she'd added another strand of pearls at her neck. The Charms were here, including Raven and another woman I hadn't met yet.

"Is that an emberwolf?" Tam asked. She must have run here—like a maniac—given her pink cheeks, exercise leggings, and red fleece jumper. "Cute little fella."

"This is Blue." I turned to the room, so Blue's face showed, like I was showing off my new baby to the world. I guess I kind of was. "Broca gave him to me for my birthday. Blue, say hello."

Blue gave a sharp yelp—a sound caught between a bark and roar—and a spear of flame shot out and singed Mandy Meadows's suit. Her eyes widened, fury rippling across her face, and I quickly patted out the small flame on her arm.

"This. Is. *Chanel*."

"He's still learning," I explained, giving her a wide berth as I crossed the room to where Tam held out her arms.

"Give me the fierce beastie. I bet you like a cuddle, don't you?" Blue collapsed in Tam's lap, and she scratched his belly, cooing over him.

"Um, so, hi." I raised a hand awkwardly at the middle-aged woman I hadn't met yet. She wore slim black trousers, a silk blouse, and a matching black jacket. Gold winked at her ears and neck, and her blond hair was sleeked back into a knot at the nape of her neck. She walked over and held out her hand.

"Deidre Valor." Two pumps, a firm grip, and a sharp nod of the head.

"Hi, Deidre. I'm Sloane."

"I own Valor Real Estate." A card materialized in my hand, and I blinked down at it, then back up at her. "I'm a house witch."

"Ah, right." A house witch typically specialized in all spells for hearth and home, particularly in the protection of an abode. It made sense for her to be a Realtor. "And one of the Charms?"

"Aye." Another brisk nod, and Deidre returned to scrolling on her phone as she flipped through a stack of manila folders.

"Is she . . . working?" I asked out of the side of my mouth.

"She's never not working." Tam shook her head. "Her cortisol levels have to be through the roof."

"Right, now that we're all here"—Mandy Meadows clapped her hands—"we can call our first official meeting of the Charms as a whole."

"Is this the entire coven?" Lyra looked around from where she sat curled on the couch, a latte in hand that looked professionally made.

Knowing her, it had cinnamon and honey, with a touch of cayenne sprinkled on top.

"It is." Broca smiled at me from her armchair, where she was stitching sequins to a purse. "There's nine of us here, and that completes the coven." Witches and their multiples of three. Go figure.

"Mandy, Felicity, Tam, Deidre, Raven, Lyra, Nova, Broca, and . . . me." I pointed a finger at myself. "The Scottish Charms."

"At your service," Raven trilled, looking fresh as a garden rose this morning in a soft navy jumper and faded wide-legged jeans.

"I brought snacks," Felicity said, from where she sat hugging her tote on a dining room chair next to Deidre. Blue poked his head up, interested.

"I think just coffee," I said, backing slowly away from the room of women as though they were a bomb that could go off at any moment. This really wasn't how I thought my birthday morning would go, and tension knotted my shoulders. Were they expecting me to perform or something in front of everyone? I was awkward on a good day, and I had barely been awake long enough to brush my teeth, let alone privately test out my magick.

I could sense it, though.

Humming, just below the surface, like that little tingle you get when you get zapped by static electricity. Waiting to be used. Calling to me. I wondered if I could just ask it what it was . . .

"Sloane." My name was the only warning I had before the tray of doughnuts and croissants slid off the counter and went flying toward my feet.

Blue roared from across the room, but my hands were already up, and . . . I felt it.

My magick unfurled, stretched, and stepped into the light.

The tray stopped before it hit the floor and hung there, levitating. I froze, uncertain what to do next.

"Tell it where you want it to go," Broca instructed.

Go back to the counter, I instructed in my mind.

The tray trembled but then floated gently back to the counter.

No way. I'd just done that. *Me.* Whirling, I looked at the group, my mouth hanging open. Blue lifted his wings and air-waddled his way over to me, and I caught him in my arms. He licked my cheek, seeming to be proud of me, and I beamed at him.

"Levitation," Tam said, giving me a pleased nod. "Well done."

"Right, then, Charms. Looks like we won't be needed here as long as we thought." Mandy Meadows sniffed and checked a slim gold watch at her wrist. "I'll see you at the cèilidh later."

"Och, I can't wait. I do love to dance." Felicity clapped her hands.

"You're just leaving?" Nova glanced from Mandy to me.

"Aye. It's a basic skill, at best." Mandy adjusted her necklace, her nose wrinkled in distaste.

"Ew." Lyra glared at Mandy.

"Did you just call Sloane 'basic'?" Nova crossed her arms over her chest, her tattoos standing out against her pale skin.

"*Yeah,*" I said. Was Mandy Meadows calling me a basic witch?

"It's a rudimentary skill. We can all do it." Mandy Meadows was already gathering her purse, a quilted cream Chanel, and moving toward the door.

"Rude," Lyra said.

"Is that true?" I asked the room, and the coven members that already had their magick all looked away except for Raven. She shrugged, a sympathetic smile on her face.

"It's a useful tool to have, Sloane. And as you grow more confident with your magick, you might be able to tap into a few other strengths down the road. Not always, but sometimes that is how it works."

Mandy Meadows struggled at the door, hissing as her hand touched the knob.

"Damn it, Broca."

"Mandy, as president of the Charms, would you say this was the appropriate manner to welcome a new member, and her newly discovered magick, to the coven?"

"I welcomed her yesterday." She blew on her hand, glaring at Broca.

"Leadership is done by a vote, isn't it?"

"You wouldn't." Mandy narrowed her eyes at Broca. The rest of us swiveled our heads between the two like we were watching a Ping-Pong match. Broca shrugged one shoulder, concentrating on a stitch.

"I would. I'll do whatever I feel like, Mandy Meadows, and you should remember that." Broca didn't look up from her sequins.

Blue leaned forward, sniffing toward the food on the counter, and I remembered my promise of cheese to him. Walking over to the fridge, I opened it with one hand and pulled out a container of cheddar cheese cubes, and then some chicken breasts that Lyra had cooked the night before. I knew I'd have to ask Raven what an emberwolf's proper diet is, but for now Blue wriggled in my arms, ecstatic at the sight of food.

"Ugh, fine." Mandy rolled her eyes and stomped back over to the kitchen and put her purse on the counter. Taking the container of cheese, she walked across the room, and Blue whimpered softly.

"It's okay, buddy. I'll get you your cheese," I promised him.

"Levitation is a useful tool for any witch to have in her bag of tricks," Mandy began, and lifted the lid on the cheese. "It doesn't require spell-casting, ingredients, charms, or any sort of ritual. Some more advanced magicks require a level of preparation that can't be done at a moment's notice."

"Like what?" Lyra asked, swiveling on the couch.

"A healing," Raven said, playing with a strand of rose quartz beads around her wrist. "A proper healing requires not only an investigative assessment, but then a gathering and harvesting of correct spell ingredients, as well as careful thought into the words you're using to ask the magick to heal. Intent is everything in magick, but preparation and research magnify it threefold."

"That's one. Divination, protection, elemental, banishing, binding, love—" Mandy Meadows ticked them off on her fingers, nails painted ballerina pink.

"You can really do a love spell?" Nova glanced up.

"There's a spell for everything. But the Charms stick by our code of conduct."

Never harm, always charm, Nova mouthed at me, and I bit back a grin.

"Most witches will be able to use several types of magick, once they learn where their specialties lie. For example, I'm not a great healer."

Surprise, surprise. Mandy Meadows was about as nurturing as Darth Vader.

"But I could heal if I needed to. I've gained enough knowledge and expertise that I could manage it. But someone like Raven, who comes from a long line of healers, will require very little effort and be far more effective than I could ever be."

"So a specialist, really." Blue wiggled in my arms, and I gave him a chunk of chicken from the container on the counter.

"Essentially, yes." Mandy held up the container of cheese. "And you may discover yours as you go along. But since it is just levitation, for now, you don't need the entire coven at your disposal."

"Agreed." Deidre sniffed and typed furiously on her phone.

"I'll stay with you today, Sloane." Felicity hugged her tote more tightly, bobbing her head at me.

"Me too," Tam offered. "Raven has to open the shop, Deidre doesn't have time for anyone that isn't a client, and Mandy must have a salon appointment."

"At least I know what a salon *is*." Mandy flicked a disparaging look at Tam, who only grinned more widely.

"So it's like popping the cork on champagne? Once the cork is out, the magick will bubble up?" Lyra asked.

"Yes, most likely. She can harness it now. We were here on the off chance she was hugely powerful, which could disrupt . . .

things . . . so to speak. We don't need the whole town rockin' and rollin' because Sloane's inherited some high-level magick. Levitation is good, though. It's a great start and a useful tool in an everyday witch's pocket."

An everyday witch.

Even getting magick made me sound boring.

I sighed.

"Now, let's practice your levitation." Mandy Meadows held the container of cheese up. "I'll toss some in the air and you direct where they go. It can be a game for Blue."

"Cheese?" I asked Blue, and he struggled to get out of my arms. I let him go, and he hurtled himself at Mandy, a drooling, depraved, flying doggo hell-bent on getting his cheese. Mandy took one look at his slobber, squealed, and tossed the entire contents of the cheese in the air. Blue howled in excitement.

"Oh no!" I exclaimed, and focused on moving the cheese.

The pieces went everywhere, and Blue gave chase.

"Damn it, Sloane," Mandy Meadows shrieked as Blue dive-bombed her, chasing a piece of cheese over her head. His wing clipped her hair, ripping out her hair clip, and she screeched as she grabbed her head. Blue dipped, snapping the cheese from the air, and swerved to race after another, hovering over Deidre's pile of folders.

"Noooo!" Deidre shouted as Blue dove at the folders, his wings scattering papers everywhere, and scooped up the next piece of cheese. Deidre slammed her body onto the table, trying to keep the rest of the papers in place, and Blue swerved onto the next.

A sharp whistle caught his attention.

"Here you go, sweetie." Tam held a piece in her hand, and he air-waddled forward, slamming into her arms with all the grace of a toddler tripping on a pile of blocks, and nipped the cheese from her hand. She held him while he panted in her arms, his smile wide and excited. "Gather the rest before I let him go."

"Sloane." This came from Broca, and I realized they were waiting on me. I reached inside for that tendril of magick again and shivered as it rippled across my skin. Imagining all of the cheese back in one spot on the counter, I blinked as pieces zipped across the room and piled themselves into a little lopsided pyramid on the tray.

Blue lunged, but Tam held him back.

"Now. One piece at a time," Broca instructed.

My magick uncoiled and curled around a cube of cheese, lifting it gently in the air so it hovered over the counter.

"Now, Blue."

Tam let go of Blue, and he careened over to the cheese, snapping it up as his wings beat lazily in the air.

"I did it!" I exclaimed. I didn't care if it was basic, it was still *my* magick, and relief filled me. I wasn't turning into a werewolf. Nor was I going to be some deeply powerful sorceress. Frankly, life could go on as normal, with just a tiny bit of added assistance from some levitation. All things considered, I'd lucked out.

Blue spied the pile of cheese on the counter and dove, devouring the rest in one massive gulp.

"Whoops." I laughed. Blue flew to me, his tongue lolling out, a contented smile stretching his puppy mouth.

"Ridiculous." Mandy Meadows grabbed her purse, and this time the door opened when she stormed out. Stroking Blue's head, I smiled, pleased he'd annoyed her.

As birthday mornings went, it was better than most.

CHAPTER EIGHT
Sloane

Later that day, I snuck away to enjoy what had begun to be a bit of a tradition for me on my birthday—going to a bookstore.

When I was younger, it had been the library, largely to escape something I hated most at the time—being the center of attention. I'd since grown more comfortable with it, but I certainly wasn't what someone would call a socialite.

Which was why books were my favorite place to escape to.

Every year on my birthday, I'd buy myself a pretty new journal to document the adventures ahead, and at least five books solely based on how pretty the covers were. It didn't matter what genre, as I read pretty much everything, so the main criterion I'd set for myself was it had to be pretty and it had to be pricey.

We all had our splurges, and this was mine.

Waving goodbye, Blue having settled down for a nap next to Broca, I zipped up my winter jacket and stepped outside, my eyes going immediately to the sky. Thick clouds tossed snow at my face, a happy birthday to me, I guess, and I pulled a wool cap over my hair. Irrespective of the snow, a calmness filled me for the first time in ages, and I considered the reason as I sauntered the fifteen-minute walk into town.

Truly? It must be because I'd finally figured out my magick. After waiting for this day all these years, the unknown hovering over my head, finally getting my magick felt a bit like a nonevent. An afterthought. I wasn't even all that deflated, though—in fact, quite the contrary.

Levitation was an easy enough magick that I could understand and be in charge of. Nothing about my life had to change, and I'd have the added bonus of being able to move things about more easily. Or reach for a book on the top shelf.

I nodded a greeting at a few tourists who wore witches' hats despite the snow, and long wool cloaks. The trees that lined the street had stopped fighting the snow, their leaves shifting from yellow to deep red, falling like drops of blood on white linen, and I whispered a silent apology to them. I knew they'd lose their leaves soon enough, but I hated they'd had to do so early because of our curse.

Passing Mystic Munchies, I waved to the woman with pink braids behind the counter who only glowered at me. The next shop, the Arcane Attic, showcased a variety of cloaks, much like the ones the tourists had just sported, as well as a fun dress with an evil eye–and–lightning bolt pattern scrawled across it. A scarf covered in butterflies and sprinkled with rhinestones was wrapped around a mannequin's neck, and I grinned at the pair of ruby-red mary janes in the front window. It seemed this was the spot for all one's witchy wear.

Humming, I stopped in front of the bookshop, painted a deep navy blue. Quill pens were painted on the outside, interspersed between moons and stars, and I looked up to see the name.

The Silver Quill.

A poster for the Halloween costume contest hung in the window, and I crinkled my nose at the huge X across the location and the words marked below it. "Moved inside to the community center."

That was our fault. I'd been told that Halloween was Briarhaven's biggest moneymaker when it came to holidays, and typically they had a huge bonfire and tons of festivities around it. The witches would celebrate Samhain, and the tourists would celebrate dressing up and getting candy.

The door opened, and I nodded to a few people who bustled out, bags in hand, and slipped inside.

Instantly, I felt at peace.

It was the kind of bookshop one wanted to linger in, where cozy corners held overstuffed chairs and colorful cushions, and fire crackling cheerfully in a small wood-burning stove. Thick, rough-cut wood beams lined the ceiling, the walls were painted that same deep navy as outside, and the bookshelves were in the same rough-hewn wood as the beams above. A thick rug in an intricate pattern of navy, white, and small pops of blush pink was thrown across wide-planked floors, and the woman at the checkout waved to me with one hand while she continued her conversation with her customer. Black hair flowed down her back, and she wore a fuzzy black sweater with a singular white circle on the chest.

The air shimmered around the woman, and I squinted my eyes. Her image blurred, and for a moment, the face of a cat looked back at me.

She was fae.

A cat sith, to be exact.

It appeared my new magick had other aspects I hadn't considered. Would I now be able to see other magickals more easily? In the past, they'd always have to reveal themselves to me first, but now I could just *see* that this woman was not human.

Fascinated, I made myself turn away, lest I be caught staring and give another member of the town reason to be annoyed at me. I breezed over to a display of books that had immediately caught my eye when I'd walked in. Gold foiling shone on the covers, sprayed edges revealed flowers, dragons, and swords, and I almost squealed in delight. They were just so pretty.

Reaching to pick one up, I paused as my phone buzzed in my pocket. Pulling it out, I saw Lyra's name and answered, ducking outside so as not to annoy anyone's browsing time. Bookshops felt like almost holy places to me.

"Hey, what's up?"

"The power's out." Lyra's voice held a note of worry, and I straightened.

"What do you mean it's out? Did you check the box?"

"We did, but it doesn't seem like anything's flipped."

"Was there anything on the news about a power outage?" I glanced around the street, but all the lights shone brightly in the storefront windows.

"Nothing we could find posted on social media. And the neighbors all have power." There was a note in Lyra's voice that took me a moment to recognize.

"That bastard," I hissed.

"Yup, that's kind of the conclusion we jumped to as well."

"I can't believe Knox would have the power cut on us. In a snowstorm nonetheless." Fury ripped through me.

"I mean, technically we're fine. The house is chock-full of fireplaces, so it's not like we'll freeze to death. Which he knows."

"What if we didn't have wood? We certainly won't have hot water. Does he want our grandmother to bathe in ice-cold water in the winter?" I seethed, digging a path in the snow in front of the bookshop.

"I think he's making good on his threat to run us out of town. And I have to say, this is fairly effective. I have to have internet to work, and we clearly are going to need hot water to function. Damn it, but this man is exhausting."

"He's an asshole is what he is."

A laugh caught my ears, and my head went up, as though scenting my prey.

Knox stood just outside a store called the Crystal Cavern, and was helping an old woman into her car.

Sure, he was going to help one old woman but leave another to freeze to death? Not on my watch.

"I've got eyes on him. I'll take care of it."

"No murdering!" Lyra's voice went up, and I clicked the phone off, tucking it back in my pocket, fury propelling me across the street without looking.

A horn sounded, and then my feet left the ground. For a moment, I was airborne, before I landed on something hard.

Not as hard as the ground, but hard enough.

"Bloody hell, woman," Knox said from beneath me. "You're going to get yourself killed. What were you thinking?"

"What was *I* thinking?" I reached back with my fist and hauled off.

Knox caught it with his hand a second before it reached his nose.

"Hey, hey, hey, now. Calm down, lass. That's no way to thank me for saving you."

"Saving me?" I sputtered, wrenching my hand from his big palm and pushing myself up from his chest. One of his arms kept me pinned against him.

I hated that I couldn't get up under his strength.

And I hated even more that I kind of liked it.

I should not be admiring his body, or how sexy he looked all rumpled and pink-cheeked in the snow, or how his muscular arm pulled me tight against his chest.

I should be trying to kill him for putting my grandmother at risk.

"You're just fine, Sloane. It's just an adrenaline spike from a near miss is all." Knox pitched his voice low, speaking to me like he was trying to calm a child with a temper tantrum, and I reached my fist up again.

He caught it easily.

"Hey, now. Violence is not the answer, my friend."

"You cut off our electricity," I finally bit out, furious with him.

Understanding dawned in his eyes, and I swore under my breath.

"Aye, a warning." His voice rumbled, determination lacing his tone.

"A warning?" I gaped down at him, refusing to notice how good he felt beneath me.

"It should be back on by now."

My phone buzzed in my pocket, and reaching down with one hand, I pulled it out and swiped it open.

"All good?" I asked without preamble.

"Yup, power's back on. No need to go on a murdering spree."

"But you know how much I like to sell organs on the black market."

Knox grinned up at me, clearly not threatened by my words in the slightest.

"I do at that," Lyra said, cluing in to what must be going on. "But you might want to keep his organs all intact. Particularly one, likely very large organ—"

I hung up before she could say any more.

"You could have put Broca in jeopardy," I said, easing back, trying to stay focused on why I was so mad to begin with.

"I'm serious about you leaving town, Sloane. But I'm also not an awful person. I'd never hurt Broca." Knox seemed sincerely upset at the prospect, and I stood, looking down as he propped himself up in the snow.

I refused to offer him a hand.

"She's just had surgery, Knox. You have no idea what she needs the electrics for. It was poor form."

"I'm sorry." Knox met my eyes, his tone sincere. "You're right. It was poor form, even if it was for a short bit of time."

"Come for me all you want," I said, pointing a finger at his face. "But my family is off-limits."

"Oh, make no mistake about it, witchling. I am *absolutely* coming for you. This is only the beginning. I can make your life incredibly uncomfortable. And I plan to."

"We need time to break the curse." I almost shouted it, but brought my tone down just in time as a group of tourists left a shop. Instead, I kicked a pile of snow by his shoulder.

"At the cost of everyone else in Briarhaven, Sloane? We're all supposed to deal with endless snow that is increasing in severity, which could potentially become catastrophic for our homes and businesses, while you just take your sweet time figuring out some ancient curse?"

Knox stood and brushed the snow from his trousers, his face set in hard lines.

Shame now mixed with fury, and I didn't like it. It had always been this way. The catch-22 of my life. If I stayed in one spot, people got hurt. But the only way to fix this mess was to stay in one damn spot—the origin of the very curse—and that meant Briarhaven would just have to freaking deal with it.

"You pride yourself on being Scotland's most magickal town. Well? *You* fix it, then." I lifted my hand and waved at the snow cascading down around us.

With that, I turned, needing to get away from him. Knox had stirred up too many emotions, and I needed to walk them off before I could think straight again.

"Oh, and Sloane?"

I glanced over my shoulder to where Knox stood, the snow swirling around him but never really landing on him.

"I forgot to wish you a happy birthday. I look forward to celebrating with you tonight." Even though frustration simmered in his eyes, he smirked.

"Absolutely not. You're not invited," I said, and he grinned, that same grin he'd shown me the first night when I tried to tell him no.

"Let me guess. You own the pub." Resignation hung low in my gut.

"Nope. My best mate does, though." Knox shot me a cheeky grin before sauntering to his Land Rover.

I looked at the Silver Quill and sighed, turning toward home. There weren't enough books in the world to soothe my turmoil today. Annoyed that my calm had been ruined by one very frustrating man, I brushed the snow from my pants and stomped toward home.

A car pulled up next to me, and I glanced over to see Knox, a smug expression on his face.

"Nice and warm in here."

"I hope you never have working batteries for your TV remote and that your tea is always cold."

"Oh, vicious. I like it. Need a ride?"

I gave Knox the same cheerful two-fingered salute my disgruntled neighbor offered me in the mornings. He laughed and drove away with a jaunty honk of his horn.

Damn him, but that stupid horn made me want to smile.

Confused and frustrated, I bent my head against the snow and trudged home.

No, not home.

Just a place to stay for a short time.

I was pretty certain that Briarhaven would never be our home again.

CHAPTER NINE

Knox

Normally, my family would host a town cèilidh in our ballroom, but since Sloane was basically persona non grata in my household, I couldn't imagine dealing with the wrath of my parents if they found out I'd allowed the birthday celebration to take place at our castle. The wind howled, shaking the windowpanes in my dressing room, and I grimaced as I wrapped my kilt around my waist. The kilt, while favorable to mucking through boggy swamp land, wasn't particularly amenable to the blistering wind of an icy winter storm. If you catch my drift.

I shouldn't even be going to this party.

I really wished the MacGregors would just take the hint and leave town. It would be easiest for everyone if they did.

I suspected that was not what would be happening, but one could dream.

My phone buzzed on the side table, and I glanced at it, sighing. Another snow-related emergency. It had been never-ending since the MacGregors had returned, and my sleep was suffering for it. Which was why I was in such a sour mood. At least that is what I kept telling myself.

A clatter of wheels on marble floors was the only warning I got before my door flew open and Haggis, my pet Highland coo, who had suffered from stunted growth and a birth defect which left his back legs immobile, came crashing through my door in his wheelchair. He was about the size of a golden retriever, with the personality of one, and had decided that I was his favorite person in the world. Oswald, my blind cat, who had been napping on the bed, jumped up and arched his back.

"Sorry, lad." I scratched behind Oswald's ear as Haggis pressed his sloppy, wet nose into my knee.

Ever since I was little, I'd had a penchant for rescuing hurt things. I'd find birds with broken wings and run to the apothecary, begging for them to be saved. I had a soft spot in my heart for those that needed a little more assistance to navigate life. It was part of what made me a good provost, or so my brothers told me, and I'd also inadvertently turned my house into a foster home of sorts for broken animals needing their hearts healed. Right now, it was just Oswald and Haggis, my two permanent residents, but at times it had expanded to everything from a phoenix to an emberwolf, and even, during one memorable summer, a young kraken. Once healed, we'd snuck him back through the loch that connected to the sea, and none had been the wiser for it.

Except for my parents, of course. They'd taken one look at the kraken, affectionately named Sugar, and hightailed to the Alps for the summer. That's what they got for raising three boys.

Haggis bellowed at me, demanding attention, and I laughed. Bending over, I scratched behind his ears as well. His shaggy fur was a burnished copper color, and he shook his head, pressing against my hand. While the healers hadn't been able to do much about his birth defects, they had assured me that he was in no pain. This was just how he was. With that knowledge in mind, my brothers and I had managed to build a four-wheeled chair for him. All we had to do was lift him into the harness that wrapped below his belly, and then the frame sat around his four legs. He simply used his front legs to propel himself around. Once he'd gotten the hang of it, he'd never looked back.

Oswald sniffed and licked a paw.

Dreadful creature.

"Is that right? I saw you curled up sleeping on him the other night, when the snow arrived."

You saw nothing, you eejit.

Oswald huffed and stalked across the bed, shooting me a dirty look over his shoulder.

"Och, are you sure about that, mate?" I looked down at Haggis, who winked at me.

He likes my fur. He kneads my shoulders when they're sore with his wee paws.

"Oh, do you hear that, Oswald? Sounds like you've been givin' your wee pal a shoulder massage."

Oswald hissed and arched his back. He bumped his head against a tassel hanging from the curtains that framed my bed. I chuckled.

My bedroom, adjoined to my dressing room, was about as castle-y as you could get. A four-poster bed in rich mahogany dominated the room, with red velvet curtains done up with gold fringe. The walls were painted a deep navy blue, the wainscoting a crisp white, and a muted tartan carpet in blues with thin threads of red and white warmed the cold stone floor. My mother had designed every inch of this house, and Oswald well knew she'd be furious if he shredded another one of her curtain tassels.

"Don't you dare."

Dare what? Oh, this? Oswald nipped at the tassel, and then swatted it lightly with a paw.

"Oswald. Knock it off."

Knock what off? Oswald batted it again. Lightly. And then, as though helpless not to do it more, he rolled onto his back and beat it up like he was punching a boxing bag.

"You know you have no self-control once you start."

I am the epitome of control. Oswald hissed, battering the tassel some more, flipping across the bed and back before going another round. *Take that! And that!*

Go on, lad! Haggis threw his head back and mooed his support, and I sighed. Crossing the room, I scooped up the cat, and he squirmed in my arms, annoyed.

I had everything perfectly in hand.

"I'm sure you did, but from the outside it did seem like you were about to shred the shite out of Mum's curtains."

I would never.

"Uh-huh. Like the six times before this, mate?" I deposited Oswald on the floor and he walked sedately down the hallway, his head held high.

Wanna play? Haggis barreled through, his wheelchair clattering, and Oswald leapt about six feet in the air.

No, I don't want to play. I don't play. I am a warrior, sent to banish evils.

Tag! Haggis bumped his nose on Oswald's bum, and Oswald hissed before Haggis took off, racing down the hallway and catapulting himself around a curve.

Like I can't hear where that snuffling beast is from a mile away?

"Still gotta catch him. It's not hide-and-seek, you know. It's tag."

Why would I remotely be interested in playing such a childish game?

"That's fine. I'll just tell Haggis he won when I see him." I proceeded past Oswald, knowing this would annoy him, and then turned the corner. When he zipped past me, swiping a claw across the back of my leg in the process, I just laughed. He was too easy.

Communicating with animals might be one of my favorite magickal abilities, and when I'd discovered it after the age of twenty-five, I'd crowed in delight. It made the largely empty castle less lonely these days. Sure, my mother had staff—a chef, a butler, a maid—

all of whom I loved dearly. But the added companionship of Haggis and Oswald was a real bonus for me.

Grabbing a long wool coat from the front closet, I tucked a tweed newsboy cap on, collected my leather driving gloves, and then stomped through the snow to my Land Rover. It was a blisteringly cold night, and it took everything in my power not to go back inside and light a fire, pour a wee dram, and curl up with a good book instead.

But the thought of dancing with Sloane was just too much to resist.

No, scratch that.

My provost duty. That was the only reason I was going.

I repeated that to myself the entire drive over to the Rune & Rose, which had a function room tucked in the back for events. The car park was almost empty, which was unusual for a cèilidh, and I pulled over beneath a streetlamp. Two snow sculptures now stood in front, one with a scarf and another with earmuffs. Warm light spilled out on the street from the arched windows, and cheerful music caught on the wind, dancing away into the snow that barreled down. Ducking my head, I made haste to the door and pushed inside, kicking the snow off my boots just inside the door. There, I deposited my coat in a pile with the others and waved at a few people as I made my way to the bar.

Music from a live band, a jaunty Celtic tune, boomed through the doors leading to the back room, and a cheerful fire snapped in the stone fireplace along the wall. The light from the lampposts outside illuminated the swirling snow in the large windows, making the fire even more welcoming, and I leaned my hip against the bar as Liam waited on a few customers.

"Mate, how's it going, then?" Liam stopped by my side.

"Brilliant." I nodded at the snow swirling outside the window.

"Och, it's a nuisance, isn't it, then? Such a shame, really. We were finally getting to see more sunshine."

"How's business been?"

"Nothing all that much today. Of course, the cèilidh helps. A little."

"Not as busy as I expected." I looked around at the mostly empty pub.

"Seems there's a touch of a protest for the MacGregors being back in town. What can I do you for?"

"Just an Irn Bru. I'm driving."

Liam nodded and bent to a small fridge behind the bar, and pulled out an orange-and-silver can. "Glass?"

"No, thanks."

Liam's attention shifted, and I glanced over to see Raven walking toward the dance floor in a shimmering slip dress that hugged every decadent curve of her body, an open wool coat thrown over her shoulders. Her hair streamed behind her, and Liam swallowed.

"Ask her out," I said. Liam had been nursing a crush on Raven for years now.

"Can't. You know that." Liam had made a promise to Raven's father that he'd look after her after he passed. They'd been neighbors, and Liam took his vow seriously. I couldn't help but wonder if Raven's dad would have been more than happy with Liam looking after his daughter as her partner, but Liam refused to speak about it. Instead, he just silently punished himself by pining for her day after day.

"All right, we're ready to start. Does everyone know the Flying Scotsman?"

The singer's voice carried over the microphone from the back room, and I straightened.

"Going in?" Liam asked.

"Aye."

"That's an odd way of kicking the MacGregors out," Liam observed, a corner of his lips quirking up. "Going to Sloane's birthday party and all."

"What do you want me to do? Haul 'em over my shoulder and toss 'em out on their bums?"

"Maybe." Liam nodded toward the windows. "If that keeps up, I reckon business will dry up. People outside Briarhaven will start asking questions. Only so long you can explain away the snow as a freak early autumn snowstorm."

"I'm working on it," I muttered.

"See that you do." Liam tapped two fingers on the bar and went to serve other customers, and I sighed.

That was the life of a provost.

I wandered back into the birthday celebration, wondering how I was going to solve the puzzle of the MacGregors. The only answer was to run them out of town. I could see no other solution for protecting the people of Briarhaven from their curse. While it wasn't the MacGregors' fault that their bloodline was cursed, their neighbors shouldn't also have to bear the brunt of it. Since they wouldn't listen to reason, I was going to have to up my ante and go all in on forcing them to leave.

My breath caught as I spied Sloane in the middle of the dance floor, a ring of women around her. It felt like I was standing on the edge of a cliff, caught between awe and the sweet terror of falling.

Her beauty illuminated the room.

A silky dress in siren red slipped over her generous curves, her lips painted a matching scarlet. My fingers dug into my palms. Hers was a body made for touching. All dips and valleys, soft curves and strong legs, a gorgeous bum that begged for me to take a bite. Her belly curved, supple and round beneath the silk, and her ample breasts shifted under the dress as she turned and caught me staring.

Sloane blanched visibly and looked away, but not before I caught . . . something . . . in her expression. Something that had my blood heating and me striding across the dance floor to examine it more closely.

Because just for a moment, I thought I'd seen interest flicker across her gorgeous face.

The dance started, the singer calling out the steps. I closed the distance between us and hooked an arm through Sloane's before she could stop me.

"Happy birthday," I said as I pulled her to the side, getting into formation with the other dancers. "It's a good thing it's not too bright in here, as your beauty lights the room."

Sloane slanted me a suspicious look, and I let her go, as the few men there lined up across from the women. The singer counted off the steps, and I almost swallowed my tongue as Sloane began to bounce in time to the music.

Everything bounced along with her.

Her body shifted under the silk, and desire shot through me. Grateful for my sporran, to hide the tinges of lust that would soon be visible, I focused on the dance as we wove our way between the other line, and then I reached for Sloane's hands to dance down the middle of the row. Music chimed, and people danced around us, but everything faded except for Sloane and her moody, suspicious eyes.

"Why are you being nice to me?" Sloane asked, her voice a bit breathless.

"It's your birthday. Aren't those the rules?"

"You've been very clear you want me gone. And now you're at my party, dancing with me." Sloane's eyebrows winged up her forehead, and I couldn't help myself. I reached out and smoothed a silky strand of hair off her cheek, tucking it behind her ear, and her lips parted ever so slightly. I wanted a taste more than anything I'd ever wanted in my life.

The craving was so strong that I forced myself to step back, to turn away and follow the movements of the dance as other couples moved down the line. Why was I doing this to myself? Sloane was public enemy number one, as my parents had made exquisitely clear, and allowing myself to lean into my hunger for her was like playing with fire. So what if I'd had a stupid schoolboy crush? That was then and this was now. Circumstances were far different, and the fate of Briarhaven hung in my tenuous grasp.

A flash of red drew my eyes as Sloane whirled past with her next partner, and I swallowed.

Bloody hell, why did she have to be so stunning?

"Careful, lad, or your mouth will freeze like that." Raven tapped my chin, forcing my lips closed, and I realized that she was my next partner. I'd literally stopped dancing as I'd gaped after Sloane, and I had to shake my head to clear my thoughts.

"Raven. Don't you look bonnie tonight."

"Thank you," Raven said, threading her arm through mine as we fell into step. "But it's not me you're pining after."

"There's no pining." Was I pining? Bloody hell, half the town was here. I hoped nobody else had noticed what Raven had.

"Maybe you should stop trying to push the sisters out, and help them instead," Raven said, as we took a turn dancing down the middle of the floor.

"It's a centuries-old curse. The Charms barely contained it years ago; what makes you think that will change now?" Surely the Charms had done everything in their power to break the curse, hadn't they? The combined force of their coven's magick, and those that came before the current iteration, should have been enough to change something about the curse.

"Because Broca had a vision. Sloane and her sisters are the first of three. It will take all three of them to break it. Give them time."

"I don't know if Briarhaven has time. Do you see it out there?" I jerked a thumb toward the outside. "What if this goes on for months? Business will dry up. There will be inquiries."

"So fix it." Raven shrugged a shoulder.

"I'm trying to. The simplest solution is usually the best." I glanced up to see Sloane glaring at me from across the room, as though she could read my lips. I startled as my hat lifted and went flying from my head, landing with a plop in the bin across the room.

"I see someone discovered her magick today," I said. Keeping my eyes on Sloane, I used my magick to lift the hat and return it to my side. There, I dusted it off in my hands, before storming across the floor and cutting off Sloane's next dance partner.

"You've got your magick now, I see. Don't you think it's time for you to go?" I lowered my head, my face close enough to hers that I could see the little flecks of gold in her green eyes. A soft, citrusy scent hit me. It reminded me of sipping sangria on a sunny beach.

"I know you live in a castle"—Sloane's breath teased my lips—"and everyone in Briarhaven loves you and bows to your every word. But you, sir, are not the king of me."

Something about the way she phrased it made me want to be, though—the king of her, in the bedroom, her silky dress pooled at the side of my bed, my hands wrapping a curtain tassel around her wrists to keep her restrained, bending her body to my will. Her defiance brought out a dominant side in me that I hadn't known I had, and I found myself craving her touch. Maybe it had been too long since I'd been with a woman, or maybe because it was Sloane Freaking MacGregor, who had played many a role in my hormone-filled fantasies in high school. But I wasn't a teenager anymore, and Sloane was all woman. It was enough to almost bring me to my knees. I couldn't say I liked it either.

"Not a king, no," I said, my voice husky. "But a protector. Of this town. And you'll do well to heed my words, Sloane. I will see you leave before your curse ruins us all."

"You really know how to show a girl a good time on her birthday, don't you?"

Goddess above, but I wanted to show her a good time. For weeks preferably. Instead, I stepped back when her sisters joined her side.

"Everything good here?" Lyra trilled, in a sky-blue dress that looked like bandages wrapped around her body.

"Aye," Sloane said, biting her lower lip and sending my libido rocketing. "Knox was just leaving, wasn't he?"

"Och, I'll go tonight, witchling." I bent close to her ear and caught her quick intake of breath. "But you'll be the one leaving in the end. Understood?"

I don't know why she brought out this side in me. If I was honest with myself, a sliver of fear rippled through me every time she was close by.

There was just something about Sloane and her witchy eyes that made me think my future would be irrevocably changed if I let the MacGregors stay. It was like I was the captain of a ship heading into a gnarly storm, and all I could do was batten down the hatches, hold tight to the wheel, and brace myself for impact.

CHAPTER TEN
Sloane

Despite my misgivings, last night's cèilidh had been surprisingly fun even with the lack of attendees.

Except for one notable moment.

Why did he have to wear his kilt?

Honestly, I'd forgotten the punch of a man in a kilt, having been away from Scotland for years, but seeing Knox stride into the party last night had conflicting emotions rising inside me. Objectively, I could admire a drop-dead gorgeous man. Yet when said man was insistent on running you out of town, it certainly leveled up the annoyance factor.

"It's a good thing it's not too bright in here, as your beauty lights the room."

I played his words back to myself, shifting under the blankets, as Blue snored at my feet.

For just a moment, I wanted to savor the compliment, like a delicious dessert enjoyed slowly and paired with a perfect glass of wine. He'd meant it too. It wasn't a reflexive comment, one thrown off the cuff to be polite. Those blue eyes had pierced me, and he'd visibly swallowed as he'd taken my dress in.

I'd done that to him.

I wasn't used to playing the part of bombshell, but when Lyra had insisted that fire engine red was the way to go, shoving a dress in my hands and refusing to hear my insecurities about how it hugged my curves, I'd given up and gone with it. Now I was glad that I had followed her directive.

There was something about putting a man like Knox on his back foot that made me feel powerful.

I rolled over and looked to where I'd plugged my phone in across the room. Wind gusted against the window, making me burrow more deeply under the covers, and I realized that now I didn't have to get out of bed in the cold to go get my phone to check my messages.

I could just use my magick to bring it to me.

A little thrill of excitement shot through me. So what if Mandy Meadows thought I was a basic witch? This magick was still mine, and I would be proud of it. Two days ago I couldn't lift things with my mind, and now I could. Which was more than the majority of the world's population could do. Far from basic, in my estimation.

I'd spent much of the day yesterday practicing my levitation skills, and frankly, I was quite chuffed with myself. I had my magick under my command, and I could quickly use it as needed.

Pushing my hair back from my face, I focused on the phone and reached for the magick that shimmered through me. I realized, now, that it had always been there. Though I'd started to notice its presence more in the years approaching my twenty-fifth birthday, this spark had always been inside me. My very essence, I supposed.

Or, my sparkles, as Lyra called it.

She was going to take to coven life like, well, a charm. I smiled to myself. Lyra had always been a girls' girl. No matter where she went, she collected friends like handbags, and ingratiated herself quickly into any new community, while Nova and I were more cautious in our approach. Nova didn't much care about appeasing anyone, aside from her clients who commissioned her art for digital prints and tattoos, and she'd spent most of the night discussing the best running routes around Briarhaven with Tam.

Broca had stayed home with Blue, insisting that she was happy to do so, and I was glad that I didn't have to leave him alone.

Aside from Knox reminding me I was unwanted, and most of the town not showing up to the party in protest of our arrival in Briarhaven, I'd had a really nice night.

Reaching my hand out, I pulled at a thread of magick and invited my phone to come to me.

The curtains covering the window behind the phone promptly burst into flames.

"Shite!" I screeched, startling Blue, who toppled off the bed and caught himself just before he reached the floor, and flew awkwardly across the room. Whipping the blankets off the bed, I kept screaming as I beat the curtains with my blankets, trying to tamp out the flames.

"Watch out!" Nova shouted at my back, and then she was there, fire extinguisher in hand, and foam exploded across the window.

In seconds, the fire was out, and Lyra stood in the door, gaping at us, while Broca cried out from below.

"Everything's fine." Lyra turned and padded down the hallway. "I'll go to her."

Blue threw his head back and howled, and I automatically lifted my arms for him. He slammed into my chest, still not great with his landings, and I cuddled him as I stared at the curtains. My heart thundered in my chest, and a bead of sweat dripped down my back.

What the hell had just happened?

"What the hell was that?" Nova demanded. "Was that Blue's fault?"

"No, not at all." Blue whimpered in my arms, and I hugged him more tightly. "I . . . I don't know. I just was going to float my phone to me, so I didn't have to get out of bed. I have no idea what happened." I flailed one hand helplessly in the air, blinking at the foam spray that crusted my window. Gingerly, I put Blue down on the bed, and he pawed at the blanket, burrowing his nose in. Stepping across the room, I wiped some of the foam off the window and peered out.

My neighbor lifted two fingers from across the street, where he shoveled his walk. I waved, less enthusiastically today, but still, we had a thing, didn't we?

"Let's go talk to Broca. Don't try to levitate anything else."

"Good shout."

"And then we'll clean this up." Nova shook her head at the mess of my bedroom wall. "I don't like this."

"Yeah, cause I'm a huge fan?" I tugged my Keep Calm sweatshirt over my head, and put a pair of wool cottage socks on, before scooping Blue up and following Nova downstairs. Blue snuffled at my neck, and then licked my chin, and I smiled despite my apprehension. He was trying to calm me, in his own way, and I hugged him more tightly to my chest. I hadn't known how much I needed Blue until I had him. Something of my own—that wasn't my sisters—to take care of.

"How did the fire start?" Broca asked as soon as we entered the living room. Lyra had helped her to her armchair, and she wore a dressing gown in acrid lime green with feathers at the wrists.

"It was me," I said, plopping onto the couch and cuddling Blue close.

Nova went to the kitchen and opened the fridge, and Blue popped his head up, torn between comforting me and the possibility of cheese.

"Go on," I said, loosening my arms, and he took off from my lap, wheeling his way through the air to Nova.

"Walk me through it." Broca clasped her hands together, her eyes steady on mine.

I took her through what had led up to the curtains exploding in fire. Lyra curled up next to me, braiding my hair like she used to do as a child when she needed something to focus on and calm her nerves.

"Let's try it again." Broca nodded toward a blue-and-white ceramic vase tucked on a side table by the front window. "Can you bring me that vase?"

A shiver of unease rippled down my back.

"What if it explodes or something?"

"I'm ready for it, Sloane." Broca waved a hand in the air. "Give it a go."

Biting my lower lip, I focused on the vase and reached for my magick, like I'd done countless times the day before, all with the desired results.

The vase lit on fire and cracked in pieces.

I didn't even know ceramics *could* light on fire.

Tears pricked my eyes, frustration filling me, and Blue threw his head back and howled, the sound morose and pulling at my heartstrings. Broca muttered something under her breath, and the fire winked out. Abandoning his cheese, Blue flew to me and plopped down in my lap, desperately licking my face as though he could take my worries away with his kisses.

"What am I supposed to do?" I asked, crestfallen.

"We'll have to see how tomorrow goes, but if this is what I think it is, well, I guess I'm not entirely surprised," Broca said.

"What is it, Broca?" Nova brought a tray of bagels and cream cheese over to the coffee table and put it down, and Blue turned toward the food, his eyes hopeful.

"Is it the curse?" I asked, my mind whirling. I couldn't go around lighting things on fire left and right. Already I had to watch out for Blue, who was still inadvertently torching things at random. We'd burn the house down before the day was over, at the rate we were going.

"It might be, if it is what I think it is. I've only known one other witch in our family to have this particular . . . affliction."

I flinched.

"'Affliction'?" I repeated. I raised an eyebrow. "I'm diseased?"

"I . . . That's not quite the right word." Broca sighed and smoothed a crease in her dressing gown. "It's still a gift, but you'll have to make the best of it."

"Please stop talking in riddles and just give it to me straight." I closed my eyes and waited, butterflies churning in my gut.

"It's entirely possible that every day you will wake up with new magick."

"What?" My mouth sprang open, and I gaped at Broca.

"Like a reverse *Groundhog Day*?" Lyra asked.

"Badass." Nova air-cheersed me with her bagel, and Blue almost fell off my lap to try to get a bite.

"Yes, like a reverse *Groundhog Day*. It's been known to happen before, though it is quite rare. Which means that just when you get a handle on your magick, you'll be given new magick the next day . . . the old one gone."

"But . . . but . . ."

"Oh, Sloane's going to hate that," Nova mused, crunching on her bagel. "She's a planner."

"Oh goddess, she's going to be a nightmare," Lyra agreed, and my head swiveled between the two.

"That's what you're concerned about at the moment? Not that I'll burn the house down around us?"

"Doubtful. Broca's got this place charmed to the high heavens, don't you?" Lyra peered around me at Broca, who nodded.

"Who was the other witch?"

"The other witch?" Broca looked away pretending to not know what I was asking. I felt the ground drop out from under me.

"It's Mum, isn't it?" I asked.

At that, Lyra and Nova both stilled, their banter dropping away, and we became a unit like we'd been for years now.

"Aye, lass. It is your mother. But she didn't particularly seem to mind. The unpredictability of her magick fed something in her that made her lean into the erratic nature of it."

My sisters and I looked at one another, each affirming something we'd seemingly chosen to overlook.

"She always told us she liked doing different things with her magick. That it made her more powerful than others." Nova's lower lip pushed out.

"Why didn't we ever question that?" Lyra's brow furrowed. "Like, now that I think about it . . . she was really, really chaotic to be around."

"She loved the drama of it all. She played into it, didn't she?" I murmured, my hand at my mouth.

"It was her way of coping with never knowing what she would be dealing with each day." Broca's face was sympathetic, even though I knew she didn't particularly care for how our mother had treated us.

"Will that be me, then? Am I going to smash plates and blow things up just to see if I can?" I asked Broca.

"Unlikely." Broca chuckled, the sound soothing some of my tension. "Your personality is far different from your mother's. She leaned into it, a rebellion of sorts, and I have to believe that is why your father finally left."

"He left?" Lyra demanded, leaning forward.

"She always told us she kicked him to the curb. Didn't need no man and all that," Nova said.

"Yes, well, everyone has their version of events, don't they?" Broca's tone was crisp.

"She drove him away." My voice was but a whisper, but it all made so much more sense now. My mother had always painted herself the victim, and for me the memories were a blur of arguments and magickal explosions, but those moments began to shift in my mind as I tried to look at them from an adult viewpoint.

"In some respects, yes. But your father wasn't an easy man either. They weren't well matched, even though their love was strong. It was fire meeting fire, and they burned each other out.

"I'd say it's saddest for the three of you, as you all got burned." We *had* gotten burned, but we'd somehow come out of that stronger.

While we were so different as sisters, we'd always been a team. And that was because of the woman in front of me.

"We had you, though." I gave Broca a warm smile. "You saved us."

"I did the best I could." Broca smiled back. "You girls have brought nothing but joy to me, and I'm honored that I've been able to be a part of watching you grow into such lovely young women."

"Och, Broca, you're going to get me going." Lyra fanned her hands in front of her eyes.

"So what happens to Sloane now? She can't use her magick?" Nova scooped up a bit of cream cheese on her finger, and Blue almost convulsed with excitement when she held it out for him to lick.

"She can use it as much or as little as she wants. It's just . . . she'll never know what she's getting until she tests it."

I looked down at my hands like they were lethal weapons.

My sisters weren't wrong. I was a planner as much as I could be, given the hand I'd been dealt, and my twenty-fifth birthday and the promise of magick had always loomed over me—the unknown keeping me up some nights. Last night, after the cèilidh, I'd come home and felt an odd sense of peace that I hadn't felt in a really long time. Even if my magick was considered basic by the Charms, I had been pleased; it had been something I could understand and easily manipulate.

I hated that I now had to be on edge, never knowing what each morning would bring.

"Bedlam," I murmured, holding my hands up. "How can I trust these two?"

"Sloane. The queen of chaos." Nova grinned at me, knowing how much I would hate that title.

"How dare you?" I sucked in a breath and Nova pretended to duck.

"Careful with those. I like my hair as is."

"Bitch."

"Messy," Nova taunted back, and I gasped, holding a hand to my chest.

"Rude."

"Girls, that's quite enough. Sloane, we need to alert the Charms."

"Do we, though?" I glared as Nova broke into laughter.

"Aye, lass. We need their help. Now that you finally have your powers, we can use them to help break the curse. The sooner we can get started on tracking down how to do this, the better."

"I think it's a good idea, Sloane. We can use the help. The last thing Broca needs is to be putting out fires, literally, all day when she's still recovering from surgery," Lyra said, playing the Broca card, and my shoulders slumped in defeat.

"Fine, call them in." I was doing this for Broca, I reminded myself. "But if they make me wear a pantsuit, I'm out."

"But pearls would look so good on you," Nova snickered.

"Bite me." Blue huffed out a puff of smoke, accenting my words, and Nova held her hands up.

"Warning received. Between the both of you, we'll never be able to say a word out of line again."

At that, I beamed down at Blue, who was circling my lap for a nap.

"Hear that, bud? We inspire fear in others. I'll take it."

"So much for being a benevolent leader."

"That comes after coffee."

CHAPTER ELEVEN
Knox

The snow was becoming a problem.

Scratch that, *Sloane* was becoming a problem.

I kept thinking of her silky red dress, my hands clenching with the need to touch her. It was undeniable, my attraction to her, and yet I knew that I needed to do what First Knight of the Iron Thistle Order would do—make her leave.

It would be one thing if all of Scotland were caught in an unexpected icy vortex, but since it was contained to just Briarhaven, I'd soon have to explain the situation to the regulatory authorities. A conversation that rarely went well. Heavy snow had collapsed the awning in front of the Familiar's Nest, a store catering to the needs of our familiars, and I'd spent all morning helping to build it back up. Tucked on the corner of the square, the shop was painted a deep blue, with yellow-gold trim and a bright red door. Sorcha, the shopkeeper, had called in my assistance as she didn't want to use her magick in plain sight to clean up the mess of her front walk.

"Thanks for cleaning this up for me, Knox." Sorcha leaned in the doorway, arms crossed over a knit sweater with bunnies on it, her gray hair braided back from her face. "I doubt we'll have many tourists with this weather, but I wanted to err on the side of caution."

"Nae bother." I shrugged and finished clearing the splintered wood, throwing it in the back of my car.

"I think Haggis and Oswald deserve new toys for your hard work, don't they?" Sorcha asked, holding the door open when I walked back to her.

"Oswald will pretend he isn't interested, but if I get Haggis a toy and not him, he'll be livid."

"Come on, then, let's pick something out." Sorcha ushered me inside, and though I had a million other messes to clean up around town, I went, unable to resist new toys for my boys.

The shop was softly lit, the walls painted a deep maroon, and wicker baskets filled with toys lined one large table. On the other side, shelves held more practical needs, like grooming supplies, medicines, and various harnesses that were more adaptable to a variety of different-shaped bodies. Like familiars with wings. I paused. I'd heard through the small-town chatter that Sloane had received an emberwolf as a gift for her birthday, and now I couldn't help but think that maybe I should also get her new arrival a gift. I was going there anyway, after this, to berate her into leaving, again—but that didn't mean I had to take it out on her new pet. And if—no, *when*—Sloane finally left, it wouldn't be like she could take the emberwolf with her. Maybe I could convince him to move in with me at the castle.

As provost of Briarhaven, it was my job to meet any new familiars and assess if they were safe for the town. While emberwolves had once been a threat to us, their domestication through the years had left them as nothing more than beloved companions. Picking up a large circular ring with a large ball inside, I held it up. "Haggis will love this."

"Aye, he will at that. Great to toss about but rolls a treat too." Sorcha held up a box with several holes in it and shook it.

"What's that?"

"A box with crackly paper inside. Oswald will love it."

"I can't believe I'm paying to buy a box," I grumbled, and Sorcha chuckled. "Cats are nothing if not contradictory. Buy them a nice toy, and they'll sit in the bag it came in."

"That's the truth of it." I idled by the baskets. "Say, Sorcha . . . do you have any toys for an emberwolf?"

"An emberwolf, is it? Have you added to your pack?" Sorcha crossed the room and studied the baskets.

"Not mine, no."

"Ah." Sorcha's warm brown eyes lit with consideration, and I did my best to head off any potential town gossip.

"The MacGregor sisters have a new addition to the family. I need to meet him and make sure he's safe for Briarhaven. Might be best to go in with a gift." There. My interest in the emberwolf was easily explained as part of my duty, and not because I wanted Sloane to look at me with appreciation. Nope, it wasn't that at all.

"Is that the way of it, then?" Sorcha continued to look at me with that light in her eyes, and I internally groaned.

"Aye, that's the way of it." I picked up a squeaky dragon toy. "What do you think of this one?"

"I think a puzzle toy would be better." Sorcha led me to another table that held a variety of structures, from a simple tray with sliding doors, to fully built castles with doors and windows that opened. "This one is particularly enchanted for emberwolves. Look . . . see this?"

Sorcha pointed to the doors of the castle. They looked to be of a sparkly, malleable material, and were a bright red.

"Flameproof. But if he does torch them, they'll open to reveal the treats hidden inside."

"That's incredible." And likely not cheap. I discreetly checked the price tag.

Sorcha caught me and gave me a knowing look.

"Aye, the price is quite dear. A present like this would certainly be considered a very nice gift for a close . . . friend."

Oh, great. Now I was stuck in the position of having inquired about a gift for Sloane's new addition, and if I didn't buy it, then I was going to seem rude, and if I did, then the whole town would think my interest was something more than just friends.

"You know, I remember Sloane's parents," Sorcha said idly as she turned and opened a new delivery of what looked to be chew toys in the shape of dragons' claws. "A one-night stand that should have never turned into a relationship. They fed off each other. Their individual magick was like a drug to the other, until they burned themselves out. Can't imagine there were too many nice gifts for the girls, though I know Broca did her best."

Sorcha was giving me an out. My heart twisted at the image of a sullen Sloane, tenderhearted and angry, slouching in an alleyway. Gifts had come fast and easy in my household, even if warmth and affection were limited.

"In that case, I'll take the castle."

"Och, and that's a grand choice. And let me know how Haggis gets on with his new ball. He should be able to toss it quite high in the air if he gives it laldy."

"Aye, I will." Sorcha rang my purchases up quickly, and before I could get stuck responding to another snow emergency, I headed toward the MacGregors' house to drop off the gift for their new emberwolf.

Raven's words had competed with thoughts of undressing Sloane throughout the night.

If Broca's vision was accurate, I needed to shift focus and figure out a solution to this endless winter. Not lust after the sexy witch. I paused outside the shop, gifts in hand, and watched as a worker hung up Christmas lights outside the Dragon's Hoard. We hadn't even gotten through Halloween yet. But I supposed it went with the theme of snow.

A memory surfaced of Sloane, standing tight-lipped as her mother picked up one item after another in the shop. I'd been shopping with my own mum, who had a veritable mountain of presents stacked on the checkout counter, while Sloane had hovered behind her mum, not touching anything.

A pretty woman with a riot of curls and sharp-looking eyes, her mother had checked the price on every item in the store before cursing softly beneath her breath.

"You'd think you'd price things a bit more fairly, Dorothy."

Sloane had winced, her eyes flying to mine, her cheeks pinkening. Immediately wanting to help, I rolled my eyes, making a goofy face. I was rewarded with a small smile, a flush of pleasure, and never had I felt more powerful.

"Mum, come on." Sloane had tugged her mother's arm, but she'd just thrown her off.

"It's a damn shame, is what it is. Robbery." Her mum spied the pile of presents on the counter, and I grimaced, knowing what was coming. "I guess only posh people are welcome here."

"Everyone is welcome in my store," Dorothy said from behind the counter, where she blithely rang up my mum's items.

"Well, *I* think they're a fair price," my mum had chimed in, trying to help.

"Och, sod off." With that charming rebuttal, Sloane's mum had sailed from the store, slamming the shop door before Sloane could get outside.

"Never you mind her, Sloane. She's just having a rough day," Dorothy called, and I could have hugged the shopkeeper.

"Um, thanks . . ." Sloane had given me one more embarrassed glance before skittering outside, and I'd never wanted to follow someone more than I had in that moment. But we didn't really know each other, and there was nothing I could do to protect her from the wrath of her mum.

"Such a shame." My mum had turned to Dorothy, her eyes alight with excitement as they always were when she knew she'd get a chance for a good gossip. "You know, I heard they're splitting up."

"None of that nonsense here, darling. We don't talk about people's marriages. Do we?" Dorothy had leveled my mum a look so severe that she'd immediately shut up and I'd been left with oh so many questions. Sadness filled me. I wished I'd had the courage to give Sloane a gift from the shop, to maybe make her Christmas a touch nicer.

Two weeks later she'd been gone.

Shaking my head of the memory, I made my way to Sloane's house, my memories making my intentions murky.

When Sloane opened the door, looking sleep-rumpled and cozy in a loose jumper and leggings, I had to pause as my thoughts scrambled in my brain, and momentarily I forgot why I'd even come here. Flashes of the red silk were burned into my brain, and the contrast of curvy, sexy Sloane draped in silk, and warm, sleepy Sloane, looking like she'd just had a proper tumble, made self-control difficult. Something I never normally struggled with. Swallowing against my suddenly dry throat, I held up a bag.

"I come bearing gifts."

"That's suspicious." Sloane crossed her arms over her chest. The wind gusted at my back, sending a dance of snowflakes into her house, but she held her ground.

"Invite the man in and stop letting the heat out, Sloane."

I grinned as Sloane grimaced, mutiny on her face.

"Aye, Sloane. Listen to your grandmother." I couldn't help but taunt her. I didn't know what it was about the stubborn set of her chin, or her absolute refusal to do my bidding, that got my back up, but I simply couldn't resist poking at her.

All curves and softness, and sharp edges and wicked intelligence. It had to be tough, never having roots, but she seemed to have managed to adapt her life to this curse, and with a resilience that had to be admired.

Sloane stood back and motioned me inside, silently seething, and I closed the door behind me, the wind battling me to do so.

"How are you, Knox?" Broca asked from her perch in the lounge chair. Her wink was as sassy and colorful as she was. Who knew a neon-yellow silk pajama set with a peacock-green robe would work together?

"Och, well enough, I suppose. The snow is causing a lot of trouble, and I've been on call with helping where I can."

"It's sorry I am for that." Broca shook her head. "Such a shame."

I opened my mouth—

"If you suggest we leave town one more time I'm going to cut a chunk of your hair out."

My eyes widened to where Sloane stood at the counter, cutting scallions with a pair of scissors, and I patted the back of my hair. I liked it just fine as it was, so it appeared I needed to proceed with caution.

"Is that a gift, Knox?" Broca eyed the bag in my hand, redirecting the conversation.

"Aye. For your wee one. I heard you had a new addition."

The scissors clattered to the counter, and Sloane crossed her arms over her chest, a mulish expression on her face.

"You brought a gift for Blue?"

"Is that his name, then?"

"Aye," Sloane said softly and disappeared through a door before returning with an emberwolf in her arms.

He blinked up at me, his tongue lolling from his mouth, a mile-wide smile on his face. His warm brown eyes were friendly and curious, and his gray-and-white coat and pearlescent wings were captivating. Wriggling in her arms, he leaned forward and swiped his rough tongue across my outreached hand.

It was clear Sloane was bothered by how quickly Blue had welcomed me, and I was secretly pleased. She likely had no clue just how loyal emberwolves were as a species. Which meant Blue had sized me up and given his approval.

His witch was another matter altogether.

"He's incredible," I breathed. I hadn't seen an emberwolf in years, and they were one of my favorite magickal beings. "How is he settling in?"

"He's grand," Sloane said, and Blue shifted in her arms, his attention going to the food on the counter.

"No fire mishaps?" I asked, and Sloane's gaze whipped to mine. Was that a flash of guilt I saw? "It's totally normal, Sloane. It takes an emberwolf a long time to have total command over their fire."

"You know them, then?" Broca asked.

"I raised one for a few years before he picked his witch. I still miss him," I admitted. Testing Blue, I reached out again, and he scrambled to come into my arms. Cradling him against my chest, I laughed as he gave my face a sloppy lick, while Sloane simmered in frustration.

"I feel like a new mom," Sloane admitted. "I have so much to learn about them."

"Well, let's start with his gift, then, shall we?" I walked over with the large shopping bag, and Blue tilted his head, interested.

"He seems intrigued. What say you, Blue? Do you want a pressie?" Sloane asked and then nodded at me to open it for him. Bending, I put Blue next to the bag on the ground and pulled out the large castle. "Is that a freaking castle? Of course you'd bring us a castle."

"You really have a chip on your shoulder about castles, don't you? I thought girls loved castles. Being a princess and fairy tales and all that."

"Are you a prince?" Sloane's mouth dropped open.

"No." I grinned. "But I am royal. I'm a knight."

"Aren't you supposed to live down in the barracks or whatever they're called, then? Not in a fancy house on the hill?"

"Nope. The knights need to be close to protect the prince, don't they?"

"And where is the prince, then?" Sloane asked, crouching next to Blue.

"Nobody knows. He absconded somewhere in the late eighteenth century, and my family took over the castle and the protection of Briarhaven. We're officially the 'royal' family, so to speak. I'm First Knight of the Iron Thistle Order and am duty bound to protect the village and its inhabitants. Hence my need to rectify this snow situation as soon as possible. I have no choice, Sloane. It's my vow."

"Huh." Sloane completely ignored my plea, nibbling on her lower lip as she watched Blue sniff the castle. "What's he supposed to do with that?"

"I've been told you hide treats inside and if he burns the doors open, he can get to them."

"Burns?" Sloane's eyebrows winged up.

"It's specifically for emberwolves. It's protected. Give it a go."

"Hmmm." Sloane gave me a suspicious look, but she went to the fridge and pulled out a container of cut-up bits of cheese, distracting Blue. He scrambled on the floor, and then took to the air in his haste to get to Sloane, almost clipping me in the cheek with his wing.

"Whoa, buddy, slow down there." I laughed, delighted to see him winging around the room like a clunky dragon. Sloane chucked me the container of cheese, which I caught while Blue gave chase, and ducked once more before he took my head off in his attempt to get to the cheese. "Hang on, hang on. I promise you'll get your cheese."

Blue landed on the arm of the couch, perching as he watched me crouch next to the castle. I looked up at him and pointed to the toy.

"So what I'm going to do is hide the cheese inside here. Your job is to find the cheese. Got it?"

Blue grinned at me. I made quick work of hiding the cheese in various rooms in the castle and then stepped back.

"Go ahead, Blue. Play with your toy." Sloane still sounded reluctant, but I could tell she wanted to see how Blue would respond.

Blue leapt to the ground and nosed the castle, wandering in circles around it, his snuffles and snorts growing in frustration until he finally torched one of the doors open and discovered the cheese.

"Oh my goddess. It's working!" Sloane grabbed my arm, and the touch was so unexpected, as was the jolt of electricity that raced up my arm, that I froze.

I wanted this woman on me, under me, around me. If my body responded to a simple touch like this, I could only imagine what it would be like to have her in my bed. Forcing myself to pull my thoughts away from Sloane wrapped in silk, again, I kept my gaze trained on Blue as he used his fire to find his treats.

"He likes it." It pleased me, more than I wanted to admit, that my gift was well received.

"I think a thank-you is in order, Sloane," Broca said from where she was scrolling an iPad in her chair.

"Thank you," Sloane said automatically. Dutifully.

"If you want to thank me, you'll come with me to the castle and help me deal with this snow issue." The words were out of my mouth before I'd even realized I'd spoken them, but now that the idea was out there, I realized just how much I liked it.

"There's nothing I can do—"

"Actually, there's plenty that you can do. I'm told you work in marketing, right?"

"Sloane's excellent at marketing. She freelances for several big companies, but her favorite is bespoke clients with unique branding challenges. Which is just what this snow problem of ours needs. Great idea, Knox." Broca radiated sunshine from her armchair.

"I don't—"

"If you're hell-bent on staying here, the very least you can do is put your skills to good use."

"I thought you wanted me to break the curse. Now you want me to work on marketing your town for you? What's it going to be?"

"Marketing first. If you think you can break a curse overnight, you clearly have a lot to learn about magick."

"Excuse me?" Sloane jabbed my chest with a finger, and I reached up and curled my hand around her finger, happy to be touching her in any way that I could, even though I knew she was infuriated with me. "I'm getting really sick of people insinuating I'm a basic witch."

"Well, you're not doing much to change our opinions, are you, witchling?" Even I internally winced at that one, but when I saw the fire of battle light in her eyes, I knew I'd provoked her enough to come with me. It seemed I would need to challenge this woman at every step to get somewhere with her, which should make things highly interesting.

"I am *not* a basic witch. And I *will* figure out a way to use this snow to your advantage, and when I'm done, I will break the curse and laugh in your face while doing so." Sloane stomped upstairs to change.

"Well done, lad," Broca said, her voice low. "Keep poking at her. She needs the challenge."

I dropped onto the couch across from her and was delighted when Blue flew to me, slamming awkwardly onto my lap, and I caught him close for cuddles.

"Why is that?" I might as well get any intel that Broca was willing to give me if I was going to be working closely with Sloane.

"She's been so focused on taking care of Lyra and Nova that she's forgotten about her own needs. And she's never going to grow into the woman, and witch, I know she can be if she, or someone, doesn't shake things up a bit."

"Understood," I said as Sloane stomped back downstairs. "It will be my absolute joy to challenge her at every step."

"I always knew I liked you, boy." Broca accepted a kiss on her cheek as I stood, Blue in my arms.

"Is Blue with us, or staying here?"

"Here. He hates the snow." Sloane slapped on a puffy navy parka and glared up at me. "All right, Knox. Let's get this over with so I don't have to deal with you anymore."

Pleased, I handed Blue to Broca, while Sloane stepped into the swirl of snow, radiating annoyance.

It looked like my day had just gotten better.

CHAPTER TWELVE
Sloane

"Land Rover, huh?" I sniffed as I climbed inside his car.

"What's wrong with a Land Rover?" Knox asked, casting me a look as I buckled myself in. The snow gusted, icy and undeterred, and I winced as my neighbor leaned on his shovel and glared at me. Pretending not to notice, I shifted toward Knox.

"Nothing at all. Fancy."

"And you have an aversion to fancy?" Knox started the car, and my bum immediately warmed as the seats heated. I refused to give any indication of pleasure and wiggled only a bit as I settled into the coziness.

"We come from different worlds, Knox." I grimaced at the sight of our car, the front end buried in a snowbank that had now doubled in size, and then I looked toward the castle. Slightly imposing, with a few turrets and towers for good measure, Knox's castle stood over Briarhaven, a stark contrast to our wee cottage. "I've dated your type before. Used to the world working in their favor. The annoying thing is that it usually does. It just makes it hard to relate to those of us who have a lot more roadblocks in our way."

Knox didn't say anything for a moment, carefully maneuvering the Land Rover through a particularly thick patch of snow before glancing at me.

"I don't doubt what you're saying is true, Sloane. But living in a castle doesn't absolve me of my own hardships."

"Hardships served on a gold plate don't seem all that difficult to swallow."

"You'd be surprised."

At the note in his voice, I paused, intrigued.

"Such as?"

"Responsibility can be both a gift and a burden." Knox shrugged, his lips pressed into a tight line, and I slumped back into my seat, intrigued by his confession. He was the town's golden boy, and everyone had sung his praises over the past few days. I supposed a golden cage was, nevertheless, still a cage.

"What's the story there? Didn't you have brothers? Your parents? Or is it just you banging around that drafty castle all by yourself?" I gestured to the castle as Knox pulled to a stop at impressive wrought iron gates, gilded interlocking *B*s on the front, thistles twisting around the letters. They glided smoothly open, and the road that curved up the hill was free of snow. "Also, why is there no snow on this road? Do your minions race out and clean off any fleck of snow that dares land on your pavement?"

At that, Knox's lips quirked, and heat bloomed low inside me. Knox was single-handedly the most enticing man I'd ever met, but he largely directed scowls and annoyed looks in my direction. Which was a good thing, it seemed, since even the hint of a smile was enough to make me want to dissolve in a pool of lust. Good goddess, but I needed to date more. There was no reason why I shouldn't have some semblance of control over my desires.

Or my magick.

I sobered as the realization that I wasn't fully in charge of my magick slammed back into me. I'd spent a good portion of my life trying to be as different from my mother as I could be, only to be gifted with the one thing that had broken her.

Super cool, Universe. Well played and all that.

"It's a spell I'm testing out. In some parts of the world where they receive heavy snowfall, they build their car parks and pavements with underground heaters. Since I'm not about to tear up all the roads in Briarhaven, I thought I'd test something that would, at the very least, make the roads passable. The gritters are working overtime, and hardly making a dent. It's next to impossible for the businesses to run, and I'm scared I'm going to have a mutiny on my hands here soon."

"Could be fun. A little rebellion always spices life up."

"It's not me they'll be after, Sloane."

At that, my shoulders stiffened. I knew the town was annoyed with us, but I hadn't thought about them turning on my family and running us from Briarhaven. Now, imagining torches and pitchforks in the front yard, I shivered.

It felt like the clock was ticking, and tension threaded my shoulders. Turning toward where my breath fogged the window, I discreetly dabbed at it. It wouldn't do to show weakness in front of this man.

"And to answer your other questions, my father is no longer a knight in the Iron Thistle Order, having passed that on to me. My brothers are enjoying gallivanting around Europe, as, apparently, are my parents, which leaves me."

"The lone man to keep Briarhaven safe?"

I'd gotten to see the world, while Knox had stayed right here and made Briarhaven a safe home for magickals. Despite my annoyance with his overbearing ways and absolute conviction that everything worked out for him, my heart softened, just a touch.

As a child, Broca had once taken us to Edinburgh to see the Royal Military Tattoo performance at the castle where military and cultural dances were exhibited from all over the world. At the very end, everything had gone dark, and a singular light had shown high up on the battlements illuminating a lone bagpiper. His song had cut through the night, silencing the crowd, as he'd stood watch over all those below him.

Knox reminded me of him.

"Something like that. Och, it's not so bad. I've largely been able to make improvements on my own without too much interference."

"Sounds quiet." And I didn't mean that in a bad way. I loved my sisters with all my heart, but a peaceful bunch they were not.

"Mmm, not always. But you'll see why shortly. Welcome to my home." Knox pulled the Land Rover to a stop in front of an impressive set of doors with deep-set Celtic carvings in the wood and massive gold unicorn door knockers.

I refused to be impressed. But damn it, I wanted a unicorn door knocker too.

A squat man in a tux swung the door open for us, and he bowed deeply, a smile on his leathery face. I could just see the magick shimmering lightly around his body, and for a moment an ogre blurred across his countenance, all moss-covered shoulders and earthy demeanor.

"Henry, this is Sloane. She's a terror, so don't let her near any sharp objects. Assume she's trying to kill me at all times."

My mouth dropped open as I rounded on Knox.

"Excuse me. I would be far more inventive with my murderous intentions than to simply knife you in the back."

"Nevertheless, best to remove the easy threats."

"As you wish, sir." Henry bowed to me and closed the doors behind us, cutting off the icy wind that pushed me forward, and warmth cocooned me as I craned my neck to look up at the high ceiling decorated with a mural of dragons in mid-battle. Flames danced in a fireplace, and I gaped at it. A fireplace. *In the foyer.* Who even knew such things existed?

"I'm not going to compliment you on your mural, but if I *were* to compliment you, I'd note the excellent workmanship." I stuck my nose in the air.

"Noted." Knox's lips quirked, and that sharp tug of lust in my core annoyed me once more. I opened my mouth to speak, but a clattering sound drew my attention.

"What's—"

My eyes rounded as a miniature Highland coo careened around the corner at top speed, a wheelchair frame rattling around him, his shaggy coat blowing back as he barreled toward us. A tabby cat kept pace at his side.

"Haggis! Stop!" Knox ordered sharply, and the coo skidded to a stop but didn't manage to catch himself in time. Throwing his body in front of me, Knox caught the coo before he took my knees out and held him tight. "We discussed this."

I tilted my head around Knox's shoulder to see Haggis give Knox an aggrieved look.

"Hi, Haggis," I said, shouldering Knox aside and dropping to my knees to scratch behind Haggis's ears. The coo tilted his head, leaning into my palm, and made a noise of contentment. "You're just the cutest, aren't you?" He bopped his head against my hand, seeming to agree with me.

"He thinks you're pretty cute too." I glanced up at Knox, amused, and froze as his eyes heated. From this angle, I knelt before him, his waist directly at my face. Remembering the gifts the goddess had bestowed upon him, my cheeks flamed. Soft fur brushed my hand, and I broke the look, desperate for anything else to take my thoughts away from my attraction to this man.

"And who is this wee one?" I trailed a finger along the back of the cat, scratching at the base of his tail as he arched into my hand.

"This is Oswald. He's quite proper, or so he'll have you told, until, of course, a curtain tassel crosses his path."

"Ah, then the warrior emerges, is that the way of it?"

Oswald bumped his head against my hand, emitting a soft purr, and I smiled. Would Blue get along with these two? It would be fun to find out. Except we might not get that chance. Surely I didn't have to come to the castle more than one time.

Knox shook a bag he'd brought with him, drawing their attention, and I watched with a small smile as he withdrew the toys for them. Haggis immediately took off after the ball, his face a picture of joy, while Oswald pretended indifference to his toy.

"What is it?" I pointed at the box.

"Crinkly paper inside a box. He's pretending it is beneath him, but wait until we walk away. He'll stomp all over it."

Oswald seemed to give Knox a narrowed look before licking his paw and ignoring the box. Threading his hand through my arm, Knox tugged me lightly down a corridor painted a soft, mossy color with a plush carpet covering the stone floors. I tried to ignore how good his body felt next to mine, towering over me, all heat and muscle. Let's be honest here. I didn't date often, so being close to a muscled man was indeed a rare thing. I liked it.

A crackle of paper sounded at our backs.

"See?" Knox hissed, and I couldn't help myself, I giggled. Knox skidded to a stop and looked down at me, eyebrows raised. "Well, I'll be damned. Was that a laugh, Sloane? Have I died and gone to heaven?"

"Oh, shut up." I shoved him, my hands pressing against the wall of muscle at his chest, and instantly retreated as heat bloomed. The more distance I kept between myself and this man would be a good thing. "It's your cat that's cute, not you."

"I believe it was 'charming' you called me, if I remember correctly?"

"A notion you've done a brilliant job of eradicating," I promised him.

"I suppose we all must fall from grace." Knox shook his head solemnly, and damn it, I wanted to laugh again. Instead, I turned and studied a painting on the wall. It showed a man with a thick beard and kilt, a bright blue wagon piled high with goods at his back. A sword leaned against his hip, casually, but the man's eyes remained alert as though trouble were close.

"Ancestor of yours?" I asked, needing a distraction to calm the fluttering of my pulse.

"Aye, he traveled as a tinker of sorts. But in reality, he was a knight. It was an easier way to protect the prince when nobody knew you were part of his guard."

Something tugged inside me, a knowing, as though this man and this place meant something to me. An echo of a memory, deep-rooted and unrealized, disappeared before I could catch its gossamer train.

"Smart," I observed, bringing my mind back to the present. Something about being here, in this hallway with Knox, staring at this old painting, was causing a trickle of unease to drift across my skin. Pushing my sleeves up, I gestured toward the hallway. "Shall we crack on with this? I have more important things to do than come up with a marketing plan for you."

"I can only assume you've never tried to hide magick in plain sight if you're so quick to dismiss the work involved." Knox continued down the corridor before stopping in front of a set of arched doors. Pushing them open, he strode inside while I did my best not to audibly gasp at the room.

Call me Belle, because I was more than ready to shack up with the beast if it came with the benefits of this home library.

Not one, not two, but *three* rolling ladders were affixed to mahogany bookshelves that lined walls painted a deep forest evergreen, the rugs done up in muted shades of green and gold. Luxurious leather couches were tucked beneath a massive arched window that overlooked the forest and a deep ravine below us. One end of the room showcased a fireplace, a very important-looking desk for what I presumed were very important people, and a long worktable with several chairs clustered around it. Knox stopped at the table and gestured to it, but I shook my head.

Those leather couches were calling my name.

It took everything in my power not to leap onto a ladder and belt out a song, and I couldn't help but trail my fingers over a few rungs of one of the ladders as I passed by on my way to the couch. Somehow, I maintained a modicum of decorum that even I hadn't known I possessed. Plopping down onto the soft leather seat, I let out a happy sigh and drifted my head back, my gaze going to the gold velvet curtains cocooning the windows.

Opulent yet understated, rich yet comfortable. I didn't want to approve, yet I couldn't help it. This room was *everything*.

"Tea?"

"No, thanks, I'm good." The sooner we got down to business, the quicker I could be on my way. But my thoughts couldn't help but shift to other, more enticing ways to be spending a morning in this gorgeous library.

And I mean curled up with a good book, you heathens.

Except when Knox settled next to me, his knee lightly brushing my thigh, my thoughts did immediately go there as well. *Guess I'll retract that heathen thought.*

"Here's the challenge." Knox waved a hand in the air, and I slunk deeper into the cushions as a 3-D image of Briarhaven appeared in the air. Cool party trick. Already I could imagine the number of spreadsheets and PowerPoints I could conjure in midair if I could harness my magick. Thinking about the fire earlier this morning, I winced and focused on the image of Briarhaven whirling gently in front of me. "Here we have Briarhaven. And around us we have villages tucked among the hills." Knox expanded the virtual map to show the surrounding villages and the main motorway that connected us all.

Ominous clouds thundered in over rolling green hills, and snow began to drift down over Briarhaven like someone having upended a jar of powdered sugar. As snow began to pile up, the sun rose and set around the town, rain billowed in, and the hills turned golden with the arrival of autumn weather.

And still the snow continued.

"While us Scots are well used to mercurial weather, and often plan for all four seasons in a day, we'd be hard-pressed to explain away the snow that has stuck to Briarhaven. You see, even if the snow popped by occasionally, that would be easier to explain away as typical moody weather than it would be to just have constant snow. There is nothing consistent about our weather, Sloane, even in our winters. The world will start asking questions, and as I'm sure you can understand, historically speaking that doesn't go well for our people."

Knox spoke of more than just us witches, but for all the magickals that had gone into hiding through the years until they learned to assimilate into everyday society. Or fled to live a hermit life tucked away deep in the hills somewhere. Which, essentially, was what Briarhaven had become.

A haven.

And I was disrupting it.

We were, but as the oldest, I did my best to shoulder the blame that came with it, even though my sisters insisted that I stop trying to protect them. If not me, then who?

And as much as it galled me to admit it, Knox was right. We had two choices: stay and help cover this curse to the outside world, or leave and figure out how to break our curse from afar.

Neither option was particularly appealing. I now had misfiring magick and was feeling completely off-kilter. Maybe I needed to be here, closer to what little roots I did have, and goddess help me, with a coven of women who might be able to have my back.

Yet I liked being the one to make the decisions for my little family. I liked being the one that kept everything together. But in one fell swoop, my newly found magick had tossed all sense of security I had in my life out the window. Now I felt bereft and powerless.

What also didn't help matters was the gorgeous provost who was making me feel things that I decidedly did not want to feel.

Largely because I was certain that every woman who crossed his path likely had the same exact feelings as I did now.

The longing to feel his hands sliding up under my soft sweater, cupping me, his hands hot against my skin.

"Sloane?" I blinked as I realized that Knox had repeated my name twice now.

Reminding myself to not look directly at him, lest I fall under his beautiful-person spell again, I stared at the floating Briarhaven.

"You need to bring in snowmakers and host a winter festival."

"Snowmakers?" Knox scoffed, and I bristled.

"Yes, snowmakers. Those machines they use to make fake snow with on the ski slopes? You need something very visible to explain away this amount of snow."

"But won't people still be able to see it coming from the sky?"

"Then shoot the fake snow high in the sky." Irritation sliced through me that he was so quick to dismiss my idea.

"Do you have any idea how many we'd need tucked around town just to keep up a fake notion that we actually planned this?"

"That's not my department. That's your job. Mine is to be the ideas person."

"Well, your idea needs work."

"So does your attitude." I couldn't believe he wasn't even considering this. How else was he going to explain away the snow? "If you're so smart, let's hear your idea."

I risked glancing at Knox and was rewarded when a scowl deepened the lines on his forehead.

"Ha!" I pointed a finger at him. "Seems Golden Boy doesn't have a great idea."

"Golden Boy? Please." His scowl intensified, and I warmed to my subject.

"I call it like I see it, boyo. Mr. Prince Charming. The town's golden boy. Saving everyone, women falling at your feet left and right. I bet you're so used to being right that you don't even know how to admit when you're wrong." I leaned forward, gleeful when I saw the light of annoyance flash in his eye. Hit a nerve there. "I'm right, aren't I? Not only about getting the snowmakers in, but that you can't admit when you're wrong, can you?"

I should have stopped pushing.

Backed off.

Given the man some grace.

Yet I absolutely could not resist needling him.

I couldn't say I was proud of that side of myself, but listen, we all have room for growth, okay?

"You know what I'm not wrong about, Sloane?"

"Very little, I'm sure. Just everyone's too charmed by you to talk back." I should have taken the warning in his tone to heart.

"This." Knox reached out and grabbed my waist, pulling me across the couch so I straddled his lap. Shocked, my heart hammering in my chest, I drew in a breath to yell at him.

But his lips found mine.

Fire erupted inside me at his touch, his mouth claiming mine for his own. It was like all of the kisses I'd had in my lifetime had been on paper, and this one was 3-D and full of life, like his magickal scale model of Briarhaven had been. Knox did that. He ignited something latent inside me, bringing to the surface needs I hadn't even known I had, and I gasped against his mouth. Holy hell, but the man could kiss. Clutching his shirt in my hands, I bore down on his kiss, opening my mouth for his tongue, and I almost melted on his lap when he tasted me, eradicating every kiss I'd ever had before from my memory.

Heat, everywhere, inside me—around me. Helplessly, I ground myself against him, riding his lap, wanting his body closer to me, in me, on me, around me. It didn't matter. I couldn't get enough of him, and my body was alive with need, screaming for more of his touch.

The scent of smoke teased my nostrils.

I wanted more. I wanted Knox, all of him, annoying ego and all. It was senseless, and ridiculous, and my feminist self would be annoyed with how I was melting into a puddle of lust over this man.

Wait—smoke?

Smoke.

Tearing my lips away from his, I whirled to see that the glorious golden velvet curtains had erupted in flames.

"No!" I shouted, leaping off Knox as he jumped from the couch.

My magick.

I'd done this.

My misfiring magick had somehow exploded his beautiful curtains in the most perfect room in the world, and he would never, ever, forgive me.

"Stay there." Knox raised a hand, and the doors of the library slammed shut behind me, even as I heard a plaintive moo from Haggis, who had clearly barreled closer at my shout. Even in chaos, Knox protected those he loved. I gasped as the flames raced up the velvet, the smoke ribboning across the ceiling, while Knox muttered a slew of words and threw his hands out toward the curtains. The windows blasted open, taking the smoke with them, and the flames winked out on the fabric.

Leaving a smoldering, ashy mess in their wake.

Shame filled me, and I pressed my hands to my mouth, horrified.

As cold showers went, it was a nasty one.

And an excellent reminder why the likes of Knox and I could never be.

"Knox, I am so, so, so sorry." I held my hands up, pleading with him to understand how bad I felt about this misstep. I should have known better than to let myself get carried away with my moods. I was a new witch, and I knew well enough that erratic emotions could cause unexpected magickal spikes.

"This was you?" Knox turned to me, his head tilted, a contemplative look in his eyes. A small tic, just above his jaw, revealed his restraint.

"Not on purpose, I promise you." I wrung my hands. "It's just that . . . um, I'm not sure how to say this . . . but it seems my magick might be a bit unpredictable."

Knox's eyes widened as he swung his head toward the decimated curtains and back to me.

"I thought your magick was levitation."

"So did I?" I stepped backward, moving closer to the door and my way out.

"And what's changed?"

"Turns out today it is fire."

"And tomorrow?"

"Um, undetermined." Goddess, I hated admitting that. The idea that I had zero control over my future, along with the obvious inability to take charge of my magick, made me grind my teeth.

The doors flung open at my back, and Henry charged in, along with Haggis and Oswald at his side.

"Sir!"

"Everything is fine, Henry. Tell Mother to order new curtains for the library." Knox paused as the cat swiped at his leg. "And make sure she knows that it wasn't Oswald this time."

"Aye, sir." Henry bowed out, and Haggis bumped his nose against my leg while Oswald leapt to a bookshelf near me and prowled the length of books.

"I'll just be seeing myself out. Truly, I'm sorry for . . . all that." I waved a hand at the mess of the curtains and turned.

A book thumped at my feet.

Jumping back, I looked at where Oswald cleaned a paw on the shelf by my head.

"He wants you to have it."

"Excuse me?" I glanced over my shoulder at Knox and then at the cat. "Can you speak to him?"

"Both of them. They're my familiars."

"No way," I breathed, distress momentarily forgotten. Would I be able to speak to Blue, then? The thought was enough to bring some cheer to ease my embarrassment.

"Aye, witchling. And entirely too chatty, if I'm being honest." Knox gestured to the book, and I bent to pick it up, pausing to give Haggis a good ear scratch on the way.

The book warmed under my hand when I touched it, as though it came alive, and I paused.

The cover was a deep cerulean blue, and when I tilted the book, it glimmered, like the dance of moonlight on the sea.

This was meant for me.

I don't know why I knew that, or what could possibly make me think such a thing, but as soon as the book was in my hand I wanted to tuck it close and never give it back. Which I should do. I couldn't possibly accept a gift from a cat.

Or Knox.

The man who had just kissed me so senseless that I'd spontaneously erupted his curtains.

"I can't take this," I said as I held the book more tightly against my chest. Right, not exactly a ringing endorsement of my words.

"Uh-huh," Knox said, seeing right through me. He stepped closer and panic set in. I didn't want to talk about what had just happened between us. I didn't want to discuss my misfiring magick or the fact that I'd been riding the man like I was a cowgirl. Nope, most definitely did not need to discuss any of that. What I needed was to get the hell out of here. Like, yesterday.

"But, since your cat is so sweet and insists, I'll just give it a read and return it once I'm finished. On loan." I waved the book in the air and backed toward the door. "Good luck with the snow festival and all that. Remember, snowmakers are the way forward. Trust me, it's a good plan."

With that, I turned and hightailed it toward the front door, only to find myself trapped, trying to pull the heavy door open.

"Damn heavy doors and damn unicorn door knockers." I glared at the huge doors. Where was the ogre when you needed him?

"Need help?"

"I most certainly do not." I tried the door again, and then winced as Knox's big body shadowed mine, and he leaned over and eased the door open for me.

"Are you going to admit there's something here?"

His voice was a breath at my ear, causing my skin to shiver as I stared out at the snow drifting from sullen gray clouds.

"There's not."

"Aye, there is."

"No, there's *not*."

"Aye."

"Nae." I parroted his Scots back and then pushed through the door without one last glance, slamming it behind me.

Outside, I welcomed the cold that slapped at my face. I'd forgotten my coat, but I didn't even care. You couldn't turn around after a back-and-forth argument like Knox and I had just had. Everyone knew that. Drawing my stubbornness around me like a cloak, I stomped down the driveway.

I'd rather set myself on fire than go back and get my jacket.

CHAPTER THIRTEEN
Sloane

"Sloane. Get in the car."

"Nope. It's a lovely day for a walk." I brushed at the snowflakes that clouded my vision.

My determined exit had been undermined by the fact that Knox had driven me to the castle, his heated-pavement trick only worked on his driveway, and the streets were piled high with snow. I'd taken to lighting fires—small, manageable fires, mind you—every few steps to melt the snow in front of me. I suppose that was one benefit of today's magick. The only issue was that the snow didn't immediately melt, and I was making very slow progress working my way home from the castle.

"I have your coat." Knox stopped his car and waited, then started again as I kept walking. He trailed after me at a sloth's pace.

Bloody hell. I realized I was being ridiculously stubborn and should take my coat. Still, thinking about how I'd lost my mind and devoured this man's kisses like a starving woman at a buffet, I picked up my pace.

"I can see your teeth chattering."

"It's a stress relief technique. Good for meditation."

I skidded to a stop when a mountain of snow dropped in front of me, easily two times higher than my head. Turning, I glared at Knox.

"I can just light that on fire, you know."

"Yes, I know. Just please get in the car before Broca reams me out for not taking care of you."

"Humph." At Broca's name, I relented. She'd be furious if she knew I was walking home without a coat, not to mention the fact I was using my magick willy-nilly with not a care in the world for who saw me using it. My stubbornness was leading me to be careless, and even I knew that I should be more aware of my actions.

"I'll get the snowmakers," Knox said, resigned.

At that, I finally stomped around the mound of snow and flung myself into the passenger seat of the car, acting much like a reluctant child after a temper tantrum. Listen, I can't always be operating at my best. It had been a tumultuous few days.

"You'll get the snowmakers *and* tell everyone you're doing a ski holiday festival." Maybe I was feeling a touch righteous, but I didn't care. It was the best idea we had at the moment.

"We don't have ski slopes here." Knox slanted me a look, and I turned away from him lest I forget that he really wanted to kick me out of town, and accidentally launched myself across the steering console into his lap.

"Call it the Sugar Drops Festival. Or something alliterative. Pinecones & Peppermint Fest."

"That's . . . that's good, actually. It sounds fun."

"Great." I stared out the window and wiggled more deeply into the heated seat. Holding my hands out to the heaters, I warmed my fingers. "Play up the magickal aspect of snow this early in the year, lean into anything cozy about winter, and maybe have games. Sledging, relay races, hot cocoa competitions. Just make it more of the coziness people like about winter but add magickal stuff too. Make a huge play for early Christmas."

"What's a hot cocoa competition?"

"Make all the restaurants compete for the best hot cocoa. Have an ice sculpture competition. Or a snowman-building contest but make it all witchy-themed. Dragons, fae, all that stuff. Everyone loves a theme."

"So the theme is pinecones and peppermint?"

"Yup. Mix fall and cozy Christmas vibes. Pinecones for fall, peppermint for Christmas . . . like candy canes and peppermint mochas. Get the pub to make some fancy drinks too."

"You know what? This sounds great. Plus, we could basically make it like an early Christmas market and keep the theme going to encourage tourism." Knox pulled to a stop in front of our cottage, and I already had my door open before he was fully stopped.

"I'll work up a list of ideas for you and email them over."

"Do you have my email?"

"Um, I don't. But you're famous here, so someone will."

"I can just give you my phone number, Sloane."

Counting to ten, I looked up at the sky and then away as snowflakes hit my eyes.

"Sure." Begrudgingly, I punched in his numbers and then turned, ready to run.

"I can't wait to see what you wear for the costume contest tomorrow." Knox grinned at me as I raised my lip in distaste at him. Halloween was here. I'd tried to forget about it, but Lyra was abuzz with excitement over her costume designs for the party. Despite the snow, Briarhaven had embraced Halloween, their biggest holiday, and had moved the annual bonfire and costume contest inside at the local community center. Broca insisted we go, in order to try to shore up our reputations in town, and there was no way I could avoid my duty to my family.

"I'm not dressing sexy," I promised him, unbuckling my seat belt.

"I'm sure anything you wear will be sexy."

I shot Knox a disbelieving look before sliding from the car.

"You need to stop. What happened back there . . ." I waved a hand in the air. "Erase it from your brain. That was just stress."

"Was it?" The corner of Knox's mouth quirked up in a sultry grin. "I'm happy to be your stress relief any day, Sloane."

"You can't." I fumed, hands on my hips. "You are the cause for my stress. Not the release. Understood?"

"I assure you, I can be both. I'm a man of many talents."

I bared my teeth at him, like a cat ready to hiss. I couldn't help it.

Okay, and maybe I wanted to laugh. But I refused to give him that because I was so not kissing him again. I'd almost burned his house down, damn it. It was one and done. Lesson learned.

I hear you, Universe.

Ignoring his pleased look before he drove away, I stomped inside, my mood foul.

I couldn't remember the last time that I'd been well and truly attracted to someone. I'd dated lightly here and there through the years, but none of my past lovers had ignited such need in me before. I paused just over the threshold as a thought occurred to me.

"Does coming into your magick make you . . ." I paused as I realized I was about to ask my grandmother if magick makes you horny.

"More irritating?" Nova offered from where she sat on the couch stroking Blue's ears.

"Hungry?" Lyra asked from where she stood at the counter mixing a bowl of something.

"Lustful?" Broca beamed when the three of us all turned and gaped at her. "What? I'm not dead yet, ladies. And I've eyes, don't I? This one's just come in from being alone at the castle with a decidedly delicious specimen of a man, her face is flushed, hair is mussed, and she's vibrating with tension. I know a cat in heat when I see one."

I bristled, literally bristled, as Nova threw her head back and howled with laughter. Blue matched her, raising his head back to howl along, and that made her laugh even harder.

"Cat. In. Heat," Nova gasped, wiping at her eyes.

"I should order him to torch you," I muttered, dropping my bag on the side table and walking over to slump next to Nova on the couch. Blue immediately abandoned Nova and wiggled his way on his belly across the couch to me, licking the back of my hand.

"Hey, buddy," I said, booping his nose. Remembering about Oswald, I decided to change the subject. "Knox says he can talk to animals. Can I do that with Blue?"

"Aye, lass. Though it will just be with Blue, as he's your familiar. Just like I can with my sweet Iris. Not everyone has the power to talk to all the animals like Knox does. We can get you sorted, though. It's an easy enough spell." Broca's eyes were alight with interest as she studied me through her sparkly glasses. "How did the meeting go?"

"Yeah, what were you doing cozying up in the castle with Knoxy boy?" Nova winked at me.

My despair must have shown on my face, because Nova instantly dropped the act and reached for my hand.

"Hey, you okay?"

"Did something happen, Sloane?" Lyra rounded the counter, wiping her hands on her apron. Even with a dusting of flour on her cheek, she looked beautiful. Like Knox. She and Knox should be the ones to get together. World domination would be an easy enough feat if they partnered up.

Thinking about Knox with another woman, even in a rhetorical sense, made my heart drop.

"Um." I shrugged, focusing on stroking Blue's soft ears.

"Don't be shy, darling. I've had far more lovers than you. I'm well aware of how Part B fits into Slot A," Broca said.

I choked, and Nova reached over, slapping my back helpfully.

"Could we not?" I gasped, shaking my head at Broca. "Bloody hell, woman. I'm doing my best to stay polite here."

"Why bother? So you shagged Knox. We all knew this was coming." Nova rolled her eyes.

"I did not—"

"It was about time." Lyra nodded.

"About time? We've been here like five—"

"Was he good? Man, I hope he was. What a disappointment if someone who looks like that couldn't deliver an orgasm." Nova clucked her mouth in disapproval.

The word "orgasm" hung in the air of the living room, and I raised both hands.

"Stop, please stop. No, we did not shag. We kissed. And during said kiss, I lit his curtains on fire and almost burned his house down."

"Oh, such a shame." Lyra gave me a sympathetic look and patted my shoulder before returning to the kitchen. "You know what would make this better? Pie. A Scotch pie, to be exact."

"I don't want food. I want to bury my head under my covers and not come out until my magick is fixed."

"That's not like you at all," Nova said, crossing her arms over her shaggy black sweater. "You're always in charge."

"When it's to help you guys, I am. But this has all been a lot for me. At once. Particularly because, you know . . ." I waved my hand in the air, refusing to give in to the lump of sadness that I swallowed past every time I thought of our parents fighting here. "It's the same. I'm the same. Just like mum."

"I will stop you right there, young lady." Broca snapped her fingers, bringing my attention to her. "You may be dealing with the same magickal difficulties your mother faced, but you are not the same. Not even close. She may be my daughter, but you three have more of me in you than she ever did. And thank the goddess for that. Let me be very clear, Sloane, that even if your mother had had perfectly working magick, she still would have been a dramatic, difficult, and unbalanced soul. It's her own karma to sort out. She made, and continues to make, her own choices, despite the guidance I have attempted to offer her. Remember, magick is a tool. And tools can and will be used in hundreds of different ways by different people."

"But what if I can't make my tool work? Isn't that what set her off?"

"Surely you must be kidding me?" Broca threw me an incredulous look. "She loved having different magick every day. Said it kept things interesting. It took all of my power to clean up her messes, day after day, and to try to shelter you three from harm. When she took you and ran, it was the hardest day of my life. I could only be grateful that you were strong enough at that point to care for yourself. Otherwise, I would have gone through hell and high water to get you back."

She did do that. She taught me a lot about loyalty and fighting for family. For what's right.

"I remember you trying." Night after night, Broca would call and arguments would erupt over the phone until my mother hung up on her. I never fully understood what they were arguing about, but I'm glad I have a better picture of that time now.

"I had no legal recourse to take you away from her. And I'm sorry that I couldn't be there for you."

"But you were." Nova leaned forward, looking past me to Broca. "You never let us lose contact. We always knew we had you."

"It's true, Broca." Lyra rolled out dough on the counter. "You've been our one constant in a sea of changes."

"Och, that does my heart good." Broca patted her chest. Her eyes were shiny, and I realized that I might be close to weeping too. "The fact that you were instantly worried you'd turn out like your mother shows just how different you are, Sloane. I'm not worried about you, or this unruly magick. We'll get it sorted, or we won't, but you're going to be just fine."

"Unless you burn down the castle. Knox might be pissed about that." Nova smirked at me when I smacked her arm.

"I'm not burning down the castle because I am not going back there."

"Girl, if you don't sample those goods, I might have to." My mouth dropped open at Broca's warning, and all of us laughed.

"Honestly, I would not want to compete against you, Broca." Pushing Blue off my lap, I went to get my bag. "By the way. I forgot that Knox's cat gave me a book."

"His cat?" Nova raised an eyebrow at me.

"Oswald. And he has a miniature Highland coo in a wheelchair named Haggis."

Nova's mouth dropped open. "You have to go back there, Sloane. I need to meet these familiars."

"We have to do this spell, Sloane. I want to hear what Blue has to say," Lyra implored me.

"I suspect his thoughts will be highly focused on cheese," I said, grinning down at Blue as I held the book out to Broca.

"Well, now, this is interesting." Broca took the book from me and turned it over in her hands, admiring the cover. But when she went to open it, the cover refused to budge. "Ah, even more intriguing."

"It won't open?" I asked, surprised. Why would Oswald give me a book that wouldn't open?

"Let me see." Nova stood and took the book from Broca. No matter how much she tried to pry it open, the cover stayed shut. "Huh, that's weird. I don't see a lock. It's not like one of those secret books that you need to slide the binding down and reveal a compartment, is it?"

"A what?" I asked as Blue clambered back into my lap.

"Like a puzzle book. Normally made of wood, but you have to, like, slide one part of the binding down, and then it unlocks a lever that opens a compartment." Nova tugged at the binding, but nothing moved.

"I don't think we're the ones meant to open it," Broca said.

At that, Nova paused and nudged the book toward me without another word and plopped back on the couch.

"Wait, let me just get this in the oven before you open it." Lyra slid the pie in, set a timer, and took her apron off before bounding across the room. "Okay, open. I hope it is a love poem."

"Oh, for fuc . . ." I trailed off at Broca's warning look. "Seriously, I barely know Knox. He most certainly is not writing love poems for me."

"The heart wants what the heart wants." Lyra nodded sagely at me. This from a woman who had men declare their eternal love to her weekly.

"I can promise you it is not that. It's more likely a list of all the reasons I need to leave Briarhaven and never come back. Certainly nothing to do with love." I took the book and held it in front of me, over Blue. "Right, let's see what the issue is."

The book opened for me . . . immediately. Surprise filled me, and a small shiver worked itself down my neck. That was odd, but magick was weird in general, so should I be that shocked?

Nova, nosy sister that she was, leaned over to try to read the page. "Huh, blank pages."

"No, it's not!" I said, rolling my eyes up to Nova. It was plain as day there was writing on the pages.

"Let me see." I turned the book to Lyra, but she bit her lower lip and shook her head.

"Sorry, Sloane, I don't see anything either."

"What part of me telling you that this book is meant for Sloane aren't you understanding?" Broca asked, as though we were all a few fries short of a Happy Meal.

"What does it say?" Nova nodded at me to look, and I brought it forward, that shiver of unease turning to excitement.

But the words just swam on the page in front of me, written in ancient text unknown to me. Not like I was some history scholar, but I'd at least be able to identify if the words were Celtic or not.

"I can't read it," I admitted. "It's not a language I know."

"Is it code? Could you copy it down and we all try to figure it out?" Lyra asked, perching on the arm of the couch.

"We'll need a revealing spell. And likely the coven to help." Broca shook her head when I went to protest. "This is very old magick, Sloane. I could feel it on the book. You can complain all you want, but your magick won't reveal what's in this book without help. We need our coven to ground us, to funnel our magick, and to unlock what's in this book."

Shite. When she said it like that . . .

"Can we at least do the spell with Blue first?" I whined somewhat pathetically. I knew I was only delaying bringing the coven about, but I wasn't sure I could handle Mandy Meadows's plastic smile at the moment. My emotions were scrambling to land—a little like Blue, actually—and my heart was still thumping from Knox's kisses.

"Are you going to admit there's something here?"

Goddess, what was I supposed to do with that? Nope, not thinking about that right now. Talking to my familiar, though? Sign me up.

"That I can help you with. We can do it right now." Broca's eyes warmed.

"Seriously?" My eyes widened.

"Can just any pet become a familiar?" Nova asked. It was a question I hadn't really considered before.

"No. Familiars are tied to the mystical world. They guide, protect, or offer you their magick throughout your life. Each holds a unique set of powers that works symbiotically with yours."

"He brings the cheese, and you bring the *whine*." Lyra changed her tone to a whining tone, and Nova snickered.

"I don't whine." I protested—*not* whined, thankyouverymuch.

"Ladies. The spell?"

"Okay, okay, I'm in. Let's do this. What do we need?" I made a zipping motion over my lips at my sisters to get them to shut up.

"A drop of blood from you both, some of my crystals, and we'll cast a simple protection circle. Or square, actually." Broca looked at us.

"Doesn't it have to be a circle?" Lyra asked, crossing the room to get Broca's dish of crystals that had been charging in the moonlight the night before.

"Not necessarily. The intent is to protect. Pentagram. Triangle. Octagon. Nae bother, really. It's about creating a safe and protective space." Broca straightened and took the bowl of crystals onto her lap, digging through them and handing several to Lyra. "There, child. Black tourmaline, hematite, and amethyst. Protection and grounding."

After Lyra laid out the stones around us, Broca looked at Blue.

"Blue, we'll need a drop of blood from your paw."

Blue surprised me by rolling over and rising into the air, hovering over Broca, seeming to understand that he couldn't land in her lap lest he hurt her hip. Broca held up a small ritual knife.

"Just a prick."

I watched, my heart in my throat as Blue held out a paw. With a gentle motion, Broca nicked his paw and collected a couple of drops of blood in a small dish. I winced, but Blue seemed remarkably unperturbed.

"Now you." I leaned forward and gave Broca my finger, and she added a few drops of my blood to the dish.

"There. Now, repeat after me." Broca leveled me a look, and I nodded.

"By claw and paw, by tail and wing, I ask the moon to let you sing. Familiar dear, your voice shall rise, with every word, no more shall you hide."

I repeated the words exactly, my eyes darting around the room in case I started any fires, but nothing came. When I finished, I just looked at Broca, waiting for instruction.

I do believe it's time for my cheese. A soft voice filled my head, warm and brash, a light growl around the edges as though the words were gently heated with fire.

My eyes widened in shock and I reached for Blue.

"Was that you, buddy? Did you just ask for cheese?"

I mean, I did just get my paw sliced open. Don't you think that deserves a reward?

"Oh my goddess. It works. I can hear him." I laughed out loud, hugging him close. "He wants cheese because we cut his paw open."

"I've closed the circle. Have all the cheese you want, Blue." Broca smiled as I carried Blue across the room to the kitchen, tears pricking my eyes.

I might only be a simple witch, but if that meant we had a chance at breaking the curse and I got to stay here with my sweet little emberwolf, maybe, just maybe, I had a fighting chance at being happy for once.

CHAPTER FOURTEEN
Sloane

"You've got to be kidding me."

"I most certainly am not." Lyra stuck her nose up, though it was hard to take her seriously in a hugely padded puffy toadstool costume.

"You look ridiculous."

"I look amazing." Lyra bounced around the room, her mushroom cap swinging about, and Blue zoomed in the air next to her, barking. "Blue agrees."

"He's just being nice because you give him snacks."

"She doesn't look as good as me." I turned to see Nova dressed in red overalls, a mustache, and a cap grinning at me.

"It's-a me! *Mario!*" Nova lifted her hand in the air and pinched it together like Italians were known to do.

"I'm not going to lie." I leaned back and crossed my arms over my chest, studying her. "This is a good look on you."

"Of course it is." Nova shrugged. "I can pull anything off, really."

It was true too. Nova exuded effortless confidence in spades. She narrowed her eyes at me, leaning one hip against the kitchen counter.

"Where's your costume?"

"Do I have to? Why can't I be Luigi?" I asked, sticking my lower lip out in a pout.

"Because I am," Broca said, coming out with her walker, wearing green overalls and a sparkly shirt.

"Are you coming to the contest?" I asked, delighted to see her up and about. It had been a challenge to get her to do her daily exercises, but she was slowly beginning to improve from her operation.

"I'm not. I'm staying here to answer the door with candy for any kids that come by. The contest is adults only, remember?"

"Is it?" I hadn't paid much attention because I hadn't honestly thought I'd be going. It wasn't like the town had much warmed up to us, and I wasn't sure our showing up at one of their parties was going to help things.

"What's your magick today, Sloane?" Lyra asked, pausing her manic mushroom dancing to snatch Blue from the air and sprinkle kisses across his face.

"I don't know. I've been able to suppress it so far," I admitted. I was doing my damnedest to try to pretend like I didn't have magick, even though it simmered just below the surface. It was like I was suddenly plugged into some universal magickal source, and power all but hummed through me. Was this how witches felt all the time? It was wild, really, knowing they just walked around with power at their fingertips.

I mean, shouldn't there be some sort of training for this? Maybe a license bureau? I worried my lower lip as I considered the intricacies of setting up such a system. It would be prudent to try, though. Maybe I needed to speak to someone about it.

"Sloane." Nova snapped her fingers under my nose. "Go get dressed. We're leaving in ten."

"Ugh, fine." I stomped upstairs. Broca had lectured me earlier about joining in the community activities to try to mitigate people's bad opinions of us, so I reluctantly stripped and tugged the costume over my head.

Turning to look in the floor-length mirror affixed to the back of my door, I sighed.

Princess Peach was not a look I'd normally go for.

There was just so much tulle. And pink upon pink. The bodice clung low, and I tugged at it, certain that the video game version of the character was not in a low-cut gown. Suspicious, I picked up the discarded package lying on my bed.

"'Sexy Princess Peach,'" I read out loud, groaning. No wonder the skirt ended two inches above my knees. Turning, I looked over my shoulder to see where the costume dipped in the back, exposing a wide expanse of skin. I wouldn't even be able to wear a bra. Surely my sisters didn't expect me to go out like this. Ignoring the awful fake wig, I jammed the crown onto my head and pulled on Ugg boots. There was no way I was wearing heels in this snow, and frankly, I wasn't sure I was even decent to leave the house like this.

"Wow," Nova said, her mouth dropping open as I came downstairs in a huff, my arms held wide.

"Really? This is what you want me to wear?" I turned in a full circle while Lyra let out a low whistle. "Don't you whistle at me. You get to wear the equivalent of a onesie out tonight, and you've shoved me into a skanky Peach outfit."

"In fairness, you look really good in it," Lyra said.

"She's not wrong, Sloane. I think you need to go find Knox while wearing this. He'll know what to do." Broca winked at me, and my mouth dropped open.

"Broca! No. I'm never touching that man again. He wants to run us out of town, remember?" I raised a finger in the air. "Do you know what he did to me earlier?"

"No, do tell. In great detail, darling." Broca leaned forward, a salacious light in her eyes, and I pressed my lips together and counted to ten in my head.

"He got me refused service at the bookstore!" I'd gone back to pick out the books I'd wanted for my birthday, and the cat sith fae woman had seen me coming and gently overturned the Open sign in the window just as I was about to walk in. I'd pointedly looked at the time on my iPhone, and then back at her posted hours. She'd shrugged one shoulder, a sheepish look on her face, and I'd known. Knox was blackballing me around town. He wanted to make life as inconvenient for me as possible.

It would almost be easier if he'd go back to outright trying to drag me out the door than these insidious attacks on our residency in Briarhaven.

"Sloane, you look adorable when you're mad like that. Like a pink puff ball of anger." Lyra grinned at me and began bopping her mushroom-cap head again to some unheard tune.

"Have you been indulging in some medicinal mushrooms tonight?" I asked.

"Nope, this is all me. I'm just excited to dance." Lyra held out her arms and shimmied, her mushroom costume gyrating around her, and I laughed.

"You're making it hard to hate you for putting me in this stupid costume."

"You look fabulous, Knox will swallow his tongue, and we're going to have a blast even if nobody else talks to us." Nova hooked an arm through mine and dragged me toward the door. "No matter what, we have one another. And we always have fun together, don't we?"

She wasn't wrong. Every year we spent Halloween in a new town, and every year we managed to make it fun for ourselves. This would be no different, even with the added layer of most of Briarhaven hating us.

Pulling on a long wool coat to cover my barely there outfit, I kissed Broca and Blue goodbye and went out into the snow. It wasn't a far walk to the community center, and there was no way I was getting through tonight without an adult beverage or two.

Despite the snow, the night held a festive air, with light from open front doors spilling onto the sidewalk as children in costumes sang or danced for their treats. I remembered that feeling of excitement as a child, not caring if it was raining or cold, just wanting to be out on the streets late, with any excuse to earn a sweetie.

"Was it all bad?" Nova murmured, as two miniature witches and a werewolf scrambled past us, giggling as they tossed snow at one another.

"No," I admitted, hooking my arm in hers, knowing she was talking about our childhood. "It wasn't great, but it wasn't all bad. We had one another. And when Mum and Dad weren't fighting, they were quite fun."

"Dad used to sing to us at the top of his lungs when we slept late," Lyra remembered.

"Mum was killer at making our costumes."

"Dad dominated during board game night."

"Ugh, he never let us win, did he?" Nova remembered with a laugh.

"Nope. No mercy." I smiled, the warmth of the good memories seeping in a bit. It had been easier to remember the bad instead of the good, as it helped to shore up my walls. If I couldn't stay in Briarhaven with this stupid curse, why should I fall in love with it?

"Mum used to give me her cookbooks to read. Remember her stovies? So good. She just kind of got out of the habit of cooking, didn't she?" Lyra murmured.

"Aye, I think it all became too much for her." Maybe that was what happened when every day your magick changed, and you couldn't rely upon anything. It was already stressing me out, and I was only a few days into this particular affliction. For the first time, my resentment toward my mother softened. She was a difficult woman, but she'd also had her challenges, hadn't she?

"Wow, this place is packed." Nova drew my attention from my thoughts, and my eyebrows rose at the line of people snaking around the edge of the community center, waiting to get inside. Music bumped, and laughter carried on the frigid night air.

"I think tonight's going to be fun," Nova decided.

"Here's hoping," I said.

Twenty minutes later, I was huddled in the corner of a large open room, clutching a glass of white wine, watching as my sisters tore around the dance floor. Despite the town professing to not like us, my sisters' sheer enthusiasm at dancing had endeared them to most of the people on the dance floor, and soon Lyra was being twirled by Hannibal Lecter, while Nova was being dipped by Edward Scissorhands. Nobody tried to talk to me, and frankly, I was fine with that. I kind of needed a moment to readjust my thoughts about Briarhaven, the talk I'd had with my sisters on the way here bringing to the surface long-buried memories. Finishing my glass, I turned to go get another and bumped into someone.

"I'm sorry. Oh—"

"Sloane." Knox grinned at me, and I gulped, suddenly wishing I still had wine in my glass to drink.

There was just so much muscle.

Everywhere.

He wore dark green fitted pants and . . . well . . . basically nothing else. A gold bodysuit, like a second skin, showcased his muscles, a pair of football-like shoulder pads dripped in fake fish scales, and dark liner coated his eyes.

Need bloomed as I remembered straddling him in the library, his mouth on mine, and I couldn't tear my eyes away from his muscular chest.

I wanted to lick my way down—

"Sloane?" Knox snapped his fingers in front of my face and my eyes darted to his. My face flushed. "Eyes up here, darling."

"I was just admiring your outfit." The lie didn't land, since I was clearly ogling his muscles, and I bustled away to fill my wineglass at the punch bowl, embarrassed at having been caught staring. But seriously . . . how could a man look that delectable?

"Enjoying yourself?" Knox asked, dogging my heels, filling his own glass. The music changed to something sharp and upbeat, and the crowd cheered. Lights from the disco ball twirled, sprinkling the room, and I suddenly found it a tad hard to breathe with how close Knox was standing to me.

"Excuse me a moment." I walked blindly through a door behind the drinks table and turned down another hallway, and then another, and then ducked through the door of an empty room. It was dark in there, a single beam of light illuminating the room from an outdoor streetlight, and I realized I'd stepped into an empty classroom of sorts. Taking a deep breath, I leaned against the wall, trying to settle myself.

"Are you okay?"

I closed my eyes at Knox's voice, but didn't move. I heard the soft sound of him entering the room, and then the click of the door closing behind him. My breathing slowed.

"Do you want the light on Sloane?"

"No," I whispered. I didn't know why I'd come here. And yet a part of me had known he'd follow.

Or maybe had just hoped.

"Are you okay?" Knox asked again, reaching out to take the wineglass from my hand. I let him. Maybe more alcohol wasn't the answer needed here.

"No." I turned my head against the wall, meeting his eyes that glinted in the darkness. "I'm mad at you."

"The shopkeepers?" Knox had the decency to look ashamed.

"It was smart, I'll give you that."

"I'll stop, Sloane." Knox came forward, leaning his hands on the wall around my head, caging me in. "I asked them to do that days ago. But now . . . I think things have changed."

"How so?" I angled my head to look up at him. "I'm still me. And you're still you."

"No." Knox shook his head, leaning closer to me, his mouth hovering an inch over mine. "I'm Aquaman, and you're Princess Peach."

I couldn't help myself, I snickered.

"Is that the way of it?" I asked. I sucked in a breath as he bit my lower lip softly. A quiet storm of need rolled through me, heavy and unrelenting. I couldn't help but arch my back slightly, desperately wanting his hands on me, and at the same time, knowing I should walk away from this man who was trying to run us out of town.

"It can be. Just for tonight." His breath fanned my throat, hot against my skin, and I shivered as he licked at the crevice of my neck.

"It's never just for a night." I angled my head, allowing him better access to kiss the delicate spot at my throat.

"Maybe I don't want it to be."

I laughed. Surely he must be joking.

"How many drinks have you had tonight?" I asked, my voice breathy, as he brought a finger up and traced it across the ribbon at my neckline.

"Would it be so bad? You and I?" Knox sounded as surprised at his words as I did.

No, no, it would not. At least that was what my body was screaming to me as heat trailed along my skin where he touched me.

"I . . . I don't even know how to answer that."

"Shall we test the waters, then?"

"Seriously? An Aquaman pun?" I groaned, but it quickly turned into a moan when Knox kissed me, full on, and pressed his body against mine. Pinning me to the wall, he reached down and gripped my wrists with his hands, sliding them up and over my head. I arched against him, loving the feel of his hard body pressed against mine, his mouth wet and hot. Slipping his tongue inside, he tasted, and molten need pooled deep inside me.

"You know . . ." Knox pulled away, and my breath came out in ragged gasps as he transferred one of his hands to my chest but kept the other around my wrists. Testing, I pushed against his hand, only to have him push back, pinning me. "This is a very naughty Peach dress. I'm going to have sinful dreams for nights after seeing you in this."

I squirmed, and the corner of Knox's mouth quirked up in a smile.

"Do you like this, Sloane? When you can't get out?" I gasped as Knox slipped a finger beneath the fabric of my dress and stroked my hard nipple. "Do you like when you have to give over control?"

No, I hated it. Everything in my life felt beyond my command at the moment, and the last thing I needed was for Knox to take that from me too.

Except...

His lips trailed liquid heat down my chest, and he moved the fabric, my breast springing free and right into his waiting mouth. His tongue was hot against me, slick and needy, and I moaned when his teeth scraped my sensitive skin.

"Or what about this, Sloane? Is this what you like?" I gasped, my back bowing as Knox's free hand slipped up my thigh and stroked across the soft cotton of my panties.

"I . . . I . . ." In my head, I knew the right thing would be to tell him, *No. Thank you, good sir, but I've had enough.* But I hadn't had enough. Not even in the slightest. When his finger slipped beneath the cotton and found me wet and ready, he groaned at my breast.

"Damn it, Sloane." Knox's head reared up, and he caught my lips in a blistering kiss before pulling back, his breath ragged as he leaned his forehead against mine. "Let me. Just let me please you."

"Oh . . . kay," I breathed out, my hips already moving against his hand, and when he slipped two fingers inside of me, I whimpered at the thick intrusion.

"It's going to be fast, Sloane. I want you to come apart around me. I want to watch you as you do. And then we're going to go back to the dance and pretend nothing happened while I drive myself crazy staring at you in that short skirt all night. Understood?"

I whimpered out a sound, likely a yes, as I was already moving against his hand, my need driving me, the sweet soft wave of release racing toward the finish line. Finding the perfect spot inside me, Knox curled his finger and pressed upward, rubbing my slick heat at the same time as he bit down hard against my nipple.

I shattered around him, and his head came up, his eyes on me as I came undone.

"That's a good lass," Knox whispered at my ear, pulling his hand out and smoothing my panties back into place.

My muscles felt liquid and loose, and when he released my wrists, my hands dropped to my sides, and my head lolled against the wall. I wanted to just flop to the floor and sleep right there.

I was supposed to walk out of here? After that brilliant orgasm?

"Right, then, shall we go dance?"

"Dance? I'm not sure I can even walk," I admitted, adjusting my top.

"Want me to carry you in, then?"

I blanched at the image and straightened.

"Absolutely not." I shot my nose in the air. I had no idea how to act around him after what had just happened. What I'd allowed to happen.

What I'd loved every second of.

"I'll see you in there." Knox gave me a rueful smile when my head snapped to his. He nodded down to his pants, and I gaped at the bulge. "I'll need just a moment."

"That's not my problem," I said, walking to the door. "You got yourself into this mess. Now you get yourself out of it."

I left the room, my legs still shaking, but needing to walk out on somewhat of a sassy note to reclaim some semblance of myself—of the woman who I thought I was. Not the woman back there in the classroom who'd melted around a man who'd pinned her to a wall. No, I didn't know her.

And that more than freaked me out.

"Maybe I don't want to get myself out of it."

Knox's words trailed after me in the hallway, and it was enough to spur me into action. Racing toward the dance, I ducked inside just in time to hear screams.

"Sloane! Where were you?" Nova and Lyra materialized by my side, covered in head-to-toe glitter.

"What happened?" I gasped, ignoring their question.

"The disco ball exploded into actual glitter. A freaking glitter bomb. Half the people are furious, and half the people are delighted. Nobody knows who did it." Nova's eyes sharpened on something over my shoulder. I turned to see Knox walk in from the hallway.

We were the only two in the room not covered in glitter.

"Yup, time to go." Lyra hooked my arm and pulled me from the room, Nova at my heels.

"Bloody hell, Sloane." Nova laughed, long and loud, as we stumbled outside. "You're going to blow up the whole damn town when you finally shag him."

I certainly hoped not. But at the moment, I was too damn satiated to care. What I needed to do was try to convince myself that it was best for everyone that I never touch Knox Douglas again.

CHAPTER FIFTEEN
Sloane

"For some reason I expected everything to be pink," Nova hissed in my ear.

"Somehow, this is worse."

The house was white.

I don't just mean white walls and furniture, I mean white, everywhere. White statues, white wood carvings, white cushions, white rugs, white chandelier, white cabinetry and countertops. It was sterile to the point of severity that I wasn't sure if signified a mental break or a rigorous attachment to a very clean house. Either way, Mandy Meadows could eat off her floor, and any offending speck of dust was likely destroyed with a ruthless efficiency to which I could only aspire in my own cleaning habits. No wonder Mandy Meadows had been so obviously disgusted by the dust and dirt in our home. She essentially lived in a sterilized laboratory.

It was the morning after my incident with Knox, and I hadn't been brave enough to try out my magick yet today. Instead, Broca had shooed us out the door for an emergency Charms meeting at Mandy Meadows's house, and now I stood, clutching my to-go cup of coffee, terrified that I'd spill a drop and trigger some sort of magickal trap that would leave me missing a limb.

Mandy Meadows, not uncharacteristically, seemed to be wound a little tight. It would be in my best interest not to push her over the edge. For now, at least while we were in her space, I needed to hang to the back. The sooner we figured out how to read this book, the sooner I could go home to curl up on the couch with Blue and badger Broca into doing her hip exercises.

"I think it's chic," Lyra murmured, glancing around the room. "But she could use a plant or two to soften the space. Some greenery. Maybe a disco ball in the corner." Lyra slid me a cheeky look.

"A disco ball requires someone to have an actual personality," Nova pointed out.

"But the light *would* be beautiful sparkling across all this white."

"Can we please not talk about disco balls?" I hissed, wincing at the memory of glitter everywhere. Nova and Lyra had been made to strip out of their costumes outside the house last night and march directly to the showers, as Broca refused to deal with cleaning up glitter.

"Ladies." We snapped to attention as Mandy Meadows ushered us from her living room through a door to a large back room. The rest of the Charms were already there. I had no idea how, as it was barely seven in the morning. They were all put together and looked fairly alert given the early hour. One would think they've all had their wake-me-up coffees too. I was in an oversized cream fisherman's jumper, leggings, and Ugg boots. Raven looked soft and lovely in a cloud-blue floor-length velvet dress, Felicity was slightly rumpled in a pastel purple sweater set and jeans, and Tam rocked a neon-yellow-and-electric-blue running outfit, while Mandy Meadows clearly slept in her in pink fembot suit.

We were a discombobulated group, to say the least. If anyone were to walk back here, they'd get whiplash trying to figure out how one of us fit with the others.

And somehow, we were meant to solve a centuries-old curse.

Either way, this was our coven, and it appeared we were stuck with them. Broca was trying to get me to warm up to the idea of having the coven help me, but it just didn't sit right with me. I simply wasn't used to asking for assistance. With anything, really.

I wanted to refuse help.

Except I couldn't. Not this time. I really did need the Charms. And it had been pointed out to me by Broca, not too kindly, either, that I was being a touch bitchy about accepting said help from this group, who had gathered at what felt like the butt crack of dawn to help me. Pasting a polite smile on my face, I took a seat at the table and looked around the room. It was more of a shed, really, an addition to the house that carried some of the white color scheme over, but here the shelves that lined the walls were piled high with what I was assuming was everything a modern-day witch needed.

Of course, it was all neatly labeled and stacked in glass containers and mason jars. Even in her magick, Mandy Meadows tolerated no messiness.

"All right, Charms, let's crack on with business, shall we? Since this is another meeting out of our regular schedule." Mandy Meadows slanted me a look, and I glowered at her. Like any of this was my fault? I'd happily be ignoring my magick and galivanting across Europe if Broca hadn't called us to come home. Did she think this was fun for me?

"Simmer." Nova poked a finger in my side, and I dropped my eyes to the table.

"First order of business will be the Pinecones & Peppermint Fest. Knox has requested we work up a spell to help shroud some of what is really going on from the tourists."

"But what about the book?" I gaped at Mandy Meadows. The only reason I'd gotten out of bed this early was because I'd been told I would get help deciphering the language in the book. And it had literally been Samhain the night before. Were we really going to jump into a Christmas festival this fast?

"Not everything's about you, Sloane."

"Meow," Lyra said, raising an eyebrow, but Mandy Meadows just rolled her eyes.

"Or in this case, it is. Because we have to fix this snow mess, which you've brought to the town."

"You're being a little harsh, Mandy. It's not her fault some witch cursed them centuries ago," Tam said, taking a swig from her water bottle.

"I'm simply stating the facts." Mandy Meadows shrugged one pink tweed–covered shoulder. "I don't have time to coddle her feelings as well."

"I don't need to be wrapped in cotton wool," I said, annoyed that this witch was getting under my skin. "If you need to do the festival spell first, by all means, go ahead."

"I wasn't asking your permission." Mandy sniffed and patted her perfectly coiffed hair, as though a strand would dare to step out of line. "Now, my thought was we needed to do a concealment spell of sorts. Knox will be bringing in snowmakers to give the illusion that we are producing all of this snow, but it won't necessarily explain away the snow falling from the actual sky. Our job is to make it so the tourists just can't see it. Or, basically, that they only see what we want them to see."

"A glamour spell." Deidre nodded. "I'd go with the fae for that one."

"I was just thinking the same." Raven leaned forward and gave Deidre a nod of approval. "They're the best at trickery."

Nova turned to me, both eyebrows raised.

"We'll need fairy moss, quartz, and bronze rings." Mandy Meadows clapped her hands together and strode to the shelves, pulling out containers of what she was looking for.

"Can you explain the ingredients to me, please, and the purpose for each?" Lyra asked politely. There was never a recipe she met that she didn't like, so this was likely just an extension of her baking. Mandy Meadows glanced over her shoulder, a smile of approval on her face, and Lyra straightened a bit in her seat. A star pupil.

I wanted to be annoyed with her, but Lyra had always been that way. She wanted to please others, and it didn't take a psychologist to figure out it came from having disinterested parents.

All three of us had reacted differently to our chaotic upbringing.

"The moss was gathered under a full moon from various fairy mounds around the outskirts of Briarhaven. With fae permission, of course." Mandy Meadows returned to the table, containers in hand. "Quartz to help charge and channel the spell, as well as direct the magick accurately. And bronze rings as an offering to the fae, as they'll use any bronze for their tools or weapons as they see fit."

"Ah, and why does quartz channel the spell?"

"It's an excellent conduit. Quartz, in itself, is your multipurpose stone. It can be used for many different spells and can help center intention. It's a workhorse of a crystal, really."

Mandy Meadows flicked her hand at the table, and a pentagram appeared. In the middle, she placed a bundle of moss, the bronze rings, and several quartz stones. She then lit a candle at the head of table, mumbled some words under her breath, and a ripple of energy moved through the air. It called to my magick, and I felt that power rise inside of me, and my palms began to sweat. I hoped whatever we were about to do didn't make my magick misfire. Broca had assured me that with the coven acting as a whole, I should, in theory, be fine to work spells. It was when I was using my magick on my own that everything seemed to go haywire.

*"By faerie sight an' faerie grace,
Hide this snow in secret place.
To mortal eye, let naught seem wrong,
Let hearts pass through, nae stay long."*

We repeated her words three times, and a light flashed in the air. I gaped down at the table, where the moss now was bundled with the crystals, the bronze rings wound around them. Four complete bundles.

"Well done, ladies. Now, we'll need someone to go to the four cardinal points around Briarhaven and repeat the spell there as well. This, along with the fae help, should cause the tourists to overlook vital details. If they do start to look or question too closely, they should be struck with an urge to leave."

"I'll go," Nova volunteered. "I'd like to see more of Briarhaven. It's been a while."

"You up for a run?" Tam asked, gesturing with her water bottle.

"I'd love nothing more. I haven't gotten a chance to go out yet, and it's making me itchy." Tam and Nova beamed at each other, and I shuddered at the thought of running on snow and ice before I'd finished my first cup of coffee.

Who was I kidding? I wasn't going for a jog even if I'd chugged ten cups of coffee.

"Great, that's you two off, then. I'm sure the rest of us can handle the little book issue together."

Why, why, did she need to speak about my issues like that? This "little book issue" might solve this curse of the snow, and I felt my back go up as I opened my mouth to speak.

"Stand down, soldier. Just get this done so we can see what the book wants you to know." Nova squeezed my shoulder as she stood. "I'm going to drop my jacket in the car. Tam, do you have an extra hat and gloves?"

"Aye. And a windbreaker for over your jumper."

"Perfect. See you back home later." The two gathered the bundles up and walked out, chattering about pacing and elevation. I turned back to the table and glared at Mandy Meadows.

She smiled at me, sweetly some would say.

Others would say she bared her teeth.

Challenge accepted.

I wasn't sure what challenge I was accepting, but as I spent more time with these women, I was starting to track the subtle underpinnings and power plays in the group. I wasn't necessarily yet sure how to navigate it, but I knew a woman who was determined to keep someone in their place when I saw one.

Too bad I was used to not staying in my place. Or any place, really. Metaphorically and physically.

"Shall we deal with this?" Mandy Meadows gestured to the book I'd put in front of me. I wanted to throw it at her face.

Not to harm her, of course.

But just to see her hair fall out of place.

She must have gauged my intention from my expression, because the book slid across the table to her. I narrowed my eyes, annoyed she'd taken it from me, but when she picked it up and it refused to open, I smiled.

It was my book.

"This is old magick." Mandy Meadows turned the book over in her hands, tapping a shell-pink nail against the cover. "Heavily charmed."

"Can I see?" Raven held out her hand, and Mandy passed it over.

Bending her head over the book, her beautiful hair curtaining her face, Raven closed her eyes and ran her hands over the cover.

"It wants to tell Sloane its secrets. It has waited to be found. For years now. I sense it's excited to finally be with her."

"A family grimoire?" Deidre glanced up from where she typed rapidly on her phone. I had no idea who was buying real estate at seven in the morning, but Deidre had been constantly checking her Apple Watch and her phone since we'd arrived.

"It might be. Hard to say. It opens for you?" Raven handed me back the book across the table, and I was relieved to have it back in my hands. It seemed to warm under my touch, happy to be with me, and I smiled gently down at its beautiful cover.

"It does, yes." I easily opened the cover. The words still swam on the pages in front of my eyes.

"It just shows blank pages for me," Lyra said, leaning close to look at the pages over my shoulder.

"Definitely a grimoire of sorts, then." Mandy Meadows nodded. "One of the first spells used when making one is to conceal the interior from anyone it wasn't meant for. It's an easy enough protection spell to circumvent, but it does take some concentration."

"Wait, why would she have to remove the protection spell from this? Isn't it more about helping her to read it? We don't need to see it, right?" Lyra pointed a finger between the women and the book.

"If you'd prefer a simple translation spell, that's also an option." Mandy Meadows studied a nail like she didn't have a care in the world. But I wondered, too, why she wanted to take the protection off my book. Filing that thought away for later, I smoothed a hand over the pages.

"Let's start with a translation spell. If that doesn't work, we can look at removing the protection."

"If you insist." Mandy Meadows returned to her shelves and studied them for a moment.

Again, why did she have to phrase it like that? I wanted to snarl at her, but Lyra squeezed my knee sharply, and Raven winked at me over the table. It pacified me somewhat, so instead I took a deep breath and tried to ignore the bitchiness that was Mandy.

I definitely was going to spill a drop of my coffee on her rug on the way out.

"A sprig of juniper and a sacred water from the enchanted burn outside Briarhaven." Mandy placed the branch in front of me, as well as a small jar of water. "Open the book, trace the juniper in a clockwise circle around the book, and then dip your finger in the water. Dab some water on your brow and then repeat after me."

"Why juniper?" Lyra piped up.

"Juniper helps with visions as well as protection. Shall we?" Mandy Meadows lifted her hands, mumbled a few words about protection, and then dropped them. "The circle is cast. Onward."

Picking up the sprig of juniper, the scent crisp and refreshing, I gently circled the book as instructed, and then dipped a finger into the water. Surprised, I glanced up at Mandy Meadows, who just nodded at me to continue.

The water was bathwater warm.

Dabbing it on my brow, I turned back to the book.

"By the gift o' Seer's sight,
Grant me now the ancient light.
Tongues long gone, words long veiled,
By this rite, let truth prevail."

I gasped as the words clarified in front of me. There was a certain section highlighted, as if the words simply hovered over everything else. Had the book chosen what I needed to see and only shown me that part? I wasn't sure if this was a temporary spell or something that would always be available to me, so I hurried to read out the passage it wanted to share with me.

"To break a curse that harms your bloodline, perform the following ritual. In a sacred circle marked by hematite stones, prick the fingers of those involved in the curse. Let their blood drip into a single cauldron with honey and whisky. Stir the mixture and place your hands over the chalice. Repeat the following three times.

"By blood that bound, by love now freed,
Let this curse be undone in word and deed.
Honey sweet, whisky strong,
Upend this heartache to right a wrong.

"The cursed must drink from the cauldron, and the ties of heartbreak will dissolve, allowing the cursed to move forward in peace. Remember, three fragments mended, a heart restored, let curse unwind, its chains no more."

I tried to turn the page, but the book wouldn't let me. I looked up, and Raven nodded at me, pen in hand.

"Got it."

"That's all we can do, then." Mandy Meadows quickly closed the circle, and I patted my fingers on the book, silently thanking it. The cover warmed in response.

"That's grand, isn't it?" Felicity, who had been surprisingly quiet all morning, bounced in her seat. "We can do the ritual and free you of the curse. No more snow! Except, you know, we'll want snow for a white Christmas."

"It seems too easy." Lyra worried her bottom lip.

"It's not easy at all." Deidre stood, tossing her phone into her leather tote bag and hitching it over her shoulder. "Unless you're still friends with the family who cursed you, that is."

"Oh no." Lyra looked at me, stricken, and my heart fell.

The house witch had a point.

How was I supposed to track down the family of the person who had cursed us? As far as I knew, they'd disappeared from Briarhaven after the witch had been thrown into prison.

"Good luck." Mandy Meadows's tone indicated she wished anything but, and I'd had enough of her attitude this morning.

"Thanks and all that. This has been enlightening. Lyra, shall we?"

"Yup, I'm good here. Thanks, this was fun!" Lyra beamed at Mandy, whose face softened as she looked at my sister. I'm telling you, nobody can bring themselves to be rude to Lyra. It just wasn't possible.

"Sloane, pop by the shop after if you're heading into town. We can make a list of people to ask for more historical information. Maybe we start at the Silver Quill?" Raven gave me a reassuring nod.

"Or with Knox. His library would hold records," Felicity added.

My cheeks heated.

"Yeah, Sloane. You could go to his library. Again." Lyra snickered as I turned and beelined from the room, even though Raven's eyebrows had moved to her hairline.

"I'm going to kill you."

"Oh, stop, it's just a bit of harmless fun," Lyra muttered at my back as I hustled through the ice queen's front room and out to our car. I was so annoyed I even forgot to spill my coffee on the way out.

An opportunity missed, for sure.

"The last thing I need is people to think we're an item."

"'An item.'" Lyra laughed so hard she clutched her stomach, and I glared at her as I started the car and waited for the struggling heat vents to kick in.

Our car had been shoveled out of the snowbank this morning.

I didn't have to ask who had done it. And I was certain it wasn't our perpetually scowling neighbor.

"What's wrong with saying that?"

"You sound like you're ninety. 'An item.' Like the gossip blogs are going to be writing about you on Instagram."

"Have I ever told you you're my least favorite sister?"

"It's not possible." Lyra preened for me. "Everyone loves me."

"Have I mentioned you're also incredibly annoying?" Pulling away from the curb, and Mandy's ice palace, I headed toward town. "Come on. Let's stop at Mystic Munchies to get Broca a surprise, and then we'll go to the apothecary to see what Raven has to say that she didn't want to say in front of the group."

"And maybe, if we're lucky, we'll run into Knox."

"Why would that make us lucky?" I glared at a gritter that passed on the street, shaking my car as it spread salt. Sir Salter Scott. Not bad, as names went.

"I don't know, Sloane. Why do your cheeks go red and you squirm in your seat every time he is mentioned?"

"I can't hear you," I shouted, turning the radio up, as Alanis Morissette raged about irony.

CHAPTER SIXTEEN
Sloane

"*Briarhaven is a cesspool of eejits. The last thing I'd ever do is be caught dead in that sad excuse of a town when there's so many more cosmopolitan and beautiful places in this world.*"

My mother's words played in my head as I drove toward downtown Briarhaven with Lyra humming in the seat beside me.

Even in the snow, Briarhaven was beautiful. And it always had been beautiful, even before Knox's makeover. It was our mother's hatred for Briarhaven, coupled with a difficult childhood, that had colored my memories of the town. But now, as I watched the shops opening for the day, snow being shoveled from walks, neighbors waving to one another, I realized that I might have a jaded view of a community that was trying very hard to be a lovely place to live.

The spell invoking the help of the fae had made the fine hairs at the back of my neck stand up and had reminded me that there were far more than witches who needed the protection of a place like Briarhaven. Knox had given everyone here a gift, the peace to live somewhat in the open, and had created a tourism industry on top of it.

Had I stayed up late last night cruising through the travel sites and reading reviews of tourists' experiences here? Maybe. Was I beyond impressed with the publicity and positive coverage that

Knox had managed to achieve for Briarhaven? Sure, but I'd never tell him that. The man was already too confident for his own good.

And unfortunately, one hell of a kisser.

My cheeks flamed again, and I looked away from my sister, not wanting her to guess what I was thinking about, and focused on looking for a parking spot in front of Pixie Dust Apothecary. Pulling the car into a space at the curb, I turned it off and paused for a moment.

"You know, it's really pretty here."

"I was just thinking the same thing," I said. The sun had broken through the clouds in a rare moment of no snow, and the landscape glittered and glimmered in the soft rays of light. The colorful shops stood out among the snow, like bright smudges of paint on a plain canvas, and cheerful tendrils of smoke wound from chimneys into the air. The village hustled and bustled as it woke up, and a few tourists with knit caps and wide eyes hurried across the street, pointing excitedly to a map. To them, this was a theme park—a destination—but to us it was just home.

Home.

It had been so long since I'd attached that word to an actual place in my mind, having ruled out Briarhaven as a spot to return to long ago. Now my perception was shifting, as memories sifted through like sand in an hourglass, and for the first time in ages I thought about what it would be like to stay in one spot.

To have an actual place to call home.

"Do you think we can stay?" Lyra wondered, echoing my thoughts.

"I don't know. I honestly don't know, Lyra. But Broca wants us to try. And I'm starting to think that I want to as well."

Lyra gasped and clapped her hands over her mouth, her eyes shining.

"You really like him, don't you?"

"What? No!" I shook my head, and when she just kept grinning at me, I reached over and tugged a strand of her hair. "I just meant that I think our perception of this town was tainted by Mum and Dad fighting all the time. We were just kids, you know? Maybe we can look at it a bit differently now that we're older."

"And in charge of our choices." Lyra pushed her lower lip out in an adorable pout that I was certain she didn't even realize she did. That same pout had earned her a gold Cartier LOVE bangle from a besotted admirer.

"There's that too. What if we need Mum's blood to break the curse?" I spat out one of the worries circling my head, and Lyra gasped.

"I hadn't even thought of that. Ugh, she'll never come back here. She was so unhappy in Briarhaven."

"We'll find a way around it. Promise. Come on, let's go see what Raven wanted to talk about."

We piled out of the car and looked both ways before crossing the street. The wind was a touch gentler today. Whatever magick the Charms had worked must be helping, because the snow situation seemed to be easing just a touch. At the very least, it would make it more manageable for tourists to access the town, and for that I was grateful.

It wasn't fun being the ones everyone in the community resented.

I didn't mind being an outcast, but I'd rather it be because of something I'd purposefully done than something that was outside my own control.

A tinkle of bells announced our arrival as we pushed inside to see Raven pouring three cups of coffee for us. Soft Celtic music lilted in the background, and a candle, scented of cinnamon and vanilla, burned at a table in the middle of the room.

"This shop is great. I haven't had a chance to get in here yet," Lyra said, turning a wide circle as she studied all the bottles lining the shelves. "You've got ingredients for practically everything in here."

"Part of the job." Raven grinned at us. "Now, what's up with you? You sent me a panicked message yesterday, then no follow-up, and today you're being weird."

"Bloody hell, Raven, it's been a lot, all right?" I grumbled, gulping the coffee while Raven grinned at me.

"Och, she's a tetchy one in the morning, isn't she, then?"

"The worst," Lyra agreed, sipping her own cup.

"I am not the worst. I'm just figuring a few things out. There's a lot on my mind."

Raven slanted a glance at Lyra, who grinned and twirled a lock of hair around her finger.

"Her magick is misfiring. Something new every day. One day it was fire. Most notably when she lit Knox's curtains on fire after climbing all over him on the couch in his library."

Raven sucked in a breath and whirled on me, and my face went mutinous.

"Such a bitch," I hissed at Lyra.

"We don't know what today's magick is because Sloane refuses to try it out again, so it's exciting times for all of us. We just get to wait and see," Lyra continued, unbothered by my fury, as every sister everywhere likely was when they purposely enraged their siblings.

I let out air, trying to calm myself, and ended up sounding like a wheezing teakettle. Raven thumped my back while Lyra laughed outright.

"And Mandy is being quite the bitch to Sloane, so I'm sure that's just adding to the fun of it all for our favorite control freak, isn't it?" Lyra winked at me when I mimed slicing her neck open.

"That I can at least offer some insight into," Raven said, seeming to understand that I needed to tackle one thing at a time. "It's because you're meant to be the next president of the Charms."

"What?" Lyra and I said simultaneously, our mouths dropping open in mirrored expressions.

"Aye." Raven laughed and ran her hands through her long hair, automatically starting to braid it. "She's been running it since you've been gone, but you, or one of you, should have been the next successor."

"Is it by bloodline? Was our mum a president?"

"Goddess, no. My mum told me everything. Your mum hated everyone and everything to do with the Charms. Refused their help.

The only reason she ended up being able to stay as long as she did in Briarhaven was because Broca battled fiercely for your protection. The Charms used to have weekly meetings to shore up the protection of this town against the curse. It took heavy magick to allow you to live here as long as you did. And then one day, your mum just gave up on the town and took you with her. After all we'd done for her to make it so she could stay."

"Gratitude isn't a strong suit of hers," I muttered, shocked at this new information. Sadness rose inside me, the same that was always there when I thought of my parents, along with a bone-deep resentment. So much she'd kept from me. Not only had I had no idea we had a coven, I hadn't known that we were meant to be running one.

"To say the least." Raven gave me a sympathetic look. "Mandy's territorial. She's run unopposed for years, and we largely have let her because we've all been fine with it. She likes to be in charge, most of us have been busy with our own lives, and it's been fine. Not the greatest, but fine. And not everyone wants to continue to be in the coven. My mum ceded her seat to me, because she didn't want to do the weekly meetings with Mandy. But now you're here."

"I don't know the first thing about magick, Raven. You know that. Mum was a horrible teacher, and I'm still learning. I don't want to challenge Mandy for the spot. I can't even rely on my own magick." A small thread of despair wound through me, and it made me even more grumpy. I didn't like feeling helpless—well, frankly, who did? But I was certainly not equipped to be running a coven.

"It sounds like you've got bigger things on your mind anyway. So, Knox?" Raven raised an eyebrow at me, and my cheeks flamed again.

I needed a spell to stop blushing. Opening my mouth to deny it all, I was saved by the tinkle of bells from the front door.

"Pub. Later. For a drink?" Raven asked, nodding toward the tourists who had come in and were exclaiming over a bowl of crystals.

"Sure, I'll see you after work." Relief filled me that I was escaping an interrogation, for now, and I pulled Lyra out of the shop.

"Mystic Munchies? Pleeease?" Lyra begged, and I relented, even though I wanted to get home and talk to Broca about the language for the curse ritual. I allowed Lyra to drag me down the street toward the colorful bakery, and stepped inside to a crowd of tourists placing their orders.

"This place seriously trips me out." Lyra looked around, a delighted look on her face, not even seeing how people gawked at her beauty.

"Truly. It's kind of like a wild mushroom trip." Not that I knew anything about exotic mushrooms, I'd just heard that certain kinds could make you see colors and whatnot, and this place looked like someone had kicked a palette of paint cans at the walls while under the influence. It didn't help that the owner, Marcie, wore tie-dye, and had neon-pink braids that reached to her bum.

Broca had told me those braids hid tiny nubs, the barest hint of horns, as Marcie's father was of an elven clan specific to the fields. Hence the name Mystic Munchies, I supposed, as I studied all the unique and natural ingredients in the baked goods, like lavender, honey, hibiscus, and rose.

The door opened, and Knox walked in, looking effortlessly handsome in a fitted tartan shirt and tweed newsboy cap. His eyes found mine, and my breath left me.

A gasp went through the crowd of people, but I couldn't tear my eyes from Knox. It felt like my heart had slowed, its beat irregular in my chest, and I rubbed at my solar plexus, where something felt tight, like I'd sucked down a glass of champagne too fast and the bubbles had lodged.

"Sloane," Lyra hissed, yanking on my arm, and I broke eye contact with Knox as he strode toward me, an unreadable look on his face. Glancing over at the glass-lined cabinets of the bakery, I froze.

Where there had once been trays piled high with every baked good imaginable, scrumptious scones, decadent brownies, glistening glazed doughnuts, there now lay piles upon piles of mushrooms.

Hundreds of mushrooms, in every color and size.

My mouth dropped open just as Knox reached us and scooped an arm through mine, dragging me across the room and through a door. Slamming it closed behind us, I blinked at the sudden darkness.

"What the hell?"

A dim light flicked on, and I looked around, realizing that Knox had pulled me into a supply closet.

"What are you doing?" I slammed my hand against his chest, only to instantly be reminded just how strong he was. Reaching up, he wrapped a hand around my wrist and pulled it to my side, forcing me a step closer to him.

"I could ask the same of you, Sloane." Knox's voice was low, barely restrained fury behind it, and his eyes heated in the soft light. "There's tourists out there."

"I didn't plan to do that. Why would I possibly do such a thing?"

"You have to be more careful. You can't just go around town without some command of your magick. There's only so much we can do to hide the tourists from what is really going on here. Now Marcie is going to have a hard time explaining away that little trick you just pulled."

"It wasn't a trick. It wasn't intentional," I seethed, fury making me punch his chest lightly.

"Walk me through what happened," Knox grit out, a tic in his jaw showcasing his annoyance.

"I don't know. I swear I don't know. We were just talking about how the place reminded us of a wild mushroom trip, and then you walked through the door."

"Ahhhhh." Knox's expression changed, the heat of anger in his eyes turning to that of hunger, and a corner of his mouth ticked up in a smirk. "That explains it."

"Explains what?" *Was it warm in here?* I suddenly felt like my skin was inflamed, and I tried to take a step back, only to bump into a bucket with a mop in it. Knox caught me at the waist before I could topple over and pulled me against him.

Exactly where I didn't need to be.

I didn't need the reminder of just how solid his body felt against mine.

Or how great his muscular arms felt wrapped around me, like I was some helpless damsel that needed rescuing.

Or how his lips felt, hovering close to mine, just like they were now.

Now? Oh, *hell no*. I made to pull back, but he held me against him.

"A witch new to her powers will often have a few stumbles in her magick. Particularly with heightened feelings." Knox hovered his mouth over mine, close enough that his breath tickled my lips, and my pulse stuttered.

"I'm sure the only heightened emotion I have is deep-rooted annoyance." I swallowed against the lie, my throat dry, as Knox's lips turned up in that devastating smile that made all rational thought leave my mind. My resolve to hate this man was weakening, and weakening fast.

"Shall we test that theory?"

"Go ahead." *Wait, what?* I'd meant to say no. Where had that come from? Before I could say anything else, Knox's mouth was on mine, and *oh my goddess*. It was even better than the kiss at the Halloween dance. Maybe it was the secrecy of, quite literally, hiding in the closet, or the dim light, or the idea that we might get caught soon, but need took over, and I reached up to thread my hands through his hair, knocking his cap to the floor.

Knox growled and angled his head, deepening the kiss. I gasped against his mouth, rocking against him, wanting to feel everything that he was making me feel. Long, languid licks of desire unspooled inside of me, making my body loose in his arms, my hips bumping gently against his, subconsciously wanting more. His hands stroked my sides and, so very slowly, came down and cupped my bum. Then, in one strong go, he pulled me tight against his hard length, and I moaned into his mouth. His tongue found mine, slick and hot, the outside world forgotten.

Knox traced a hand at my waistband, and I shuddered in a breath when his fingers met skin, and he trailed them up my side beneath my jumper. Cupping my breast with one hand, he thumbed a nipple, laughing softly against my lips as he caught another moan with his kiss.

"By the goddess, Sloane, you'll be the death of me. All fire and brimstone one moment, and molten lava the next. I want to make you melt under my touch. I want to watch you come undone again, because of me. Because of the pleasure that only I can bring to your body."

I sucked in a breath, shocked at how much my body seemed to want the same, and then I arched my back to press my breast farther into his palm.

"Tell me you want this too. Tell me that I'm not absolutely out of my mind with lust for you and you don't feel the same. Say it." Knox bit at a sensitive spot behind my ear, tweaking my nipple slightly, and I gasped at the light bit of pain spiking through my lust. Bloody hell, but I wanted him. Consequences be damned.

A sobering hammering at the door brought us back to reality.

Knox swiftly stepped back, smoothing my shirt and pulling his jacket over where he very obviously still showed signs of wanting me.

"I don't mean to break this up, guys, but we have a problem." Lyra poked her head in the door, her eyes gleaming in the light of the closet.

"Could Marcie not get the mushrooms fixed?" Knox blew out a breath and picked up his cap from the floor from where I'd knocked it off.

"She can. But something, ahem, keeps changing them back. The tourists are starting to take videos, so I'm guessing it has to do with what's going on in here."

"Just getting a few things to help clean up," Knox said loudly, grabbing the mop and bucket and pushing past Lyra into the store. "Sorry, folks, the bakery will be closed for the rest of the morning. Our spell machine is a bit out of whack. We need to fix the projector."

"See? I told you it was all fake." A man elbowed his wife as Knox pushed the tourists from the room, promising them a free muffin if they came back later. Once they were all gone, I crept outside into the room and gave Marcie a small smile.

"I'm so sorry, Marcie. I didn't mean to run your business away. I'm still figuring out my magick."

"Well, get it sorted, then." Marcie glared at me, a terrifying woman almost six feet tall, with muscular arms from kneading dough. "It's bad enough we have to deal with the snow. We don't need you terrorizing our businesses too."

"She said she was sorry, all right?" Lyra said, striding forward to get in Marcie's face. Typical Lyra. She could pick on me, but nobody else could.

"No, she's right, Lyra. She's right. I'd be upset too. I truly am sorry, Marcie. I'm new to all this and struggling. I'll do better, I promise."

Somewhat mollified, Marcie nodded briskly at me as Knox swept his hand over the glass cases and the baked goods reappeared.

"Here." Marcie put a few lemon poppy seed scones in a bag. "Poppy seed for protection."

"Thank you." We accepted the bag gratefully and hurried from the store. Knox caught me just on the way out, as Lyra was already at the street.

"Do you know what else poppy seed is for?" Knox asked, a glint in his eye.

"Actually, I don't." I didn't know anything about anything, it seemed, at least when it came to magick.

"Love and attraction." Knox winked at me as my mouth dropped open, and before I could stop him, he dropped a quick kiss on my lips.

In full daylight.

In front of the entire town.

I could have killed him.

"Absolutely not. I'm not doing this."

"You say no now, but you were the one climbing me like a tree two minutes ago."

"Climbing you like . . . I most certainly was not," I began, and Lyra shouted up at me from where she stood shivering by the car.

"Come on, Sloane. It's freezing out. You two can have your love squabbles later."

"This is not a thing." I pointed between him and me before turning and storming down the street to the car. "And can you please stop shouting 'love squabble' across the entire town?"

"Why not? The whole place could hear you moaning from the closet."

"Shut up," I gasped, horrified, and Lyra fell back into her seat, laughing.

"Okay, maybe not that bad. But you should see your face right now."

"Again, not my favorite sister. The worst, actually."

"You might be my favorite. You definitely are keeping things interesting." Lyra dug in the bag and ripped off a piece of scone. "Scone?"

"Fine." I grabbed it from her and took a bite, before remembering Knox's predication about poppy seeds being good for love.

But it was a *really* good scone. Sighing, I held out my hand for another piece and prayed that he'd just been messing with me.

Love was not something I could deal with on top of the rest of the chaos in my life.

Not in the slightest.

CHAPTER SEVENTEEN
Sloane

We were on our way later that afternoon to meet Raven at the Rune & Rose for our promised drink when a conversation stopped me in my tracks.

"You can't help but try to fix broken things, can you?" a voice boomed from a car speakerphone.

"She's not broken, Mum," Knox spoke, his car door cracked open as though he had meant to get out before his mother had called.

I put my hand out to silence Lyra, and we stood in the parking lot, just out of sight of where Knox spoke to his mum.

"It's always the same with you. You see a wounded animal, you bring it home and nurse it back to health. And now a damsel in distress. You've got a hero complex; it's what you do."

"I'm a knight, Mum. It's kind of in the description, wouldn't you say?"

"That's to protect Briarhaven and our esteemed heritage. Not to save a MacGregor."

My fingers dug into my palms at the way she said our last name, as though we were cockroaches that had infested her fine castle. And, sure, I'd probably be pissed if someone had lit my gorgeous curtains on fire too. But still.

Lyra sucked in a breath next to me.

"Bitch," Lyra whispered.

"Sloane doesn't need saving." Lyra gripped my arm, eagerly nodding her head in approval at Knox's words. "What she needs are friends who will help her work through her trouble."

"You could do so much better," Knox's mother continued on, unperturbed by the note of warning in her son's voice. "I can tell you're infatuated. But, really, darling. A MacGregor? Do you really want to muddy our royal bloodline with the likes of them?"

My mouth dropped open.

"The good thing is you have two other sons who can carry on the bloodline just fine, don't you? I'll remind you, Mother, that I'm an adult who makes my own decisions. You've disappeared from Briarhaven, handing me all of the responsibility to take care of an entire town. And I've been great at it, haven't I? Briarhaven has thrived under my guidance. I pride myself on making good, well-thought-out decisions. Why would that change when it comes to who I choose for a partner?"

Knox's mother grumbled on the speaker.

I slammed a hand over my mouth to stop my audible gasp.

Lyra's grip tightened on my arm.

Partner, Lyra mouthed to me, her eyes huge in her face.

"But . . . a MacGregor, Knox? Surely there is another—"

"I don't have time for this. Either you trust me to make good decisions or you don't. Which is it?"

"It's not so simple—"

"Fine. If you don't, then come home and run Briarhaven yourself. I'm sure I can find better things to do." Knox clicked off on his mother speaking, and I could just see him run a hand over his face in the light shining from the pub.

"Hide," I hissed, pulling Lyra around the back corner of the pub before Knox could get out of his car and see us. We huddled in the cold at the back door, waiting as the car door opened and slammed shut and then footsteps crunched.

"Did you catch all that?"

Lyra and I screamed as Knox's head appeared around the corner and we clutched each other, trying not to slip in the snow. My heart hammered in my chest, my thoughts still tripping over the word "partner."

Nobody had ever asked me to be their partner before.

I'd never let anyone in far enough to let them.

And now here was this impossibly beautiful man who had somehow skipped a few steps forward and was thinking of me in a light that I wasn't sure I was ready for.

Or wanted.

And yet.

And yet . . .

The thought of him claiming me so freely to his mother made my heart go all ooey and gooey in my chest, and honestly, I wasn't even sure what to do with that.

"Your mother sounds *lovely*," Lyra said, raising an eyebrow at Knox. I elbowed her in the ribs.

"She's not." But some of the tension left Knox's face. "She's stubborn to a fault, an absolute snob, and allergic to any concept of real work. How my father puts up with her, I do not know. Yet she loves me and I her, and she's my cross to bear."

"Well, family Christmas should be fun." Lyra winked at me, and I felt embarrassment creep up my face, heating my cheeks.

"Not to worry there. They rarely come home. Most holidays I spend with Haggis and Oswald while Henry snores by the fire."

"Right, then. I'll just . . . see you two inside?" Lyra exited stage left, abandoning me, and I made a mental note to murder her later.

Knox stepped forward, leaning one arm against the wall over me, and I felt like every teenager in a rom-com where the handsome star football player leans over her after a game.

And damn it, but my heart went all fluttery at his nearness.

"Did that freak you out?" Knox asked, a corner of his mouth quirked up in a knowing smile.

"Me? Freaked out? Not at all?" I made to cross my arms and dropped my purse on my foot. "Oh, dang it."

I bent over at the same time Knox did, slamming the top of his head with mine, and I stumbled. He caught me with his arm as I swore, bringing my arm up to pat at my head, narrowly escaping elbowing him in the nose.

"Easy there, killer." Knox dodged my blow and held me against him as he dipped and picked up my handbag.

"Sorry, sorry, sorry. I didn't realize I was so clumsy." I wasn't usually, but nothing had gone to plan since I'd arrived back in Briarhaven. Everything was off-kilter, and I wasn't doing well with this level of upheaval in my life. Not in the slightest. Add to that the town's golden boy was now calling me his partner to his mother, and yeah, right, okay . . .

This witch needed a drink.

"Do I make you nervous, Sloane?"

I swear every time he said my name, my insides melted, and I wanted to cuddle into his arms.

"Um." I really hated to admit that anything, or anyone, made me nervous. "Not really, no."

"Is that right?" Knox grinned over my shoulder, and I turned, gasping at the back wall of the pub. The bright white brick was now covered in vibrant orange mushrooms.

"Are these poisonous? I'll just put myself out of my misery." I reached for one, but they disappeared before I could pick it off the wall.

"No need for dramatics, darling. You can admit you like kissing me."

"Has anyone mentioned you're a touch overbearing?" I looked up at his perfect jawline and exquisite eyes. Seriously, could anyone stay mad at this face? I wanted to, on principle, just because I really felt that Knox needed to learn that not everything went in his favor all the time.

My body, on the other hand, was putting up a strong argument against that particular decision. That betraying bitch wanted me to pull him into the back seat of his Land Rover and see if he wore boxers or briefs.

"Maybe. But I get things done." Knox grinned, and I realized that I was fighting a losing battle here.

"Right, I'm late to meet Raven. Have a nice night."

"We're going to the same pub." Knox threaded his arm through mine and helped me over a snowbank. Several snow figures of all sorts now dominated the front lawn of the pub, ranging from the original snow couple, who seemed to have birthed a small army of snowpeople, snow dragons, and even a snow giraffe.

"We're not walking in together."

"Why not?"

"Because everyone will see us together and think things."

"And?"

"I don't want my love life gossiped about around town." I whirled on him at the front door. Another devastating smile lit his face.

"So, it *is* love?"

"What? No. *No.* Knox. Go away." I stomped inside, his chuckle following me, and beelined toward where Lyra sat next to Raven at the bar.

"I took the liberty of ordering you a drink," Lyra said, just as a very handsome barman appeared with a purple drink. He put it in front of me with a flourish, and then held out a little machine that poured smoke into a bubble on top.

"A witch's brew."

"Sloane, this is Liam." Something about the way Raven spoke, a softness to her words, had me giving a quick glance between the bartender and her. His eyes lighted on Raven's face, warming, and I realized my instinct was correct. There was something here. "He runs the best pub in the Highlands, and we're lucky to have him here."

"Stop, you'll make me blush." Liam grinned. He wore a waistcoat over a shirt rolled to its elbows, and tattoos of runes and Celtic designs covered his arms. This was not a man who blushed, but anyone who was sweet on Raven was a good man in my book.

"It's true," Raven insisted, turning to me. "He built this place up from scratch, with help from Knox when he redesigned the town, and we couldn't be prouder of him. It's become the hub for, well, everything really. And the drinks are truly magickal. Try it."

I lightly popped the bubble on top of the glass, laughing as the smoke curled into the air, and then sipped the cocktail.

"Oh, wow." I nodded approvingly at Liam, who bowed his head in acceptance of my compliment. "It's incredibly refreshing."

"Lavender and basil paired with sweet mint. It's a gin-based cocktail, and a popular one with the tourists." Liam slid us a few menus and then disappeared to attend to other people standing at the bar, while I glanced around the pub, studiously ignoring where Knox was speaking with a group of men who had flagged him down.

While I'd been here the other night for my cèilidh, I hadn't spent any time in the actual pub itself. Now, I nodded in approval. Large arched front windows looked out onto the colorful shops of the street, letting the outside in, and giving clientele the opportunity to people-watch. A fire burned merrily on one wall, and a variety of seating options, from low-slung leather chairs and couches to tables for eating, gave patrons a choice of seating. It was sleek, both modern and quaint, and gave a cozy welcoming vibe. And the magickal elements were just right—nothing too in your face, and yet the artwork all featured dragons or mythological creatures and framed runes and spells, and a tartan witch's hat was tucked on top of a fake stuffed coo head that hung on the wall.

"He's cute," I said, giving Raven a meaningful look.

"Isn't he? And he's just the sweetest too. He's really been a good friend to me."

Lyra and I exchanged a look over Raven.

"I don't remember him from school."

"Och, he moved here after you left. You just missed him. Nice family too." Raven slid a glance at where Liam leaned on the bar, chatting with Knox, and then tucked her hair behind her ear. She'd unraveled her braids from earlier, but still wore the same pretty velvet dress. "So. Knox?"

"Ugh." I took another sip of my drink and settled in, truly unsure of what to say. It felt like a million contradictory thoughts whirled in my head, and I wasn't sure which one to land on. Frankly, I wasn't sure I could even trust my feelings. I'd kind of felt like Alice down the rabbit hole ever since I'd arrived in Briarhaven, and what I likely needed was a few days by myself to just process all that was happening.

Unfortunately, it didn't seem like I'd get a quiet moment anytime soon.

"Is that a good 'ugh' or a bad 'ugh'?" Raven asked, sipping a frothy concoction in a tall-stemmed glass.

"I don't know. He's sexy as sin, kisses like the devil, and wants to throw me out of town. What the hell am I supposed to do about that?"

"Shag him," Lyra and Raven said together. They both laughed and clinked their glasses.

"I can't just . . ." I waved a hand in the air. "He's, like, the town's golden boy. I highly doubt he's been running around having one-night stands. It's too small of a town. We all would have heard about it."

"No, you're right. He gets tons of attention, but I rarely hear about him dating. I mean, he does, occasionally, but he doesn't have a bad reputation for it or anything. He's not a guy I'd warn you away from," Raven said, pursing her lips as she thought about it.

"See? And I'm a love-'em-and-leave-'em type of girl. We don't really have a choice. We always end up having to move."

Lyra nodded her head sadly in agreement. "It can be fun, but also tiring, because you always have to leave. Goodbye gets a little old after a while, I guess. I try to be good about picking my men now.

Ones that I will enjoy but not become too attached to. Even then, it's not easy."

"No, I can't imagine it is." Raven tapped a finger on the bar, considering our plight. "But if you break the curse, then you can stay here . . . and have a future with Knox."

"A future . . ." A lump formed in my throat. I'd never really been in the position of truly being able to consider a future with anyone before. It made me feel all sorts of things. The saddest of which was hope.

I'd long ago learned to bury that particular emotion.

"Oh my goddess," Lyra gasped, and I looked to see her staring at a third man who had joined Knox and Liam. If possible, he was even more handsome than Knox and Liam combined, and I was surprised the women in the room didn't pass out from their collective good looks. Or, frankly, the men either.

"Is that Rab?" I asked, leaning over Raven to gape at Lyra. Rabbie Barclay had been Lyra's first love at age sixteen, and things had ended on a very sour note when we'd left. She'd only spoken of it once, and I'd only seen her cry over him once, as well. After, it was like she zipped up whatever feelings she'd held for him, tucked them away in the bottom of her mind, and had never mentioned his name again.

His eyes locked on hers, and I held my breath. The two most singularly beautiful people in the room, locked in an unspoken argument.

Finally, he gave Lyra a small nod.

It wasn't a friendly one.

Lyra seemed to understand whatever he was conveying, and she shifted, giving him her shoulder.

It looked like their past was going to stay buried.

"Do you want to—"

"Nope. So, back to Knox?" Lyra said, her smile too bright, and not reaching her eyes.

"There's no 'me and Knox.'"

"Yet you were snogging him in the closet at Mystic Munchies today."

"What?!" Raven exclaimed, her face lighting up with interest. "Tell me more. In great detail, please."

"I don't know what to say." I rushed out in one breath. "My brain short-circuits around him. All rational and reasonable decision-making abilities fly out the window, and suddenly I find we're attached at the lips. And then I don't want to stop, and if my magick weren't misfiring left and right, I probably wouldn't stop. And what does that mean? I have no clue. Like, I can't possibly consider a future with this man. I can't live in a castle. I'm not fancy. It's just not . . . No. This is not a viable or smart option for me."

"And yet." Lyra patted my back, trying to soothe me. "You lose your mind when he's around, and he clearly does with you. He told his mum he wants you to be his partner."

"He said what?" Raven screeched, and the men all glanced at us.

"Shut up." I grabbed Raven's arm and bowed my head, surprised to find a giggle bubbling up in my throat. I couldn't even remember the last time I'd giggled about something, let alone about a man. This was . . . well, it was fun. It was fun to sit and have a drink with a girlfriend and giggle about our relationships. Here, in Briarhaven, I could be myself. I had a history here, people who knew me, and we didn't have to constantly cover our tracks or try to explain away weird occurrences that our blood curse made happen. This felt . . . safe. And right.

Oh my goddess, did I want to actually stay in Briarhaven?

Mum would have a fit.

The thought alone cheered me a bit.

"Sloane, that's serious. Knox does not have long-term relationships. If he told his mum that, he must really like you."

"Oh, please, he barely knows me. I've been home all of five minutes, and I'm just the shiny new toy in town."

"I don't think so, Sloane. I think he's serious," Lyra said, stirring her drink, which had come served in a copper mug.

"Well, it doesn't really matter if he's serious or not. If we can't break the curse, we'll have to move on."

"Unless we can get the coven on board to do whatever magick they did to keep your mum here as long as they could," Raven pointed out. "I'm told it was exhausting, but they did it because she was part of the coven."

"Are you saying that even if we can't fix this curse, maybe the coven will be powerful enough to help us stay in one spot?" Lyra speared to the heart of the matter.

And for once, I felt optimistic.

"Aye, assuming Mandy will sign off on it. She'll be a hard one to convince."

"And you need the president of the Charms to be the one to have the last say?" An idea bloomed—not a comfortable one, and I'd need to discuss it with Broca.

"That's the nature of the coven. Head boss has final say and all that."

"Duly noted." Raising a finger to signal Liam that I was ready for another, I leaned back in my chair. Despite my determination to ignore Knox, I couldn't help but glance at him as he gestured animatedly to Rab.

I wanted to lick that man up like an icy scoop of pistachio gelato on a hot summer's day. Forcing those particular thoughts from my head, I refocused on the conversation.

Bloody hell, but it looked like I was going to give this a go. I was going to actually try to help us stay in Briarhaven.

"But why did they stop helping Mum, then?" Lyra asked, drawing my attention back.

"She chose to leave the coven. Once she'd given up on it, they didn't feel the need to keep doing the magick to help her, so the curse forced her to leave."

Lyra and I wore equal expressions of shock.

"Wait. *That's* what happened?" Lyra held a hand to her heart. "She always told us it was because of our dad. That once he'd left, she didn't want to stay in this stupid town anyway. That's why she took us and left."

"*What?*" Raven blew out a breath, her face a picture of shock. "Um, so your dad didn't disappear. He lives up in the hills outside town."

"He *what?*" My heart twisted, like it was a punching bag taking too many hits, and I picked up my drink, finishing it in two gulps.

"He's . . . here?" Lyra blinked at me, her face wrecked.

"Aye, though largely a hermit. Your mum had a falling-out with the coven. I remember because my mum was raging about it. After all they'd done for her and all that. Came home just up in arms over it. Your mum seemed pretty ungrateful, got into it with everyone, threw a huge fit, and the coven revoked their protection. Everyone was pretty fed up with her behavior at that point, but none of them thought she'd take you three with her. It's why the town hasn't full-on tried to boot you out. Most of them remember what you all dealt with growing up." Raven's eyes were sad. "And your dad, well, he just went to the hills. I think he needed the peace, to be honest."

"I can't . . . even. I just can't wrap my head around this." Lyra's eyes filled.

"That arsehole. No-good bastard of a man," Mum shrieked.

"What's going on?" I asked as I came downstairs and noticed that Mum had once again smashed some plates.

"What's going on? What's going on is your father is gone. Just left us all. I knew he wouldn't last. Men never stay," she growled.

"Mum, what? What do you mean he's gone? On a holiday?" I asked, although, for some reason, I knew it wasn't just a holiday.

"No, Sloane. He's gone and never coming back. Not that I'd have him back."

"She always said Dad was the devil." I put my arm around Lyra's shoulders as she dabbed at her eyes with a napkin. Glancing up, I caught Rab giving her a worried look. "But maybe we're old enough to make that judgment call for ourselves now."

"We have to tell Nova." Lyra nodded, her movements jerky.

"I'm so sorry. I truly thought you knew," Raven said, her face wreathed in sympathy.

"It's not your fault. It's not the first of her lies we've gotten caught in. I'd rather know than not know. At the very least, maybe we can make a plan to approach him on our terms."

"Och, *Dad*." Lyra shredded the napkin. "Do you think he'll even want to see us?"

"If he doesn't, the man's a bloody eejit." Raven waved a hand at Liam. "I believe we need another round, ladies."

"Och, aye. That we most certainly do."

CHAPTER EIGHTEEN
Knox

"Help her." Henry's voice sounded at my back.

I turned from where I stared out the window in the library to see Henry holding Oswald in his arms. A plaintive moo sounded, and Haggis clattered in behind him, shaking his horns.

"What's got you in a huff?" I asked Haggis, ignoring Henry's statement.

Oswald swiped my nose. His claws hurt.

"Oswald, was that really necessary?" I asked, bending to examine the wee scratch on Haggis's snout.

He ran me over! Oswald flipped his head backward over Henry's arm, the picture of a dramatic, fainting damsel in distress. Except he was no damsel, and I suspected he'd caused his own accident on this one.

"You know he doesn't corner well. Did you cut it too close?" I asked him, scratching the scruff at Haggis's neck.

Of course not. I'm blind, remember? How am I supposed to know where the big oaf is?

The cat had a point, and I sighed. Crouching, I kissed Haggis on the forehead.

"Try to be more careful of the cat, will you? And Oswald, next time you swipe Haggis with your claws, you're sleeping in the barn for a night."

Oswald hissed at me, jumping from Henry's arms and onto my desk. There he settled down, his eyes slits, and I knew I was in for it.

"We'll get it sorted and have ourselves a nice evening while you're off to the pub," Henry promised.

Oswald reached out a paw until it connected with my pen and he swiped it from my desk.

Rolling my eyes, I took a deep breath, pinching the bridge of my nose.

"See that you do. I'd like to not have every last pen of mine lost under the couch." I stomped over to the desk when Oswald swiped another pen off and picked him up, carrying him with me to a lounge chair. There, I sat and scratched behind his ears until he gave up his mad and began to purr in my lap.

"What are you going to do about the lass?" Henry stopped at the mini fridge hidden behind wood paneling in a bookshelf and opened a bottle of beer. Settling across from me, he took a sip, waiting to hear what I had to say.

"Och, Henry. I don't know. I truly don't. She's got me all twisted up." I pointed at my head.

"And in here?" Henry tapped a finger against his chest.

"I don't know," I repeated, noncommittal.

"It's nice, you know, to see you challenged. To have to put some work in. Women have always come easily to you."

"Excuse me?" I glared at Henry. "You're enjoying this?"

"I'm just saying—she matters. Which means none of this is going to be comfortable for you. But that's where the good stuff happens, you ken? Outside your comfort zone. You need to have a long, hard look at what you want, Knox. Not what is best for Briarhaven, not what is best for your family. You. You've done a good job here, but it's time you put yourself first. What do you want?"

"Her." My mouth went dry when I admitted it, and Oswald turned, slanting me a look.

And yet you try to make her leave?

"Her curse is bad for the town," I protested, defending myself to the cat.

Pretty Sloane! Haggis wheeled himself to Henry for a pet.

"There's a lot of magick in this town, boyo. It might do you some good to realize that folks can well take care of themselves, and have been for centuries. The snow is annoying, that's the truth of it, but we're a resilient and resourceful bunch. We'll find our ways around it. We always do. Might be time for a change in your stance when it comes to the MacGregors, don't you reckon?"

With that, Henry lifted his bottle to me in a salute, clucked his lips, and left the room, Haggis at his heels.

If the opinion had come from my parents, I would have ignored it. But Henry had acted as a de facto father to me for years, and I took his musings much more seriously. A forest ogre, Henry had started work in our gardens, quickly working himself up to helping with the magickal creatures in the stables, before finally settling in the house as one of our family. He seemed to enjoy the airs of being a butler, even though there was really no need for such pomp and circumstance with me. Once a month he disappeared for a deep mud bath somewhere on the shores of the loch and returned rejuvenated and ready to dispense all advice—asked for or not.

It had been Henry who'd consoled me when my family had ordered me back to work, while they'd taken a holiday together. I still remembered it, being left at home to watch the keep, while they'd all gone to the Cayman Islands together. I'd been told that one Douglas family member must always remain at the castle, ostensibly to protect Briarhaven, but really, we weren't in a time of war anymore. Why couldn't I have gone with them to parade around on sunny beaches and dive in azure waters? Instead, Henry and I had taken our meal by the fire every night, playing brutal games of chess, while my family had regaled me with tales of their holiday.

I reminded myself I should be grateful. At least I had a somewhat functional family. Unlike Sloane, who'd grown up where screaming matches were the baseline of her existence.

I wished I'd done something. That day I'd run into her in the alley.

I wished I'd established a connection then, to show her that I could be there for her. I'd been too tongue-tied, full of teenage attraction, to do much more than mumble a few words.

I was beginning to see she'd always been it for me.

My heart stumbled every time I saw her. It always had. And now that I was a man, and had tasted her kisses, I was ready to overthrow centuries of Douglas leadership simply to keep Sloane by my side. After many a sleepless night, where I battled with my responsibility to my town and my responsibility to my heart, I realized that I couldn't bear it if she left.

You'll find a way. Oswald stood, arching his back, before hopping off my lap and sauntering out the door.

He was right. I'd find a way. I was a fixer, and Sloane's curse was one big, fat problem that I was going to solve.

It had been a busy few days since I'd kissed Sloane in the closet of Mystic Munchies, and it aggravated me just how much I missed her in the time since I'd last had her in my arms. Calmly, I had listened to stories left and right about the MacGregor sisters and did my best to reassure Briarhaven that we'd sort this out. All while constantly looking around to see if I could catch a glimpse of Sloane on the street. She'd been lying relatively low, from what I'd heard, and I wondered if the bakery incident had freaked her out.

I could still taste her kiss.

It surprised me just how much real estate this woman had taken up in my brain. I wasn't usually one for soft yearnings or angsty pining, but I couldn't believe just how many times I'd picked up my phone to call her on one excuse or the other and then put it down. And frankly, I was surprised by my own rapidly growing feelings for Sloane. I don't exactly know when the change from wanting to make her leave to wanting to make her love me happened, but here we were.

Thoughts of how to help Sloane consumed me on the walk into town, but by the time I arrived at the pub I was no closer to a solution. Only half-frozen, covered in snow, and distracted by remembering the heat of Sloane's mouth on mine.

"Hi ya, mate. Sorry I'm late." Rabbie Barclay, a good friend of mine, stopped at where I stood on the sidewalk outside the pub, having lost myself in a train of thought.

"No worries, mate." I shook my head and brushed the snow from my face, and we stopped to ogle the veritable army of snow sculptures that had now expanded to both sides of the walkway in front of the Rune & Rose. A snow fairy held hands with a witch, a tiger kissed a snow frog, and there was even a wee snow ladybug. Things were getting out of hand here.

On Tuesday nights the pub closed early, and I usually stopped in for a round of darts with Liam and Rab. We stepped inside from the cold to find Liam behind the bar.

"What'll it be tonight, lads?" Liam asked, from where he stocked beer cans in a cooler. I loved the pub like this, when the main lights were off, and it was highlighted just by the fire and a few lamps in the corners. The ambiance made it easy to chat about our lives while we played darts, and I was lucky to have Liam and Rab as my mates.

"Common Gin and tonic for me," Rab ordered.

"Sure, same. I heard Munroe's building a distillery in Loren Brae," I said, settling onto a stool. Common Gin was owned by Munroe Curaigh, a respected businessman who had thumbed his nose at his posh parents and gone into making gin for the working class instead of working for the fancy whisky brand his parents owned.

"Aye, that's the way of it. Heard good things too. He's engaged." Liam placed three glasses on the bar and bent to building our drinks.

"Another one bites the dust," Rab said grimly. I glanced at him. He wasn't usually so bitter when it came to the likes of love, having dated far and wide. It wasn't surprising, as he basically was a stand-in for David Beckham, but with a bit more muscle.

"Hopefully, he's happy." Liam slid us our drinks.

"Doubtful," Rab murmured into his drink.

"What's up with you?" I asked, taking a sip and angling myself toward Rab. He was a fairly cheerful sort, and usually wished others well.

"The same thing that's up with you." Liam snorted and put the darts on the bar.

"Me? I'm fine." I pointed a finger at my chest. "This one over here seems a bit tetchy."

"It's the MacGregor sisters. Got you both tied in knots." Liam grinned when both Rab and I stilled. "Uh-huh. See that? That right there. That's what I'm talking about."

"Which sister?" I turned on Rab, ready to fight.

"None of them." Rab glowered at me.

"Lyra," Liam said, smirking when Rab swore under his breath.

"Och, no, that's right." I'd honestly forgotten that Rab and Lyra had been an item for a moment back in the day. We were all so young, and relationships were fleeting in high school. But judging from the look on Rab's face, maybe not so fleeting.

"It's nothing."

"Doesn't seem nothing. Your face looks like Wolverine's," Liam said.

"If he sat on one of his claws." I outright laughed when Rab's expression soured even more.

"Like you're one to talk. Sniffing around Sloane."

I took a sip of my drink, steadying myself. I wasn't sniffing around her, exactly, and I knew that Rab had used that term to get me angry. Which would deflect from any discussion of him and Lyra.

"She does smell good. Like a sangria on a sunny beach." I beamed at him when he swore, downing his drink.

"What's going on with you two anyway?" Liam asked, pulling Rab's glass over to make him another.

"I don't know," I said, because these were some of my oldest mates, and if I couldn't be honest with them, then I wasn't sure who I could be honest with. "She's dug into my brain somehow. All I can do is think about her."

Rab snorted, tapping his fingers on the bar, nodding in agreement. I took that to mean he felt the same about Lyra.

"But?" Liam asked, sliding a fresh drink to Rab.

"I'm meant to get her to leave town. This snow is too much. Bloody hell, mate. Scotland has unpredictable weather, but this is beyond anything we've dealt with before. My job would be to make sure they leave. It's what my parents want as well."

Rab snorted again, taking a sip. He well knew how domineering my parents were.

"I'm sure they've offered an opinion?"

"Naturally. The official decree is to run the MacGregors out of town. Like, yesterday."

"Is that your plan, then?" Rab looked down at the bar.

"Aye. And no." I sighed, running a hand through my hair. "I don't reckon I can do it. There has to be another way."

"You want to help solve the curse," Liam said, crossing his arms over his chest.

"I do at that. The issue is, I'm just not sure how long it will take. I may have a revolt on my hands here soon enough if I don't enforce their leave."

"I'll help." Liam met my eyes. "I talk to everyone here. I'll put in a good word for them."

"You will?" Some of the tension that banded my chest eased. "That might make a bit of a difference."

"Aye, nae bother, lad." Liam shrugged. "It's easy enough to remind people that it's not their fault they were cursed. I know I moan about the snow and whatnot, but still. They've been dealt a bad hand. Would be good to remind a few people of that."

"I can help too." Rab tapped his fingers against his glass. "Unofficially."

"Does that mean you want Lyra to stay?" I asked.

"Don't go there." Rab shook his head, and I eased off. He'd talk when he wanted to talk, and that was the way of it.

"Does your mum know you fancy Sloane?" Liam asked, picking up the darts and motioning toward the board.

"It's none of her business." It wasn't, that was the truth of it, but Briarhaven was a very small town, and I didn't care to hear my mother's complaints about the gossip.

"And when has that ever stopped her before?" Liam asked, hitting a bull's-eye for his warm-up shot.

"Never," I admitted, wincing as I hit a three.

CHAPTER NINETEEN
Sloane

I felt like I was unraveling at the seams.

It had been a week since the coven meeting about the curse, and in that time, my magick had continued to go off the rails. The revelation about our father had rocked my sisters and me, and with the added stress of the snow continuing to pile up, I was like an unwatched pot on the stove, ready to boil over.

Thank the goddess for my sweet grandmother. Broca was doing her best to make me see the levity in my ever-changing magick. Her favorite had been the day when my magick turned every light bulb into a disco ball, and '70s music had blared through the house. I would have been annoyed by it, but it had made it easier to get her out of her chair and moving around, which was exactly what her physical therapist required for her to move forward with her hip recovery. We'd had to badger her into the local gym each day, since walking outside was out of the question with the heavy snowfall, and she was slowly making strides—pun intended.

One morning, we were busy making decorations for the Pinecones & Peppermint Fest, tying pinecones onto twine, and wrapping candy canes in bows, when all of the pinecones had turned into hedgehogs and chaos had ensued. I was never going to look at a pinecone the same way again.

Another day, which still made me hot and bothered when I thought about it, my shadow had become extra clingy. All day long, it had tripped me up, like a scared child hanging on to my leg every time I made a move. It had also happened to be the day that I'd gone into town for a few things for Broca from Pixie Dust and had run into Knox on the street. Quite literally run into him, because my shadow had lost its mind, apparently, and pushed me right into his chest. He'd caught me, and once he'd realized my issue that day, he'd insisted on carrying me home and installing me in my bedroom until it was safe for me to move again. And had decided to babysit me in the process.

Knowing the house was full of people made our kisses all the more stealthy in my bedroom, and even though I had put up a small fight about not wanting to be with him, my resolve was weakening. *Anyone's* resolve would weaken around that man. His biggest flaw that I could find at the moment was his absolute confidence that things would work out in his favor. And as much as I tried to disavow him of the idea of us as a couple, somehow I still found myself wrapped around him every time I saw him, my lips on his, my body aching for more.

We hadn't crossed that line yet, but I wasn't sure how much longer I could hold out. Knox was cheerfully open to telling anyone and everyone about his interest in me, which I found beyond irritating, while I continued to grumble and ignore any questions that came my way about Briarhaven's favorite golden boy. I'm sure that didn't endear me to anyone, but I was not used to answering questions about my private life. Particularly when I didn't even know the answers myself.

It turned out, Broca hadn't known our father was still around, either, or at least that's what she told us, and I believed her. She had nothing to gain from hiding that information, and she'd been just as upset with our mother for hiding that from us. As far as she was concerned, children had a right to know about their parents and make their own decisions, and Mum shouldn't have kept our father's whereabouts a secret. I wondered if he knew we were back.

We discussed going to the hills, just my sisters and me, to see if we could find him. There were just a couple small issues with that plan. The first being that the snow was growing worse every day, and none of us were experienced in winter hiking or camping. It would be foolish beyond belief to just trudge up into the mountains and try to find this man. And second, we realized that we didn't really know if he wanted to see us anyway. If he'd wanted to, wouldn't he have reached out? Even though Nova was still pretty mad about it, we'd agreed to wait on any decision about moving forward on trying to find him until we could seek out more information.

I'd yet to confront Mum about any of this. Lyra and Nova wanted me to say something, but a part of me was beginning to realize that the less contact I had with her, and the more I distanced myself from her narrative, the better I was becoming at making decisions that suited me. And, at the end of the day, if we decided to stay in Briarhaven, our relationship with our mother would remain fractured anyway. What the three of us needed to do was to reach these conclusions about our own future for ourselves, without the lens of a bitter and toxic mother coloring our views.

All of this meant I had a lot of big feelings pinging around inside me, and no particular outlet for them at the moment. So why not try more spell work? It would either go entirely off the rails or potentially solve everything. With that in mind, I'd summoned my family to the living room.

"You think we'll be okay to try this . . . just us?" Nova asked, settling onto the floor in front of the coffee table. She'd stayed at home a lot this past week, aside from her morning runs, after learning about our father, and had spent much of her time drawing. It was Nova's way of coping with her reactions, and her tattoo designs flourished whenever she was in a mood.

Lyra had baked to the point where I might just be winning over the curmudgeonly neighbor who gave me the two-fingered salute every morning. Granted, he still slammed the door when he saw me coming up the walk, but we'd left a container of treats at his door each day, and this morning I'd even found the empty container back at ours. It was a small step, but maybe, just maybe, we were starting to change a few people's minds about our presence back in Briarhaven.

"I think it is worth giving it a go, just us, and we'll see what's what. I need to feel the magick of this spell. I'll be able to get a better read on it if we follow it exactly or if the magick requires different needs now," Broca said.

"Wait, why?" That was interesting. I felt like I was in preschool when it came to magick, our mother having refused to teach us anything of its history, with Broca filling in limited tutorials where she could. It was a large reason why I'd spent so long dismissing all things magickal, while Nova and Lyra had spent far more time delving into our magickal history.

"A spell or ritual that was suitable hundreds of years ago may not be the same now." Broca smiled at me, her tone gentle, endlessly patient. "Think of it this way. As we learn and grow as people, our needs change. Our understanding of the world changes. For example, words that may have been used fifty or one hundred years ago, which were common vernacular then, are now understood to be slurs. So people stop using them, society adjusts, and collectively we move forward with a better understanding of how to coexist. The same goes for magick. We have technology now. We have quicker ways of doing things. There are some shortcuts we can use that help in our magick, while in other ways the original ritual is best. Witches can adapt to modern times, just like anyone else can. I'd like to just give this ritual a go, see if I can feel if something in particular needs tweaking, and if it does, we'll call in the Charms and make it a bigger thing. Make sense?"

"Aye, it does at that." I nibbled my lower lip as I thought about modern-day witches googling how to perform rituals.

Cheese? Blue bumped his head against mine, and my heart warmed. Having the ability to talk with him had strengthened our relationship significantly, even though a large part of our conversations were based around his deep and abiding love for cheese.

"In a bit, buddy. We're going to do a ritual first."

Won't work.

"Why not?" I scratched behind his wings, a spot he struggled to reach with his paws, and his face went delirious with pleasure.

Need Vaila's family.

"Who is Vaila?"

The witch who cursed you.

My mouth dropped open. To my knowledge, this was the first we'd ever had a name for her, any record of her involvement having been destroyed long ago, or so my mother had told me. Until the people of Briarhaven had been able to make the village a stronghold for witches, long before Knox had made it a coveted destination, there had been a lot of witch hunts and burning of homes.

Which also included books, records, and magickal tools.

Even having a name was a start. This could seriously help us in our search for a way to break the curse. I wasn't sure why I hadn't asked Blue more before, but now I leaned back on the cushions and studied my wee familiar.

He grinned up at me, his tongue lolling out.

"What else do you know about Vaila? Do you know her last name?"

I quickly told the others what Blue had said, and Broca leaned forward, excitement in her eyes, while Nova and Lyra crowded close around the coffee table.

No. Just that she had a broken heart. And her family can never love. Not truly.

"He says that Vaila had a broken heart and none of her bloodline can ever truly love someone."

It's part of the curse. She hurt others. Which means she hurt herself.

"How do you know this?" I asked Blue.

We get information on our witches before we pick them.

My heart warmed. He'd picked me. Me. It was quite an honor, and I pressed a kiss to his wee forehead.

Blue rolled in my lap and took off across the room, his wings flapping lazily as he lumbered toward the kitchen cabinets to see if any spare cheese had been left on the counter. I repeated what he'd said.

"I'll get him a wee snack. For being such a good boy."

The best emberwolf in all the land, Blue corrected from where he perched on the counter, snuffling in the sink.

"Does that mean we're looking for someone who is single? Never married? How can her bloodline continue if she isn't in love?" I wondered out loud, and Nova snorted.

"I hate to break this to you, Sloane, but science has proven that babies can be made without the presence of love."

I threw a cushion at her head.

"Shut up. I was just thinking out loud."

"But it is a good starting point. Not to say that people who are married are all in love and all that, but we could maybe start narrowing down the bloodline by those that are single." Lyra fed Blue a few pieces of chicken, and he did a wee dance on the counter, his paws making a fun little tippy-tapping sound against the Formica.

"Assuming they even live here." Broca tapped her finger against her lips as she thought. I wasn't sure how I'd missed the fashion gene, but she always looked good, and today's lemon-yellow silk pants, lime-green top, and bright orange–rimmed glasses just worked. She looked like a citrus plant—in the best way possible.

Blood magick. Dark curse. Keeps them close.

"Blue says dark magick will keep the person close."

"He's not wrong." Broca nodded thoughtfully. "You pay a great price for using dark magick, and oftentimes it can bind you to the area of your ritual."

"How can that be?" Nova protested, closing her drawing pad and leaning back on her arms. "I've read enough accounts of witches who are extremely savvy in the dark arts and travel all over the world."

"Och, I said oftentimes, but not always." Broca nodded her approval at Nova. "The thing with magick is that there will always be outliers. There will always be people who practice and grow to such a level that they become the exception. Those practitioners are the scariest, so they are. The stronger a dark witch becomes, the more they know how to offset the potential repercussions of using power to harm. But in this case, from my understanding, it was a young witch new to her magick. She wouldn't have had time to protect her own bloodline from harm revisited on her for using such a curse. She wouldn't have likely learned how not to be tethered to this place. It's highly probable her bloodline is still here because of that. Nothing is for certain, but I'd lay money on it."

"Which says a lot, considering you only like to spend on name brands." Lyra blew a kiss at Broca and came to join me at the couch, Blue bobbing along in the air behind her, still hopeful for more food.

"So shouldn't we be spending time trying to find them?" Nova asked.

"I guarantee they'll be well shrouded. It's not just like looking up a name in the phone book."

"What's a phone book?" Nova fluttered her eyelashes at Broca, who glared at her.

"Och, this one's got a smart mouth, doesn't she? Like nothing existed before Google."

"Learned from the best." Nova held up her arms when I threatened to throw another cushion at her.

"Right, let's crack on, then, shall we?" Lyra said, casting an eye at the timer on the oven. "I don't want to burn my pie."

"Oh, aye, let's hurry this ancient blood ritual that might take the curse off our bloodline in time for Lyra's pie to come out of the oven." I rolled my eyes as I slid to the floor next to the table we'd pulled close to Broca's chair. On it, I'd put a small bowl above a Bunsen burner–style candle, and with a dash of honey and whisky inside.

"Are the hematite stones in place?" Broca asked, looking around the room. Lyra had created a circle with crystals she'd picked up from the Crystal Cavern.

"Aye," Lyra said, leaning forward over the table.

"Heather bloom and thistle's thorn,
Shield me now from harm unborn.
Circle o' light, fierce and bright,
Keep all ill beyond my sight."

A shimmer in the air, almost like the surface of still water being disrupted by a dragonfly, and Broca had cast the circle.

"Sloane?" Lyra offered me a gold pin to prick my finger. I did it quickly, keeping my mind clear, and dripped my blood into the dish. The rest of the women did the same, and then Lyra stirred the mixture with a small silver spoon with Celtic insignia on the handle.

"By blood that bound, by love now freed,
Let this curse be undone in word and deed.
Honey sweet, whisky strong,
Upend this heartache to right a wrong."

Three times we repeated the spell, passed the cup around for a wee sip each, and then we waited, our breath holding.

Nothing happened.

"How will we know when, or if, it has worked?" Nova asked.

"Look out the window," Broca suggested, and we all turned. If anything, the snow had intensified, not lessened, and the wind howled as it battered our wee cottage.

Told ya. Blue rolled over and pawed me, wanting his tummy scratched.

"Just let me close the circle," Broca muttered a few quick words, and that same disruption in the air shimmered around us before we were free to move about. Standing, I picked Blue up because I needed a cuddle. A part of me had really hoped it would be that easy. A quick ritual to ease this curse that haunted us, to stem the hatred flowing our way from those of Briarhaven who resented us, and to maybe, just maybe, allow us to finally put down roots. I stood at the window, Blue nuzzling into my neck, and watched as the snow attacked Briarhaven.

There was only so long we could stay here before the whole town turned on us.

It was inevitable, really, and I'd seen it many times before. I was used to this. Moving on, packing up, saying goodbye. That was our norm. We weren't cut out for putting down roots, building lasting friendships—hell, even falling in love. Unless our partners were ready for life on the road, and that was a lot to ask of someone, particularly if they already had a good thing going in their own life.

It was just . . . for the first time in, like, ever, I wanted to stay. I wanted to get a drink with Raven at the Rune & Rose, and pick out new books at the Silver Quill, and shop for gifts at the Dragon's Hoard. I hadn't even been to Whispering Woods, the garden center, yet, and I had to imagine they probably hated us the most. Autumn would be a booming time for their business, as everyone prepped their gardens for winter. Feeling dejected, I turned back toward my family.

"I think we're going to have to go." I hated to say it, I truly did, but it needed to be put out there. The girls needed to start thinking about packing up, not settling down, and we needed to see about getting a more comfortable car for Broca to ride in so she could join us. Maybe a van would be the best option.

"You give up so easily." Nova jumped up, stomping a foot, her face contorted in frustration.

"I'm not giving up." I wasn't giving up, was I? It was just the reality of the situation. "I'm not. It's just . . . the writing might be on the wall, Nova. We need to be prepared. We need to be thinking about buying a nice van, maybe even a camper van, so Broca can travel with us. We need to be thinking about food supplies and amenities for Blue. We can't just up and go in the middle of the night. Not like this. By failing to prepare—"

"You're preparing to fail," Lyra and Nova finished for me, their expression of frustration mirrored on each other's faces.

"Well, I'm not wrong," I shouted after Nova as she stomped upstairs.

"A camper van." Broca snorted, and then shook her head sadly at me. "Have you met me?"

"It's a viable solution to keeping you comfortable while on the go," I protested.

"Listen to yourself. Viable solution? Sloane, you are twenty-five years old. When did you become so mired in the pragmatics of things?"

"When I had to be the one to make sure they were actually fed." I flung my hand out in the direction of Lyra.

"It's true, you did." Lyra jumped onto the couch next to me and hugged me. "But we're not kids anymore. And it's time for you to maybe be a bit selfish."

"Beyond time," Broca agreed.

"You do know, don't you, that we don't always have to stay together now?"

My mouth dropped open at Lyra's suggestion, because honestly, no, I had not considered that. We'd always traveled together. The MacGregor sisters were stronger together, as a unit, and just thinking about one of them being on the other side of the world from me caused my heartbeat to speed up and my mouth to go dry. Blue leaned up and licked my face, sensing my distress, and I cuddled him closer.

"So you're going to leave me?" I asked, a bead of sweat breaking out and dripping down my back. I honestly couldn't imagine being away from them. Maybe it wasn't the healthiest thing in the world, and yes, I realized that codependency came out of the trauma we'd experienced as children, but knowing something in your head and facing it were two totally different things.

"We didn't say that." Lyra smoothed my hair back from my face. "But if you try to leave here, we might decide to stay."

"But we don't have a solution." The protest was weak on my lips, but still, my brain couldn't wrap itself around not having a solution. Were we meant to just exist here, throwing Briarhaven into increasing harm, with no way to ease the torment for ourselves and our neighbors? Surely my sisters could see the insanity in that.

"One might show up. In time."

"Like it did with our mother? You heard it yourself. The Charms kept her, us, here for as long as they did with an extraordinary amount of work. And magick. And they hated it. They resented her, resented the toll it took on them to do so, and where did it leave them? With an ungrateful witch who ran from town anyway." I stood, anxiety coursing through me, needing to move around the room.

"They didn't do it for your mother, Sloane." Broca's voice cut through my anxious thoughts. "They did it for you and your sisters."

At that, the enormity of what we owed this town rose inside me, and I choked back tears. Turning, I looked helplessly at Broca.

"Which is exactly why we have to leave. We failed them then, and we'll do it again. Our curse is hurting Briarhaven. Whether we do the stupid festival or not, it won't be enough. Don't you see? We aren't repaying them by showing up here again. We're just screwing them over. *Again*." I grabbed my coat and wrenched the door open, Blue still in my arms.

"You were just children, Sloane." Broca's voice was quiet at my back as the snow swirled inside the door. "They didn't expect anything of you three other than to grow and prosper. It's not your job to break the curse, alone, without help. We can do this . . . together. You just have to be patient and believe a solution will present itself."

"I already know the solution. The safe solution. And that's to leave. I need . . . I just need some space to think."

I slammed the door behind me and crunched through the snow, my shoulders bent to protect Blue until I reached the car and bundled him into the front seat. Rounding the car, I glanced back at the cottage to see Broca standing in the window, Lyra at her side.

They didn't have to say anything, because I could see what they were thinking. They thought I was coward for wanting to leave, but I thought it was more cowardly to stay and let other people fight your fight for you. Frustrated, and slightly distracted, I started the car and pulled it gently into the recently plowed street, no specific direction in mind. My thoughts churned, my feelings rioting around me, and I was so stressed by the discussion that I'd forgotten one warning that Knox had given me.

An emotional witch new to her magick can wreak havoc.

Just like the witch who cursed my bloodline.

And just like now, when all of a sudden, my car morphed around me and no longer were Blue and I cozied into the front seat.

No, now we were tucked inside a sleigh, wrapped in blankets, while a dragon bucked its head against the reins.

The reins that I was now holding.

My mouth dropped open in a silent scream as the dragon blew out a breath of fire and took flight.

CHAPTER TWENTY
Knox

"Of course, Mrs. Stuart. I understand completely." I stood patiently outside the Dragon's Hoard, our local curiosity shop, and listened as Mrs. Stuart listed all the reasons why we needed to make the Mac-Gregors leave. I'd meant to just pop into the shop quickly to pick up a wee bauble for my mum's birthday, and have it sent off, but like everything in Briarhaven, it took double the amount of time to accomplish. It was part of the job, though, listening to the concerns of the citizens, so I kept a polite smile on my face.

"Those MacGregors are a menace to Briarhaven," Mrs. Stuart warned, clutching her wool coat more tightly to her neck.

"I can't say that I agree with that. Have you met them? They are all lovely people, and I do believe their intention is to break the curse," I said, going to bat for the MacGregors, as I had been increasingly called upon to do.

"Surely they could have managed it by now. This is ridiculous." Mrs. Stuart turned to the sky and sniffed.

Her eyes widened and she froze.

I whirled, hands already up, prepared to protect her from any incoming danger.

But I was not prepared for what I saw.

A green dragon with iridescent scales that shimmered with an underlay of orange writhed through the air, fighting the restraint of being tethered to a sleigh. Snow swirled, clouds concealing the dragon, but I knew what I'd seen.

A sleigh that held a shrieking Sloane and an exuberant Blue.

Shop owners ran into the street to look, and when the dragon opened its mouth and shot flames, they raced back inside, their screams deafening as the dragon whirled in the air, dragging Sloane behind it.

She was clearly *not* in charge.

"Bloody hell," I murmured, and ran out into the street. Invoking my elemental magick, I pulled from my very core. *"Fires obey, in my command stay!"*

The dragon swung, its tawny eyes on me, and swooped low, slowing enough that I was able to grab the side of the sleigh.

"Knox." Sloane's face was a picture of abject terror, and I swung myself inside the sleigh, prying the reins from her hands and squeezing next to her on the seat. With one steady pull of the reins, the dragon lifted us once more and I waved cheerfully from the sleigh at the shop owners gawking below.

"Everything's fine. Just fine," I shouted down, the icy wind stealing my words, but they got the gist. I directed the dragon toward my castle, bending my head against the icy wind. Fury rippled through me at the thought that Sloane might have been hurt.

How had she even *found* a dragon? I had a million questions for one Miss Sloane MacGregor, but I kept them inside as I focused on landing the dragon on the front lawn of the castle. The moment dragons suspected they could take command, they would. Once the sleigh lurched and skidded to a stop, the dragon stomping its feet in the snow and melting small patches of snow with its breath, I grabbed Sloane's arm.

"Come with me. Slowly."

Blue leapt into the sky and buzzed about, and to my utter astonishment, he flew to the dragon's head.

"Blue," Sloane shouted, worry in her voice.

When the emberwolf zipped forward and licked the dragon's snout, my knees went weak.

But instead of incinerating the wee pup, the dragon bumped its head against Blue's, sending the wee emberwolf spiraling into the air. Blue promptly righted himself and barked excitedly, looking eagerly between Sloane and the dragon.

"I think he wants to play," Sloane said. Her mouth gaped open, and fine tremors ran through her body.

Turning, I held my hands in the air and released the dragon from the reins.

"Just a quick one," I warned the dragon. "The tourists have already seen too much. Keep it low if you can."

The dragon bowed its head, and Blue bounded over to Sloane.

"Yes, but be careful. He can light you on fire."

Blue eagerly took off in his fat bumblebee air waddle, doing his best to quickly reach the dragon who had soared into the air. They tumbled around each other, Blue barking ecstatically.

"Why does the littlest dog in the park need to befriend the biggest?" Sloane murmured, her hand at her heart. "It's terrifying."

"Looks like Blue's the one in charge here," I pointed out, as the dragon followed Blue at a demure pace, allowing the wee emberwolf to bark and wheel erratically through the air, terrorizing a couple of birds out of the trees. Blue gave chase, and the dragon followed, happy to have a game on.

Sloane shivered, and I drew her close, wrapping an arm around her.

"Care to tell me what happened here?" I bit out, not even wanting to think about what other catastrophes were in store for me so long as Sloane's magick kept misfiring.

"You warned me . . . about erratic moods and magick. That"—Sloane nodded toward the dragon, who was looking over its tail midair, waiting for Blue to give chase—"is our car."

"Right. That's . . . *interesting*." And an entirely different type of alchemy. Sloane may be new to her powers, but she certainly wasn't weak. Turning a car into a sentient being was advanced magick, the type that took years to learn, and she'd done it while distracted. But since her teeth chattered, and her body shook with adrenaline next to mine, I figured now likely wasn't the best time to discuss such matters.

"And terrifying. Like . . . I just can't. I can't." The shaking increased, and I decided it was time to get her inside. Particularly because the snowstorm was now reaching blizzard-like conditions. Giving a sharp whistle, I motioned for the dragon to return, with Blue at his side.

"Blue, want to come meet some new friends?" Blue gave the dragon one last head bump, and then flung himself into the arms of Sloane, who caught him with a soft grunt.

"There's a large outbuilding around back," I told the dragon who eyed me balefully. "Big enough for you to cozy up in some hay if you want a dry spot from the storm. I'll instruct that food be brought out. If that suits?" You always walked a fine line with dragons. You wanted to show you were in command, but at the same time, it was only because they allowed you to have it. Respect was the most important piece of the relationship. When he bowed his head to me, I knew he was happy with the offering. Without another glance, he took off, his large wings spiraling snow into our faces, and I bundled Sloane toward the front door. Henry stood, blanket in hand, and immediately wrapped it around Sloane and Blue as we stepped over the threshold.

"Thank you, Henry." Sloane's voice was muffled under the blanket, and I flipped a corner down so she could see. Blue peeked his head up, and his grin widened when he caught sight of Haggis barreling into the front hall.

"Blue, this is Haggis."

Play? Haggis looked at me.

"If he wants to." I grinned at where Blue scrabbled at Sloane's arms, wanting to be released, and she let him go. He flitted into the air, and Henry gasped.

"I haven't seen an emberwolf since you were a lad," Henry said, his eyes glowing with excitement.

"Pretty great, isn't he?" Blue dropped to the floor, and Haggis wheeled forward, sniffing him.

Blue looked at Sloane.

"His back legs don't work. The wheels help him get around. No flying, though. At least I don't think so?" Sloane glanced at me, and I nodded.

"No flying, but Haggis is great on his wheels. You two have fun."

Oswald strolled into the foyer, languid as could be, until he caught scent of Blue.

Blue froze.

"Blue," Sloane warned.

Oswald's back went up.

Blue gave us such a cheeky grin that I had to laugh, and then he took off after Oswald, Haggis happily joining the chase.

"Oh no," Sloane said, "Will he be okay?"

"Oswald is excellent at protecting himself. This is good. Will give him a little shot of excitement, plus some extra exercise. Let them work it out. Come on, let's get you into some dry clothes."

"I can just go home. Honestly, it's fine. I don't want to put you out." Sloane's eyes took on a bit of that panicked look that I was beginning to regard with such fondness. Every time she got that look in her eyes, it meant she was thinking about things she didn't want to be thinking about, which usually meant that I would get to steal a kiss very soon. One of these days she was going to accept that she and I were a great match.

I'd been thinking more and more about why I wanted Sloane in my future. As my partner. She was passionate, empathetic, fiercely loyal, sarcastic, strong-willed, gorgeous—and each of those traits lit me up inside. I admired how her hard edges balanced her soft side.

Beyond that, Sloane was also stubborn, smart, and resilient. All traits that complemented my role as provost perfectly. She took care of everyone else, ignored her own needs, and basically hissed at me anytime I helped her. It only made me want her more.

Soon I'd make my intentions perfectly clear, but I had to convince her about me first.

Striding back to the front door, I opened it, and about a foot of snow fell inside.

"The storm's the worst I've seen yet. What makes you think you're going anywhere?"

"Seriously?" Sloane came to the door and peered out. Even though it was late afternoon, it was almost as dark as night, and the snow raged with the intensity of, well, a dragon. There was no way anyone was going anywhere at this point. Pulling out my phone, I put a village-wide alert out to shelter in place, and then sent a text to Broca that Sloane was with me and safe.

"Just telling Broca you're here with me." I held up my phone, and Sloane bristled.

"I'm capable of checking in with my family, thank you very much."

"Aye, lass, but now you don't have to. Come on. Let's get you some food."

"I'm not hungry."

"I am."

"So eat." Sloane shrugged out from under my arm, and I grinned, already knowing where this was going. I'd allow her to keep pushing me back, but when she came to my bed, it would need to be by her choice.

"Come on." I nudged Sloane down a hallway toward my dressing room, and her mouth fell open when she walked through the door.

"Is this how you live?" Sloane twirled, looking at the massive dressing room attached to the bedroom, a meal already set up at a small table by the fireplace.

"Such a shame, I know. It's a wonder how I get by." I smirked at the irritation that flashed across Sloane's face until she realized I was joking.

"Must be nice."

"'Tis. No complaints here. But I would like to get you into warm clothes." I pointed toward a pile that the maid had left out. "Go on. I won't look, I promise."

"Like I'd change in front of you." If Sloane's lips weren't tinged blue, I was certain she'd have denied the clothes, but instead she grabbed the bundle and stomped into the en suite, mumbling about how stupidly gorgeous everything was. When she came back out, her hair tied in a knot on her head, in a soft robe wrapped around knit pajamas, I wanted to go to her. My arms ached with wanting to hold her close, but there was tension in her shoulders, and a sadness in her expression that I needed to get to the bottom of. Something had happened today, something significant, that had allowed her magick to create a dragon.

"Do you know the best meal for a storm?"

"What's that?" Sloane asked, skirting along the walls of the bedroom and staying as far away from the four-poster bed as she could. Which meant she was absolutely thinking what I was thinking, and lust tugged low inside me.

"Cheese toasties and tomato soup." I pulled the cover off the food and held it up, and Sloane's expression softened.

"A fan favorite. And one of the few things I can cook." Sloane glanced at the door to my bedroom and then back to the table. "Will Blue be okay?"

"Blue is currently being roundly spoiled by Henry, I can promise you that. Henry has a soft spot for emberwolves, and he has one of the gentlest hands with animals I've ever seen. Despite my parents' great annoyance with me bringing home every animal under the sun, Henry was always there to help."

"Do your parents get annoyed with you a lot?" Sloane slipped into the chair and I held the wine bottle up. She nodded, and I poured us both a glass of a rich cabernet sauvignon and waited until she took a sip and nodded her approval. Sitting across from her, I relaxed. She looked so warm and lovely by the firelight, more vulnerable than I'd ever seen her, and I wanted to know this side of Sloane too.

"Aye, they do. And yet, somehow, they've entrusted everything to me, and not my brothers. Even though they critique every last thing I do." Compliments were few and far between in my family.

"That seems counterintuitive. Either they trust you or they don't. If they don't, they should be here taking care of things. If they do, they shouldn't get to weigh in on every choice you make."

"Yes, but then what else will keep them busy in their retirement?" I'd meant it as a joke, but Sloane leveled those all-seeing eyes on mine.

"No, Knox. It's wrong. You're doing a great job with Briarhaven, and despite your whole hero complex you've got going on, the town is lucky to have you. Your folks should realize that."

"Thank you," I said, oddly touched. I hadn't been seeking compliments from her, but her approval meant something to me. It settled around my shoulders, a warm blanket on what few insecurities I did have, and I beamed at her. "I think you're finally warming up to me."

"I wouldn't go that far." Sloane sniffed and then took a bite of her toastie, made with thick sourdough and oozing with melted cheese. I was certain Blue would be pestering her for a bite if he were in here. "You still want me to leave town."

"Och, not anymore, lass. I want to reverse the curse. I'd be a much happier lad if you stayed."

"Seriously?" Sloane arched an eyebrow at me. "It could take months, nae, years before the curse is fixed. Look what's happened already. You can't possibly say you're willing to put up with this nonsense for much longer."

Nobody else had.

The unspoken words hung between us, but I could read the underlying meaning as loud as if she'd said them. My mind flashed back to the sullen-faced girl, her parents screaming inside, and realized that nobody had really stood up for her before. Which meant I had to. Sloane was mine, and I realized I needed to show her that not everyone would leave the moment they faced a hardship.

"So?" I said, keeping my tone light, suspecting she needed it. "We figure it out."

Sloane stood abruptly, outrage on her face, and threw her hands in the air.

"Why does everyone keep saying that? Like it's so easy? We spent years here and nothing came of it except my parents almost killing each other. Who is to say the same won't happen again? I have the same magick as my mother, Knox. It misfires *every* single day. I have no idea what will come, no control over anything, and I'm supposed to just . . . to just . . . to just *accept* that?" Sloane's lower lip wobbled, and I went to her. Pulling her against me, I tilted her face up with a finger to see her eyes swimming with unshed tears.

"Why don't you let go for a little bit?" I asked, brushing my lips lightly over hers.

"I can't." Sloane half sobbed against my mouth.

"Why not?"

"Because if I do . . . it could all fall apart. Who will take care of everyone? Of me?"

"Your sisters are adults. They can manage. And I'll take care of you."

Sloane reared back, blinking up at me, but I held her tight against my waist.

"You? You'll take care of me? Listen, buddy, I don't need a—"

"I know, Sloane. You've proven to the world you don't need anyone to rescue you. But what if you let go . . . just for a little bit?"

"What happens then?" Suspicion rose on her impossibly lovely face.

"Why don't you find out? What say you, Sloane? It's just you and me in here. There's nowhere to go. Nobody needs you for anything right now. This is about you. What do you want? Right now, in this moment?"

I could see the flames of the fire reflected in her eyes, and I waited, the moment drawing out, tension snapping back and forth between us.

"I want you."

CHAPTER TWENTY-ONE
Sloane

As the words left my mouth, I could already feel it, a loosening inside of me, like a knot untying. How nice would it be to hand the control over to someone else, if even for just a moment? I felt safe here.

Knox had been there for me, repeatedly, every time my magick had gone astray.

But it was more than that.

He was more than that.

Knox wasn't just a fixer; he was steady. He showed up for people, for this town, and even for a family that had left him behind. We were not so very different, him and I, even though I was certain the bed he was about to lay me down on was covered in sheets of silk. His eyes had darkened, something unfathomable and yearning swimming in their depths, and need rose inside me, demanding an escape.

I wanted to feast, but when I reached for his neck, wanting to pull his mouth to mine, he angled his head back.

"Nuh-uh, Sloane. I'm the one in charge now."

"But," I said, confused. Intrigued. I was used to taking the lead in the bedroom, having my needs met exactly as I wanted, leaving a lover sleeping and sated in the bed as I slipped out and moved to the next town. Not that I took lovers all that often, but when I did, I made it count.

"Let it happen." Knox swallowed my next protest with a kiss, hitching me up against him, rubbing my body against his as he dropped me lightly onto the bed. I looked up at him, just simply admiring the view, as he stripped off his shirt. He'd changed into gray sweatpants at some point, slung low at the hips, and already the material was tented from where he wanted me. It was staggering, really, the number of muscles he had rippling across his abdomen, and his thick arms bunched as he reached up and ripped off a silken cord attached to the curtains around the bed.

"Knox!" I gasped. "Nooo, I can't get in trouble for ruining another pair of curtains."

"Don't worry." Knox loomed over me, the golden cord dangling lightly in hands. "Oswald already beat you to these."

"What are you planning to do with . . ." I trailed off as Knox bent over and brushed the softest of kisses across my lips as he angled one of my arms over my head, and then the other. My hands brushed the cool wood of one of the posts on the four-poster bed, and I shivered as I realized his intentions.

"I get the sense that you won't actually let me take charge unless I stop you from doing so." Knox knelt, one knee pressed at the apex of my thighs, and I moaned as he pushed gently up, rubbing his thigh against where I wanted him most. I rolled my hips, my body arching, craving his touch. "But I'm going to need your permission first, Sloane."

"You want to tie my hands up?" I gasped as I rocked against him, surprised at the need that had already built inside me. What was even more surprising was how unopposed I was to having him tie me up. Everyday Sloane would have balked at such a suggestion, but there was something about him that made me willing to try this. In fact, I was even becoming quite excited at just the thought of it.

"Aye, lass." His timbre was low, a growl at my throat, and I couldn't tell who was more surprised when a nervous giggle escaped from my lips.

"Um, yes, I think that would be nice," I said, still rocking against his leg.

"Your safe word is 'silk.'"

"Bloody hell." I gaped up at him. "Do I need a safe word? What do you plan to do to me?" Half-intrigued, half-terrified, I watched as he raised the cord over my head.

"I want you to feel safe, Sloane. That means you need an out."

"Right. Silk." Immediately, Knox stopped all movement and backed off, and I whimpered as his thigh left where I burned for him.

"No?" I asked stupidly as a soft grin crossed his face.

"If you say it, I stop," Knox explained gently, firelight flickering across the hollows of his cheekbones.

"Oh. Right. Right. Um, you may proceed." My throat went dry, and my nerves kicked up as he wound the silken cord around my wrists, pulling it tight enough that even when I tugged, I couldn't easily slip my hands out. I was well and truly tied up, and a shiver of panic slipped up my back, making me a touch uncertain of what I'd just agreed to. I swallowed again as Knox leaned back and traced a finger sensually down my cleavage.

My clothes vanished, and I cried out.

"Knox!" Pulling at the cord, I writhed as I realized I had nothing to cover myself, and that I was just laid bare for this man, feeling exposed and uncertain. Embarrassment made my skin flush.

"Shhh," Knox said, trailing his hands down my sides. His touch was warm, his caress insistent, and some of the nerves lessened as he devoured me with his eyes. "Stunning, sexy Sloane. I've dreamt of you."

"You have?" I blinked up at him, derailed from my embarrassment, as he stood and walked to the table to get my glass of wine. Returning, he held it to my lips, and I gulped, grateful for the luscious wine to wet my throat.

"Och, about every night since you've been home. I've ached for you, Sloane. Touched myself over and over, craving this very moment. And now? It's even better than my dream. Just look at you. Every man's fantasy, laid out for my pleasure."

"I don't know about that," I began, but Knox stopped my words with a kiss, his lips wet with wine.

"Maybe not every man's, but mine. The only man who shall be fantasizing after you. You're everything I've ever wanted, Sloane, beautiful both inside and out, and I can't stop thinking about you."

"Oh." I wish I could have come up with something more eloquent, but all conscious thought left the building when he dipped a finger in the glass of wine and dripped some of the liquid onto my nipple. The cool liquid hit my burning skin, and I gasped as his mouth followed, hot and moist against my breast, his tongue swirling the peak as I arched into his mouth. Somehow, the man managed to drive me crazy, and I bucked under him, while he held the wineglass steady and away from where he bent to my breasts, his dark hair gleaming in the firelight. I wanted to run my hand through his hair, to keep him there, pressed against me, pleasure rocketing through me. But the fact that I could do nothing made it that much worse.

And somehow so, so, so much better.

Pleasure spiraled through me, like one of those whizzy firecrackers that burst out and buzzed around in circles, and I exploded under his touch, sobbing as he sucked my nipples, scraping his teeth lightly over me as I rode his thigh into oblivion. When I shuddered to a stop, gasping for air, Knox knelt above me, a cheeky grin on his face.

I gasped at the hundreds of silky pink plumeria flower petals on the bed.

"Did you do that?"

"No, darling. Remember, your magick tends to go a bit haywire when you're . . . stimulated." His hands traced languorously up and down my thighs.

"Whoops," I said, but I couldn't bring myself to feel bad about it. The flowers added an exotic flair to this moment, spicing the air with their sweet scent.

"And we've only just begun, witchling. When was the last time you took pleasure for yourself?"

It had been ages, really, since I'd done anything. Self-care, in any form, had fallen to the back burner.

"Um." I couldn't really answer that, not when he dribbled some wine on my stomach. Putting the glass aside, I watched as he casually stripped, and almost swallowed my tongue at the sight of him. Long, thick, and supremely well equipped, as I'd assumed the first night I fell on him. But seeing him now, at full length and ready for ravaging, so to speak, my insides went liquid. I wanted him inside me, all over me, and I mewled in distress as he prowled around the bed.

"Soon, love, soon." I watched as he protected himself with a condom—modern conveniences for modern witches, after all—and then dropped between my legs. His lips found the wine on my abdomen, and he kissed his way gently down, ignoring where I wanted him most. I bucked, and he placed one strong hand on my stomach, holding me down as he sunk his teeth into the soft flesh of my thigh.

"Ouch," I hissed.

"Shhh," Knox said, licking across my abused flesh. He lifted that gorgeous face of his to mine. I had to take a moment, just to revel in the view of this insanely handsome man kneeling between my legs, a sexy grin on his face. "Do you not like when I bite you, Sloane?"

"No, I do." In fact, I'd liked it more than I'd realized, and when he bit again, likely bruising my skin a bit, the soft tremors of another orgasm rose inside me.

"*Mine*," Knox said softly, biting again. "I want to mark you as mine, Sloane, in any way that you'll let me."

The comment was so basely male, so extremely egotistical, that I wanted to rear up and smack that cheeky grin off his face. And at the same time, it was so intensely hot that I collapsed back against the cushions as a sharp wave of lust spiked through me. Damn it, I didn't want it to excite me so much. But having someone claim me as their own?

Nobody had ever said those words to me before.

And now, here was this gorgeous man, chanting them against my thighs, burrowing his head between my legs until his tongue found me in one glorious slide of heat. My back bowed, and I whimpered as his mouth assaulted me, the slick, warm deliciousness of his tongue on me dragging me sharply to the edge once more.

"Stop, stop, stop," I breathed until finally he pulled back.

"That's the not the safe word, Sloane," Knox said idly, and slipped a finger inside me as I gaped down at him. Trying to stay focused, I panted as he toyed with me, sliding another finger inside, widening me, as he found the sweetest bit of delight inside me. "What were you wanting to say?"

I was pretty sure my eyes had rolled back in my head at this point, and I was actively riding his hand as he loomed over me, patiently waiting for me to speak.

"I want you," I finally gasped out, trying desperately not to orgasm yet. "Inside me. I want you, Knox."

"Och, that's a good lass. Those are the words I've been waiting to hear." Knox pulled his hand from me, and shifted, positioning himself against me. His hand was slick at my side, and when he lowered his lips to mine, I could taste myself in his kiss. It was heady, erotic, and deeply intimate, and I moaned against his mouth, pulling against the ties that bound me back. Knox rubbed against me, toying, just the tip, as I kissed him, desperate for more.

"Say it again, Sloane."

"Bloody hell, Knox."

"Say it."

Annoyed, beyond aroused, and desperately aching for him, I glared up at him.

"I want you inside me."

"Not that." Knox laughed as I fumed, letting out the sound a kettle makes.

"What exactly do you want me to say?" I ground out, shifting my hips, trying to get him to slide inside me, but still he teased me, sliding himself over me, but never in me. My need was an overfilled balloon, ready to pop, and I wanted to scream.

"That you're mine, Sloane. Tell me you're mine. Not just now, not just in this moment. But for real."

"I . . . I . . ." I blinked up at him, and for a moment, I saw the vulnerability there.

A yearning.

That matched my own.

We both wanted to belong somewhere, didn't we? I could understand this emotion, even if it scared the ever-loving hell out of me, and I could only do the one thing that made the most sense at the moment.

Be one hundred percent honest.

"I'm yours." I whispered it, unsure if I'd be able to say it comfortably to his face in the light of the morning, but here, as the storm raged outside and the flames flickered in the grate, here I could show him the shadows of my heart.

"There you are," Knox said. His lips claimed mine in a searing kiss, and he entered me in one long stroke, filling me so completely that I shattered against him, my body convulsing around his hardness, loving the feeling of being completely covered and filled by him. He pumped into me, my hips rolling, matching him thrust for thrust, as my pleasure built once more.

Not being able to touch him was the single most infuriating and erotic experience in my life. There was nothing I could do but give over to him as he pounded against me, hard against soft, the slick rhythm throwing me over the edge once more, and I broke around him as he bent his forehead to mine.

"Bloody hell, Sloane. You've ruined me." Knox caught my lips in a searing kiss, his words imprinting on my heart, and then he shuddered against me as he found his own release.

He rested beside me, just for a moment, his breath hot at my throat.

"Incredible." Angling up, and over me, Knox peppered sharp short kisses against my lips. "Stunning. Immaculate. Mind-blowing."

I blushed, even though a giggle threatened to bubble up. Knox reached up and untied my wrists, kissing the skin there gently. Once I was released, a wave of shyness swept over me, and I crossed my arms over my chest.

That had been *so* outside my comfort zone.

No man had ever taken control of my body and owned my pleasure like one Knox Douglas had.

"Come here." Knox patted the crook of his arm, and when I hesitated, feeling uncertain now that it was over, he sighed and pulled me close, rolling me easily so he was the big spoon.

I had no idea what to think, no frame of reference for how to explain just how he had made me feel. He'd completely unraveled me and put me back together again, shined a light into all of the shadowy corners of my soul. And I wasn't sure what to say or do after an experience like that. If he was any other person and this had been any other situation, I would have patted him on the bum and thanked him for a nice time before strolling out. But since the first time I'd seen Knox again, he'd put me on my back foot and kept me there, and now I was struggling to reconcile my feelings for him.

When I opened my mouth to speak, to say anything that could shore up my walls, he just tucked me closer and pulled the blanket over us.

"Rest a bit now, Sloane. You can fight your battles another time."

I smiled at the windows, loving and hating how well he already knew me.

And despite it all, my lids fluttered closed, and I fell into the first deep sleep I'd had in ages.

CHAPTER TWENTY-TWO

Knox

I woke before Sloane, comfortable and cozied at her side, and took a moment to just savor how great I felt. Waking up, with her next to me, made me feel complete in a way that I hadn't known I'd needed.

Her dark lashes fanned across her cheeks, and her hair was a tumbled mess around her head. I shifted, moving closer, and her eyes fluttered open, her gaze shifting to me.

I could see the instant she put her walls up.

It was almost physical, the way she protected herself, her expression going from sleepy and vulnerable to guarded in five seconds flat.

Which was fine. This was all fine. I had patience and I believed in my ability to gain someone's trust. Sloane just needed to give me time, and I'd show her that I could be a constant in her life.

I grinned as she pushed up, rumpled and awkward, and made use of the bathroom, likely checking if there was another door out so she could slip away undetected. I rolled in the breakfast cart that I had called for, let a happy Blue in, and brought the food to the table with him at my heels.

When she came out, dressed once more in her own clothes, hair knotted back on top of her head, she skidded to a stop when she saw Blue sitting in his own chair at the table, a small plate of food in front of him.

"Oh," Sloane said, her eyes darting around the room. Everywhere but my face, really. Smiling, I strode across the room and cupped her chin in my hand. Bending, I took her lips in a searing kiss that left no doubt about how I felt about her, and she moaned gently into my mouth, softening against me.

"Good morning, witchling. I wasn't sure what you liked for breakfast, so I ordered a bit of everything."

"Coffee," Sloane said, swallowing thickly. Taking her hand, I nudged her into a chair.

"Did you have a nice night, buddy?" Sloane said, reaching out to scratch behind Blue's wings, and he wiggled in his seat.

Oswald ran from me for part of the night, but once we ignored him, he came back to play.

"That sounds about right for Oswald." I laughed and poured Sloane a cup of coffee.

"I love that you can hear Blue speak," Sloane murmured, her face buried in the cup that I had handed to her.

The dragon left early this morning, before light, but said to tell us he'd be around if we ever need him. He was happy with whatever meal Henry fed him.

"Henry has a particular affection for dragons. As a forest ogre, I think his kin often interacted with them," I told Blue.

"I really have so much to learn about this place. Like, I know we grew up knowing magickals were about, but I guess maybe it's just that myopic nature of youth at times? I think I was just so focused on my own stuff that I didn't really ask too many questions about the others that lived in Briarhaven."

"Understandable." I was pleased that Sloane was talking, sharing more about her past with me, and maybe I would be able to help her break down that wall she'd so carefully erected after she'd awoken. "I think kids can be forgiven for not seeing the world around them more clearly. They're still learning. I only knew about most of the magickals because they were constantly in and out of the castle."

"I still can't believe you grew up in a castle." Sloane slanted me a look.

"It had its perks."

"I bet." Sloane quieted, her expression tightening as she eyed the drapes pulled back from the window to reveal softly falling snow. I sat across from her and crossed my arms over my chest, waiting.

"So." Sloane took a few healthy gulps of her coffee, and I let her gather her thoughts.

This was where she was going to try to tell me that once was all we'd get of each other.

"So," I repeated when the silence drew out, knowing she was struggling. "Why don't we skip the part where you try to push me out of your life, and you just accept that I'm around for the long haul, and we take it day by day from here?"

Sloane's mouth dropped open, and I wanted to pull her back to bed and kiss her until she forgot all of the insecurities that had crept back in this morning.

"I wasn't going to push you out of my life," Sloane grumbled, burying her face in her coffee again.

"Weren't you?" I raised an eyebrow.

"Maybe just a wee bit of space," Sloane conceded, and I laughed.

"Yeah, all that. Why don't we skip it? Let's just give this a proper go and see what happens. I reckon we'll be quite happy if we do."

"You make it sound so easy." Sloane gulped her coffee at an alarming rate, and I filled another cup for her. "But I'm cursed. Nothing about dating me is easy. Why would you want to deal with all that?"

I couldn't say aloud what I'd been thinking: *Because I want you and feel as though I've been waiting all this time for you to come back.*

"Because nothing great in life comes easily, Sloane. The hard work makes the reward that much sweeter."

I beamed at her when she just stared at me, caught on my words, her brain trying to come up with some solution. At some point, she'd have to understand that I was the answer, not the problem. I'd just have to wait her out until she saw that I really meant what I said.

"But you don't know me all that well, Knox. I'm fiercely independent. Difficult. Bitchy. Annoying. Ask my sisters."

"And I suspect they'd all say a lot of great things about you too. Nobody's perfect, Sloane. And I like your sharp edges. They challenge me. I don't need everything in my life to come easily to me. Will you give us a chance?" There, I'd laid it bare, holding my breath. I wasn't going to push her, not yet at least, but I really hoped she'd consider dating me.

"Like a trial run?" Sloane asked tentatively.

"Sure, a trial run. Some would even call it 'dating.' Let's date, Sloane. No pressure. After you deem the trial run to be over, you can let me know if you're keeping me or returning me."

"Returning you to whom?" Jealously spiked in Sloane's impossibly beautiful eyes, and I suppressed my grin.

"Just a turn of phrase, witchling."

"Knox." Sloane gave me a look. "I don't stay."

"Maybe you will . . . this time."

"And if I don't?"

"We can figure it out. There are always solutions, you know that."

"You can't leave here. Briarhaven is your home."

"Maybe it is time for someone else to come run it a bit while I stretch my wings." Reaching over, I patted Blue, who grinned up at me, a happy wee emberwolf.

"You make it sound so easy. But it's not."

"And you're creating troubles for yourself before they're here. Listen. You said it yourself. Trial run. We'll take it a day at a time. Deal?" I reached my hand out to Sloane, and when she finally gave it to me, I turned it over and placed a kiss on her palm. She shivered in her seat, and when I licked the skin, blowing a breath across it, she shivered again. Slanting a glance at Blue, she pulled her hand back.

"Not in front of the children." Sloane reprimanded me with a small smile, and I was grateful to see it. She was warming up to the idea of us, on her terms of course, and I'd take what I could get.

"Understood. Shall I give you a ride home?"

Sloane groaned and slapped her hands to her face. "I forgot! We don't have a car anymore. Bloody hell, now what?"

"Take one of mine." I shrugged and snagged a piece of bacon.

"What?" Sloane's eyes widened.

"I have several. Just take one."

"Oh my goddess. Is this what it is like dating rich people? I can't just take a car, Knox."

"Fine, I'll gift it to you."

"Have you lost your *mind*? You don't just give someone a car."

"I have it on good authority it happens all the time. They even make these massive bows to put on cars. It's a thing. Look it up."

"I know it's a thing." Sloane sighed. "It's just not our thing."

"It can be." I grinned when Sloane made a frustrated noise.

"No, it can't. You need insurance, and title stuff, and all the adult things that go with getting a car. You can't just give someone it."

"Would it be easier if I buy you one? They'll do all that at the dealership right then."

"What? No." Sloane rose, frustrated, and began to pace. Blue's gaze followed her, his ever-present smile on his face. "You don't need to buy my love, Knox."

"I'm well aware of that."

"So why in the world would you offer me a car?"

"Because I'm your friend and you need one? I can just lend you the use of it if that makes you feel better. Insurance should cover driving in my car."

"Just a loan?" Sloane eyed me suspiciously.

"Sure. We'll call it a trial run."

Sloane's expression turned mulish, and I waited, hoping she would laugh, and when a smile broke through, I sighed in relief.

"Damn it." Sloane shook her head and waved for Blue to fly into her arms. He slammed into her chest with the grace of a toddler hopped up on too much sugar. "Fine, Knox. I will accept your extremely temporary loan of a car until we figure out a better solution."

"You're welcome." I grinned when Sloane slanted me a look.

"Thank you," Sloane added, stiffly at that. I wanted to hug and kiss her until she relaxed, just eased up a bit, but I knew this wasn't the time. Not yet. It was going to be incremental, with her, and I well understood why. So long as she gave us a fighting chance, I'd be happy.

On the way downstairs, I hummed softly to myself, feeling happy and relaxed for the first time in a long time. Sure, we had a curse to break, and the town was raging about the constant snow, but I liked challenges. I know it didn't make sense, but it was nice to feel needed, to be able to fix things, and having problems meant I could find solutions. Call it a hero complex, or just a life of someone who didn't like to be bored, but either way, obstacles were my thing. I was going to help the MacGregors, one way or another, because I think they deserved it. The sisters *deserved* an honest chance at a happy life. This curse was unfair to them, and to the towns they tried to live in. It had gone on long enough.

My phone rang, and I pulled it from my pocket, swiping up as my mum's name came up. It was a video call, and I angled so Sloane was on the screen.

"Say hi to Sloane," I instructed my mum, and I could see the same expressions of shock on each woman's face as they stared each other down on the phone.

"Um, hello, Mrs. Douglas." Sloane nodded.

"Why is she there so early in the morning?"

"Because we are dating. Do I need to provide more detailed information?" I raised an eyebrow at my mother as she gasped, and Sloane elbowed me in the ribs, ducking out of the screen.

"Knox, how uncouth."

"Get used to it. Sloane and I are dating, and what you just said was rude. Do better." I hung up and Sloane rounded on me.

"Knox! You can't speak to your mother like that."

"Sure I can. If she has an issue with what I do with my life, she can get back here and say it to my face. Until then, I quite simply do not care. I have taken care of this house and this town for years now, while they travel and do anything they please. It's my turn to enjoy some happiness, and I'll be damned if she gets to suck the joy from my life."

"Oh." Sloane's mouth rounded.

"And yes, that happiness means you." I brushed a kiss on Sloane's lips, and then continued on down the hallway. I only paused when I realized she wasn't following me. Turning, I caught her cuddling Blue close, her eyes caught on a painting. Wandering back, I looked at the painting she was staring at.

It was the one with the man standing by the blue cart.

"What's caught your eye?"

"Look." Sloane pointed, and I leaned closer to see a blue book in his hand. The same blue book that Oswald had given her.

"Ahhh, that makes sense. Eoin always regretted not being able to help Bonelle."

Sloane gave me an odd look.

"So the hero complex runs through generations?"

"We're knights, baby, can't really train that out of us." I grinned at Sloane's annoyed huff of breath.

"But look, there are a lot of people in the background. And the emberwolves! See, there's one." She angled Blue so he could look at the painting too. "I wonder if this is the day it happened."

"It might be." I strained my eyes as a thought occurred to me. Many of the people featured at the festival in the background still had family lineage here.

"It feels meaningful. But I'm not sure why." Sloane worried her bottom lip, and I dropped a kiss on top of her head.

"Maybe because Eoin couldn't save Bonelle all those years ago, but I might be able to save you now." I had an idea how to help, but I needed to dig a little further first. Not wanting to set hope alight quite yet, I decided against telling Sloane my thoughts.

"Oh," Sloane breathed, her eyes caught on the painting. "I didn't realize. That's your ancestor. Duh, of course. Did he help Bonelle?"

"I think to a point, but in the end, I'm told he had to choose between the village and her. So she ran."

"Poor thing," Sloane said, her face wreathed in sadness. "So young to be on her own."

"But unlike her, you're not on your own now. And we'll fix this."

"You say that so confidently." Sloane shook her head and moved away from the painting. "I wish I could feel the same."

"Fake it 'til you make it, witchling."

"Is that what you do?"

"Sometimes, if I have to. Everything has an answer. In time. We just don't know it yet. But we have a lot of smart people who care about you in this town."

"I think you're being optimistic on the 'care about me' part of this. They care about Briarhaven."

"And you're a part of Briarhaven." Sloane opened her mouth to argue with me, but I cut her off with a kiss. Hunger unfurled in me, and I braced one arm over her head, leaning into the kiss.

A whisper of wind was the only warning I had, and when I looked down, my clothes had turned see-through. Even better? So were Sloane's. Blue took off from her arms, making a chortling noise that sounded dangerously like he was laughing, and I raised an eyebrow at Sloane.

"Something on your mind, love?"

"Oh. My. Goddess," Sloane breathed. Her cheeks tinged pink, and her eyes widened as she stared down at me.

At where I was very much reacting to where her magick had taken her today.

"It looks like we may be a touch late to starting our day." I scooped her into my arms, and even though she let out a small shriek of protest, she didn't tell me to stop. Bounding back to my room, I kicked the door shut behind me.

"You know what, Sloane? This misfiring magick might be quite a bit of fun after all."

"Nooooo," Sloane moaned, even as I ran my hands under her clear jumper, lust pinging crazily through my brain. "It's the worst."

"Is it?" I cupped her breasts in my hands, delighted with the clear view.

"Knox, I need to get..." Sloane's voice trailed off as I tapped my finger against her breastbone, pulling at my magick, and her clear clothes disappeared. Her mouth fell open. "I will never get used to that."

"Magick certainly has its uses," I said, pushing her back against the door and threading my fingers around her throat.

Whatever Sloane was about to say died at her lips as I lightly tightened my hold, delighting as her eyes dilated with lust.

Oh yes, my fiery Sloane liked when I took command. Her throat moved under my palm, a nervous swallow, and I grinned as I brought my mouth to a pert nipple and bit lightly. Sloane sucked in a breath and arched against me, but I held her pinned.

"Knox." Her voice was shaky with need.

"Aye, lass?" I traced a finger down the soft slope of her stomach and found her seam. She shifted, automatically widening her legs, and I laughed against her breast. "Och, that's a good lass, isn't it, then?"

"I should hate this," Sloane admitted, swallowing a moan as I slid a finger inside her, finding her wet and ready for me.

"Should you, though?" I lifted my face to find her expression caught between stubbornness and hunger, and I reached deeper, finding that soft spot inside her that made her legs buck and tremble.

"I..." Sloane closed her eyes, leaning her head back against the door, her hair tumbling over her shoulders as I worked her quickly to the edge. When I thought she was close, I eased back, barely able to stop myself from driving deep inside her. Stepping back, I wrapped an arm around her waist and guided her to the bed, turning her so her hands were on the mattress.

"Stay."

"I'm not a dog, Knox." Sloane turned and glared at me over her shoulder, and I winked as I sheathed myself with a condom and bent over her. Gripping her hips, I positioned myself at her tight entrance and nudged lightly inside. Playing.

"No, you're certainly not. What you are is mine, Sloane. Mine to do what I want with." I shoved deep inside of her and her moan came out long and keening. "Mine to claim. Mine to bring to pleasure over and over. Because that's how you like it, don't you, witchling? You like it when someone else takes over, for once, and you just get to let go. Am I right, my beauty?"

"Yes," Sloane gasped, pushing back against me as I drove into her, rocking her sweet round body against mine. "Yes, please."

"Please what, Sloane?" My fingers dug into her flesh, and I increased my speed, sliding fully out and slamming back into her.

"Faster," Sloane gasped, throwing her head back so her hair fell down her back. "Harder. Please, Knox."

"As my lady wishes."

We exploded at the same time, and I gasped as a pleasure so pure and bright shook my body.

Damn it, but I wanted this woman.

Every day.

By my side.

Arguing with me over dinner.

In bed with me.

Now I just had to convince her that this whole dating thing was meant to be oh so much more.

CHAPTER TWENTY-THREE
Sloane

"Oh, good morning, Sloane. Don't you look . . . rested." Nova fluttered her eyelashes at me.

Three grinning faces greeted me when I walked in the door with Blue, and I pursed my lips, wanting to be annoyed with all of them. We hadn't left on the best of terms, and yet my body was sated from two rounds of extraordinary lovemaking, and despite my doubts about finding a solution to this curse, if anyone could do it, it would be Knox. He exuded a quiet, and sometimes not-so-quiet, confidence about handling trouble, and he had somehow managed to kick-start a small spark of hope in my gut.

"I am, thank you." I lifted my chin, determined to buzz past them and their nosy faces and go enjoy a nice hot shower. Blue launched from my arms, doing a lazy circle around the room, and went to the kitchen to investigate for any leftover snacks.

I slammed into an invisible wall.

"Ow!" Luckily, my hands had caught the brunt of it, and not my face, and I turned to glare at the only witch powerful enough to pull off that little trick.

My darling grandmother, who was dressed in screaming fire engine red today and pointing with one finger at the couch.

"Sit."

"I'm an adult, Broca. I can do what I want. I'd like a shower, and then I can come chat."

"Gotta wash all the nasty off her from last night," Nova whispered to Lyra, and the two giggled while I sucked in a breath, ready to flay them with my words.

"Enough." Broca continued to point at the couch. "Sit, Sloane. You'll have time to shower before the festival. We need to sort this out."

"Also, I would dearly like full details of your night with Knox." Lyra raised her hand with a cheeky look on her face.

"Is it true you conjured a dragon?" Broca cut right to the chase when I dropped to the couch, arms crossed over my chest, determined not to spill any details about my time with Knox. Embarrassment crept in.

"Aye." I hung my head. "I don't even know how I did it."

"High emotions." Broca tapped a finger against her lips, her glasses a deep cobalt blue today. "But your mother was never this powerful. I've been treating this like you two are much the same, but now I'm seeing you're anything but. Most witches in total command of their full power would never be able to summon a dragon, Sloane. And you did that without even trying. You need to understand the intensity and severity of your power, and we need to train you to put safeguards in place until we figure out how to reverse this misfiring magick curse."

It was a relief to know I was nothing like my mother, even if it frankly terrified me to no end to hear how powerful I was. Maybe that would be fun once I was in command of my power, but as of now I felt like my magick was a ticking time bomb.

"This afternoon, you and I are going to work on a containment spell. This is basically a way for you to take your magick, shove it down in a little box inside of you, and keep it under wraps unless absolutely needed. I think it will be the best solution going forward until we figure this out."

"And if we don't?" I looked around at my sisters, their faces crestfallen.

"We will."

"Everyone keeps saying that. And yet." I waved a hand in the air. "How many generations haven't been able to break this curse? Why us? Why now?"

"Three sisters, eleven months apart. It's your destiny." Broca's eyes softened behind her glasses. "I'm certain of it."

"And you think Briarhaven is going to put up with our curse on the town for the next two years until these two come into their magick?" I rolled my eyes. "It's only been a few weeks, and already people want to run us out of town."

"Yes, but we can handle this. Like we did last time. We just need to get the Charms on board to help."

"Yeah, Sloane. Give this a chance. Please?" Lyra begged me. Nova just crossed her arms and glowered.

"Fine." I couldn't believe I was saying it, but a part of me that I wasn't ready to examine too closely yet wanted to stay too. Not just because I'd had some of the best sex of my life last night, and this morning, with what seemed to be a genuinely good guy—but because my wee family seemed to be happy here. Lyra was filming more content than ever for her baking channel, and Nova's sketchbooks were positively booming with new art. Broca's face wasn't as troubled, and she laughed freely in a way she hadn't when both my parents had been around. She had lifelong friends here who had been visiting her each day.

And then there was me.

I had Blue to think about now. He needed a safe, magickal place to live.

I had Raven, my childhood friend who had forgiven my absence.

And the Charms were even starting to grow on me a bit.

The way we'd always lived might not be the solution anymore. If I was going to appoint myself the unofficial leader of this little faction of ours, then I also needed to learn when to bend. It might not be easy, particularly with the snow that continued to assault our little town, but I was beginning to actually believe that we might have a chance at beating this thing.

And I would never know if I didn't at least try.

"Seriously?" Nova sucked in a breath.

"Aye." I nodded, surprised when both my sisters jumped up and piled on top of me, squealing. Their sudden attack sent Blue into a tizzy and he wheeled around the room, barking loudly between little shots of fire, and we all screeched as he nearly burned our hair off.

"Blue, buddy, come here." I waved him over so he would stop singeing us, and he slammed onto our cuddle pile, worming himself in between all of us, his tongue slathering my face with smoky-smelling saliva. "Ewww."

"Do we have Knox to thank for this change of heart?" Broca asked as we righted ourselves on the couch. Did they?

"Nobody's perfect, Sloane. And I like your sharp edges. They challenge me. I don't need everything in my life to come easily to me."

Yes, Knox Douglas was definitely one reason I wanted to try to stay.

"A bit, maybe." I shrugged, uncertain how to articulate all the feelings pinging around inside me. "It's just . . . he really seems to think we can break this curse. He's full on. And he carries this absolute conviction that everything will work out for him. It's hard not to be swayed when someone like that tells you everything is going to be just fine."

"His track record is pretty good so far. He's not a bad guy to have on our side." Broca waved a hand in the air. "Now let your sister go shower. We need to pick out our outfits for later."

"Are you going too?" I asked Broca as I rose.

"Of course. One doesn't miss a festival simply because one has a bad hip. Knox has commissioned a sleigh just for me."

I winced, having a good idea just where that sleigh had come from, and dearly hoped it would be drawn by regular horses this time. Retreating to my room before I had to answer any other questions, I stopped by the window to look out at Briarhaven. Gray clouds blanketed the sky, a permanent fixture these days, and snow barreled down relentlessly. My neighbor frowned at me and raised his hand. It was just a quick jerk, but for the first time, he waved. A salute almost.

To my surprise, the gesture brought hot, sharp tears to my eyes. Returning it, I ducked into the shower and laid my cheek against the wall while the warm water sluiced down my back, mirroring the tears that ran the length of my face.

The hardest thing to admit, at least to myself, was that I wanted this more than anyone. It was easier to avoid the painful memories here, to stay on the move, and to never set down roots. Settling down in one spot was a siren song I'd long evaded. Even the thought of having a chance to start over here, to make a real life for ourselves, was enough to crack open the lid on those long-ago-buried dreams.

My own house.

A love life.

A family, even.

Such simple things, and I know my ancestors before me had managed them, but they'd had to do so always on the go. We made the best of it, us MacGregors, but we were not nomads at heart. We were made for quiet mornings and restful routines. Easy friendships and cozy fires and weekly meetups with friends. My soul craved it, but I'd ignored these needs for so long because I'd had no other choice.

But now it seemed like I did. Hope was dangerous, I knew, because it made you believe that another way could be possible.

And yet.

And *yet*.

Was I just going to repeat this cycle the rest of my life? Dragging my sisters along with me? Forever on the move, forever saying goodbye, forever unhappy? It went against everything that I'd been taught, but now was the time to stay.

To stay and fight.

Broca said I was powerful.

And I believed in Broca. My silly, impossibly elegant, steadfast grandmother. I'd do this. Even if it hurt. Even if it made me uncomfortable. Even if the whole town ended up hating us.

By the time I'd returned downstairs, hair dried, resolve hardened, Lyra had laid out our outfits.

"What in the world?"

"Aren't they great?" Lyra beamed at me from where she stood over three pink tartan ski suits. Like the one-piece ski suits from the '80s, with a zipper up the front. I gaped at her.

"Seriously?"

"I promise. We're going to look super cute. Plus, with these hats?" Lyra held up a white knit hat with a matching pink pom-pom on top.

"Very chic." Broca nodded in approval.

"Everything is going to be outside tonight and this weekend. We'll want to stay warm, and I figured matching would kind of show the town we come as a set, you know?"

I slanted a glance at Nova, who glowered at the ski suits.

"You're okay with this?"

"She's right, and I do wear pink well even though it's not my first choice of color."

I lifted my chin in surprise. If Nova was okay with it, then I had no choice.

"Pink tartan it is, then."

Broca walked into the room, relying on a cane, decked out in her pink tartan. Naturally, her pink glasses were covered in rhinestones, and diamond hoops winked at her ears.

"Well, ladies? Shall we show Briarhaven that the MacGregor witches are back and back for good?"

"Let's do it."

"Charm on, witches," Nova crowed, and despite myself, I laughed.

"Charm on indeed. Let's make this town fall in love with us."

CHAPTER TWENTY-FOUR
Sloane

It was a weekend for the books, as they say. Briarhaven showed up and showed off.

The whole town turned out, determined to give the best Pinecones & Peppermint Fest they could, and I have to say, they did a fabulous job of it.

They managed to take a catastrophe—almost blizzard-like conditions—and turn it into something magickal for everyone to enjoy. I could only imagine the amount of concentrated magick it took for them to do so, but according to Broca, it was significant.

Our arrival at the bonfire Friday night was met with mixed reactions, but we'd expected that. The MacGregors had planned ahead. We were going to kill everyone with kindness, even if it went against my ingrained response, particularly to assholes, and show our town that we should be allowed to stay.

The Rune & Rose was hosting the opening party with a massive bonfire in their car park, along with spiked hot chocolate, and marshmallows for all. Twinkle lights had been strung up, wind shelters built, and speakers bumped out party tunes. The place was packed, with both magickals and tourists alike, and Liam was doing a brisk business at his hot chocolate hut. The collection of snow sculptures in front of the pub had expanded into the festival, and two large peppermint striped candy canes made of snow were crisscrossed at the entrance.

"One mystic mocha, please," I said, ordering at the hut. Liam gave me a smile, but when his eyes danced over my shoulder, caught on someone else, I glanced behind me to see Raven laughing with someone by the fire. I wanted so badly to say something to him about her, and yet I forced myself to ignore the quiet yearning in his eyes.

One way to start endearing myself to others would be to not bring up their vulnerabilities.

"This is really great, Liam." I gestured around at the bonfire, and the well-lit pub behind it. "Your pub is fantastic. You've created a really warm and welcoming spot. For me, and my family as well." He'd been the first to allow us to have a party at his place, even when a huge chunk of the town had ignored the invitation to my birthday cèilidh.

"And you'll always be welcomed here, Sloane MacGregor. So long as you stick by my rules, you'll have a seat at my bar." Liam winked at me, and my heart sighed a bit for Raven. Why was she not dating this cutie?

"What are your rules?" I asked, accepting the takeaway cup of hot chocolate, piled high with pink marshmallows and a candy-cane-striped spoon.

"Dannae be an arsehole." Liam leaned into his Scots, and I laughed, charmed by him. As I'm sure many women were, judging by the growing line behind me. I took a sip. Refreshing peppermint mixed with rich mocha with just a smidge of Baileys for an edge.

"Delicious," I said, tipping my cup to him.

"Cannae have a wee peppermint festival with nae peppermint, eh, lass?"

"Truth." Tipping my cup to him, I wandered toward where Raven stood by the fire, instructing some children on the best way to toast marshmallows. When a few of the mothers saw me approaching, they tried to draw their children away.

"Sloane is the best at roasting marshmallows. Isn't that right, Sloane?"

Was I? Doubtful. But I was about to become an expert marshmallow maker if that was what it took to win over this town. Bending over, I whispered in one girl's ear that she needed to ask for sprinkles with hers, and her eyes widened with the excitement. Straightening, I bumped shoulders with Raven as we looked over the festival.

"This is pretty incredible," Raven said, turning to smile at me. She looked adorable in a maroon coat with a faux-fur-edged cap on her head. "I know the snow sucks, and I know it brings your family a lot of stress. But just look . . . We've really turned it around."

I paused and looked out over the festival with fresh eyes.

Briarhaven could have whiplash from the shift of focus from Halloween to Christmas and Hannukah decorations. In fact, there were still skeleton decorations with Santa hats hastily thrown on their heads at the hardware store. But here, it was as festive as could be. Elaborate strands of lights wound around the ancient yew tree in the middle of the square, and hundreds of strands of twinkle lights strung out from it, connecting to poles around the square, created a canopy of sparkling lights above us. Booths lined the square selling everything from ornaments to crafts to jewelry. Chopped logs had been rolled close to the bonfire, with wool blankets tossed over them to make for comfortable sitting. Carolers warmed up by a bandstand, ready to take the stage, and children screamed and chased one another with snowballs.

My breath caught as I spied Knox, talking to a woman in front of a mulled wine stand, a child laughing on his shoulders.

Oh, my ovaries.

Honestly, I'd never been one to think much of having children, nor did I particularly want them. But there was something about seeing a big strapping man with a small child in his arms that did funny things to my insides.

"How's that getting on, then?" Raven asked, following my line of sight. Knox swooped the child off his shoulders and hung him upside down, and the child's squeals echoed across the square.

"It's . . . getting on." I wasn't sure what to say, really, or what to think. The man had ravished me six ways to Sunday, and I should feel embarrassed by how much I loved how he dominated my body, and yet I couldn't quite work up any shame about it. Frankly, that was antiquated thinking. So what if I liked a man to dominate me in the bedroom? It was hardly uncommon. Maybe it was time for me to learn to give up a bit of the control I so favored.

But only just there. In the bedroom.

And to him.

Surprised at the thought, I realized that I trusted him. Completely.

And wasn't *that* the scariest thing of all?

"I truly cannot decipher the emotions running across your face. You're either going to eat that man alive or run like hell from him," Raven decided, watching me.

"That's about right," I admitted.

"Well, if I had any vote—I'd say eat him alive. Bloody hell, Sloane, he's gorgeous."

"Goddess, he really is, isn't he? I'd be annoyed by it if I weren't too busy craving his hands on me." Shocked at my words, I slapped a gloved hand over my face and Raven laughed outright.

"Girl, I do not blame you. He's a mighty fine snack."

"Who is a snack?" I jumped at Knox's voice in my ear.

"Oh, Liam is," I said, neatly throwing Raven under the bus, and her mouth rounded in a perfect O shape.

"Och, all the ladies like Liam. Do you fancy him more than me, Sloane?" Knox pulled a sad face.

"Of course not."

"That's what I thought." Knox shocked me by pulling me close for a searing kiss, and then tucking me under his arm. He grinned at Raven's raised eyebrows. "We're dating now."

"So it's official?" Raven gave me a look.

I squirmed under his arm, nervous at the term. "It's a trial period."

"That's what dating is, isn't it?" Raven looked confused now. "Did you, like, set an end date or something?"

"Nope. Sloane's just not ready to admit she likes me publicly. Thank goddess, my ego is strong enough to hold up under such disdain and neglect."

"You probably enjoy being her dirty little secret," Raven said, and Knox threw his head back and laughed.

"That is fun—maybe we can role-play that later."

"And that's me out . . ." Raven laughed and waved. "Bye, lovebirds."

"'Love'?" The word sent a shiver down my spine.

"Nope, don't start panicking. Not yet, at least. We have to go to the photo booth."

"There's a photo booth?"

"Aye, look." Knox turned me, and to my surprise, I found Broca, dressed as Mrs. Claus, handing out bags of treats to kids who sat with Santa by a sleigh. A sleigh that looked remarkably familiar.

"Is that my sleigh?" I hissed, leaning into Knox.

"The one and only. Come on, let's get a picture with Santa."

"He's not the real Santa, is he?" I asked as we drew closer. If he wasn't, he did a damn good impression of him. Rosy cheeks, a rotund belly, and a beard that reached to his waist completed his look.

"Awww, that's cute. Do you still believe in Santa, Sloane?" Knox dropped another kiss on my forehead before I could dissuade him, and I bristled at his words.

"Listen, buddy. This town is so damn magickal, it wouldn't surprise me, okay?"

"That's fair. But no, this is Jan, Henry's cousin."

I squinted at the Santa, and just for a moment his countenance blurred and I could see the ogre he was masking.

"Ah, right, okay. I can see it now."

"Are you getting better at that now? Knowing who is magickal and not?" Knox kept his voice low, as there were tourists in line with us. We inched slowly toward the front.

"I am. I think it happened . . ." I looked around and changed what I was going to say. "On my birthday."

"Aye, that makes sense. You're much more plugged in . . . after." Knox gripped my hand and pulled me forward when our turn came, and Broca beamed at the both of us.

"Here's your sweeties, dears." Broca held out two treat bags tied with mini candy canes that we'd compiled on our dining room table. I waved them away.

"Save them for the kids."

"Speak for yourself. I love sweeties." Knox plucked a bag from Broca's hand, and she chuckled.

"A man after my own heart."

I raised an eyebrow. Was my grandmother flirting with Knox?

"Don't give me that look." Broca shook a finger at me, and I turned, concealing my smile, only to find Knox sitting cheerfully on the older man's knee.

"You're sitting on him?" I asked.

"Trust me, lass. I'm strong," Santa promised me and patted his other knee. Knox's grin only widened, so I shook my head and went with it. The picture was as ridiculous as I expected, but I won't lie when I say it made my heart warm when Knox immediately tucked it in his wallet. Damn it, but maybe I did want the cutesy dating stuff that other women raved about when it came to their relationships.

Something I'd have to think about more later.

"Come on, we have to go decorate our pinecones."

"We do?" Distracted, I allowed Knox to drag me to where several picnic tables were sheltered beneath a canopy. There, baskets of pinecones were arranged, along with a myriad of craft supplies. I gave the pinecones a suspicious glance, still shaken from when they'd all turned into hedgies that one day at our house, but these all seemed fairly benign. The woman from the bookshop, the cat sith, beamed at her cat-shaped pinecones, while a man across from her built a Christmas tree out of his pinecones.

"What, exactly, am I making here?"

"An ornament." A woman in a sparkly knit cap with kind eyes sat across from us at the table and held up her bedazzled pinecone. I recognized her as Dorothy, the owner of the Dragon's Hoard. Leaning forward, she lowered her voice. "Say, is it true you summoned a dragon?"

"I did." There was no point lying about it. Half the town had seen me screaming through the air.

"We haven't seen one in ages. They keep to themselves, tucked away in the hills, but I do try to convene with them when I can. They accept me, you know." Dorothy's golden eyes, much like a cat's, regarded me seriously. "The fact you brought one here means they accept you as well."

"Is that right? Tell me, how do you convene with them?" I asked, fascinated. Picking up some glue, I began to coat my pinecone.

"See, the dragons are tricky. Not like the fae, but still tricky nonetheless." As Dorothy shook her head at me, I counted five different sparkling earrings in one ear. "Obviously, you can't go to them empty-handed."

"Naturally," I agreed with her, gently teasing. But also, where did the dragons live exactly? I had *so* many questions.

"The more sparkles, the better. They also like anything unique or amusing. The last time I was granted a visit, I brought a mother-of-pearl secret chest. It was a puzzle of sorts, you see? They had to unlock several mechanisms to open each secret drawer or panel. And then inside that, I'd added a glorious bunch of Sri Lankan sapphires—pink ones, mind you—and they'd been delighted. I took my tea there that day, and it's still one of the best afternoons of my life."

"Are there many of them? Or are they solitary creatures?" I realized my knowledge of dragon communities was sorely lacking.

"Och, there's a good bunch tucked away up there. They have families and live together as a community. Quite a peaceful bunch, really. They fancy themselves protectors of Briarhaven, as I'm sure you know better than anyone."

"Me? I don't really know, actually." Imagine that, dragons protecting our wee town. I wondered why she thought *I* would know. "Are they related to emberwolves?"

"They are. And I heard you've been lucky enough to gain one as your familiar. Is that right? Will you bring him to me?" Her eyes lit up, and I took a step back, imagining her on a throne, screeching, *Bring me your emberwolves!*

"I'm sure he'd be happy to meet you."

"Och, that would be the best." Dorothy clapped her hands, and then her face fell into worried lines. "Oh no, I'm going to have to research the best gift for an emberwolf. I wouldn't want to offend him."

"Cheese," I said, and laughed when she looked at me like I was putting her on. "I promise you it's cheese. He'll be your best friend for life if you feed him cheese."

"Cheese it is, then. You'll bring him next week?" Dorothy flicked a hand on the Apple Watch at her wrist and brought up her calendar. "Thursday suits."

"Um, right. Sure. I'll bring him Thursday. He'll enjoy getting out."

I wasn't sure how much Blue would care one way or the other, but when Dorothy rounded the table and threw her arms around me in excitement, I realized I'd made the right decision. I may be making a lot of people in Briarhaven angry with the incessant snow, but I might have other tools in my wheelhouse to start winning more people over. And my sweet boy, Blue, looked to be one of them. After she walked away, I smiled up at Knox.

"There you go, Sloane. Winning the town over, one dragon lover at a time."

"You think they'll come to accept us?" I leaned in as the carolers took to the stage and began to sing.

"I think they already have." Knox kissed my forehead, and I snuggled close as the carolers sang about their wish for a white Christmas.

At this rate, they'd have it and more.

CHAPTER TWENTY-FIVE
Sloane

I missed Knox.

I was surprised just how much I'd come to rely upon him, in such a short time.

By Sunday, I wanted nothing more than to strip myself out of this pink ski suit, curl into a cozy blanket, and read a book by the fire. Blue missed me, as I'd made the decision to let him stay with Henry over the weekend, keeping Haggis and Oswald company. From what I was told, he was having the time of his life, but I was ready for him to come home. I hadn't spent another night at Knox's, despite his attempts to take me home after the festival because I was nervous about being seen going home with the town's shining knight. It was one thing to ingratiate ourselves by doing good for the community, it was another thing entirely to be taking one of the most-loved bachelors in town for my own.

To my surprise, Knox not only handled my rejection well, he also called me once he got home to video chat with Blue. We ended up talking for hours, curled on our sides in bed, hashing over all the experiences we'd had each day. It was nice. And a part of me had ached to be next to him. I could see it, already: our days winding down curled up in bed, having these talks face-to-face.

I wasn't so sure that I wanted just a trial run with him anymore.

Restless, I went downstairs, ready for a cup of tea before bed, needing to unwind from a whirlwind weekend. I hadn't thought much about work in the past few weeks, having finished my last major marketing gig a few weeks before we'd arrived to Briarhaven.

But I realized after meeting so many people this weekend that I wanted to do something else.

I wanted to tell their stories.

It was really just an offshoot of marketing, wasn't it? Working on helping a brand showcase themselves was simply storytelling. And I'd met so many fascinating and deeply magickal people over the weekend that my hands itched to work the tidbits and snatches of what I'd heard into something more. Something tangible.

At the very least, it gave me some direction for the first time in ages. Being back in Briarhaven, my creative energy was starting to come alive again. At some point, I needed to speak to the woman at the bookstore—I suspected she could tell me if anyone was cataloging the stories of Briarhaven's people.

"I'm knackered," Nova said from where she and Lyra were sprawled on the couch. Broca snoozed quietly in her chair, the festival having knocked everything out of her.

"Me too. But I think we did good, didn't we?"

"Did you know that Marcie at Mystic Munchies weaves spells into her baked goods? She has an entire holistic section that is specific to certain needs." Lyra waved a finger in the air. "I need to see if she'll share some of her secrets."

"Maybe you could apprentice there," Nova suggested, and Lyra perked up, slapping Nova's arm.

"That's not a bad idea."

When a knock sounded at the door, I glanced at the clock on the wall as I veered toward the door. It was a bit late for a visitor.

I opened the door and froze.

Snow swirled inside, blisteringly cold, and the streetlights shone weakly against the intensity of the storm.

My father offered me a tentative smile.

"Dad?" Tears pricked my eyes.

"What?" Nova shrieked from behind me.

"What . . . what's wrong? What's happening?" Broca screeched, waking up from her nap.

"Best to come in," I said, stepping back, feeling . . . nothing. Nothing at all. It was like my emotions had gone totally numb inside me, and I stood back and watched as my sisters crowded around him.

Time slowed, and my magick unfurled, simmering on low. I realized Broca was staring at me, not at my father.

"Put it away, Sloane," Broca ordered, her voice quiet but firm.

"I'm trying," I hissed, easing closer to Broca's side.

My one constant.

"Try harder. Now is not the time."

I'd been so good all weekend. Broca had taught me a spell to lock my magick away. At any times of stress, I'd recited it to myself, visualizing my magick as a glowing little ball locked away in a box. It had helped, and there hadn't been a single mishap the whole weekend. I was proud of myself for that, but now, as I tried to hide from the pain of seeing my father again, the lock on that box of magick jiggled, threatening to fall open.

Nova, the youngest of us, hugged my father openly. Lyra and I had shielded her from the brunt of our parents' fights, and she had a much shinier view of our father than I did. Lyra stood back, a welcoming smile on her face. At her heart, Lyra wanted to believe the best in everyone. I knew, without a doubt, that she wanted to give our father a chance to explain himself, at the very least.

I didn't know what I felt.

Since coming back to Briarhaven, some of the shades had lifted on my memories. I now understood that my mother was a toxic and unreliable witch, one who leaned into the chaos of her magick. I also now understood that she and my father were a horrific match, and never should have been together long enough to conceive three children, let alone raise them into their teen years.

I was well aware of how I felt about my mother, but I still wasn't sure where that left me with my father. Years of resentment had built inside me and were now clogging my throat. I stood with my arms crossed, studying the man who looked past my sisters to me.

If he'd wanted to, he would have. I reminded myself of this, hardening my heart against him. People either showed up or they didn't, and he'd quite literally disappeared into the hills.

He'd aged, but we all had, and he was still a handsome man in his own right. Gray threaded his hair and beard, his eyes were the same shade as mine, now with lines tucked at the corners. He looked healthy enough, though a bit worn around the edges, and he held his cap in his hands.

"Sloane," Dad said.

I shrugged one shoulder, not sure what to say.

"Well, then, Russell. Best to come in. I suspect you'll have some explaining to do."

I kept silent. It was a tool I'd learned years ago. People weren't comfortable with silence, and often the best way to find out their true intentions was to remain quiet and let them speak.

Nova looked between me and him. Her face twisted.

"Are you going to push him away? When we've just found him again?" Her pain was real, and I turned to her.

"No," I promised. I wanted to. I wanted to slam the door in his face. But it wasn't my choice to make. My sisters were adults now, as they'd taken to reminding me, and I could shelter them no longer. They would need to make their own choices when it came to our father. I wouldn't stand in their way. "Tea?"

"Ah, please." Dad bobbed his head, and Broca waved him to the dining room table. He sat, Lyra and Nova across from him, while I put the kettle on.

"Where have you been?" Lyra asked the million-dollar question on everyone's minds, and I busied myself with getting cups out, wondering if he was going to lie.

"The hills." His voice was rusty, like he didn't use it often. "I had, *have*, a job to do. One that I stayed away from while I raised you girls."

The kettle popped, and I poured the tea, my mind mulling over what kind of job would call him to the hills. Away from his family. As matriarchal witches, we carried both the MacGregor name and the curse, and I wondered if it had all become too much for him. Carrying the tray to the table, I sat down and wrapped my ice-cold hands around my cup of tea.

"They deserve an explanation." Broca's words were sharp.

"You let her take us." I held my father's eyes, challenging him.

"I had no choice. You were already gone." Dad looked around at each of us, his eyes sad. "She took you when I was . . . away. She didn't return my calls, and I had no way of tracking you."

"And you didn't have a cell phone?" I'd always wondered why I couldn't call him.

"They never last. At least in what I do."

"At the very least, be honest with them. These are your daughters, who have grown into some pretty remarkable and resilient young women," Broca said.

"Ah." Dad looked us each in the eyes. "This is a family secret, but you should know, as it runs in your blood, though we won't know if any of your magick manifests in this way. It's hard to say, but even so, it's a powerful magick to have access to."

"What does that mean?" Nova pushed her lower lip out.

"The reason I disappeared on so many trips when you were growing up, why I can't have cell phones, and why I live in seclusion in the hills, is that I'm a keeper. A keeper of dragons, to be exact. I care for them, protect their home, and see that their royal bloodline will never be extinguished."

"Dragons," Lyra breathed, her eyes lighting up.

"Aye." Dad bobbed his head, taking a sip of his tea.

"I wonder if that's why you conjured a dragon," Broca said, and Dad angled his head toward me.

"Is that right?" He looked at me with a considering light in his eyes.

"And it's why you can have Blue." Broca nodded to me.

"I heard. An emberwolf. Quite rare to have as a familiar but not unusual for our bloodline. The dragons know their own."

"But . . . how? Mum never once mentioned this," I asked, confusion filling me.

"No, she wouldn't have. She resented me, my connection to this town, and my absolute refusal to leave with her. For a while I thought we had a fighting chance of staying here, if we both could compromise."

"Mum doesn't compromise." Nova snorted.

"No, she doesn't at that."

"So instead of a fighting chance you just . . . fought?"

"Constantly." Dad nodded, his finger tapping against the teacup. "It was the best and worst time of my life. And I'm sorry that you three were collateral damage in that."

"Are you?" I asked, uncertain if I could believe him. "Are you really?"

"Sorry? Aye, I am. I had no choice but to let you go. She knew that too. I can't leave here. Just like you three can't stay. It's an awful curse, and we were the wrong people to meet, to fall in love. A fire that burned too hot, consuming everyone around us."

"And there was no way to reach us?"

"No. While your mother's magick was unreliable, it was still strong. She blocked me. But when I heard you were back, I came here to give you this. It doesn't make up for not being around, but I hope it's a start."

Only then did I notice the bag at his side. Unzipping the backpack, he pulled out an accordion-style file folder and slid the top open.

A pile of letters spilled out.

"What are these?" Lyra picked an envelope up. "December 2022."

Nova picked another one up. "June 2021."

"Letters. I wrote you all a letter each month, even though I had nowhere to post them. In my own way, I hoped you would one day know that I cared, and still care, about all of you."

My heart twisted, and something warm and hot rose in my throat. I stood up, uncertain what to do, but knowing I needed space.

"Sloane." Dad looked at me as I turned to walk away. I paused, looking down at him as he held out a hand to me. "I know you dealt with the worst of it, and for that, I'm sorry. I can't give you your childhood back, but I hope I can give you your father back. If you'll have me."

"I don't know," I answered honestly, even though his face fell. "It's going to take time. I'm not saying that I can't get there, but I can't just pretend like we are suddenly one happy family."

Dad nodded, accepting my words. "I hope you'll stay and we can make that time."

I nodded once more and then disappeared upstairs, my misgivings churning in my gut. If I didn't tamp down on my feelings, I might blow the entire house up.

And when Knox video called to show me Blue at his side, he took one look at my face and knew something was wrong.

"I'm coming."

"No, no, it's fine." I waved him away, but the screen was already black. I shouldn't have answered. I should have known better.

A tap at my window five minutes later had me blinking into the storm in surprise. There, Knox hovered in the air, Blue in his arms. Sliding the window up, I pulled him inside, shocked.

"You can fly?"

"Hover for short bursts as needed." Knox collapsed on my bed, and Blue launched himself at me, deliriously happy. "Things looked intense downstairs, so I thought to bypass whatever had put that look on your face."

"You didn't need to come," I said, trying to look everywhere but at him as Blue licked my face.

"Yes, I did, lass." Knox patted the bed next to him. "Come here, love. Tell me about it."

"I . . ." I paused as I realized that instead of hiding it all, pushing it all down as I usually did, I genuinely wanted to tell Knox about it.

Plopping down on the bed, I curled into his side.

And told him everything.

CHAPTER TWENTY-SIX
Sloane

Despite our best efforts, the snow had intensified and was approaching catastrophic levels. While the Pinecones & Peppermint Fest had done good things for tourism, and people had been happy with all the snow-filled games, another week had passed and the onslaught of bad weather showed no signs of weakening. The Charms told me everyone was working at full effort now to make the village even somewhat passable, and it was hard to say how long they'd hold up under the strain.

We were also no further along on our break-the-curse path.

And while I hadn't quite come to terms with our father's sudden reappearance in our lives, I also hadn't frozen him out. Talking to Knox had been surprisingly helpful, largely because he hadn't pushed me in one direction or the other. Instead, he'd suggested that I take all the time I needed to feel my feelings and reminded me nothing had to be decided in that instant. Hearing that had loosened some of the tension, because he was right—I could take my time. It had been years since I'd seen my father, and now that I knew where he was, I could ease into our relationship again on my terms.

Each night, I read one of his letters, as did my sisters, to varying reactions.

But the dragon revelation had to be one of the biggest surprises. Now, all of Nova's sketchbooks were being filled with increasingly intricate dragon designs, while Lyra was researching the history of the dragon keepers.

And I went to see Dorothy at the Dragon's Hoard, Blue along for the ride. We went after she'd closed the shop for the day, on Thursday as requested, and she'd all but flung the door open and wrenched us inside when we arrived.

"I've been so nervous, I've been pacing!" Dorothy exclaimed, waving a finger at the wall of snow behind us. "I was worried you wouldn't make it."

"The Land Rover's been pretty reliable. I just went extra slow." As much as I hated to admit it, I was in love with Knox's car and might have a hard time giving it back to him. At least he had several options in his garage to choose from, surely he wouldn't miss it?

"I'm just so pleased you're here." Dorothy clapped her hands together, her face alight with pleasure as she beamed at where Blue's wee nose poked out of my coat. "An emberwolf. My, what an honor. Even though you are a keeper's daughter and all. It's just rare to see."

"How did you know I'm a keeper's daughter?" My father had said this was a family secret. I followed Dorothy as she waved us through the shop and up the stairs to a small second-floor flat. Here, a rich navy-blue color on the wall made the colorful chairs, abstract paintings, and shelves full of intricate baubles that rivaled the likes of a museum pop. She directed me toward two velvet armchairs in pale dusky gold, a low-slung coffee table between them.

On it lay an entire platter of cheese.

Blue poked his head out, struggling to get out of my coat, but I held him tightly.

Snacks.

"Yes, I know there are snacks. But it is rude to go eat it all. So you are going to wait and be polite and eat the cheese slowly. Understood?"

But, why?

"Why do you have to wait to eat the cheese? Because you'll get a sore stomach otherwise."

Never. Dragons don't get upset stomachs.

"I do believe you were a wee bit windy the other day," I murmured in his ear, reminding him of his gas that had almost blown me off the couch.

I'm certain that I can't recall.

Blue turned his nose in the air, and I laughed as I unzipped my coat. When he spread his wings and took flight around the room, Dorothy crowed in delight.

"Oh, would you just look at him? He's incredible." Dorothy's eyes shone brightly as Blue circled, adding a few dips and dives for her.

"Show-off," I murmured.

I am a majestic beast, Sloane.

I grinned as he buzzed past me and then hunkered down on the floor. Sliding me a glance, he reached a paw out and knocked a piece of cheese off the table.

Oops.

"Blue," I warned.

Another brick of cheese went flying.

"Oh, cheeky monkey." I shook my head at him, and he looked up, a mischievous expression on his face.

"Please, go on, sit." Dorothy dropped into a chair, indicating I do so as well, her gaze fixated on Blue. "He's really just so incredible, isn't he? Just look at those wings. They blend perfectly with his coat, but his face is just the cutest."

"It really is." Blue snuffled the ground, searching for his cheese, and I eased back into the chair. "Thanks for having us over."

"Oh, it's my pleasure. It's not every day I get to spend with a keeper's daughter."

"So you know about us, then? My dad? How is that possible?"

"I'm a historian for the dragons." Dorothy beamed at me when my mouth dropped open. "I'm granted certain privileges others aren't.

And even then, I still have to beg and plead my way into having an audience with them. Even if it is to record their own history. Your father has the great honor of keeping them tethered to this world."

"'Tethered'?" I raised an eyebrow at the word.

"Aye, lass. Without him, they'd float right through the veil to another realm. But they like it here and want to stay. Which requires someone affixed to this world. Your father, in this case. It's why he can't leave Briarhaven."

"Surely they have a backup? What if he, I don't know, slips on a rock and hits his head and dies? Would they just disappear?"

"Not instantaneously, no." Dorothy pressed her lips together. "But eventually, yes. If they couldn't find another who understood the role. And the heavy responsibilities of it. He's a good man, your father. He's given up a lot to keep the dragons here. I admire him."

"Aye, he gave up his daughters." I couldn't help that my words were bitter at my throat.

"Did he, though? Or were they taken?" Dorothy's tone held no censure, just curiosity.

I shrugged, uncertain how to respond, when a huge crashing sound exploded from outside. Metal crushed, sharp and cracking, and the sound of glass shattering shot me to my feet.

"Oh no," Dorothy cried. We both ran to the window, and Blue followed, scrambling to land on my shoulder until I reached up and tucked him into my arms.

Below, a minivan was wrapped around a tree, its front end smoking and crumpled like an accordion.

"*No*," I breathed, turning. "That's Felicity's car. We need to call for help."

"Already on it."

"Keep Blue with you." I put Blue on the couch. "Buddy, stay here. It could be dangerous."

Grabbing my coat, I raced outside.

The sight that greeted me was dire.

Felicity sat hunched in the driver's seat, blood pouring down her face, unconscious. I was the first to arrive, though shouts greeted me through the swirl of snow and sleet that hammered the car. Wrenching the door open, I pressed my palms to the blood at her head, hoping to stem the flow. My breath caught in my chest.

"Felicity," I called, hoping she would wake up. "Honey, I need you to wake up. You've had an accident."

I wasn't even sure if she was breathing. Did I need to check that? Maybe I should be administering CPR instead of stopping the flow of blood. Panic clenched my throat.

"Sloane, move back."

"Raven," I gasped, immediately making room for the healer. "I don't know . . . I'm not sure if she's okay."

"Just move," Raven ordered, and I slid out of the way. Shifting my coat from my shoulders, I held it up, trying to block Raven and Felicity from the sharp shards of icy snow that hammered down from above. Raven put her hand on Felicity's chest and closed her eyes, her face going as still as a statue's. A moment later, her eyelids fluttered open.

"She's alive, but she's seriously injured. We need to get her into surgery."

"What can you do?"

"I'm going to work on the internal bleeding. The broken bones will have to wait. Now wheesht." With that, Raven closed her eyes and went to work, murmuring spell after spell until sirens pierced the air and an ambulance slid to a stop next to the car, Knox right behind it.

Everything was a blur of movement as the officials took over, and we were pushed back, back, back, until we could barely see through the snow as they strapped Felicity to a stretcher and whisked her away.

"Is she going to . . ." I grasped Raven's arms, unable to say the words.

"I don't know. But I have to call her family."

"What can I do?" I asked Raven, feeling helpless.

And Raven, despite her loyalty to me, couldn't help but glance at the snow that barreled down from the sky and then back to me. I winced.

Even if it hadn't been intentional, the meaning was clear. The snow was becoming a true threat now, and if we didn't do something to fix this soon, I might not have any choice but to leave.

I'd been handed a cold, hard slap of reality in the form of one friend's van wrapped around a tree.

What I needed to do was go home, pack everyone up, and get out of town before all of Briarhaven descended into chaos. It was clear we were running out of time. Raven squeezed my arm once, understanding on her face, and my heart fell. She knew as well as I did what we had to do. It wasn't fair to ask people to live with this. Staying in Briarhaven to break the curse had been a pipe dream at best.

Tears threatened, and I swallowed them back, pushing them down, down, down, behind that wall that I'd been so good at keeping up most of my life. Dorothy handed me Blue, and I bundled him into my coat and beelined for the Land Rover, ostensibly ignoring where Knox stood speaking to the police.

I couldn't face him.

Not now. Not like this. With the blood of an innocent victim on my hands. It wasn't my curse, but it was mine to bear.

But as I made to close the driver's door, a hand stopped me. Already I knew who it was.

I struggled in a breath and then swung my gaze up to his.

"Sloane. No." Knox's voice was ragged, his face ravaged with grief.

"Knox," I said.

"You can't do this. You can't leave. Not now. Not like this."

"I have to go, Knox. Don't you see?" I swept a hand out, tears blurring my vision. "This is only getting worse. We were stupid to think we could fix this. We've barely made any headway, and now someone is seriously hurt. How many people will have to break their faces against steering wheels before you let me go?"

"There has to be a way around this," Knox argued, his eyes wild, burning through me. "You can't just leave."

"I don't have a choice. Look at me," I shouted, and Blue whimpered on the seat next to me. I held up my hands, still covered in Felicity's blood. "Look at this! Her blood is, quite literally, on my hands. I don't have a choice."

"Please don't go, Sloane." Knox leaned forward until his forehead touched mine, his breath tickling my lips. "I need you. I . . ."

"You what?" I said, his nearness calming me despite it all.

"I love you, Sloane. If you leave, you'll take my heart with you."

That box of emotions cracked open inside me, my heart shattering open, and tears poured down my face. A future here now truly felt insurmountable.

"I have to go, Knox. It's what we do. We don't get to stay, can't you understand?"

"Then I'll come with. Take me with you."

"No, Knox. Your home is here. Briarhaven needs you."

"Forget Briarhaven, Sloane. When do I get a chance at my own happiness?"

My heart cried for him, for us, as I stared at him, frozen with the impossible choice in front of me.

But I did know one thing, now that I'd finally allowed my emotions to escape. I loved Knox, irreparably so, and I knew two things. The first? If I told him now, he'd leave everything behind and follow me to the ends of the earth. And the second? He'd never be happy if he did so.

Raven appeared behind Knox.

"Emergency meeting of the Charms. At your house. I'm coming with you." Raven slid into the back seat, ignoring Knox, and I looked up at him, helpless.

"I have to go." And I didn't mean just because the Charms had called a meeting.

He knew it, and I knew it.

"Coward." Knox turned and spat on the street behind us before storming away, the snow swallowing him up as he went. Blue whimpered after him, and I slammed the door, agony rippling through me.

"There's time to deal with that later, Sloane. Pack it away," Raven ordered, and I nodded, my hands gripping the wheel.

"Is she going to make it?" I asked, starting the car and easing it past the squad cars that had blocked off the accident scene.

"I believe so."

"You're not just saying that?" I shot a glance in the rearview mirror to see Raven sitting, her head thrown back, eyes closed, all color drained from her face.

"No, I wouldn't lie to you."

"I need to leave, don't I?"

Silence greeted me, but that was all I needed to hear. I know Raven didn't want to be the one to say it, to send me packing, but I also knew her code of "first do no harm" as a healer wouldn't allow her to encourage me to stay here any longer either.

"Understood," I said.

I stared at the blood drying on my fingers, and my resolve tightened. I would get us home, get us through this meeting, and then I was packing my sisters up and leaving town. We'd been happy enough traveling the world before, and we'd figure it out again. I wouldn't allow anyone to die because the MacGregors simply wanted an easier life.

CHAPTER TWENTY-SEVEN
Sloane

Mandy Meadows was already at my house, in pink snow pants and a pink jumper with Après Ski knitted across the front. The rest of the Charms gathered around the dining room table, including Broca, who had left her lounge chair to join the meeting. Felicity's absence was louder than her presence.

Blue flew to his pile of blankets in the corner and dug his nose in, burrowing until he found a perfect spot, ready to warm up after being out in the cold.

"Sloane, you're bleeding." Lyra jumped up, concern on her face, but I just waved her away.

"Not mine." Toeing my boots off, I stomped to the kitchen sink and rinsed my hands under the hottest water I could, not even noticing when my tears joined the blood that ran in thin rivulets down the drain.

An arm came around my shoulder. And another around my waist. My sisters. Forever at my side.

"We heard," Lyra said softly.

"I'm so sorry," Nova said.

"I think we need to leave," I choked out. I hated saying it, I hated admitting defeat, I hated uprooting everyone. But this was why I never let myself hope. This was why I never let myself get too attached. It just hurt, impossibly so, when inevitably we had to move on. I don't know who we were kidding this time around, but nothing had changed.

Nothing.

"Broca has called an emergency meeting of the Charms." Mandy Meadows sniffed, her disapproval clear, as she tucked a piece of blond hair behind her ear and eyed the tray of biscuits in front of her like they were crack. Drying my hands, I took a seat at the table with my sisters and tried to gain control over my feelings. But still, tears tracked down my face.

"So I did. I'd like to introduce an emergency ordinance. Like the one we did for my daughter years ago." Broca smiled.

"I'm certain I don't know of which you speak." Mandy Meadows sniffed and stared harder at the plate of biscuits, ignoring eye contact with Broca.

My magick escaped, unable to stay tamped down with my swirling emotions, and the tray of biscuits exploded into a pile of frogs, leaping every which way. Mandy Meadows screeched as one landed directly on her face, its little webbed legs splayed out across her cheeks, holding on for dear life as she clawed at her face.

Tam laughed, catching one and putting him on her shoulder.

"There's a good lad." She booped another on its nose and bent to gather them up.

Raven pressed her lips together and spoke sharply when Mandy Meadows went to slap one off the table. "You'll do no harm." Muttering under her breath, Raven gathered the frogs, and then Broca raised her hands over them. In moments, they'd returned to biscuits, though I was certain nobody would dare take a bite of the snacks now.

"As I was saying, I'd like to invoke Ordinance 33.3, wherein the Charms band together to help one of theirs in need. In this case, four of us in need." Broca swept out her hand to encompass all of the MacGregor witches sitting at the table.

"Wouldn't this be the time to focus on helping Felicity?" Deidre asked, tapping away at her phone.

"What could you possibly be discussing right now?" Surprising us all, Nova shot out of her seat and swiped Deidre's phone from her hand. "There's no way in hell you're selling real estate in this snow. For once, just focus."

"My, my, this witch doesn't even have her power yet and she's getting mighty feisty." Deidre focused on the phone in Nova's hand.

"Ouch," Nova hissed, dropping the phone to the floor, and shaking her hand. "Stupid witch heated it."

"That was dumb," Lyra said, smiling at Deidre. "You'll likely just melt the internal components."

"Worth it," Deidre muttered, reaching into her bag.

"I swear to the goddess, if you pull out another phone I don't know what I will do. Remember, we can't trust my magick." I slapped a hand on the table, and Deidre stopped, glaring at me.

"*Brilliant* to have you all back," Deidre muttered, and I winced. Making more enemies was probably not the best idea for us at the moment.

Mandy Meadows beamed, delighted with the exchange, and it was hardly any wonder why. She'd been pretty clear about not wanting to help us from the start.

"Deidre's right. We need to figure out a collective way to help Felicity, not to invoke some ancient ordinance that requires us to put in unnecessary work."

"Felicity is going to be fine." Raven held up a hand, stopping Mandy Meadows from talking over her. "I healed her internal bleeding. She needs some help from the doctors, but the intense healing is done."

"Och, you poor thing. Why didn't you tell me?" Tam sprung up and went to her bag, rummaging around until she pulled out a vial. Coming back, she poured a few drops in Raven's tea. "Drink."

"Thanks." Raven gave Tam a grateful look, as did I, because within two sips, color had returned to Raven's pale skin.

"Tell us about this ordinance?" Lyra asked, turning to Broca.

"We used it once before. Back when Mandy wasn't a part of the coven," Broca said, adjusting her red glasses. "For the first time in decades, the MacGregor witches had been able to stay in one place without bringing harm to anyone. But it did require sacrifice on behalf of the Charms."

"What kind of sacrifice?" Tam leaned back and quirked an eyebrow. "Human?"

"Unfortunately, no." Broca looked directly at Mandy Meadows.

"Savage," Lyra said under her breath.

"The ordinance requires not only that the Charms meet each week, but we also must do withholding spells each week. On top of that, wards must be placed around the town, checked, and recharged on a biweekly basis."

"What does the withholding spell do?" I blinked at Mandy Meadows when she sneered at me.

"Withholds the curse from landing on our town?" Mandy Meadows spoke as if I were a toddler who was still learning my words. My lip curled in distaste. "As you can see, this will be an incredible amount of work, not just on behalf of the Charms, but even more so on the Charms who already have their magick. We'll be picking up the slack of those who aren't yet of age." She sniffed in the direction of my sisters.

"You're saying there is a solution, but it just takes hard work?" Tam shrugged a shoulder. "So what?"

"It's tedious, time-consuming, and with very little benefit." Mandy Meadows took a small sip of her tea, sitting rigid in her seat.

"I beg to differ, Mandy. A full coven has a huge benefit, particularly for the leader. If I remember correctly, won't a full coven amplify your powers tenfold?" Broca leaned back in her chair and took her own small sip of tea. All eyes bounced back to Mandy.

"Goodness, while that sounds lovely and all, I'm already quite powerful." Another sip of the tea accompanied by a rigid smile.

"As am I," Broca said. She sipped. "A factor you should consider. Without my help, those beauty spells of yours might slip a bit." Another small sip.

"I don't use beauty spells." Something flickered in Mandy Meadows's eyes, but she took a measured sip of her own tea. "Though I'm sure you must need plenty of them."

I sucked in a breath.

"Luckily, I don't. I've been blessed with good genes. Strong genes. Remind me about your mum again, Mandy? Why didn't she make it into the coven?" Broca's eyes were steely behind her glasses, and she took another long sip from her mug.

The head of our coven stilled, her face a mask.

"We'll put it to vote," Mandy Meadows finally said, her voice as cold as the storm that raged outside.

"Please, by all means." Broca waved a hand to the table, ever gracious, and then took another small sip of her tea as if to punctuate the win.

"All in favor of enacting Ordinance 33.3, please raise your hands."

Everyone at the table raised their hands except for Deidre and Mandy Meadows. Mandy smirked.

"Unfortunately, without a unanimous decision, the answer to your motion is a resounding no."

"Hardly resounding," Nova muttered.

"Wait, doesn't the majority win? Isn't that more democratic?" I asked, confused. We finally had a real solution, and it was just being ripped away from us before we'd even had a chance to explore it.

"A coven is not a democracy." Mandy Meadows stood and picked up her pocketbook. "And, frankly, we shouldn't have even called a vote, as one of our members is currently in the emergency room. As president of the Charms, I declare the motion denied, and also that no other motions may be called until we are once again all present."

"What happened to your motto, 'never harm, always charm'?" I couldn't help but ask.

"I'm not the one harming people here, Sloane." Mandy Meadows slanted me a look as she strode to the door, flipping her hair over her shoulder. "It's your curse that put Felicity in the hospital."

"Och, come on, Mandy. That's hardly fair," Tam called, but the slamming door was the only answer.

My heart dropped. Mandy was right. We *were* hurting people by being here.

"Give it a few days. Felicity will be feeling better, and we'll call another vote. It'll be okay." Raven stood and stretched.

Nova opened her mouth, but Broca raised a finger, effectively shushing her. The Charms hurried out, the meeting over, and I limped to the couch to hug Blue.

"Blue, buddy, I think we may need to leave Briarhaven," I spoke into his ear, sadness filling me. I wondered if it would be better if I left him with Henry, so he could be happy with his magickal buddies here. Otherwise, I'd always be hiding him, and he'd constantly have to wear a jumper to hide his wings.

No. Stay.

"But what if I can't?" I wrapped my arms around where he'd buried himself in the blankets.

Knox will figure it out.

"Yeah, you both seem pretty confident about that." I sighed and rolled over, looking up at my sisters standing in front of me.

"If they won't invoke Ordinance 33.3 . . ." Lyra said, her hands at her heart.

"Then we need to disappear," I finished, hating the sadness that swept across their faces. "Even if just for a bit, to give the town a break from this awful weather."

"It's never just a break." Nova kicked her toe at the couch, her face sullen. "We never end up going back."

"I know." I wasn't sure what else to say, my heart was breaking too.

"Ladies, it's late. It's been a big day, lots of high emotions. Let's table this for tonight. Another day or two of snow won't destroy the town, and knowing Knox, he'll have an alert out that everyone takes extra caution. There's nothing more to be done tonight but to rest."

With that, we all retired to our rooms, and Blue was soon snoring at the foot of my bed. And still I couldn't bring my brain to rest. My mind kept flashing back to Felicity's blood on my hands, and when I finally did sleep, I slipped into a gnarly dream where I was ripping Knox's heart from his chest and kicking it across the pitch like a football. By the time I jerked back awake, sweaty and crying, I'd made my decision.

CHAPTER TWENTY-EIGHT

Knox

"Like hell they're going to leave," I snarled out loud, pacing the library, Haggis wheeling behind me. I'd barely slept the night before, and Sloane hadn't answered my call. I'd only tried once, and when it had gone to voicemail, I didn't try again.

I'd said what I needed to say.

But now I needed her to believe it.

Stay, stay, stay.

"Damn right they need to stay." I looked down at Haggis, who peered up at me, his eyes concerned behind his shaggy scruff of bangs.

Whatever happened with the blood curse ritual?

This from Oswald, who sat on the back of the couch, near the half-burnt curtain sash that hadn't yet been removed from when Sloane had set it on fire. I was oddly sentimental over that sash. He prowled forward, pretending indifference, but I knew where he was headed.

"It didn't work."

Oh? Did they have all the people they need to perform it? Oswald rolled on his back and licked a paw, the picture of calm.

"I'm not sure."

Don't you think that might be something you could help with? Oswald stood and stretched, his tail brushing the hanging cord, and he whirled, ready to swipe.

"Oswald," I warned.

It's already ruined.

"Fair point." I ran a thumb over my chin as I considered it. It was the same thought I'd had the other day. But I'd forgotten about it in the flurry of the festival, and then with Felicity's accident last night. "I might have to convince a lot of people."

And? Don't you think it is time to call in a favor after everything you've done for this town?

At that, I paused, not even caring when Oswald went into full attack, ripping the curtain cord down from the hook and pouncing on it on the floor. He was right, as he often was.

I never asked anyone for favors. In fact, I spent my life serving others. It felt . . . out of pocket, against the grain, uncomfortable—but if I wanted Sloane to stay, I needed to give her a fighting chance.

She needed Briarhaven.

As much as I needed her.

In the time since she'd come home, she'd worked her way into my heart, and now I couldn't picture a future without her. I wanted her at my side, bossing me about. Then in my bed, with me taking control behind closed doors. I wanted Blue to join our pack, knowing how much fun he'd have living here. I wanted a chance at making a real family. Together.

Yesterday, I'd been infuriated when she refused to say the words back. Adrenaline from the crash had spiked, causing me to shout, but now I could see what I needed to do. Not only did I need to call in favors, but I also needed to show her, again, that I wasn't going to leave her.

I needed to show Sloane that people would turn up for her.

When most people in her life had failed her, it was time for her to learn a lesson about community, about friendship, and about love. And

I was going to be the one to teach her, even if I had to shove the damn lesson down her throat and keep her tied to my damn bed for a week.

You look a little scary.

"Oh, sorry." I gave Haggis a scratch behind his ears and smoothed out my expression. Probably shouldn't go into Sloane's screaming about tying her to my bed and refusing to let her leave until she understood that people who loved each other showed up for each other. Instead, I picked up the phone and clicked on Liam's name.

"Liam, mate. Need a favor. Today."

By the time I arrived at Sloane's house, my plan was well in motion, and I was a warlock on the warpath. When Lyra opened the door and looked up to see my scowling face, she beamed.

"Ah yes, our knight in shining armor has arrived."

"Where is she?"

"In her room. Packing." Lyra moved back, letting me inside.

"Here's a spare key to the Land Rover. Get yourselves to the pub. I'll follow with Sloane shortly."

"My, my." Nova fanned her face as she stood. "I do love this alpha-male thing you've got going on, Knox."

Despite myself, I smirked.

"Bring Blue with you, too, so she doesn't worry."

"Blue, cheese!" Nova called, and there was a clamor of noise, a curse from Sloane, and then Blue wobbled his way down the stairs, zooming heavily toward the kitchen. Nova had grabbed a container and walked toward the door. "This way, bud."

I stomped upstairs, ready for the fight of my life.

"Knox." Sloane held a hand to her chest when I burst through the door. "What are you doing here?"

"Saving you."

"Damn it, Knox." Sloane shook her head, a wistful expression on her pretty face, and folded a jumper. A worn suitcase lay on the bed, already half-full, and seeing it made fury rise inside me. "This is for the best."

"The best for whom?" I asked, stepping close and wrenching the jumper from her hand. I tossed it on the bed, and Sloane's mouth dropped open.

"Okay, Mr. Caveman and all that. No need to be rude."

"You haven't even seen me begin to be rude. You want rude? Here." Picking up the suitcase by one hand, I upended it as Sloane gasped, furious. All of her carefully organized piles landed in a mess on the floor.

"Now you've crossed a line." Sloane lifted her chin before stepping forward and reaching for the suitcase, but I held it out of reach.

"I plan to cross a lot of them. Over and over. You know what I've figured out, Sloane?"

"Give it back," Sloane hissed, fury rippling across her face as she lunged for the suitcase.

"I've figured out that nobody ever pushes you. You're always the one calling the shots. You've got everything planned, and once things get messy, you leave."

"I leave so we don't destroy people's lives." Sloane tugged the handle of the suitcase, and I pulled back. We locked in the middle, Sloane pulling hard on the handle while I just held it, and Sloane's scowl deepened.

"Aye, and you'll destroy mine if you go."

"Knox." Sloane's face softened, but I couldn't stand to see the pity in her eyes. Instead, I bent forward and scooped her over my shoulder.

"Knox!" Sloane screeched, slapping my bum with her hand. "Put me down. This caveman routine is not hot. Not at all."

"Lies." I clambered down the stairs and walked us directly into the snow. She had no coat, no shoes, and likely no bra on, and I did not care.

"What the actual hell?" Sloane raged at me as I dumped her in the back seat, hit the child locks, and hopped in the driver's seat.

"Put your seat belt on."

"I will not." Sloane battled with the door, her chest heaving, as she scrambled.

"Fine, I'll do it for you." Reaching over the seat, I shoved her back and wound the seat belt over her, all while she batted at me with her hands.

"Knock it off. I'm not going anywhere with you," Sloane seethed.

Catching her chin with my hand, I forced her to meet my eyes.

"You will. If you care even one-tenth as much for me as I do for you, you will sit in this bloody car and keep your mouth shut until we get to where we are going."

Sloane's mouth worked, opening and closing, and then she slumped backward, her expression still mulish.

"And then what?"

"You'll just have to wait and see. I'm serious, Sloane. I'm at my wits' end with you right now, and I don't suggest you push me any harder or you'll just see what happens when a warlock as powerful as I am loses his ever-loving cool."

"Are you threatening me?"

"With violence? Never. But with consequences of your own choices? Absolutely."

Sloane gratefully fell silent, and I shifted the car into gear, trying to drive as fast as I could to the Rune & Rose before she decided to give me hell again. Bloody hell, but life with her was going to be fun. Once there, I parked on the street, as the lot was full, and disengaged the locks.

"Knox, I can't go in there like this." Sloane looked down at her leggings and baggy T-shirt and slippers. She was likely freezing.

"Put on my jumper." Peeling off my coat, I handed her my jumper, and then zipped my coat back on over my long-sleeved shirt. She pulled it over her head, looking adorably rumpled in the brown jumper, and then I hopped out. Opening the door, I unbuckled her and lifted her into my arms, carrying her like a man carries his bride over the threshold. The mountain of snow figures on the front lawn had grown to a terrifying amount, and they seemed to watch our every move as we passed.

"Will you tell me what is going on?" Sloane asked, craning her neck to hide her face from the snow.

"Nope."

I walked us inside to a huge crowd staring at us.

"What's happening?" Sloane asked, her body tensing against mine.

"We're here to help break the curse." Raven stepped forward, pointing to the cauldron hanging over the fire.

"But how?" Sloane slid to the floor and looked around at everyone.

"Everyone here has lineage back to the days of your curse. These are the founding magickal families of Briarhaven." I swept my hand out to the room.

Sloane's mouth dropped open, and a sheen of tears filled her luminous eyes.

"And they all came out? To help?" Sloane looked around, overcome. "I thought they hated us."

"We hate the snow." This was a shout from the back.

"Don't take much issue with the MacGregors."

"Sloane?" Broca asked, leaning on her cane by the fire.

"Och, I'm overwhelmed." Sloane fanned her face, looking around at everyone. "You all didn't have to do this. We would have figured something out eventually. I can't thank you—"

"Save it until you know if it works." Dorothy cut off Sloane's rambling, and laughter went through the room. "Let's get this show on the road."

I stood watch as every standing founding family member I could find came forward and added a drop of their blood to the cauldron, along with honey and whisky.

"Mandy's not here. Is she not from a founding family?" Sloane looked up at me, and I nodded toward a woman dressed in muted turquoise who stood quietly at the back of the room.

"Her mum is. Mandy refused to be here."

"Is that right?" Broca's look sharpened, her eyes meeting mine.

"That is correct," I said, not wanting to get into coven politics at this time. But I knew what it could mean when a member of a coven, particularly the president, didn't participate in a ritual of this magnitude. Mandy had pulled a risky move, and the payoff might not be what she hoped for.

"Sloane, I'm Felicity's mum." A woman with messy hair and tired eyes gave her finger to be pricked.

"Oh my goddess, how is she?" Sloane's eyes filled with concern.

"Much better today, thank you. A few broken bones, but nothing that won't heal with time. Thank you for being there for her."

"I didn't do anything. Raven did." Sloane gestured to her friend.

"You brought comfort when you could. It mattered." She squeezed Sloane's hand and stepped back as member after member of the town came forward to support Sloane.

Until the very last person stepped forward.

"Dad!" Sloane exclaimed.

I'd never met Sloane's father in person before, and I straightened my shoulders as he came forward. We'd seen each other in passing, when I was growing up, but once the girls had moved, he'd disappeared into the hills.

I'd sent Henry to find him. Even though Sloane was of the same bloodline, *I'd wanted her to see that people would show up*.

And he'd come. Just as I expected he would.

Sloane's eyes filled again, and this time the tears spilled over as he gathered her in his arms, kissing the top of her head.

"I'm not sure my blood will add much more to the ritual than yours, but I'm putting a whole lot of love in there with it." His voice was low, gruff, against her hair, and even I felt like I might cry. We all looked discreetly away as they hugged, and then Sloane pulled back, wiping at her tears as Russell stepped forward and added the final drop to the cauldron.

"Right, shall we?" Broca raised a hand, but a bark interrupted her.

Blue erupted from the other side of the room, and Sloane gasped, her hands going automatically into the air as he swooped across the room in that lovely, wobbly, funny way of his, landing clumsily in her arms. He looked up at her, his smile on his face, and raised a paw.

"He wants to add his blood." Sloane half laughed through her tears.

"A drop of dragon's blood. That's a mighty gift," Russell said.

"I agree. What a gem wee Blue is," Dorothy said.

"I don't want to hurt him, though," Sloane said, turning to look at me.

"Won't hurt him a bit. Their paws are scales. See?" Russell turned Blue's paws to show the vibrant scales, and then quickly pricked it before Sloane could protest any more. A drop of iridescent blood splattered into the cauldron, and the contents began to move of their own accord.

"I think that means it's ready." Broca stirred, and then tilted the cauldron, pouring the drink into a quaich to be passed around among everyone. Broca called the circle, and placed the hematite stones.

Together, the descendants of Briarhaven recited the ritual.

"By blood that bound, by love now freed,
Let this curse be undone in word and deed.
Honey sweet, whisky strong,
Upend this heartache to right a wrong."

Three times we recited it, our voices united, many of us reading from the text message I'd sent with the ritual earlier that day. At the end, light flashed inside the empty cauldron, the air shimmered, and then quiet descended on the pub.

"There's something in the cauldron," Broca said.

Sloane bent over and reached in, pulling out a stone.

"It's a piece of pink quartz." Sloane held it up. "But it's broken."

"Is it part of a heart?" Nova said, stepping forward to examine it. "See how it curves? It looks like a piece of a broken heart."

As one, the MacGregor sisters slumped, their eyes filling.

"It didn't work," Lyra muttered, her huge eyes sad. "What are we supposed to do with a piece of broken quartz?"

"'Three fragments mended, a heart restored, let curse unwind, its chains no more.'" Sloane turned, hugging Blue to her chest. "The line that didn't make sense. In my book."

"That's your piece," Broca said, nodding knowingly. "I told you. 'Three sisters to right a wrong, a heart shattered, once again strong.'"

"This is part of the heart," Sloane murmured, turning the piece in her hand.

"The snow . . . It's gone." Lyra clapped her hands to her mouth, and we all turned to look.

That had been the silence that had fallen, I realized.

I'd grown so used to the howling of the wind outside that I hadn't realized that the storm had not only disappeared, but it had taken the rest of the snow with it.

Not a single flake remained. Sunlight filtered through the tree branches, a few still stubbornly having held on to their amber leaves, and fluffy clouds dotted the azure sky.

The army of snow sculptures were nothing but puddles on the front lawn.

We all gaped out the window, and then cheers erupted.

"Drinks are on the house," Liam called, and we all cheered again.

I turned and scooped up Sloane, pressing my lips to hers in the kiss of all kisses. I needed her to feel, down to her very stubborn toes, how much I loved her.

"Ahem." A throat cleared behind me, and I lifted my head from Sloane's to grin at her father. "I love her, if that's what you're wondering."

"Right, that'll do." Russell tapped two fingers to his head in a gentle salute, and then faded away, likely slipping back to the quiet of the hills he now called home.

"I love you too," Sloane said, and Blue bobbed his head in her arms, before barking once. "Blue says he does too." A lightness filled me, like a thousand champagne bubbles exploding, and the remaining tension that threaded my shoulders eased. She was really mine to keep.

"How do you feel about joining our pack, Blue?" I asked, bending down to kiss his furry little forehead. He swiped his rough tongue up the side of my face, and I took that to mean he approved. Then he wriggled out of Sloane's arms to launch himself around the room, and I pulled her close.

"You're staying." It wasn't really a question, but still I needed to hear it.

"I'm staying," Sloane agreed, and laughed when I pulled her tight. I just needed to hold her close, to know she was mine, forever, hopefully, but for as long as she'd give me for now. "I'm worried, though. It's only one part of the heart. Which means . . . we haven't fully broken the curse, have we? Something else will happen, won't it? With Lyra?"

"Hush, darling." Broca stepped forward, having overheard Sloane's words. "We'll have a respite for now. Lyra has some time until she gets her magick. I suspect the curse will rear its head the closer we get to that. For now, just breathe. Tonight we celebrate. But tomorrow?"

"What's tomorrow?" Sloane leaned forward, hanging on Broca's words.

"Tomorrow, we have a wee fight on our hands." The light of battle shone in Broca's eyes.

"What's happening? Tell me," Sloane, my little control freak, demanded. Broca turned and raised an eyebrow at me.

"Right, on it." With that, I tossed Sloane over my shoulder and took her out the door and home to my castle, where, for once, she didn't need to be in charge of everything.

And tomorrow, we'd fight whatever Broca's battle was. Together.

CHAPTER TWENTY-NINE

Sloane

Waking up in Knox's bed was as delightful as I remembered.

Particularly when his hands roamed down my body before he was even fully awake.

Well, one part of him was.

Desire bloomed inside of me, and I slipped across his chest, straddling him and taking him deep inside me, my lips against his.

"Good morning," I whispered into his mouth as he speared up, his hips lifting me as he came fully awake. Knox laughed into my kiss.

"Nice try, witchling." He flipped me so easily, while still staying inside me, that I gasped into his mouth, marveling at his singular strength. He covered me, one hand sliding up to pin my wrists over my head, and bit lightly at my collarbone. I hummed out a soft cry of need, arching against him, as pleasure heated inside me, long and liquid and lovely.

It was both thrilling and easier than I had imagined, this being *together*. For all the aggravation he'd brought me at the beginning, there was now an ease to our relationship that made me feel safe. It was as though he'd seen all the worst sides of me, and even when I showed him the scary bits, he hadn't been turned off. It was an incredibly exhilarating place to be in with someone.

Not to mention someone as ridiculously handsome as he was.

Not that I planned to feed his ego *too* much.

He teased me with long, lingering strokes, and I arched my back, rolling my hips to meet him, as he hummed against my lips.

"Mine."

"You're so controlling." I laughed into his mouth.

"Only here, witchling. Only here."

And when we crested together, soft and easy, on a quiet morning with no snow battering the windows, my heart was full.

"I've dreamt of this, you know," Knox said, after, as he carried me to a massive shower.

"Dumping me under a shower when I've already told you that I wanted coffee first—"

I glared at him as he pushed me under the warm spray, and then followed me into the shower, closing the glass door behind us. Puffs of steam billowed around us, and I swiped my hair out of my face, annoyed with him.

"I don't have any of my hair products here," I griped.

"And this is a problem . . . why?" Knox slicked his hair back under the spray, and I momentarily lost all meaningful thought as I watched water sluice down the expansive muscles of his chest.

"Um."

Knox grinned and braced a hand on the wall over my head in the shower. I should hate when he did that, I really should. But there was something about a strong man caging me in against a wall that, apparently, seemed to get me excited. I licked my bottom lip as he angled his head closer.

"What's the issue, Sloane?" Knox nipped at my lower lip and I groaned. In this moment, I couldn't quite seem to remember what I was so fussed about, as his hard body pressed against mine.

"Nice, um, shower," I gasped out as he found the soap and ran his hands down my body.

"I renovated the bathroom myself. I wanted something that fit me. Scotland is too cold for me to be ducking to fit under a tiny stream of water. I wanted dual showerheads, full steam, and lots of room. There's nothing better after a long day in the cold to come in and warm up like this."

I had to agree. The dual showerhead was quite nice, the water warm against my back, as Knox took careful attention to soaping my breasts.

"I'm quite sure they're clean now." I gasped, laughing as his mouth found mine again for a slippery kiss.

"Better safe than sorry."

Laughter burst out.

And so did my magick.

I grabbed Knox, pulling him to one side of the shower, surprise causing me to freeze.

"Do you . . . do you see that?" I asked, squeezing his arm tightly as we stared.

A perfect sphere of fire hovered in midair.

Directly beneath the rainfall showerhead.

And it was not extinguished by the water.

"I do. My, my, Sloane. You do continue to impress, don't you?"

"But how can this be?" My heart hammered in my chest. "I've already had fire. If I'm meant to have different magick every day, wouldn't I not get fire again? Unless . . ."

"Unless we fixed your magick." Knox grinned down at me as I gaped up at him.

"Do you think so? What if we did? I mean, this could be different fire from the first fire, right?" Excitement made me do a little shimmy in the shower, taking care not to touch the flame.

"Och, lass, I guess we'll need to try to find out." Knox tapped a finger on my nose.

Focusing on the ball of flame, I reached for my magick, and to my complete delight, the ball of fire disappeared. "I did it! I shut it off."

"You did. And if you're what I think you are, then you just might be a very powerful witch indeed. Come on, let's dry off and go find Henry. He's just the man you need for this situation."

"He is?" I blinked up at Knox as he wrapped a luxurious bath sheet around me. I had to admire a man who invested in good towels. None of those little bath towels that barely fit around my body. No, these were quality, and I felt instantly cozy as my feet touched the heated floor. Honestly, I could get used to this luxe life.

"He might be. Henry has great depths, you see." Knox picked up a towel and rubbed it over my hair.

When his hands came away, I gaped in shock at my dry hair in the mirror.

"How the hell did you do that?" I asked, reaching up to touch my dry strands. Screw fire, I wanted beauty magick. This would make life so much easier.

"Didn't I tell you? My strengths lie in elemental magick. Your hair was wet, and water is an element. I just asked it to move on."

"You asked the water in my hair to move on." I shook my head, my dry hair flying around my shoulders, amazed at this new life full of magick I could now study. Where once I'd shunned it because I was scared I'd end up like my parents, I now found that I was genuinely interested in approaching magick with an open and curious mind. There was just so much to learn. "Then why didn't you ask the snow to move on?"

"Even my magick has its limits, witchling." Knox tugged a lock of my hair.

Pulling on my leggings from yesterday, Knox's oversized jumper, and thick fuzzy socks of his, I followed him down to the library, where Henry had laid out breakfast on the table near the desk. The room was quiet, the large windows cracked open to a soft autumn breeze, and sunlight dappled the trees, a few amber leaves dotting their branches.

Until pandemonium broke loose.

In the form of three very chaotic familiars bursting through the doors. Blue swooped above Oswald, who streaked through the door, his eyes wide in a panic, while Haggis brought up the rear, his wheelchair rocketing across the soft rug in the library.

"Halt!" Knox shouted, holding up a hand, and they all skidded to a stop. "That's enough. Play outside. We're trying to have a nice breakfast here."

Cheese? Blue drifted to me, and I caught him for a cuddle.

"Morning, buddy. Did you have a nice night?"

I did. I love it here. Haggis and Oswald are fun. Can we stay?

"Mmm, we'll see." I didn't want to bring up the subject of moving in with Knox. As far as I saw it, we were still in a trial period of sorts.

Henry says if we stayed, I could have the entire garden to play in. With my new friends. I might even meet some of my ancestors.

I hadn't thought about Blue being lonely, and I tilted my head to look down into his sweet eyes.

"More emberwolves?"

No. Dragons. My ancestors.

"And Henry thinks they'll come here?"

He said they have the space for them. Dragons are curious by nature, so they may come by to check on things. Please, can we stay?

"Blue, sweetie, I don't know. That's a lot to ask." I tried to keep my voice low, but the library was quiet, and Knox was standing close, petting Oswald, who had hopped up on top of the desk.

"What does the lad want?" Knox looked at me, but before I could answer, Oswald bumped his head against Knox's hand. "Ah, he wants to stay here."

"Och, right. The three of them can communicate, can't they?" Here I was trying to be quiet when Haggis and Oswald were listening to everything Blue said.

"Aye, lass. And with the right magick, I think we can swing it that we can hear all of them. If they become a pack."

"Really?" Intrigued, I stepped forward to scratch behind Haggis's ears. The mini coo smiled up at me.

"Really." Knox moved forward and stepped close, running a hand over Blue's head before cupping a finger under my chin and tilting my face up to look at him. My breath caught. "What do you say, Sloane? Would you like to move in here? On a trial basis, of course."

My heart fluttered in my chest, my pulse beating like a hummingbird at my throat, and I swallowed. "Um, but what about Broca and my sisters? They need me."

"Do they?"

"Of course they do." Didn't they?

"Or do they need some space to grow?"

"Are you implying that I smother them?"

"I'm not, but you could start to, now that you're in one spot." I opened my mouth to argue with Knox.

He's right. Let them grow.

I looked down at Blue, who turned and swiped his tongue across my cheek.

I like happy Sloane.

Blue was right. I was happy. And I also needed to stop seeing my sisters as people I needed to take care of. They were already incredible women, but they still defaulted to looking to me for leadership. And though it chafed a bit to think about letting go of those reins, I also knew it wasn't healthy to hold so tightly to them. I knew I'd hated it when my mum had made all the decisions for me until we were able to get out from under her thumb. The last thing I wanted was for my sisters to end up resenting me.

"Fine, I suppose I'll move in here. On a trial basis, naturally." I affected a snobby accent.

"Naturally. Only if it meets with your approval." Knox grinned, and then his lips were on mine.

"Ahem, good morning, sir." We turned to find Henry at the door, a tray of tea in his hands.

"Henry. Just the man we wanted to see. Will you join us for breakfast?" Knox asked and pointed to the table.

"I've already had my brekkie, but a spot of tea will do nicely." Henry settled the tray on the table and gestured for me to sit in front of a plate with a warming cover on it. My stomach rumbled in appreciation when he lifted it to reveal a full Scottish breakfast.

"Toast is in here." Henry nudged a basket with a napkin covering it toward me. "Tea?"

"Please." This was far nicer than any breakfast I usually had.

"Sloane likes coffee," Knox said, and picked up a different pitcher.

"Oh, but tea is fine too." Henry was being so incredibly nice, I didn't want to offend him.

"Nae bother. Coffee it is." Henry switched out and poured me a cup of coffee. Once we were all settled, I dug into breakfast, dancing lightly in my seat as the delicious food warmed me.

"Henry, I think you may be able to help us." Knox leaned back and took a sip of his tea, his expression thoughtful. "As you know, Sloane's been dealing with discovering different magick each day. But after last night's ritual, she discovered she had fire this morning. But she's had it already."

All of our gazes swept to where the beautiful gold curtains had once hung by the windows, and heat bloomed on my cheeks.

"Sorry about that," I muttered, forking up some eggs.

"Nae bother, hen. Time for a refresh anyway," Henry promised me, reaching out to pat the back of my hand lightly.

I highly doubted that, but then a thought occurred to me that made my blood run cold.

"Knox." His name came out a choked gasp. "Am I going to have to live here with your mother?" There was no nice way to say it, and I hoped I hadn't insulted him, but the way I'd heard his mum speaking of me didn't bode well for our future potential familial relationship, let alone that of roommates.

Henry laughed softly into his napkin.

"No, Sloane, you won't. While, of course, they'll come back to stay once in a while, my parents have no wish to be in Briarhaven anymore. They've made that abundantly clear. The castle is mine."

"What about your brothers?"

"There's plenty of room for them if they decide to come back, but I think maybe we cross the bridge if we come to it? They're having too much fun at the moment to dip their toes in the responsibility pond anytime soon."

Relieved, I sat back and took a sip of my coffee, my pulse returning to a normal rate.

"And, about the fire?" Henry looked between Knox and me. "You're concerned she's repeating magick now?"

"No, we think that with ending her part of the curse, we also broke that particular malady. I think she may have landed on her actual magick."

"Ah." Interest bloomed in Henry's eyes. "Tell me about the fire."

"Glowing ball. Hanging out in a stream of water like it wasn't bothered in the slightest." I gestured with my cup.

"That's . . ." Henry's gaze darted to Knox and then back to me. Happiness flushed across his face and he stood, unable to contain himself. "Do you know what that means? You're a Fireheart witch. Och, it's been ages since we've had one of those here."

"A Fireheart witch?" But even as he said the words, I felt a physical click inside me, like the final piece of a puzzle sliding into place, and I rubbed at a spot on my chest.

"You're not just a keeper of dragons, like your father, miss, but you can pull from their magick. Transmuting fire, in all ways, is a massive power."

"Transmuting how, exactly?"

"You can summon the power of dragon fire. This can transmute into many things." Henry's eyes gleamed. "One of my favorites is that you'll be able to communicate through fire."

"That sounds . . . terrifying." I gaped at him.

"No, like whispers through the fireplace. Not fireballs at their head." Henry chuckled. "Though you can do that too. You'll also be able to use fire to imbue elemental magick to mundane things. A fork or a piece of jewelry, for example. You'll also be able to pull from other elements, like Knox can, but yours will be specific to all things dragon. It's quite exciting." Henry clapped his hands. "Och, just think! They'll likely visit us more now if they know we have a Fireheart witch. I must ready the stables. We'll need to build a bigger opening, more space."

Henry whirled, his eyes wide, and Knox gave him a nod.

"Do as you see fit, Henry. We welcome dragons here."

More friends?

I looked down at where Blue pawed my leg and smiled.

"Aye, sweet baby. More friends. It looks like Broca was right. It seems my abilities are quite strong." It felt good to say that. For the first time, I was no longer scared of my magick. I'd spent years worrying over what would happen with it, then when I'd finally gotten it, it had immediately malfunctioned. But now I could finally say I was proud of my own powers and feel it in my very soul. I was powerful. Me, Sloane MacGregor, a strong witch who was going to use her magick for good, help others, and break the curse on her bloodline. It made me feel a bit like a superhero.

Of course you are. You're a Fireheart.

"Thanks. That would have been helpful a while ago, you know." I laughed down at Blue, but then slipped him a piece of cheese. "He knew what I was all along. I should have just asked him."

"Ah well, sometimes things have to come to light in their own time, don't they?"

I looked across the table at this impossibly handsome man, who was so consistently certain that things would always work out for him. And I had to admit that maybe there was something to be said for just believing that the world wasn't out to harm you.

A sweet trill came from outside the window, and I looked across and saw a stunning goldfinch popping about. The loch stretched out, glimmering among the verdant hills in the distance, a swipe of blue paint on a master's canvas. Briarhaven spread before me, colorful cottages and stores clambering over one another, tendrils of smoke curling into the air from chimneys, people bustling on the pavement. Life was so charming here, especially now that the snow had stopped. It made me realize that I'd spent my childhood years so busy trying to avoid the potholes that I'd forgotten to look up at all the beautiful scenery surrounding me.

It was time for a change.

And not just on a trial basis.

Sloane MacGregor, Fireheart witch, was finally going to learn to grow some roots.

EPILOGUE

Sloane

"I thought Mandy had banned her from calling emergency meetings?" Nova opened a bottle of champagne and poured the four of us a glass each. Broca stood at the door, ushering in the Charms, who came in looking decidedly different not all bundled up and covered in snow.

"I guess Broca does what she wants," Lyra said, leaning forward to wave at Diedre, who immediately veered off to commune with her folders at the table.

"I can't believe you're a Fireheart witch," Nova said. We waited to cheers until Broca returned to the couch and took a glass. She was standing more, her enforced physical therapy slowly giving her more mobility, and now her daily walks could be taken outside instead of on the treadmill.

"I don't fully understand what that means, but I'm pleased about it too. I think. I just have so much to learn." I leaned back against the cushions with a soft sigh, the glass of champagne still in my hand. The black crystal dragon figurine I'd coveted from Raven's shop sat on a side table, eyes glittering red in the sunlight, a gift from my sisters for solving my part of the curse. "But the good thing is that Knox has a massive library and Henry has already pulled some books for me. I'm going to throw myself into research mode and see if we can uncover anything else about our past."

"Particularly since the ritual only broke the curse for you." Lyra bit her lower lip, her eyes worried as she gestured with her glass. "You know what else we realized, last night after you left?"

"What's that?"

"Someone in that room had family ties to the original witch that cursed us." Nova's eyes were serious on mine.

"Oh . . . but *of course*." I hadn't even thought about that, but I realized they were right. That was why Knox's one-fell-swoop approach had worked so well. Instead of trying to figure out which family had cursed our ancestor, he'd just included everyone. It was an expedient, though some may say sloppy, way of achieving his goal.

"Because the way the ritual was worded, it did seem to indicate that everyone involved in the curse should be a part of the unbreaking," Broca agreed, her expression thoughtful.

"It was clever on Knox's part, indeed," she added.

"And because we just have one piece of the quartz heart, it does mean it's likely a ticking time bomb on when the next curse kicks in."

"Something like that." Broca moved to the door when a knock sounded. "Felicity."

"Och, she's out of the hospital?" Putting my glass down, I sprang up and rounded the couch to greet Felicity. Raven stood at her side, carrying Felicity's emotional support tote, and a white bandage stood out on Felicity's forehead. She used crutches to help her inside, but the color was back on her cheeks, and her eyes were bright.

"I'm so glad you're okay," I said, gently pressing a kiss to her face.

"Thank you for your help," Felicity said, and I waved it away, guilt filling me. Had it not been for the snow, she wouldn't have been hurt.

"I didn't do anything. Raven healed you. This was all my fault. It was the snow that caused all this."

"No." Felicity shook her head. "No, it wasn't, Sloane. I was being stupid. I dropped my phone and reached for it. I know better."

"Wait, that's what happened?" I'd been convinced the snowstorm had caused her car to skid out.

"I mean, the snow didn't help the situation, but it wasn't the cause. I was being reckless." Felicity pursed her lips. "A lesson I likely won't forget."

"We are all learning and growing, aren't we?" Tam appeared behind Raven, water bottle in hand, running shorts on.

"Ladies. To the table?" Broca waved us over, and we all sat.

Except for one Mandy Meadows.

"It's not like Mandy to be late," Felicity looked around.

"She's not. I wanted to make sure you were all up to speed on coven code of conduct prior to her arrival," Broca spoke and all eyes turned to her.

"Oh boy." Raven sucked in a breath.

"Not only did Mandy refuse to participate in a ritual meant to benefit a coven member, as well as the entire town of Briarhaven, but she also universally rejected an ordinance vote yesterday. Despite her insistence that covens are not democratic, that is untrue. We are allowed to put any matter to vote, and the winning choice is the path forward."

"I see someone's been reading up on the coven rules." Mandy Meadows stood at the door, resplendent in a blush-pink pantsuit and pearls.

"I didn't have to read up on them," Broca said. "Won't you come in, Mandy?"

"Of course I'll come in. *I'm* president of the Charms." Mandy strode inside, slamming the door behind her, and Blue jumped up from where he'd been snoring lightly on the couch. He was worn out from his playtime with Haggis, and he gave Mandy a grumpy look before burrowing his head back in his blankets and tucking his wings around him.

"This is an unsanctioned meeting of the Charms, and thus anything here does not go on public record." Mandy put her Chanel handbag on the table and sat, her body stiff.

"There is no public record," Tam said, taking a slug from her water bottle. "Not sure what you're talking about, but if you're trying to sound fancy or something, it's not landing."

I could have hugged Tam.

"Either way, as president of the Charms, I will be the one to call the meetings. Is this about the ordinance, Broca? I already told you that it is too time-consuming. There is no way you can ask us to dedicate our lives to making sure the curse doesn't hurt Briarhaven when it would be much easier if you all would simply leave."

My mouth dropped open. She'd finally come out and said it. As welcoming as Mandy Meadows had pretended to be when we'd first arrived, the sheen had worn off her glamour.

Broca raised her chin, her eyes steely.

"As is my right as a standing member of the Charms, I am invoking Ordinance Thirteen, a forced vote to elect a new president of the Charms."

A gasp went up around the room, and everyone sat back in their chairs, Mandy included.

"You . . . you . . . you can't," Mandy said, her hand fluttering in front of her face.

"I can and I will." Broca's voice was like steel. "You've shown that you don't hold goodwill toward all members of the coven, you're willing for harm to befall them, and you've acted against the wishes of the group as a whole."

"But—"

"I nominate Sloane MacGregor as coven president of the Charms."

A second gasp filled the room, mine the loudest of the bunch.

"But, Broca, I don't know the first thing about running a coven." I whirled on Broca, my hand on her arm. "Are you sure you know what you're doing?"

"Sloane. I've watched you take care of everyone else around you since you were far too young to do so. You're a natural leader, you genuinely care about others, and you're good at thinking long-term. All elements of what is needed by a coven leader. The history of magick can be taught."

"She can't even control her magick," Mandy protested, two red spots appearing on her cheeks. "This is ludicrous. You'll turn this coven into a joke."

"Actually, she can," Lyra said, her expression fierce. "She's a Fireheart witch. And that's pretty badass, in my opinion."

A third gasp went around the room, and I was pretty sure I'd have to get smelling salts soon if we kept it up at this rate.

"A . . . a . . ." Mandy stammered, her hands clutching the handles of her purse. "But we haven't seen one in—"

"Centuries. Since Bonelle MacGregor was cursed in this very village by one very dark witch." Broca's eyes sharpened as she looked around the table. "Now I will repeat myself. I nominate Sloane MacGregor for coven president. I will now call the vote."

"You can't . . . without a majority . . ." Mandy hissed, her face contorting.

"What makes you think Sloane won't get a majority?" Broca asked, and the room went silent. I looked around the table and realized everyone was looking anywhere but at Mandy. "All those in favor of Sloane as president, say aye."

"Aye." Raven raised her hand. As did Broca, my sisters, Tam, and Deidre.

Felicity looked between Mandy and me, her eyes filling with tears.

"I'm sorry, Mandy, but they may be right. It might be time for a change. She's a Fireheart, after all. Her magick will help all of us."

Mandy's mouth dropped open when Felicity raised her hand.

"Nae." Mandy stood, her purse clutched in front of her. "You don't know the first thing about running a coven, Sloane MacGregor. Do you even know what casserole to bring for a crystal cleansing? Or what spell keeps spirits away from a newborn? You'll make a mockery of this coven, I can promise you that. Disgraceful."

Mandy turned on her heel and stormed out, slamming the door after her, while I gaped at the table.

What had just happened?

"I didn't even vote," I said.

"You can't," Broca said cheerfully. "Not when you're the candidate. Congrats, love. You just became president of the Charms."

And made myself a powerful enemy in the process, it seemed.

"I'm the new president?" I blinked around the table, and my eyes landed on where Nova smirked at me. Bringing her hands beneath her chin, she fluttered her eyelashes at me.

"Just remember . . ."

The entire table joined her: "Never harm, always charm!"

AUTHOR'S NOTE

"*Anam cara*" is a Gaelic term that loosely translates to "soul friend" or "soul companion." It's a perfect term for Blue, my sweet soul puppy, whom I lost earlier this year. This is the first book I've written without both my boys by my side, and I hope my love, and theirs, shines through in my words and that I can continue to honor them with my stories. It may seem odd to some, a dedication such as this, but I never would have started writing books if not for my dogs. You see, the very first book I wrote was about my stolen Boston terrier, Briggs, and how I recovered him and rescued Blue along the way. It's a story of my heart and propelled me into taking a chance on writing more books of my heart—such as the one you read today. So, if you get a chance, enjoy a bit of cheese today with a smile on your face thinking of the pure joy that these sweet animals bring to our lives.

A huge "Thank you!" to Christina, Casey, and Allison at Jane Rotrosen Agency for guiding me on this new path of traditional publishing and helping me to bring this story to life. Many thanks to Ghjulia and Carrie at Gallery Books for giving my stories a new audience and enjoying my worlds as much as I enjoy creating them. To the rest of the team at Gallery Books—Christine, Sally, Sarah, Fallon, Mackenzie, and Olivia—thank you for making my book shine and championing it to the world! I can't wait to see where our journey goes together.

To the Scotsman, who embodies the term *anam cara*, but of my heart, I'm so lucky our destinies intertwined.

And, if you're already missing Sloane and Knox, be sure to pop by my website for a free bonus scene where Sloane gets to meet her dragons: www.triciaomalley.com/free.

KEEP READING FOR A SNEAK PEEK AT THE SECOND INSTALLMENT IN THE SCOTTISH CHARMS SERIES, COMING IN 2026!

Magick runs in my blood. So does bad luck.

One second, I was hurrying down Briarhaven's main street, my head ducked against the light mist of rain that had shadowed the autumn days of late. My mind was fixed on Mystic Munchies and the nerve-racking question I was about to ask, when I slammed into something solid. Some*one* solid, that is.

I barely had time to gasp before I was knocked off my feet, landing hard in the mud.

"Bloody hell, Lyra."

That voice.

I blinked up, my breath stolen, as Rabbie Barclay loomed over me, offering a hand I wasn't sure I wanted to take. My first love. My biggest regret.

And then, as if the universe wanted to drive the moment home, the skies opened.

Cold rain pelted my skin, soaking into my dress, into my bones, into the deepest part of me that already knew—my curse had arrived.

Want to be the first to know about Lyra's story?
Sign up for Tricia's newsletter at
https://www.triciaomalley.com/newsletter
and follow along for updates!

ABOUT THE AUTHOR

Tricia O'Malley is a New York Times, USA Today and Wall Street Journal bestselling author of contemporary, paranormal and fantasy romance. Her books have sold over three million copies worldwide. When she's not writing, Tricia can be found scuba diving, travelling, or debating the best popcorn topping. She splits her time between Scotland and the Caribbean, loves fun vacation reads, and thinks life is better with a little bit of sparkle. To see some of her Scotland or island life photos, visit her on Facebook, on Instagram, or at www.triciaomalley.com.

booksandthecity.co.uk
the home of female fiction

NEWS & EVENTS | BOOKS | FEATURES | COMPETITIONS

Follow us online to be the first to hear from your favourite authors

bc
booksandthecity.co.uk

X
@TeamBATC

Join our mailing list for the latest news, events and exclusive competitions

Sign up at
booksandthecity.co.uk